MEANT TO BE

Emilynne cupped Bryan's cheek. "I know I am grateful for the providence that compelled me to seek your help in Limerick."

Bryan gazed at her for what seemed to be both forever and but the merest tick of the clock. Living doubt, wizened mistrust, and a flicker of hope warred in the depths of his penetrating gaze. "Despite—"

Emilynne stilled his question by sliding her fingers over his lips. "We have both been guilty of dissemblance. I cannot censure your reasons without condemning my own.

"It would seem we were fated to meet over this matter." She smiled as she continued. "I am grateful that at least now, I trust that you seek not only the right thing, but what is right for the children."

Bryan closed his eyes as deep emotion flared within him. His hand clasped her wrist with a grip that sent shivers racing down her arm. Instead of pulling her hand away, he turned his face into it and pressed a kiss to her palm.

Emilynne flowed into him like water seeking the shore. "Kiss me," she whispered. "Kiss me as if you truly mean it."

Dear Readers,

Desire, dreams, and destiny—with a healthy dose of betrayal, villainy, and adventure—are the very things songs have been written about for centuries. And Ballad Romances is our love song to you: a brand-new line featuring the most gifted authors in historical romance telling the kinds of stories you love best.

This month, we launch the line with four new series. Each month after that, we'll present both new and continuing stories—and we'll let you know each month when you can find subsequent books in the series that have captured your heart.

Joy Reed takes us back to Regency England with the first book in *The Wishing Well* trilogy, **Catherine's Wish.** In this enchanting series, legend has it that, when a maiden looks into the Honeywell House wishing well, she sees the face of her future betrothed—with decidedly romantic results. Next, celebrated author Cynthia Sterling whisks us off to the American West with **Nobility Ranch,** the first in an uproariously funny—and sweetly tender—series of *Titled Texans* who have invaded America with their British nobility intact, and their hearts destined for life-changing love.

An ancient psychic gift is the key to the *Irish Blessing* series—and a maddening, tantalizing harbinger of love for the Reillys of the mid-nineteenth century. New author Elizabeth Keys weaves a passionate tale of the family's middle son in the first book, **Reilly's Law.** Finally, Cherie Claire invites us into the world of *The Acadians* in the 1750s, as **Emilie**—the first of three daughters of an Acadian exile—travels to the lush and sultry Louisiana Territory—where desire and danger go hand in hand. Enjoy!

Kate Duffy
Editorial Director

Irish Blessing

REILLY'S LAW

Elizabeth Keys

Zebra Books

KENSINGTON PUBLISHING CORP.

http://www.zebrabooks.com

ZEBRA BOOKS are published by

Kensington Publishing Corp.
850 Third Avenue
New York, NY 10022

Zebra and the Z logo Reg. U.S. Pat. & TM Off.

First Printing: July, 2000
10 9 8 7 6 5 4 3 2

Printed in the United States of America

Prologue

Beannacht Island, Western Ireland
1842

"Ye must be ready fer The Blessing at any time. And ye must heed it, fer a blessing missed is a curse indeed."

Quintin's tones echoed across Granny's too-silent room as the three Reilly brothers huddled together by the brick hearth. The eldest of the boys, he was charged with the telling this night. He recounted the oft-told tale reverently—with all Granny's inflections—missing not a word nor glimmer of magic, missing nothing.

"But how will we know?" Devin, the youngest, asked in a hushed voice, his question a necessary part of the ritual.

"You'll know." Bryan, the middle one, answered with unembellished brevity.

"We'll all know." Quintin shot his brother a quelling look. " 'Tis a sound once heard that lingers on. A sight once seen and never forgotten. A feeling once felt, always remembered. 'Tis in the blood of all Reillys.''

He ruffled the dark curls on Devin's head. "Aye, you'll know, young Devin. And it will be up to you to make of it what you will. Capture The Blessing or suffer The Curse."

The distant rumble of a storm over the ocean deepened the night's gloom. A hint of lavender puffed by on the breeze from the window they'd cracked open. Devin shivered, his eyes round with wonder though still red-rimmed from a day of tears. "I wish Granny could tell us the story."

His forlorn tone, hollow with the loss keening through them all, rolled across the hardwood floor. As one, their gaze flew to the empty rocker still draped with Granny's favorite green shawl. Devin loosed a shuddering sigh.

Bryan elbowed him in disgust, though his own lip trembled a bit. "We promised we'd remember, Devi. Don't start now—we promised."

"Aye." Quintin's tone returned to that of the boy he was. "And you promised Gran you'd not mewl like a babe."

Tears dripped over Devin's chin. "I'm trying, Quin. But . . . I miss her." The last came in a watery whisper.

A gust of wind burst against the window, rattling the panes. Quintin and Bryan exchanged a look. The image of a windswept hillside and a freshly dug grave seemed to hover in the air between them.

With a sigh Quintin knelt next to Devin. "We all miss her, Devi, and we always will. Gran knew we would miss her. Why else do you think she made us promise to retell The Blessing?"

"Because it is important?" Devin hiccuped.

Quintin grinned. "Aye, boy-o, but it is also a way to stay close to her." He lightly cuffed Devin on the chin. "Now,

buck up, will you? We canna get through a telling if you're going to blubber."

"Aye." Devin wiped his nose on his starched Sunday jacket and struggled to smile. "I'll not cry."

"Much." Bryan muttered, earning a halfhearted kick from Devin for his efforts.

Before they digressed into a full scuffle, Quintin intervened. "The Blessing has been in the family for generations. Nine unto nine."

"But won't that mean it stops with us? We could be the ninth generation." Devin's anxious whisper blended with the atmosphere Quintin was creating.

"No, you dolt." Bryan shot his younger brother a superior look. "Nine unto nine means eighty-one generations."

"Nine unto nine." Quintin repeated, ignoring Bryan's comment. "Reillys take heed and Reillys beware, for unto ye is delivered a great gift. A token of esteem, a promise, a fearsome gratitude."

The firelight flickered over his solemn face. "For nine unto nine, ye must make the choice. Only ye can direct the course to joy or sorrow. Only ye decide if it is Blessing or Curse."

"I hope mine's not a curse." Devin shivered.

The elder two ignored him.

"It can roll in with the thunder or seep in like the dew. It might fly past in a flash or dance by on a song. The knowin' is up to us. The doin' another part."

"Aye." Bryan's reverent whisper lingered in the air. "The joy of yer heart, the wish of yer soul, the direction of yer life, the path of yer choosing."

"The choice, once made, cannot be undone," Quintin intoned.

"The decision, once forged, cannot be altered," Bryan and Devin returned with urgent half-whispers.

"Blessing or Curse for all time."

Three pairs of mirthless green eyes glistened with new tears.

"For all time," they repeated together.

The three voices died away, leaving only the solemn tick of the clock on the fireplace mantel and the murmur of the adult voices from the parlor below. Devin sighed. "I still wish Gran were here to do the telling. I especially like the way she talks of The First Blessing. And the Druids."

"Aye. We all wish Gran were still here." Quintin's agreement held equal sorrow. He fisted his hands and chewed his lip. His gaze flew to the Bible sitting on the nightstand by the massive four-poster.

"Did you count how many carriages were in the procession after the Mass?" His choked effort to pull back from the grief threatening to undo his thirteen-year-old's pride came out as a whisper.

Bryan nodded. "Forty-two. Near everyone on the island. She would have been proud. She told Da she expected him to close the shipyard, but I don't think she meant for three whole days."

"How come Da never likes to talk about The Blessing?" Another of Devin's favorite questions shifted their attention.

"He speaks of it," Bryan countered.

Quintin shook his head. "Only if you force him. Mayhap you're not to talk of The Blessing once it happens to you." He shrugged.

"But Gran spoke of The Blessing," Devin pushed into the conversation.

"Aye, but Gran was a girl," Bryan offered as though that answered everything. "Girls don't get The Blessing."

"Sometimes they do. I asked her when Meaghan was borne," Devin insisted.

"It is a rare event for them, Gran said." Quintin smothered a yawn as he banked the small fire they'd coaxed earlier. "Come on, we'd best get to bed before they discover we're not there. It will be a long time till any of us experience The Blessing."

They stood for a moment in the doorway to the bedchamber, loath to leave, as though that meant Granny truly was gone.

"Good night, Granny," Bryan offered.

"We love you." Devin sniffed again.

"And we'll remember." Quintin picked up the lamp and they trudged out into the corridor.

The last glow from the fireplace died away, leaving the room awash in pallid moonlight and the lingering scent of Granny Reilly's lavender perfume.

Chapter One

Limerick, Ireland
1858

"She's ready when ye are, Captain Reilly."

Bryan Reilly winced as his honorary title rang out across the docks from the *Caithream*. The courtesy never failed to serve as a painful reminder of the dreams he'd lost through his own reckless folly.

He brushed by a young woman dressed in widow's weeds standing alone on the pier and nodded to Michael, the sloop's true shipmaster, signaling permission for imminent departure as his gaze ran the ship's length. Though small, she was a beauty from her foremast to her stern. He surveyed her sleek hull against the shifting sway of the river in Limerick's harbor. Swiftest of their small fleet, graceful and clean, the *Caithream* was Reilly-born and Reilly-built, just as he was—a symbol of everything he once aspired to master and now sought to protect with all the persuasive acumen he possessed. If only his mission to England would go as smoothly as she sailed. If only.

A cry from behind him caused him to turn just as he stepped foot on the gangplank.

"Darling, you're safe after all. Thank goodness!"

The young widow, only slightly taller than his shoulder, flung herself into Bryan's arms. Her embrace engulfed him in the fresh scents of lemon and freesia, at odds with the heavy tang of the docks. Her lips brushed his and set blood pounding at his temples with a wave of desire so profound, it shook the irritation that held him rigid against her assault.

Before he could recover, she pressed herself tightly against him, molding tempting curves against his worsted suit as she whispered in his ear. "Please, help us, please."

The desperation in her plea quivered through him. Her distress manifested as a near-palpable thing in the gray light of early morning. The silk of her gown sighed as she pressed closer, and his body tightened in response to hers. *Damn.* The feel of her in his arms evoked emotions best left unstirred and betrayed a promise he'd made to himself long ago. He'd no time for delay caused by a stranger's troubles. And however desirably packaged this woman might be, she was definitely trouble.

Whoever she was and whatever her motives, she'd cracked his solicitor's prudence in an instant. As he held her closer, he sensed he had to get rid of her as quickly as possible before his life changed in ways beyond imagining.

"Shhh, it is all right, lass." He'd only a hazy impression of dark blue eyes and full lips beneath the brim of her bonnet. He tried to pull back from her embrace, but she wouldn't release her hold of him and he didn't wish to draw any further attention.

"Husband, what must you think of your silly wife believing you'd drowned?"

She spoke loud enough for the entire quay to hear and clutched his shoulders with her gloved hands so tight, she made him wince as much from her grip as her words.

"Are you daft?" he bit out. Heads turned as the inhabitants of the busy docks paused to observe them. The normal bustle of ships being loaded and unloaded seemed to pause as if listening to what she'd just proclaimed. What game could she be playing?

"Kiss me," she begged; terror bordered her hushed tone as it quavered against his ear. "Kiss me as if you truly mean it."

He held perfectly still, stunned as much by her request as by his sudden wish to comply. What kind of fool allowed dallying with a wayward tart to take precedence over urgent business? He tightened his grip on her arms. Finally, she drew back.

"Please." Her gaze, an unwavering lapis blue that breached his soul, threatened any ounce of resolve he'd ever claimed to hold.

He had the sudden unnamed certainty that he could not ignore this woman, no matter that logic demanded he set her aside. The sharp sting of desire pierced him, this time in a red-hot haze, blotting out everything else. He wanted to kiss her, hang the consequences.

"Gladly."

He anchored a hand in the cloud of soft blond tresses gathered at the nape of her neck, then dragged her lips to his.

"Oh."

The sound escaped her as he covered her waiting mouth and drank in her soft, sweet warmth. The honey-and-cream taste of her sang through his blood. Music rippled over his mind and heart. Lilting strains of an unseen harp. A melody he'd never heard before yet recognized on so deep a level, he shuddered. The notes shivered through his soul and roared through his limbs in sweeping chords of fractured color and fragmented light.

It was the Reilly Blessing, to be sure, provoked by the woman in his embrace. He'd thought he'd fallen afoul of that legend long ago. He groaned. Every story he'd ever heard echoed through his thoughts in a wild blur. Past regrets, ancient guilt, and years of carefully constructed defenses sluiced away like sea salt after a cleansing rain, leaving him vulnerable to this family fable reborn in the feel of her lips. To salvage his future he should thrust her away, but to save his sanity, he could do nothing but pull her closer still.

She stiffened in his arms as though his onslaught were more than she expected in response to her demand. Then, after a moment, she melted against him and made a little moan in the back of her throat. He tasted raw desperation and unnerving desire on her soft lips. The fiery clamor of The Blessing deafened him to all rational concerns.

"Muirneach." The Gaelic endearment pushed from his depths. Passion flared between them, so bold and hot, Bryan could easily imagine it burning away the very docks beneath their feet.

Wouldn't that be a sight for all of Limerick to see?

The thought dumped a bit of cold lucidity over him. He released her from his hungry kiss and tilted her chin up to study her face more closely, noting her rosy lips and the daze that lingered in those beautiful blue eyes. His doubts thundered back with biting reality. What game was this enticing stranger playing, and why had she chosen him?

He loosened his hold on her, regret and anger warring inside him, ripping at the slender threads he yet held on his control. For one tiny moment he had lost all of the control he had worked so hard to attain.

He dropped his hands from her.

"Mayhap you'd like to explain this brazen display?" His tone came low and even, betraying none of the desire she roused in him. Good.

A flush rose over her cheekbones, coloring her pale skin the delicate pink of new spring roses. She lifted her chin. Her gaze slid toward the harbormaster's office at the end of the dock as she swallowed and leaned close to his ear.

"I need your help. *We* need your help."

Her gaze bespoke truth. Whatever her predicament, she saw him as the only answer. And deep inside him lurked the need to allay her fears. He squashed it back, determined to question her.

"We?"

"Myself and my"—she turned her gaze back toward the street at the opposite end of the dock—"two children."

At her stumbling admission, guilt twisted through him, cold and heavy. He clenched his hands at his sides. Children? What folly had indulging an impulse led him into this time?

He'd just kissed another man's wife into glorious submission. An Englishwoman too, if her heritage ran true to her delicate accent. He'd called her beloved in the language of his forebears for all to hear. Physical desire had swept away years of training in the finer points of business demeanor and public bearing.

What would Gill O'Brien have to say about that? His stomach tightened as he pictured the senior partner's frowning censure. Gill's highly visible courting of English business brooked no scandal from the junior members of O'Brien & Mallory. Bryan could imagine more than mere condemnation, relation or no.

Blessing be damned.

"Madam." Cold reality iced his tone. "I don't know what dramatic role you are enacting, but I'd suggest you ply your talents elsewhere. Good day."

"No." Her impeccably gloved fingers clutched his arm as he turned. "Please, this is no act. I'm deadly serious. We need safe passage to England immediately. That is your destination, is it not?"

Her glance slid back toward the harbormaster's office. "I . . . I can pay you."

Again the honest tremor in her voice shook him, twining her concern through him despite his need to be done with her. Either she was a very good actress or she was truly in danger. The aura of The Blessing and all that it entailed seemed to linger in the air between them. He thrust the idea away and tried to concentrate. Michael had said some unsavory characters were hanging around the docks, looking for a lone woman traveling with two small children. Was she the one they sought? And, if so, could he afford to involve himself further in her dilemma? The answer to the last was a bald no. Still, the effects of The Blessing beckoned otherwise, and his own honor demanded he not turn his back on someone in trouble.

"Payment is not the question." He glanced back down at her again, realizing his mistake as her gaze caught his. Deep sea blue, turbulent with a rising storm. He couldn't form the words to send her on her way. And deep inside him a voice demanded he help her any way he could.

"Please don't deny us. I must get the children home safely."

Lingering chords from a distant harp seemed to hover in the air between them. *A blessing missed is a curse indeed.* He could hear Granny's warning ringing through the years. *The knowin' is one thing, the doin' another.* He could neither leave this woman here to face her fears alone nor delay his own departure. Too much was at stake.

"Why are you being hunted?"

Her fingers tightened on his arm, signaling her continued distress. But her chin rose with an air of defiant pride that bespoke an underlying fortitude despite her apprehensions. Admiration stirred within the heart he'd thought long dead.

"I have broken no laws. I'll . . . I'll explain everything, anything you want, but please tell me you'll give us passage. I cannot stay visible on this dock for much longer: The risk is too great."

"Do you flee your husband?"

That brought her up short. She blinked in surprise. Then the tiniest smile curved the soft lips he'd bruised with his kiss.

"I assure you, sir, I flee no husband." Again her cheeks pinkened. "I seek only safety for myself and the children at our family's home in England."

He looked at her, dressed in black from head to toe. Despite his misgivings, he'd known from the moment he kissed her that he must help her. Still, he needed to be sure he was not abetting some crime. "Are you in debt?"

"The only debt I plan to incur is yours. *If* you will take us on board and leave at once. Your crewman did say you were ready, did he not?" Honesty still laced the worry behind her breathless answers.

"Hey, Captain, those scurvies I told ye about yesterday be making the rounds of the docks again." Michael's measured tones came from behind Bryan. There was little Michael McManus missed; it was why he was of such value both as shipmaster and friend.

The woman turned to look down the quay, releasing a little moan that echoed in Bryan's heart despite his best efforts to shut out the sound. Two rough-looking characters stood grilling the purser of a large brigantine moored nearby.

"Please." There were tears in her eyes when her gaze returned to his. "Help me."

"Are we set to go, Michael?"

"Aye, Captain, we'd best catch the tide."

"Then we'd better bring your children aboard, madam. We're casting off."

"Oh, thank you." Her relieved smile dazzled him. His mouth went dry. Then she stood on tiptoe and brushed her lips against his cheek. "I am in your debt."

Her tears dampened his cheek. Bryan held himself back as desire knifed him again. "Now, lass," he growled.

"This way." She turned in a flurry of black silk and white petticoats to lead him back down the docks.

The steady pace of the sea captain's boots echoed a reassuring tattoo through the morning mist as he followed Emilynne down the bustling quay.

The intrusive sounds from the strangers surrounding them tore at her self-possession, aggravating her fear of discovery. She found Captain Reilly's presence oddly comforting despite his silence. Blessing or curse? She could have sworn he'd muttered the words as he set off behind her. His hesitation before agreeing to give them passage had nearly had her expiring on the spot. Especially with those thugs so close by.

"Please, let us get away. Oh, please." The prayer broke from her in breathless gasps for the hundredth time in the past fortnight as she hurried toward the carriage. Her heart hammered the plea against her ribs. She must protect them at all costs. She'd promised Robert—and Wellesleys always kept their word.

She'd never expected to seduce her way out of Ireland to keep that word. Having made Captain Reilly's acquaintance in such an unconventional manner should have left her filled with disquiet, yet she could not shake the idea she had done the right thing. Her lips still tingled from the intense kiss they'd shared.

Grateful as she was that the captain had not denied her, her desperate move shattered her own reserve. Disturbing waves of warmth still rippled deep inside her, threatening her concentration on the dangers still at hand. This would never do. She needed all her wits about her if she was to get them all safely home.

The hackney's shadowed interior appeared empty at first as Emilynne opened the door. Her breath froze in her chest until her eyes adjusted and she saw the two irresistible imps that made the struggle to leave Ireland so necessary.

She turned back toward the captain. "They're still asleep. I'll carry Christian. Can you manage Abigail?"

"Aye." Captain Reilly nodded, his gaze unreadable. She could not guess the thoughts hidden in the depths of his startling green eyes. Was he thoroughly scandalized by her behavior, flinging herself at him as she had? Heat crept into her cheeks. What did it matter what he thought so long as he helped them escape?

She gathered Christian into her arms. The little boy sighed and murmured against Emilynne's neck.

"Mama." Soft and happy, his tone burned tears in Emilynne's throat. She choked them back.

"Hush, darling," she whispered against the child's sleep-warmed cheek, and reached for the carpetbag that held the meager belongings they'd escaped with.

She watched as the captain easily swept Abby into his arms, then turned and headed back toward his ship. Emilynne smiled her gratitude to the hackney driver, thankful she'd paid the man in advance as she hurried after the captain.

"Good luck, ma'am." The driver's words trailed after them.

She glanced around. No further sign appeared of the men who'd been asking questions about a woman traveling alone with two children on the quay the day before when she'd booked passage to London for herself, the children, and her fictional parents.

They must have seen through her ruse. She'd arrived at the docks at dawn only to find the men skulking near the larger ship she'd planned to board. She'd overheard several of the seamen in the harbormaster's office speak highly of Reilly Ship Works and its owners. When she'd heard his name called out and seen the signet ring on his hand that matched the ship's crest like a blessing beckoning to her, desperate invention had struck.

"Please, God, please let this work."

The small ship was a bustle of activity as she followed the *Caithream*'s captain up the gangplank. He offered no words to his crewman, just a nod, but that seemed all that was needed as the man shouted brisk orders to his small crew.

"Thank you," she breathed as she followed the silent captain across the deck and down a small set of steps.

Shifting Abby on his shoulder, he offered his hand to brace her elbow as she descended into a dark corridor. The contact of his fingers through her sleeve warmed her far more than it should have, heightening the echoes of their kiss. He paused in the closeness of the ship's passageway, his gaze locked with hers for an interminable moment while her eyes adjusted from waterfront sun to the dimness of lamplight. He flicked his gaze down to her lips. Her cheeks burned again beneath his dark perusal.

"This way." His voice came low and rough as he turned away and led them past a comfortable-looking salon.

Did Captain Reilly regret his quick agreement to help her? Too late if he did. Emilynne had no intention of retreating from the sanctuary this ship offered. She lifted her chin and held the sleeping child closer as she followed him.

He opened a door at the opposite end of the corridor and preceded her into a small cabin. From the desk with charts laid out she surmised this to be his personal quarters.

"This should do for the moment," he offered over his shoulder as he settled Abby at the far side of a wide bunk.

Emilynne leaned down and relinquished her own precious burden, laying Christian next to his sister on the pillow. She covered them with the opposite end of the bunk's oversized down quilt.

"Thank you so much. Abby, Christian, and I are in your debt."

"Don't thank me yet." He lifted a sardonic brow. "I've a feeling we shall both pay dearly for this bit of folly." He bowed ever so slightly. "Madam."

Without another word he turned and left her alone with the children.

As the door closed behind him with a cool metal click, the tension of the last weeks caught up with her and her knees gave out. She swayed against the bunk containing the sleeping children. Days and nights had become a blur of fear and running. Beyond the dark black of her mourning gown, she'd not had the time to spare so much as a thought to grieve poor Robert.

Pain welled up inside her as she gazed at his children's sleeping faces. Christian, with his hair so like his father's, and Abby, who had Robert's deep brown eyes and determined chin.

Silent tears rolled down her cheeks and fell unchecked onto her bodice for the brother she missed so desperately.

"Nothing and no one will get to your children, Robert. I swear it." Her whispered vow echoed back to her from the confines of the captain's well-ordered cabin. No matter what she had to do and no matter whom she had to fight, she would do what she must to provide security for her niece and nephew.

"Where are we?" A sleepy voice drifted from the folds of the quilt.

Emilynne wiped the tears from her cheeks.

"We're on board ship, Abby," she whispered back, unwilling to wake Abby's brother just yet. The tension and travel had exacted a toll on the children's reserves as well.

"The ship to England?" The little girl sounded more awake now.

Emilynne stroked Abby's cheek. "Aye, one and the same. Soon we'll feel them get under way and we'll be heading toward home. Are you hungry?"

Abby nodded, her gaze far too somber for her age. After

her recent losses and their headlong flight, Emilynne could not blame the child, yet the sight twisted her heart.

"I must go make some inquiries on deck and see what provisions have been made for us. Will you be a brave girl and keep an eye on Christian for me?" Emilynne patted the child's hand, refraining from giving Abby a hug for fear she'd never let go if she gave in to the emotions churning through her now.

"I won't be long." Emilynne closed the cabin door behind her and leaned against it, biting her lip as weariness threatened to overwhelm her. The prospect hovered of a few hours or days without having to worry at every turn. The sounds of creaking wood and thuds of sailors' feet overhead reminded her—not yet—she must bear up awhile longer.

They were not out of Limerick's harbor yet. In fact, they had not yet moved from the wharf. She ran a worried hand over her brow and straightened, drawing once again on reserves of strength she hadn't known she possessed.

When they were out of the harbor, she would spare a few moments to rest. She couldn't relax even a little until they were far away from any possible discovery. Her boldness on the docks had surprised no one more than herself. Though she'd never have planned such an act, she knew at that moment when discovery seemed imminent, she'd kiss the devil himself if it would get them to safety.

"And I'll do it again if I have to." She lifted her skirts as she reached the steps and then felt the gentle sway of the ship change. Not enough to make her sick, though she couldn't stop the reflexive action of pressing her hand to her mouth, but just enough to send the message that they were finally under way. She breathed a sigh of relief in spite of the twinges in her stomach.

She leaned forward and peered out from her position on the steps, grateful to watch the dockside buildings gradually recede. High in the rigging several of the sailors shouted their compliance with the orders being issued below.

"Thank heaven, we are away." She spoke her thought aloud.

"Indeed, madam." The captain's voice came from just beyond the top of the steps. She jumped.

"Would you care to join me?" His tone made the words a command. "Mayhap you could now spare an explanation for your rather hurried departure."

For a moment Emilynne was tempted to turn back toward the cabin. She had a few biscuits tucked in her reticule, enough to satisfy Abby for the moment.

With a lift of her chin she pushed the temptation to plead fatigue aside, and she tightened her lips. She'd had enough questions over the past few weeks to last a lifetime. Still, she had promised to tell him, hadn't she? She could at least provide enough details of her story to satisfy a ship's captain—the man had become their savior, after all.

The fetid breeze off Limerick Harbor mixed with the fresher scent from the Shannon River as Emilynne emerged from the corridor. Sunlight pierced the gray clouds overhead and sparkled on the water. Her stomach twinged again. Emilynne averted her gaze and sought the captain. He was easy enough to find, leaning with his back against the ship's rail and watching her with that unfathomable dark gaze of his.

"Madam." He straightened as she approached. He was dressed strangely for a man of the sea. His tailored suit and bowler proclaimed him more ready to negotiate the shoals of business than the waters of the Shannon. Still, his crew had identified him as such.

"Captain." She resisted a ridiculous urge to curtsy as she looked up at his frowning visage. "I know you don't want my thanks, but . . ."

"Nay, madam, a simple elucidation will do." His lips quirked over the words.

He was far better educated than the captain of the vessel that had brought her family to Ireland so many months before. Her throat constricted again at the memories of happier days. Not that she remembered much of that passage; she'd been too ill to leave her cabin much. Still, she'd promised this seaman his explanation, and so elucidate she must.

"Yes, of course." She swallowed, uncertain just where to begin and made the mistake of looking down into the blue-green waters of the Shannon. "Oh, my."

She pressed a hand to her lips and closed her eyes, doing a slow mental count to twenty. *No, better make that twenty-five.* It took a moment before she realized he was speaking.

"I beg your pardon?" She held her gaze level to his with an effort. His eyes were a deep forest green beneath brows as dark and inky a black as she'd ever seen, far preferable to the swirling colors of the river. She bit her lip at that thought and wished she had not come up on deck.

"Are you all right?" His brows drew together in concern and she wished they had not. She concentrated on his dark, wavy hair instead, but that rippled in the breeze and reminded her too much of the water slapping against the hull of the ship.

"Yes, quite," she managed to say, trying not to cover her mouth again. Seasickness had plagued her all her life. It was an inconvenience at best, and most oftentimes horribly embarrassing. Robert had teased her for being a poor sailor. Pain seized her heart as she looked down at Captain Reilly's polished boot tips. "I'm just tired. That's all. Would it be too much of an imposition to acquire some victuals for the children before too long? I awoke them before they had any breakfast."

"Mmmm." His disapproval stung as the ship's mainsail snapped into the wind and the ship picked up speed. He turned Emilynne's face back up to his and examined her with the eye of a judge about to render a verdict. "When did you last eat? Or is it the motion of this vessel. You're as pale as new parchment."

He sounded disgusted—as any good sailor would be at someone who could not tolerate the easy motion of a ship on calm water. Mortification stung Emilynne's cheeks. "I—"

"Get below, madam, and rest before you fall. It is not in my nature to bully the infirm no matter their secrets." His cool tone did nothing to soothe her embarrassment. "I'll seek your testimony later."

She nodded and hurried toward the steps, unwilling to show further weakness in front of him or the rest of the crew, who watched them so intently. Wind filled the sail over their heads and the ship pitched forward. Emilynne grabbed for the stair railing and nearly missed.

The captain's hand covered her gloved fingers atop the rail, cutting short her sigh of relief. The scent of sun-warmed oak and fresh-cut sage surrounded her as his other hand steadied her around the waist.

"Do you require further assistance?" His breath warmed her temples as he spoke.

For a moment his nearness struck her dumb. She could neither think nor move away as she turned to glance up into his face. He was so close. A warmth that had nothing to do with seasickness flooded her stomach. She had a curious urge to run her fingers over his hard jaw, trace the tiny dent in his chin, and feel again the touch of his firm lips.

His brows knit together, an inky black line across his forehead. "I do not even know your name."

His words came low and soft, as though he had not meant to give voice to them.

"Emilynne," she offered, her quiet tone matching his. "Emilynne Wellesley."

"Emilynne," he repeated as though he'd no idea what to do with the information he'd sought.

Again their kiss on the docks seemed to hover in the air between them, an unspoken intimacy between strangers. Heat crept into her cheeks, vying for dominance against the swirl of warmth in her limbs. The pressure of his fingers on hers burned through her gloves.

She shivered. "I think I can manage. I must see to the children."

He straightened, releasing her from the strange sensation of his touch. "As you wish, madam."

She descended the steps and traveled the corridor, feeling his gaze upon the back of her neck with each step.

Bryan watched her until the cabin door shut behind her. Only then did he become aware of Michael's presence beside him.

"Lovely woman, that," Michael McManus, shipmaster, captain, and longtime friend offered.

"Aye." Bryan took off his bowler and raked a hand through his hair.

"Seems ta me ye might have at least mentioned ye'd

gone and gotten married though. I'd have loved ta be there and offer my felicitations.''

Bryan searched Michael's features for humor or sarcasm. Beneath his cap, his friend's eyes were narrowed as he looked out over the water, giving no clue.

"Indeed," Bryan answered, wishing he couldn't still taste the honey-and-cream sweetness of Emilynne Wellesley's kiss. Wishing he could ignore the fire that raged through him when he touched her earlier as well as just then. Trying to convince himself he had not really heard the harps of The Blessing there on Limerick's dockside. He'd put the end to his chance at that family legend years earlier. "An old salt like you knows not to believe everything he sees and less of what he hears."

"Aye. That's true enough," Michael commented around the stem of his pipe. "She's married though, eh?"

Bryan's stomach knotted anew. "So it would seem." *I flee no husband*, her assurance hovered.

Silence held for a moment before Michael added, "And a mother."

"Pity," Michael observed when Bryan said nothing more.

"Have you something on your mind, Captain McManus?" Bryan prodded. "I find I'm in no mood for cryptic rejoinders. We've got to get to Liverpool as swiftly as you can manage."

Michael muffled a suspicious-sounding cough, though his face remained impassive. "You'll be bunkin' in the fo'castle, then, Captain?"

"You know I hate that title. I gave up all pretensions to earning it long ago."

Michael shrugged. "It is a tradition I'll not be the one

ta break. Ye'll survive a few days of respect. And hard work."

Michael transferred his twinkling gaze to Bryan and smiled. "A stiff run through the ocean waves is jest the thing ta blow out some of those staid cobwebs clogging yer innards. Any that are left after kissing a lass pretty as that one."

He strolled away, his shoulders shaking, though no laughter carried back on the breeze.

Bryan gritted his teeth. There were times Michael's observant nature grated on him. This was one of those times. No good could come from hungering after the young widow in his cabin.

If indeed she were a widow.

He knew next to nothing about Emilynne Wellesley save her desperation and the very real fear that drove it. It was no longer in his nature to act so impulsively as he just had on the docks. The last time he'd acted on his feelings had led to disaster. He quashed old pangs of guilt and remorse over the rash actions that had exiled him from his family and the call of the sea, setting his course toward a more stable career in law.

Yet, he could no more have left her behind than deny the pleasure he'd found in her kiss. The Blessing had seen to that. He intended to question Michael further about the men asking after her. Just as soon as Captain McManus was over his current bout of humor.

And then he would have an in-depth discussion with Emilynne Wellesley.

Chapter Two

"Keep the rest of that hot, will you, Jimmy?" The aroma of Granny's special ginger tea filled the galley, engulfing Bryan in his grandmother's tales of The Blessing and surrounding him with her determination that he and his brothers learn from them.

The past has much ta teach the future, my dears. And I aim ta see ye take heed. Granny's warning, issued from her rocker by the fire each night when they begged for another tale of mighty Fians and fey creatures, echoed in his ears.

"Aye, Captain Reilly. I'll set the pot by the fire." The *Caithream*'s cook broke into Bryan's thoughts. "It will be hot fer yer guest when she needs it."

Jimmy chipped a small piece from the wood figure he whittled. "Let's hope the queasies don't bother them little uns. They made short work of the chocolate and biscuits I brung 'em when we cast off."

Picturing the chaos three seasick passengers would create stopped Bryan in the galley hatchway. He'd cursed himself for a fool a hundred times in the past hour after allowing them on board. How could he believe lust engendered by a single kiss could have anything to do with The Blessing?

He gripped the mug's heated handle, searing a needed dose of reality into himself, hoping the pain would provide armor against strange callings from a heritage he'd abandoned long before. He made the wrong choice bringing Emilynne Wellesley with him. He'd be cursed to regret his impulse for the rest of the trip and God knows how long after.

He steadied himself against the bulkhead and took a deep breath, needing to pull his thoughts into logical order before he saw her again. He required a fuller picture of the situation he had so foolishly involved his ship and crew in, that much was certain. Especially to assess any possible interference in his own quest. With any luck he could deposit Emilynne Wellesley on Liverpool's wharf and be on his way with no delays.

At least the utter desperation leading to her unconventional arrival on board seemed confirmed. Michael's accounting provided the disturbing information that she must indeed be the person the rounders in Limerick sought. Their somewhat forceful inquiries dealt with a young woman with blond hair and blue eyes traveling with two young children. Michael had gained little beyond that in his efforts to question them except for the fact they had money to offer for her—a purse of gold coins. It would seem someone of means had sent the scurvies after her, but who? And why?

Perhaps it was not too late to turn back to Limerick.

Even as the thought sprang forward, he discarded it.

The distress haunting Emilynne Wellesley's gaze still twisted inside him. He couldn't abandon her to the fate she so feared until he knew for certain what she faced. Heaven knew, he needed no more hurdles or distractions placed between him and his goal. The possibility of securing new financing for Reilly Ship Works was too important to be delayed by nostalgia for childhood tales of Druid blessings or curses. Or a schemer's haunting eyes.

"Do ye want me ta warm that up a might, cap'n, afore ye actually take it ta yer *wife?*" Jimmy tried for a sober tone, but his shoulders heaved from his own jest.

"She's not . . ." Bryan winced, halting further protest before it could leave his lips.

Jimmy waved him away as he coughed through his laughter. "Course not. A woman as pretty as that would have ta be desperate indeed ta wed the likes o' ye. I jest pray she's not so poor a sailor as Master Devin."

The cook's hearty chuckle followed Bryan as he moved down the passageway. Mention of his younger brother always brought a smile. Though he struggled valiantly and drank gallons of ginger tea, Devin was indeed a poor sailor. Granny's recipe never failed to help, at least a little.

Wisps of ginger blended with the smell of sea-soaked wood and salt spray, scents all three Reilly brothers had been weaned on. Perhaps he should secure a mug for himself as well, to quell whatever had come over him at dockside earlier. He'd brew barrels of tea if it would help. Anything to dissolve his interest in the mysterious and troubled Emilynne Wellesley.

He shook his head as he started toward the salon. The high-pitched hum of childlike voices vied with the familiar creak of well-weathered timbers. An impossible hint of Emilynne Wellesley's freesia and lemon drifted in the air.

Her scent reached into him, twisting his stomach and knotting his resolve. He grimaced and raked a hand through his hair. Banked longings burned inside him with a ferocity he had no intention of investigating further. He tightened his lips and reached for the door handle. He was there to interrogate her. Nothing more.

His fingers hovered over the latch as he shored up his determination. He'd faced far tougher witnesses in his day and known beautiful women before—though none had ever made him feel that his life changed within seconds of their meeting.

And none had filled his soul with more color and music in a matter of seconds than he'd ever imagined could exist in a lifetime. He opened the hatch to the salon. "I see you." Words lilted into the passageway, followed by a cheery giggle, halting him in the entrance.

Bonnet abandoned, Emilynne Wellesley knelt on the floor. Her voluminous black silk skirts and petticoats bunched around her knees and bared her slender calves and shoeless feet.

The sight slammed into Bryan like a fist, cutting off his air, creating a tightness in his chest that was part pain, part pleasure. He'd expected to find her wilting in a chair, not engaged in children's play. Obviously her attack of nausea had passed. Had she feigned illness in order to avoid fulfilling her promise to tell him her story?

He tightened his lips to keep the accusation from bursting forth and ruining any chance he had of coaxing the truth from her.

The remembered feel of her pliant lips and soft curves threatened to steal away his resolution to get to the bottom of her predicament.

She was hardly the picture of proper English womanhood approved by Queen Victoria. She looked more like a carefree country lass than the cultured nobility her speech and manner conveyed. Bright color bloomed in her cheeks as her entire attention focused on the child in front of her. Her toes flexed and curled as she laughed. Beckoning.

Bryan's mouth went dry. He swallowed. He couldn't remember ever thinking a woman's feet, her toes, the slightest bit sensual. Now the sight of hers, bared for all the world, lent an incredible intimacy, a heated sensuality, to his presence in the salon. Hot blood rushed through him. Was her skin really as soft and creamy as it looked in contrast to the drab black of her gown?

The memory of his fingers tangling in the white-gold silk of her hair rose unbidden, the taste of her rousing him far more than it should. He'd never reacted so quickly to any woman before. And certainly not in the open company of others on the public docks. He caught back a groan and tried to dampen the desire this vixen in widow's weeds tore from him with such careless ease.

"Christian, I'm coming to get you." Feet arched, toes curling tighter still, she sang the words, eliciting more giggles from just beneath the old blanket the boy had draped over himself.

The child was not at all hidden, yet he seemed to think he was. The blanket quivered, beset with chubby chuckles. Vague memories of just such sport with Devin and their younger sister, Meaghan, sprang to mind.

Without warning Emilynne pounced on the blanket with an exaggerated cry of victory and gathered the child into her arms. A tantalizing glimpse of thigh flashed from beneath the lacy layers of her petticoats. Bryan nearly dropped the mug, managing to slop hot tea over his fingers as he clutched the handle tighter. The liquid's sting could not begin to compete with the heat burning in his belly.

Predator and prey rolled to a giggling stop at the tips of Bryan's boots, a tangle of arms and legs, enticing him with the gleam of Emilynne Wellesley's pale skin and supple figure. Bryan cursed silently and forced himself to focus on the child sprawled happily atop his mother. Stubby fingers tangled in loose ringlets of glossy hair that fell free from her coiffure during their mock tussle.

"Got you." The words came suprisingly clear from so small a boy.

"Indeed you have me, sir. I yield." Emilynne continued to smile up at him as they laughed together.

Bryan gritted his teeth, his whole being caught up in a silent groan. He fought the urge to gather her into his arms and taste the lilt of her words on her tongue. To savor her laughter and lose himself in her free spirit as she forgot any pretense at proper society. The sheer, ungoverned desire snaking through him fisted his free hand at his side. Enough of this.

"Feeling better, I see, Mrs. Wellesley." Brian didn't attempt to thaw the sarcasm icing his tone. The more distance he kept between them, the better off they would both be.

"Oh, my." Emilynne Wellesley's gaze focused upward from her incongruous position at Bryan's feet, her wide blue eyes, dark and luminous with some emotion he couldn't read. Surprise? Regret?

He raised an eyebrow, squashing his own disappointment as her smile disappeared. This woman rent his self-possession too intimately and far too easily. He must retain control.

She planted a quick kiss on Christian's cheek and set him down. "Go see Abby, darling."

The little girl sat stone still on the bench, watching the scene with solemn brown eyes. The boy appraised Bryan too before toddling to his sister's side, his eyes a blue the same shade as Emilynne's.

Emilynne shoved her skirts down over her bared legs in a rustle of silk and petticoats. "I beg your pardon."

"Allow me." Bryan offered his hand.

After a moment she slipped her hand into his waiting clasp. Cool and soft, he resisted the sudden urge to stroke his thumb over the back of her hand as he helped her stand. The black gown's hem settled toward the floor, hiding her feet. He suppressed a pang of regret.

"Thank you." Her tone grew wary as she gave him a far more sedate glance. Intelligence glowed in the blue depths of her eyes. He must proceed with care if he wished to get the truth from her, he told himself.

Bryan offered the mug of tea. "I brought this for you."

She took it from him as if happy to have something to occupy her hands.

"Thank you for this too." She inhaled a deep breath of the pungent brew. "What is it?"

"Ginger tea. An old family recipe." Bryan paused as she took a quick sip of the brew. "For seasickness."

"Oh." The roses in her cheeks bloomed anew. Embarrassment? Or shame for a deception? "How did you—"

"My family has been building ships for generations. I've seen many a green-gilled seaman. No Reilly ship sails without a supply of our granny's ginger tea."

She sipped again, her gaze not quite meeting his. "It is quite good. Soothing and stimulating at the same time. Your grandmother must be someone very special."

"Indeed." Bryan swallowed over the sudden tightness in his throat. *The choice once made cannot be undone.* Echoes of Granny gently chiding him shifted his suspicions. He tried to thrust all thoughts of The Blessing aside. Granny would have approved of his impulsive actions this day. "Very special."

Emilynne Wellesley's gaze met his, questioning and patient as though she would listen to whatever he wanted to say about Granny. As though she had all the time in the world to listen just to him. He was almost tempted to answer the questions he saw in her eyes.

It was a neat trick. He'd seen it used in many a deposition. If she had no intention of sharing information about herself or the children, she need only shift the focus back to him. A flash of annoyance over falling for such a simple tactic stung him.

He cleared his throat and reached for the impassive manner that availed him in court. "But you seem to have recovered on your own."

"Yes." She nodded. "Motion on the river, once I get used to it, doesn't seem to bother me as much as on the open sea." Her loose curls caressed her cheek. The movement caught her eye, and she hastened to tuck the strands back into place in her chignon before slipping her bare feet back into her shoes.

A swift knock from the passage stemmed an irrational surge of relief that her feet were now totally covered. The implied intimacy of her bare feet no longer threatened his tenuous control.

"Oh, beggin' yer pardon, Captain. Missus." Jimmy managed a nod to them both. "I brought this for the little miss." The cook held up a small, detailed carving of a unicorn.

Bryan lifted an eyebrow, caught between irritation and amusement. "I never took you for the fanciful type, Jimmy."

"Aye, well . . . ah." The cook's cheeks went a darker shade of their usual ruddy hue. "I've a houseful of young uns at home, sir. They like tales of strange beasties."

He turned his gaze toward Emilynne. "Do ye mind, ma'am?"

"It is a kind gesture." She offered him a hesitant smile, though her posture stiffened and her grip on the tea mug tightened enough to whiten the tips of her fingers.

Jimmy returned her smile with a sheepish one of his own and then made his way toward the children. She was silent as she watched the big cook kneel down between them. When he brandished the intricate unicorn, Christian's eyes widened. Even Abby, who seemed to be reserving judgment, smiled, drawn in by the little creature. She reached out a tentative finger and touched the little horn.

"Now, this here be fer yer sister, her bein' the eldest and all." Jimmy spoke quietly to the two children, so somber in their own black mourning. "What kind of creature would you like old Jimmy ta fashion fer ye young master?"

Emilynne's face paled a bit, heightening the dark circles beneath her eyes. What had happened to leave her so fearful? Bryan's need to resolve the puzzles surrounding her heightened.

"Jimmy's a bit rough around the edges, but he's got a gentle heart," Bryan offered in a quiet tone. "He'll not harm them."

She exhaled slowly, her gaze reflecting pensive caution and weariness barely held a bay. "We've been running so long, it is not easy to rely on anyone."

Her breath caught as the words left her. Her gaze turned

to his and locked there for a moment. She had not meant to speak her thoughts aloud. The knowledge blazed there on her delicate features.

He could no longer delay his questions.

"We need to talk, Mrs. Wellesley. Would you like to come up on deck?" Bryan prompted, sensing an opening in the mystery she held wrapped around her like a warm cloak.

She glanced back toward the children and then met his gaze. Her chin lifted just a bit. Her eyes darkened with unvoiced doubts and her gaze slid back to them, both busily engaged in play with the little unicorn.

"We can leave them with Jimmy for a few moments." Bryan raised his tone just enough to catch the cook's attention. Jimmy nodded without breaking the intent conversation he was having with Christian about unicorns and the purpose of their horns.

She gave him a rueful glance and tried to smile. "Very well, Captain. Though I did not fare well the last time I ventured on deck."

With a lingering glance at the children she moved to the hatchway. "I'll return in a moment, Abby and Christian." Though louder, her tone as she called back over her shoulder held a warmth he envied for a flash.

He held the door as she moved into the passageway. "Look toward the horizon this time. It will help you over the seasickness."

She preceded him up the steps and out into the sunlight. He followed her to the rail and waited until she had focused out beyond the water to the lush green banks of the Shannon. She braced herself against the ship and nodded, tensed and ready. Her posture reminded him of a reluctant witness determined to testify yet reveal as little as possible.

"What brought you to Ireland?"

Bryan hid a smile as Emilynne forgot to focus on the horizon and glanced up at him. Her own questions sparkled in her eyes. She had not expected casual conversation. So much the better. An indirect approach often yielded more answers.

Sunlight glinted on the water and danced along her silvery-blond tresses. Bryan kept his face impassive beneath her scrutiny. Worry, caution, and weariness fought a battle behind her deep blue eyes. What was she hiding? He offered her a polite smile and raised a brow as he waited.

After a long while, Emilynne looked back toward the horizon. She took a deep breath and said, "I came to study the standing circles."

"The what?" Surprise rippled through him, taking him off guard. He narrowed his gaze at her. It wasn't often objects of his scrutiny managed that.

She smiled. "Stone circles." Her tone held a hint of humor. "They date from the time of the Druids. Or maybe even before that. They are quite a passion of mine."

"Indeed?" Yet one more thing Granny would have approved of. He pushed renewed twinges of guilt aside and turned his grandmother's teachings to his own ends. "You're looking toward the peninsula where most of my granny's stories from the time of the Druids took place."

Again her gaze flew to his. Approval glinted there. Bryan decided to press his advantage as he gestured toward the distant purple hills. "It is called The Burren. Home of Polnaborne, Granny called it The Well of Sorrows."

She gazed toward The Burren with marked interest as he continued. "My elder brother and I visited the great stone table once. It was fascinating and a little overwhelming for a sixteen-year-old boy who thinks the world should be at his feet. I couldn't look away for the longest time."

"I know just what you mean." Her tone rippled through him, hushed and reverent. "Our family estates are in Wiltshire, close to Stonehenge. Even when I was a child I would beg my father to take me there. I used to think the stones could speak to me. Poor Papa, he spent a good deal of time among those ancient stones with never a word of complaint."

"How successful were you in your studies here?" He kept his tone low and even so as not to disturb the flow of her words.

"I spent an entire day at Athgreany in County Wexford. The locals call it the Piper's Stones, but that was before"— she swallowed and visibly forced herself onward—"we had to leave."

The sunlight reflecting on the water seemed to dim with the rush of sorrow that clawed her voice. Silence held between them for a moment.

Bryan could almost feel her pain. Sympathy welled, jolting him with unexpected strength. Ignoring his impulse to stop, he pressed for the answers he needed.

"What caused your flight from Ireland?"

Emilynne's breath caught at the directness of the captain's question. She clutched the tea mug, wishing the tin cup could lend her a small portion of its strength. She sought the words to begin, but the story seemed too overwhelming. Her stomach rolled and she managed another sip of tea. He was right. Looking toward the horizon did help—a little. But her stomach churned as much from fear as from the motion of the ship. Ginger tea could do little to ease that.

Silence drew out between them.

"What reason for this urgency?" His polite tone had gained a decided edge. She dared not glance up at him. He'd made their escape to home possible, and all he'd asked from her was the truth. A truth she'd promised him. A truth she could trust to no one until she'd made it to her destination.

Tension coiled ever tighter between her shoulder blades as she debated how much she should entrust to this stranger, no matter how gallant he appeared. The situation was complex, and hard for one of her own countrymen to fathom, let alone a foreigner, a man used to skimming the waters unfettered by the demands of family or property. She shifted her shoulders and forced herself to begin.

"I need to get the children out of Ireland. To England. That is where they will be safe."

"Why?"

Again a bald question, no longer couched in the polite terms dictated by genteel society. But then, their meeting had been far from any societal norms. Her cheeks burned and she bit her lip. What she had done she did because she had no other options. She didn't care what polite society thought.

"Because Robert is dead," she answered in a flat tone, not bothering to hide this one horrible truth. Tears sprang, hot and quick, burning her eyes and throat with her own unvarnished admission. She choked back the sob that threatened and swallowed hard. "Because there is nothing for us here and no one for us to turn to."

Silence again, broken only by the creaking of the ship and distant snap of wind-filled sails overhead.

"I'm sorry." His hand covered hers against the mug, warm and solid and capable. Yearning seized her, swift and unexpected. She wanted to lean against him, to rest against his shoulder and seek comfort. To pour out the whole of her tortured suspicions and bitter anxieties.

A tremor quaked through her as their embrace at the dock swirled into her thoughts again. Enfolded in this man's arms, she'd felt her first modicum of relief after days and nights of running with nowhere to turn. And no one to trust. Surely, that had to be the reason behind this desire raging through her like flames devouring dry kindling to seek his solace again. If only she dared.

But she didn't. Couldn't. No matter how kind Captain Reilly seemed, he was merely a means to an end. She should no more depend on him than she had any number of others.

She closed her eyes, trying to block out the sea of faces. Robert . . . Gail . . . Thaddeus . . . solicitors hovering like vultures . . . even the numerous draymen and farm wives who'd offered her transportation or a meal during their flight from Kildare . . . never knowing what or how much to tell.

Blast Thaddeus Whyte and his insidious plans.

"Why must you leave Ireland?" Bryan Reilly's question pulled her away from the tumult of her memories.

"In England we will be home," she told him, despising the tremor in her voice. "Away from Thaddeus Why—" She caught herself and realized his hands still covered hers on the mug.

She pulled way. "With people who know us, people who can help."

"Why are you running, Mrs. Wellesley?" His tone was low, but the question singed her like hot ash. "And from whom?"

She paced away from him, forgetting the horizon in her agitation. "There are things better left unsaid, truths better unspoken."

"Why?"

Because too much is at stake. She swallowed as her throat tightened. "My reasons are my own affair."

"I believe your method of achieving passage aboard my vessel makes your plight my affair as well. Or is it your custom to secure travel by offering yourself in such a fashion?"

Her breath caught in her chest. His words delivered a slap that rang in her ears. A bold affront, yet she could not deny what she had done. No one would have approved of her introducing herself to a man in public, let alone beg for his intimate embrace. Hot blood scalded her cheeks.

She held herself so straight, she felt sure her spine would snap from the effort. "No, sir, I assure you it is decidedly not my custom to do so."

He stepped closer, locking his gaze with hers. "Then, what forced you to do so today? And why did you pick me?"

He caught her shoulders in the warmth of his palms, gentle even as his tone grew harsh. Her heart pounded a traitorous warning as she searched his face, trying to discern which angered him more, her behavior or her choice of victims.

"Has it occurred to you that had you picked a man of lesser principle, you might even now find yourself flat on your back, paying for your passage?"

Ice trickled through her. Her blood seemed to rush out through her toes, leaving her light-headed as his meaning came home to her. She swayed and he steadied her. A myriad of possible outcomes ran through her dazed imagination in the span of a few heartbeats. She had been foolish to trust him. To trust anyone. She had placed three lives in his keeping without stopping to consider the consequences of her actions.

Where had her scholarly pursuits and careful planning been then? Just how weary and desperate had she become?

"Oh, Robert, what have I done?" The question slipped from her in a despairing whisper. Tears burned again at the back of her eyes, but she refused to give in, to show yet another sign of weakness.

Bryan Reilly's intent gaze searched hers for a moment. "Damnation," he cursed under his breath, releasing her shoulders only to cup her face and hold her gaze to his.

"I did not tell you this now to have you fear me. I wish to hear only the truth from you, devoid of games and hidden motives."

She could drown in the deep green of his eyes. His touch, so warm and alive, made her throat tighten, and she swallowed again. "Is there such a thing?"

"Aye, there always is. Tell me."

She closed her eyes and shuddered as the husky timbre of his voice unlocked her deepest yearnings. She held her lips closed against the urge to tell him everything in a rush. She could not. Not when she'd already been so foolish. She needed to rest and collect herself before she did something that put all of them in further peril. Abby's life depended on it. Christian's too.

With his hands so gentle against her skin she could not think. She pulled away from his touch and struggled to focus on the horizon once more.

"I must resolve a legal matter," she offered, trying to give him bits of truth without revealing the whole.

"Indeed?"

Was there a touch of disbelief to his tone? She blew out a tense breath as she warmed to her subject.

"Yes. I could no longer wait for the solicitors in Ireland to deal with . . . the matter. There is nothing worse than waiting for a firm full of greedy vultures delaying something that is of paramount importance to you. To them it is merely another pile of papers and the source of hefty fees."

That at least felt good. She drained the remainder of Granny Reilly's excellent but now cold ginger tea. Venting her ire and frustration about Thaddeus's solicitors was something she could handle without revealing everything.

"Indeed."

His tone made the word noncommittal despite his using it a second time. She supposed that as a ship's captain he hadn't much need of those in the legal professions. Lucky man. Perhaps if she carried her rant far enough, the rest of his questions and suspicions would drown in the tide of her wrath.

"Yes." She thumped the empty mug against the rail for emphasis. "Robert always dealt with the same firm at home, the same man. And no wonder, it must be next to impossible to find a reputable firm and even harder to find a responsible solicitor. One who will actually work to seek the truth. Such an advocate might actually be worth the exorbitant fees the rest of the profession gouges from the unwary."

Her host remained silent beside her. She watched the lush Irish landscape drift past for a moment. How she longed for sight of the English coast. She'd dreamed of nothing else but a visit to this mystic isle since she was a girl. She'd never be able to test her theories now. She'd never dare to return to these emerald shores; too much was at stake.

"And your flight? Is that a legal maneuver on your part? Is it legal at all?"

Tension underscored the sharpness of his questions. She could feel the same tension rippling toward her from the rigid stiffness of his posture. If she looked into his eyes, she was certain she'd never be able to carry off her answer. She avoided his gaze.

"Yes." She did not consider keeping the children in her care illegal. Her raising them was as necessary as her next breath, or Christian's or Abby's.

"Are you certain?"

She lifted her chin and met his gaze again; something in his tone told her she must. Challenge burned in the depths of his eyes, doubts and uncertainty. Her evasions had been for naught. He did not trust or believe her.

As long as he carried her home to England, that was fine, for she could not afford to trust him either.

"I'm quite certain that what I'm doing is both right and necessary, Captain. Else I would not be doing it."

He said nothing, his face an impassive mask. Gone was the gentle stranger who cradled her cheek just moments earlier. A pang of loss stung her.

"There ye are, Captain Reilly. Madam." The sailor, Michael, strolled over to them, breaking the tight lock they held on each other's gazes. "We're making good time, sir. We should be leaving the Shannon behind in short order. Did ye want to discuss our course?"

"If you will excuse me, I should get back to the children.'' Emilynne decided to take advantage of his timely interruption. ''I don't like to leave them alone for too long.''

''Of course.'' The captain nodded, but his dark gaze told her their conversation had not yet reached its conclusion.

Chapter Three

Michael joined Bryan at the rail and tamped tobacco into his pipe before lighting it, his actions smooth and easy from long habit. The pipe's aroma snapped in the crisp breezes off the Shannon to mix with a hint of brine from the sea. They would reach the river's mouth soon.

"Why consult me on our course, Michael? Rescuing a damsel in distress?" If Bryan was to do anything with his passengers other than take them to Liverpool or maroon them in a remote portion of his country, he'd have until well past Dingle and Bantry bays to decide.

"From the looks of the pair o' ye, ye both were in need of rescuin'," Michael answered. "I thought ye might want to reevaluate the course ye'd chosen with yer guest. She may not realize it, but ye looked stymied."

Bryan watched Emilynne Wellesley retreat down the aft hatch. He could almost read the relief spurring her nimble escape. Adding in the fact that she had yet to answer all but the most basic of his questions, he viewed her with new respect. And irritation. Stymied was right. If only he could think so clearly standing next to her.

"The lady had no love fer yer questions?" Michael observed.

"Aye. And the lady certainly has no love for solicitors. In fact, I'd say she positively loathes them." As the last whisper of her blond tresses disappeared from sight, Bryan turned back toward the river and the Irish coast.

"Does she know yet that she's beholden to one of Limerick's finest fer her passage?" Captain McManus offered with a touch of humor.

"No." Bryan shook his head, wondering just what her reaction to that news would be. "Not yet."

"This promises to be an interesting voyage. Mayhap ye'll have a better chance of keepin' yer secret if ye change out of yon fancy duds. There's not many a seaman who dress like they were due in court at any moment." Michael's amusement skipped across the Shannon's sparkling waters.

Bryan couldn't join in Michael's laughter. Her comments stung even as he tried to shrug them off. What possible difference could it make to him that she didn't care for men who practiced the law?

"I'll change once my gear is stowed in the fo'castle. We'll use the mate's berth for storage and charting. Now, did you really want to discuss possible routes to England?"

"No," Michael admitted, completely unabashed as smoke curled up from his pipe. "Although I do need to know if our passengers mean any changes to our destination."

"I hope not." Bryan still churned over everything Emilynne Wellesley had just said, along with all the things she had not. One partial admission stuck out beyond the rest.

Thaddeus Why— She'd stopped herself there.

Familiarity with the name had startled Bryan out of his own line of questioning. *Thaddeus Whyte.*

Certainty niggled that somehow the firm's newest client was tied into Emilynne's problems. Was he the man seeking her? With gold and hired ruffians? The notion seemed ludicrous. Gill O'Brien would be beside himself at the thought. Thaddeus Whyte was a noted horse breeder and trainer with a fine reputation for business that had reached all the way from County Kildare to Limerick.

As senior partner, Gill's job entailed enticing new clients to the firm. He had been trying to lure the famous horse breeder's business for years. He'd practically glowed when he announced they'd been given a small custody matter to attend for the man he'd pursued so long. The fact that the matter involved working with one of Bristol's most respected firms had been an added fillip to the deal.

Custody. The world telescoped to a fine pinpoint of fact as Bryan's legal senses twanged.

"She's on the run with two little ones." *I flee no husband,* she'd said. He groaned. "And all I felt was relief."

"What's that ye say, boy-o?" Michael clapped him on the shoulder. "Ye're relieved she's got children?" Puzzlement quavered in Michael's tone.

"There's many a man prefers a worldly-wise widow ta an untried miss. Still, I'm surprised ta hear it from ye. As well as ta see the impulse that set her on board yer ship. Ye've always been a might cautious since . . . well, fer quite a while."

Michael subsided to puff his pipe and stare at the Irish coast as his unfinished reference hung in the air between them like stale smoke. Michael knew firsthand the reasons driving Bryan's caution. He'd been the one to find him and Devin that night. If not for Michael's timely rescue, things would have been worse.

Much worse.

The pulse in Bryan's temples that had beat off kilter since Emilynne Wellesley ran into his arms pounded with the boldness borne of old wounds. He rarely allowed himself to dwell on the wreck that shattered his future while fissuring his past.

After all these years he thought he had learned control. Yet, capriciousness had once again landed him in uncertain waters. In an instant he'd surrendered to raging lust disguised as a family legend.

Blessing, indeed. He caught back a groan and cursed silently.

His previous indulgence in acting on heedless impluse cost him his father's respect and nearly ended his brother's life. What price would he pay for this new folly? Everything in him rebelled at the possibilities. What strange lunacy had convinced him he heard The Blessing when he held Emilynne Wellesley in his arms?

The sails billowed overhead, fluttering with the swirling crosscurrents of air as they neared the end of the Shannon. He forced himself to concentrate on the mess his ill-advised actions had created.

If Reilly Ship Works was going to have any chance at the expansion they so desperately required, he needed to reach Harland in Liverpool before the deal for Belfast's yard closed. He wanted to be the one to pull the family business back from the brink. To wipe out the mistakes of the past and show his father and brothers he was still one of them.

But he couldn't sabotage his firm in the process nor willingly circumvent the law by aiding and abetting a fugitive's flight. He hated the idea of turning back to Limerick if he was wrong. He hated the thought that all his careful planning and common sense had blown away on the harbor breezes, prompted by the sweet passion in a lass's kiss and the phantom strains of a ghostly harp.

What was the name of the firm Gill was consulting in Bristol on this custody matter? Jefferies, he thought. He exhaled long and slow.

"It is as well you asked about the course, Michael. I'm afraid we will be making an unscheduled stop. Head us into Bristol first. I've a few details that need attending."

"That'll back up our landing in Liverpool by a full day or two, more if we run into weather." Michael scrutinized Bryan from the corner of his eye, as his pipe released fragrant smoke swirls into the air. "Must be important details."

"Aye. I think I know why our Mrs. Wellesley is running. And from whom." Bryan wished the echoes of The Blessing did not still reverberate through him. He reached a hand up to grasp the rigging. The rough hemp chaffed his palm with a welcome sting of reality. "If I'm right, the man is a client of O'Brien and Mallory's."

"Should we stop now?" Michael followed the direction of Bryan's thoughts with the ease of long familiarity. "Mayhap we could still get to Irish authorities before we hit the open sea."

Bryan shook head, making his decision even as Michael voiced the course he had privately considered. "I'm still only formulating my theory. There are too many unanswered questions. And too little time to guess wrong."

Bryan tugged on the rope. "I need to get to England. At least there I can telegraph Liverpool to explain my delay."

"It is not the only reason spurring ye ta continue on, is it?"

Michael's question hit too close to truths Bryan hesitated to face. The Blessing, if it existed, and if that was what he'd felt on the docks, was not to be lightly taken. Still, he could hardly explain away the gut certainty that had shaken him to his core when he'd kissed Emilynne Wellesley.

He sought a reason he could share more openly. The sparkle of the afternoon sun on the water reminded Bryan of Emilynne Wellesley's deep blue gaze. "When she came on board, one thing struck me beyond all else. She was frightened to death. When she looks at me, there's fear and desperation in her eyes. I don't think any of that's a lie."

Michael was silent for a moment. "Aye, well, that's not all that struck you."

Bryan sent Michael a quelling look. *Trust an old friend to see right through my evasion.*

"Beggin' yer pardon, Captain." The smile lay heavy in Michael's tone, though his nod was deferential. "But it was plain for all Christendom ta see, the lass knocked the wind out of yer sails. She gave ye a kiss to sizzle the socks off the Pope."

"Her kiss was borne of fear and despair, not passion." Lemon and freesia and the soft feel of her in his arms. Sizzling, indeed.

Michael took a long draw from his pipe. "Mayhap, but if that's true, remind me to give my missus a good scare the next time we make Limerick's harbor."

Michael's shoulders shook at his own humor, though he had the sense to hold his laughter mute. He puffed in silence for a moment.

"I'm blessed with the funniest captain ever to put to sea," Bryan said under his breath.

"Aye." Michael blew out a long string of pipe smoke. "Ye are that, Bryan Reilly. It is lucky ye have meself to show you the humor in life when ye are so disposed to look at the darker side of things."

"I've had enough humor to last me for the moment."

"So it is to Bristol first, then. Ye're sure?" Michael squinted again.

"Aye. There is no help for this. If her troubles stem from a matter my firm is involved with, I'm honor bound to handle this."

"As you wish, Captain. I'll chart the necessary changes. It will be a long while till we pass Bantry and have any course corrections." Michael offered a cocky salute as he went back to his duties.

Bryan shook his head and turned his gaze out across the water toward the island they would pass just after sundown. Beannacht Island, home of Reilly Ship Works, birthplace of the Reilly Blessing legends. The deep blue of Emilynne Wellesley's troubled gaze blended with the sea ahead. "I wonder what Granny would have to say about all of this."

Emilynne descended into the relative safety of the *Caithream*'s dark passageway. Her breath felt trapped in her chest and her heartbeat drummed in her ears. Every inch of her seemed to hold the imprint of Captain Reilly's determination to wrest the whole truth from her. Truths she dared not trust to anyone until she had the children safely ensconced at home.

Had she said too much? How much was too much? The

same questions she'd been dodging for weeks ran around and around in her head like a terrier chasing a rat.

She rested against the bulkhead and counted very slowly. To ten. To twenty. To twenty-five. Gradually her heartbeat calmed and her breath came easier.

She was so tired of this constant alert. The perpetual fear. Returning home would at least grant her a respite from the subterfuge she'd been husbanding for far too long. She wished for what seemed the thousandth time that they had never come to Ireland in the first place.

But wishing could not make it so. She closed her eyes. If only she didn't react to Bryan Reilly the way she did. There was something about the captain, in his tone, his manner, that reached inside her and coaxed forth a tumult of longing.

His words echoed in her mind. *You might even now find yourself flat on your back, paying for your passage.*

Dark images of unthinkable acts followed by a stranding or even murder haunted her. What might have become of the children? She shivered again. Why had none of that occurred to her when she'd seen Captain Reilly on Limerick's docks?

Because she'd been too tired and too desperate, she answered herself. No wonder her brother had doubted her ability to take charge of his children on her own. Robert had said he didn't want her burdened with looking after the children and running the estates when she had her own pursuits. That was his explanation for giving his friend Richard charge over the lands and accounts. Richard would even be named co-guardian, he'd said, should the unthinkable happen and Emilynne be unwed at the time.

"If the proof is in the pudding—I'm a disaster. Oh,

Robert, you were right not to trust me. I'm not good at making decisions. And I'm a terrible judge of people." Green eyes and wavy black hair that unleashed wild longings were no basis for trust, no matter the appeal of the cleft in his chin or the broad strength in his shoulders.

Years of never quite fitting in blended with the terrors of the past months. She'd always preferred her studies of ancient scrolls and texts over the normal pursuits for society's young ladies. Her family had teased her indulgently about her lack of worldly knowledge. If only she'd tried to muster the interest—paid more attention—she might have been better prepared for making travel arrangements and judging who was a cad and whom she could trust. But her parents, and then Robert, had always smoothed the way for her.

She knew Robert and Gail wanted the children to remain with her, but had they intended to push her now toward the decision they'd quietly approved in life? Richard Andrews had always been a part of her life, like the air and the Wiltshire countryside. Almost as close as her own brother since their estates marched side by side. A match between them had long ago earned everyone's approval. Everyone's except her own. The tacit understanding had been to allow her more time to complete her latest project and reach her decision upon their return from Ireland.

She wondered what Richard's reaction would be to her return. The children needed a stable home. A substitute father. Would he be happy that she was finally ready to accept his proposal? One of them should be. She was too numb.

The gentle sway of the boat on the river picked up speed with a slight jolt. She could hear orders being shouted and feet scampering across the deck in rapid compliance. Soon they would be at sea. She prayed her good fortune with keeping her nausea at bay would continue but doubted such would be the case. She should hunt up another cup of that ginger tea before they hit open water. But first she wanted to make sure the children were all right. They hadn't been separated for this long since they'd left County Kildare. In truth, save for her one day's journey to the Piper's Stones, not since they'd come to Ireland. And look how disastrous a day that had turned out to be.

She gathered herself together and fought to keep her balance as the ship rose and fell with the new current. "Abby? Christian?"

She opened the salon hatchway to find her niece and nephew wedged tight against the vessel's cook as he hummed a tuneless ditty, his own eyes closed as tight as theirs as they sat together in the captain's chair.

Relief mixed with sadness in a bittersweet pang tensing her throat. This rough-made seaman couldn't possibly know how often Abby and Christian had sat just so with their father. A tear burned its hot pathway down her cheek. Robert had a lovely voice, and though Jimmy's was much deeper, it appeared to be enough to satisfy two heartsick, weary children. Abby's face, though drawn and tired, looked relaxed. Christian looked to be asleep.

A sigh escaped Emilynne as she brushed the telltale droplet away with shaky fingers.

The cook's eyes drifted open. "Oh, Missus." He eased his bulk out from between the two children who snuggled against each other in the warm spot he left behind.

"I hope ye don't mind. It has been almost a month since I snuggled me own little uns." He cleared his throat.

Underneath his gruff bulk there did indeed beat a tender heart. "No, Jimmy." She smiled at him even as the ship's rolling momentum gripped her stomach. "I don't mind."

"Are ye quite all right?" Jimmy peered at her with a worried frown.

The squint of his eyes seemed only to tighten the queasy swirl in her stomach.

"Yes." She bit off her answer as her stomach clenched and the room swirled. "Well, no. Is there any more of that ginger tea about?"

"Oh, aye." Jimmy hurried toward the door. "Sit yerself down. I'll be right back."

Emilynne braced herself in a corner of the salon, trying for as little movement as possible while her stomach rolled in opposite pitch to the ship's motion. Closing her eyes helped a little, but experience told her the relief wouldn't last long.

Within moments Jimmy reappeared with a tin cup in hand. The scent of hot ginger stung her nostrils as he came closer. "Ye look whiter than the ship's sails, Missus. Even Master Devin doesn't turn that pale."

He pressed the mug into her hands, and she forced herself to take a small sip. Surprisingly, just the scent helped a little. The hot tea burned its way into her stomach, and she counted slowly. Perhaps distraction would help. "Devin?"

The cook stood poised for action before her, watching her face with the intent expression of a man who knew how to read seasickness through long experience. "Yer pardon, ma'am?"

"You mentioned someone named Devin just now. Is he one of your sailors?"

"Master Devin's Captain Reilly's brother. Youngest of the three Reilly boys, he is. He'll ne'er be a true sailor, pluck as he is. He's yet ta gain his sea legs, though he's a whiz with the sextant.''

Emilynne took a deep breath. The distraction was not helping. Cold beads of moisture broke out over her lips, and her stomach rolled in a long, hot wave. "Oh, my."

"Here ye go, lass." With a quick gentleness that belied his girth, Jimmy maneuvered her toward the bucket he'd placed by the door. "It's all right."

Her face flushed hot, cold, and then hot again as she emptied the meager contents of her swirling stomach into the bucket, once again mortified by her lack of control. Already she could feel the dark void racing toward her. Soon she would be as useless as a lump of stone. How humiliating.

"I'm sorry," she managed to say as Jimmy offered her a cool cloth. "And thank you."

"Aye, lass, don't fash yerself." The cook patted her shoulder before scooting the bucket into the passageway. "Ye're no' the first person to suffer, and ye'll no' be the last."

Emilynne groaned as the ship pitched across a large wave and a brisk wind caught her sails. She closed her eyes and rested her head against the *Caithream*'s cool oak wall.

"I'm sorry. Could you please ... I can't ... the children ..." Darkness rushed up to meet her before Emilynne could finish. The floor tilted severely to the right, and she could feel herself falling, free and weightless. Why was it taking her so long to hit the floor?

Bryan stood with his feet braced on the deck, at ease with the feel of the ship rolling beneath him. There was nothing like being at sea and still nothing better than being at sea aboard a Reilly vessel. Pride tugged his shoulders taut as the *Caithream*'s bow sliced easily through the water.

"Captain Reilly?"

The title grated a little less with the waves below him and the wind filling the sails above. "Aye?"

"Sir, it's Mrs. Wellesley."

Bryan glanced behind him. Jimmy stood ramrod straight, a worried frown creasing his weathered face.

"What about her?"

"Well, sir, ye'd best come below. She's a mite . . . under the weather, if ye get my meaning."

Bryan sighed, pulled back to reality by the cook's hesitant admission. How could one woman cause so much trouble? He headed toward the stairs. "All right, Jimmy. Is the ginger tea still hot?"

"Oh, aye, it is that. But I don't think that's going to help." The cook's words came in a tone of dire lament.

Bryan turned to fix him with a hard stare. "What do you mean, Jimmy? Out with it, what's wrong?"

"One moment she was fine, though sick as a lad that's ne'er put ta sea, then she slumped over." Jimmy spread his hands. "She fainted dead away on me, Captain. I only just caught her afore she hit the deck."

Bryan took the steps at a run. He burst into the salon, only to find Abby and Christian asleep in a chair.

"Where is she?"

"In yer cabin, Captain." Jimmy followed him as Bryan changed direction. "I thought it best ta put her in yer bunk seein' Cap'n Mike already strung ye a hammock in the fo'castle with the rest of us."

Bryan blew out a long breath and pushed into the cabin. The sight of her lying pale and limp against the coverings sank tenterhooks of concern deep into his flesh.

"What happened?" He crossed the cabin in two long strides.

"Like I said, Captain, she was fine, then sick, then out so quick, I almost missed her."

Bryan stroked damp tendrils of hair away from her forehead. She was far too warm. "Get me some cool water, Jimmy."

"Aye, sir." The cook disappeared through the hatchway.

Bryan braced his thigh along the edge of the bunk and leaned down to look at her more closely. Even ill, she was lovely. He swallowed.

"Emilynne." Her name came out in a rasp. He cleared his throat.

"Mrs. Wellesley—"

"Here ye be, Captain." Jimmy appeared at his elbow with a basin and a clean towel. He placed them on a small table, then hovered nearby, like an oversized gull fretting over a pier.

Bryan dampened the towel and soothed it over her face and neck. After a moment her eyelids fluttered open. Her gaze focused on him, filled with confusion.

"Richard?" Hope as well as chagrin laced her question. "I'm so sorry, Richard. Robert is gone. We are so lost."

Robert was the name of the children's father. Who was this Richard?

"It is the captain, lass," Jimmy offered in a gentle tone. "Ye're safe aboard ship."

"Captain?" Her brow furrowed and she closed her eyes. "No, no more ships, please. Richard, can't we just go home to Newbury Manor?"

"Yes." Bryan couldn't stand the plea in her tone. All the worry that lay trapped behind her eyes now shivered through her weakened tones. "Yes, we'll go wherever you feel safest, Emilynne."

Her brow cleared and some of the tension left her body as two tears tracked over her cheeks.

"Thank you." She shuddered. "I have been so worried. So many nights. All the running."

"Whom are you running from, Emilynne?" Guilt twisted through Bryan even as he asked the question. She was not really aware of her surroundings. He should not be asking and yet he had to know the answer.

"Thaddeus." The name came from her in a mix of loathing and fear. She shuddered again and a low moan escaped her lips. "You remember, Gail's uncle. Thaddeus Whyte."

The fine hair at the back of Bryan's neck rose. He found himself gripping the side of the bunk so tightly, his fingers ached and he forced himself to relax. She *was* connected with Thaddeus Whyte.

What caused her flight with the children?

"What happened?" he prompted, needing to hear whatever she would say.

More tears squeezed out from behind her closed eyelids. "Richard, it was so awful—"

Her voice drifted away. She lay pale and still against the pillow for a long while before continuing. "The children are in danger."

Whether what she said was the truth or the result of her illness, she believed it now. Bryan could feel that as strongly as if it were his own conviction. And the danger emanated from Thaddeus Whyte.

"Emilynne—"

Her hands gripped the coverlet as her eyes opened,

pinning him in a gaze of tortured, storm-tossed blue. "Promise you will protect the children."

The intensity of her gaze reached inside him. At that moment it did not matter that the promise sought was not his. The connection between them thrummed so strongly, it blocked out everything else. Blessing or curse. As he looked into her eyes, her very soul, the promise became his.

He took her hands in his. "I will protect the children, Emilynne. I always stand true to my promises."

Her gaze searched his for a moment, and then, as though she found what she sought, she sank against the pillow, exhausted by the exchange.

"Blimey, Captain." Jimmy's whisper barely registered as Bryan continued to look down at her. His heart pounded with raw protective emotions, leaving him dumbfounded.

"Indeed." *Blimey* didn't begin to cover it.

"What do you think—"

The hatchway opened behind them with a slight creak. "Excuse me." A young voice spoke and Bryan turned to find the girl, Abby, at the entrance. "I can't seem to find—"

"Mama? I'm hungry." The boy appeared beside her. He frowned into the cabin, sighed in disappointment, and then stepped toward the bunk.

"What's wrong with Aunt Emilynne?" Abby's cheeks went pale beneath her dark brown lashes as she followed her brother across the cabin.

"She's having a wee touch o' sickness," Jimmy answered.

"Will she be all right?"

"Oh, aye, lass, she'll be fine. She—"

"Wait." Bryan dropped to one knee beside Abby. "Your aunt?"

The girl nodded.

"Emilynne Wellesley is your aunt?" Bryan couldn't stop himself from repeating the question. Hidden relief surged followed by more questions. All would have to wait closer examination later.

She nodded again, downy auburn curls brushing her shoulders. "Yes. Our parents are . . . were . . . Robert and Abigail Wellesley of Newbury Manor. Aunt Emilynne takes care of us now. She's taking us home."

The child looked up at Jimmy again, then back at Bryan. "She won't die, will she?" The question came with deadly calm and seriousness though the girl braced as if for bad news.

Bryan took her hand and matched her tone as he held her gaze with his. "No, Abby, she will not die. Your *aunt* will be fine as soon as the seasickness passes."

The girl met his gaze with a maturity far beyond her years, her manner grave as she measured his words. "Just Aunt Emilynne's usual seasickness?"

"Yes."

"Supper?" Christian's voice piped up from the bunk. He had crawled up beside Emilynne and was tugging at her sleeve.

"Oh, aye, boy-o, supper it is." Jimmy chuckled. "But ye'll no' get it in bed." He scooped the boy up, turned to Abby, and offered his arm. "Would ye be so kind, Miss, as to accompany us to the galley?"

After giving Emilynne one last worried glance, she nodded, accepting Jimmy's hand as the cook headed toward the salon, already spinning tales of the delicious supper he would serve them.

Bryan looked back toward the bunk as the hatchway closed behind them. Emilynne lay deep asleep, her hair in loose waves across the pillow. He couldn't resist the urge to brush his fingers against her cheek beneath the dark signs of weariness marking her. So very soft and so vulnerable. Traits he was quite certain she had no intention of revealing to anyone.

I flee no husband. That part of her story seemed true. And from young Miss Wellesley's innocent revelation, he gathered that Robert and Abigail were deceased. Added to what little he knew of the Whyte matter, the question of who should care for their children must be open to dispute.

"Not very thoughtful of your brother, leaving things in a muddle. What made you decide to take matters into your own hands, *Miss* Wellesley?"

He wiped the cloth across her brow. "And why did you have to thrust them so squarely into mine as well." More questions to be examined later.

He loosened the buttons at her cuffs and collar. His fingers lingered on the creamy softness of her throat. Just feeling for a pulse, he tried to convince himself; after all he had a vested interest in her recovery. The sooner she roused from her illness, the sooner he'd have his answers and the sooner he could set about putting things to rights.

He wiped her brow again. "So far ye're turning out ta be far more curse than blessing, Emilynne Wellesley. That's for certain."

Chapter Four

Blue Hills Stud
County Kildare, Ireland

The rumble of hooves echoed across the meadow, a frenzied tattoo both felt and heard. Thaddeus Whyte gripped the fence post and leaned over, eager to see which of his latest class of two-year-olds would lead out of the far turn. If he was any judge of horseflesh, and he prided himself on his ability to pick the best, it would be Ramses, the big bay he'd bought the previous October at Goff's yearling sale.

"Beg pardon, sir," his groundsman's timid voice sounded behind him. Irritation pierced Thaddeus as he lost sight of which horse made the turn first.

"Blast it! What is it, O'Toole?" The Irish were an ignorant lot, possessing no sense of timing. The distasteful trait had never ceased to grate on him through his years of stewardship at Blue Hills Stud. "And it better be good since you've interrupted me now."

He swung around and stopped his tirade short as he squinted against the setting sun. Two men stood in the stable yard. His anticipation rose. "So you're back, Wilkins. Have your men run that chit to ground at last?"

Wilkins's sly gaze slid toward the stable for a second before he shook his head.

Thaddeus barely contained the surge of frustration coursing through him. The man's reports had changed little over the past three weeks. "It is most definitely time to engage someone more capable of concluding this business."

"We almost nabbed her in Limerick, Mr. Whyte," the man said. "We traced to her to a ship bound for London. Only she never boarded."

"Damnation. How can one woman prove so difficult to locate? Especially one dragging two children." The blood in his temples thundered so loudly, Thaddeus barely felt the horses passing on the track behind him. Why had she fled to Limerick of all places? "Where is she now?"

"We think she slipped onto a smaller boat."

Thaddeus's fists clenched at his sides. A smaller *boat* indeed. Emilynne Wellesley had proved a thorn in his side ever since she'd arrived in Dublin with her precious brother and his brats. And Gail. After years of delay he'd tried to entice his niece home on her own, but her husband insisted on accompanying her and dragging along his entire family. More's the fool.

"Beg pardon, sir?" O'Toole spoke up, interrupting Thaddeus's thoughts yet again. "But couldn't ye jest wait fer her ta turn up at her own home in England?"

Thaddeus bit back frustrated anger. Such a display

served only to make the dolts on the estate less likely to cooperate with his needs. And just then it looked as if he needed every man he could muster. A snicker flicked across Wilkins's deceptively smooth choirboy's face. He understood the game at least.

"I've told you." Thaddeus forced patient reason into his tone. "Told all of you here how important it is to get Miss Gail's children away from Miss Wellesley as quickly as possible. She is a dangerous woman prone to fits and hysterics, not at all suitable to take two innocent orphans on some nonsensical flight across Ireland."

Until the custody of the two brats was fixed here, he daren't let her reach England and gain ungoverned access to the legal system there.

"A farmer outside the city gave them shelter one night," Wilkins rejoined. "He remarked he'd never seen such quiet children. It was unnatural-like. She's most likely got them tykes scared ta death." A cunning smile slid across Wilkins's lips. Thaddeus appreciated the insertion. The man had potential despite his failures to date.

The small Irishman still carried a doubt-filled wrinkle over his brow. Thaddeus caught back a sigh of impatience. Charm and guile had gotten him much further in life than bluster and bellowing. He needed his men to be as eager to find the fugitives as he was, through greed or trickery. Whatever worked faster.

"She had us all fooled when she first arrived, what with her sweet manners and angel's face. I could scarce give credence to the stories my niece had written to me regarding Miss Wellesley's flights of fancy and vile temperament."

"I don't know, sir. She was right nice ta me the day I took her over ta them Piper's Stones," O'Toole shared with halting reluctance yet truly irritating Irish stubbornness.

"Even let me wait by the rig when I told her them ruins give me the creeps."

"There you have it." Thaddeus pounced on the man's superstitious fears. "What kind of hobby is it for a gentlewoman? Measuring stone ruins and writing stories of pagan ways and devil worship?" He snorted and took a step closer.

"I only pray," he continued, dropping his tone as O'Toole leaned closer, "she hasn't taken those poor innocents off to use them in some ungodly sacrifice."

A look of open horror crossed O'Toole's face. "Heaven forbid." He quickly crossed himself.

Thaddeus hid his smile and spread his hands, striving for a worried expression. "You can see the reason for my urgency in locating the children. After she attacked me and laid me low with that vase and then locked your sister in the linen closet, O'Toole, I'm afraid Miss Wellesley is capable of anything in her paranoia and delirium."

O'Toole nodded in agreement now. The fool. It was sometimes too easy to manipulate simple minds. "Come with me to my study, Wilkins, and tell me everything you've learned and how much more it will cost me to bring them back to Blue Hills. I'll spare no expense if it means my great-niece and -nephew will come to no harm at her hands. It's what Miss Gail would have wanted."

Thaddeus took the path toward the house, his two minions shuffling in his wake. He'd get those urchins back and under his control by any means necessary. He'd expended too much effort and too many years to cede control of the stud farm to anyone at this point. If only Gail had understood that. She and her headstrong husband might be alive to raise their miserable progeny themselves.

Emilynne Wellesley would soon come to understand

those brutal facts. Thaddeus smiled to himself. A year or two in an Irish prison for kidnapping would hasten her desire to accept his clemency, and perhaps the occasional offer of a reunion with the children, in exchange for certain personal considerations.

The vision of the elegant blond begging for his goodwill warmed him. She was one filly whose spirit he'd truly enjoy bringing to hand.

An hour later, after digesting the nuances of Emilynne's apparent departure from this country, Thaddeus handed his man a small sack of gold with an envelope and new instructions.

"Wilkins, return to Limerick at once. Tell Mr. O'Brien that I expect him to get me that guardianship immediately. The confirmation my niece and her feckless husband did not make any provisions for their children is enclosed."

Using an entirely new firm for this custody matter had worked out rather well expediency-wise. His other firm was too well informed regarding the efforts he'd required to keep control of Blue Hills from passing to Gail.

Wilkins nodded his agreement to what they both knew was a sham and shoved his hat on his blond curls. "Aye, sir, I'll ride all night if it will help save them little tykes." His lips twisted over the words.

Thaddeus favored him with an approving smile. Wilkins was so apt at playing the innocent. "Good man—young lives are at stake. When you've delivered my missive, I want you to learn as much as you can about Reilly Ship Works and the captain of the vessel you think the children were spirited away on. I want to be certain Liverpool was their only destination. Then meet me in Dublin if you can."

Wilkins touched his cap and strode out of the room.

Thaddeus turned to his groundsman. "O'Toole, have

that lad of yours bring around the carriage. I will go to Dublin and send word to my man in England that he must be alert for Miss Wellesley's arrival. With any luck, a Dublin cutter can make landfall in England before the ship she's taken passage on rounds this side of the coast. I want to go over at once to fetch those dear children back here, where they belong.''

"I'll see to it meself, sir. Mr. Wilkins sent him ta apprentice at the ferrier's down Waterford well. Seemed strange him takin' an interest, but it is jest as well, the lad's been a might skittish 'bout carriages ever since Miss Gail's accident.'' O'Toole bobbed his head and left.

Ah, yes. Wilkins had mentioned a potential problem there. An accident to the blacksmith's assistant would go unnoticed once the matter at hand was settled.

Thaddeus steepled his fingers before leaning back in his chair. If O'Brien & Mallory delivered the goods, he'd have a warrant sworn out for that chit before seeking her on the other side of the realm.

He grabbed for his tumbler and tipped back a triumphant swallow from his stock of excellent whiskey. He could hardly wait to see Emilynne Wellesley in chains.

Bristol, England

Heels thudded against the gangplank through the thick fog shrouding Bristol's waterfront.

Please, let this be Captain McManus with news. Sharp memories of the two roughcuts looking to snatch the children from her on Limerick's docks pricked Emilynne. She shivered at the base of the steps by the aft hatch, hesitating before exposing herself to any prying eyes or ears skulking behind the nightly activities plied along the wharves despite the damp weather.

Surely, Thaddeus would have men watching for her here of all England's ports. She'd been too grateful to escape Ireland, and then too ill, to dwell on the danger of their destination. Though for some reason she'd thought the vessel was headed to Liverpool.

Thankfully, Bristol's dual waterways were long and crowded. She could only hope waiting by every one of them would be an impossible task—even for Thaddeus and his almost limitless resources.

Emilynne shivered again, her teeth chattering as she drew her black wool cloak tighter about her shoulders. Despite her recent incapacity, there was no time to indulge in further weakness or faintness of heart. Getting the children safely home was paramount. Even alerting the authorities that Robert's and Gail's deaths were not accidental was secondary to that goal.

She had felt too ill before they docked in Bristol to do more than nod her assent to Captain Reilly's proposal that he see her safely settled there. What had she gotten them into?

She'd felt off kilter ever since they'd reached the Bristol Channel and the waters had calmed a trifle. She'd tried but still could not fit the pieces together. Somewhere on the open water he'd turned from addressing her as Mrs. to Miss just as she thought of him almost exclusively by his first name. When had this intimacy been forged?

Not to mention that somewhere in between bouts of nausea she must have told him about their connection to Bristol.

She truly owed this crew a debt of gratitude, but if Bryan's plans did not meet with her approval, she would take matters back into her own hands now that they were so close to home. Thaddeus Whyte would need an army to pry them out of Wiltshire if she could just get them there.

"Greetings ta ye, Captain," Captain McManus's voice called out across the planks as he thudded onto the deserted deck. Two captains on one ship. Images and voices from her seasickness swirled and faded.

"Hello, Michael."

Emilynne smothered a gasp as Bryan Reilly's deep tones answered from close by. She halted in the hatchway and watched his silhouette ease away from the ship's central mast. She hadn't seen him since he'd brought Abby and Christian belowdecks when the ship left the Bristol Channel and entered the Floating Harbor. He'd warned her then to stay below until he came to fetch them and escort them ashore. But that had been hours earlier.

Captain McManus struck a match as Bryan drew near, lighting his pipe with several long pulls. The flickering flame revealed the bearded man's merry eyes even as it chased shadows across the chiseled planes of his companion's clean-shaven features. A pang of loneliness stung her as she realized how much she was going to miss these two captains. Despite her misgivings, she'd come to depend on them far more than she cared to admit. Yet another loss to face.

Emilynne closed her eyes and took a steadying breath. She'd no time to indulge in a bout of emotions that could not be remedied. The gentle sway of the ship in its moorings made her stomach lurch anew and forced her eyes open once more. Fighting to keep her equilibrium, she hesitated in the hatchway, knowing she'd never convince these men she could manage on her own if she staggered on her way over to them.

"Any news? Are there any inquiries being made regarding Miss Wellesley?" Bryan's questions put voice to her own concerns. "She is quite certain she will be sought for here."

She shouldn't eavesdrop. She should step forward and declare her presence to the men. No good comes from listening at keyholes, long-ago lectures from her governess echoed as she hung back. But then she doubted Miss Brown had envisioned life-threatening situations during her instructions on polite behavior. Thaddeus had fooled them all—with disastrous results. She could not take the chance it would happen again. She'd be better off trying to steal away with the children than to walk into a trap through ignorance or misplaced trust.

"Aye. There's news, and then again there's not." McManus nodded and took a long pull on the bowl of his pipe. It glowed red in the gloom.

"There's been inquiries here and there about one of the quality traveling alone with two children. Just as she feared. Gave a fair description of the lass, too, from what the tap man at the Llandoger Trow was a'tellin me."

Emilynne gulped a deep breath of air. The smell of rotting food and raw waste from the harbor water washed through her in a nauseating rush pushed by fear and panic. Thaddeus must be spreading his gold—*Gail's gold*—pretty generously for her description to be known at Bristol's busiest tavern.

Her heart pounded and the fog seemed to thicken, obscuring her thoughts as well as her vision.

"Not now," she whispered. When she was home in Wiltshire—home and all of this was settled—then she could indulge in a case of the vapors. She gripped the cool wood trim of the hatch and fought for control.

"What else?" Bryan's terse response helped her get a grip on her rebellious stomach.

"That office ye sent me to was locked up tight. I nosed about instead. None hereabouts that recognized the name had anything but the highest praise for Robert Wellesley. He's known as a man of integrity and fair dealings. No hints of anything untoward."

He'd been checking Robert's credentials? Confirming her story? In a flash, ire displaced a portion of the nausea still threatening her. *How dare anyone question the honor of a Wellesley?* Who in bloody blazes did Captain Bryan Reilly think he was?

The total stranger into whose arms she had flung herself.

That thought brought her rolling emotions to a halt and warmed her cheeks. The memory of his lips claiming hers by her own insistent demand on the Limerick wharf stilled her outrage. In that one instant she'd tasted a lifetime of solace and reliability she'd never dared to dream could exist for her. She held herself in check by the hatch. She dared not dream it existed at all.

Bryan . . . Captain Reilly had behaved in nothing short of a chivalrous manner since she'd foisted herself on him. Of course he'd need to verify for himself that what little she'd told him was the truth. A gentleman's principles and honor would demand such. She could almost hear Robert chastising her.

"But?" The wary edge to Bryan's tone echoed her deeper fears. She gulped a deep breath.

"None spoke of him as having passed. Gone ta Ireland a few months back, they could say. None seemed over-anxious that he's not been heard from since, Ireland bein' such a wild, uncivilized land and all.''

Both men shook their heads over that observation. "Settlin' an estate matter fer his missus, a few recalled, but nothing else.''

The situation she faced was worse than she feared. No news seemed to have reached home of Robert's and Gail's deaths. Her stomach seized anew. Thaddeus had lied to her on that count too. She would have to convince the authorities on her own.

"Damn. I was afraid of that." Bryan paced over to the railing for a silent moment before turning back to face his friend. "What arrangements have you made for lodgings?"

When Captain McManus moved forward to join him by the railing, Emilynne could no longer make out what was being said.

She stepped out onto the deck, searching for the right words to greet them without revealing that she had been listening. Neither man seemed to hear her approach as they peered out into the fog.

Michael's words drifted through the fog as she approached. ''. . . It is out of the way of things, but still within easy distance of the commerce district. Seemed the best place fer ye and yer wife.''

Bryan had a wife? Surprise ripped through her, followed by a conflicted muddle of disappointment and the undeniable sting of jealousy.

"You have a family in Bristol?" The question popped out of its own volition. The two men turned to face her as she groaned inwardly. Hardly the smooth entrance she'd been trying to conjure, let alone any of her business.

Bryan Reilly and the *Caithream* provided the means toward her end of getting the children home to England.

Nothing more. Grateful as she was to him and his crew, she had no further claim on either. She would just have to ignore the hollow feeling threatening to sap her small store of confidence and settle all that she still faced on her own. She'd gotten them this far after all.

"It would appear you know more about my marital state than I, Miss Wellesley." Bryan's deep voice seemed to pierce right through her. "Or have you forgotten how you introduced yourself to all and sundry when we first met?"

The sparse light from the lamps on the deck did little to show the set of his features, but she couldn't miss the amused twist in his tone. Embarrassment flooded her. Colors and light and the intimate warmth of his hard chest against hers. She'd called him husband before begging his kiss on Limerick's busy dockside. No, she'd never forget their meeting—more's the pity.

"I beg your pardon, Captain Reilly, Captain McManus. I should not have intruded on your conversation." She winced, her mortification at the curl of heat those memories evoked robbed all humility from her apology. That would not do. The children's safety still depended on the good graces of these two men and their crew.

"No harm done, ma'am." Michael McManus spoke first, a rich chuckle underscoring his words. "Though being the captain and ye will be sharing the lodgings I arranged, ye might want ta consider callin' him by his Christian name. Havin' two children and all betwixt ye, as it would seem."

"Anyone seeking a woman traveling alone will not bother to look twice at a family," Bryan inserted before she could question this development. "We thought it safest for you to continue the guise of being my wife until other arrangements can be made."

"And the landlady assured me she'd save two rooms fer ye," Michael hastened to add.

Seemed sensible enough, but the intimacy of the situation set her pulse racing.

"Very wise. Thank you, Captain, er, Bryan." Her cheeks heated as she used his name outside her private thoughts. Relief that she would not have to face the night or the city alone with just Christian and Abby tumbled through her. Coupled with a small inexplicable shot of joy that she would not have to say good-bye to him just yet. "If you are certain it will not inconvenience you. However, I insist on bearing all the expenses."

Again her words came out frosty and stiff as she struggled to contain her wayward reactions to this man.

"I know you English tend to think of the Irish as a shiftless lot. But as I told you earlier regarding your passage, I have no need of your money," he answered stiffly.

Oh, Lord, she'd insulted him again. Who would have thought a seaman would be so touchy? Tight-jawed indignation rippled through the quiet timbre of his words, and she wished she could bite back the last of what she'd said.

"Now, Captain, there's no call ta clamber up in yon crow's nest." *Bless Michael McManus for trying to dampen Bryan's ire too.* "Come down from yer rigging."

If only she did not turn so awkward in Bryan Reilly's company. They would never be able to pass as a family if they could not manage to be civil for more that a sentence or two. This plan did seem to be a sensible one, at least until she could get in touch with Robert's solicitor. She had to try harder for Abby's and Christian's sake, at least.

She forced a little warmth into her explanation. "I simply did not wish you to strain your resources on our account."

Bryan's gaze roamed her face for a moment as the ship's

creaking filled her ears. Something almost imperceptible softened in the set of his jaw and the tension in his shoulders before he nodded. "I assure you, Miss Wellesley. I am capable of providing for my family. Even if it's only a sham one. You can stop waving under my nose those pitiful few pence you received from selling your mother's cameo."

Emilynne clutched the edges of her cloak to stop her fingers from instinctively seeking the carnelian and ivory heirloom she'd left behind in Limerick. She pressed her lips together. It was not possible for him to know she'd been forced to pawn her remaining jewelry, including her favorite brooch and Gail's betrothal ring. Unless she'd told him in some feverish ramble while she was ill.

Cold fingers of fear clutched her heart. What else had she revealed in her delirium on the Irish Sea? "How did you . . ."

"Abby informed me of the circumstances regarding your loss when your fingers kept questing at your collar." He supplied the answer before she could finish her question. "She is a child who has witnessed too much heartbreak in too little time. She needed to tell someone."

She had hazy memories of Bryan talking to the children in the cabin while she drifted through the fog of her travel sickness. His deep voice wove tales laced with Irish legends and with stories of a boyhood spent on an island, providing an anchor for her own chaotic thoughts and dreams.

"Except in play with Christian, Abby has spoken so little of late." Disquiet as to how much he had lured from the child's confidences underscored Emilynne's curiosity. She needed to know just what Abby might have revealed of their circumstances. "What else did she tell you?"

As Bryan moved closer, his wood and sage scent mingled with the wisps of vanilla smoke curling from Michael's silent pipe, surrounding Emilynne with a sense of dependable masculinity she'd missed since Robert's death. How she yearned to trust this man.

The glitter of a lamp across the deck sparkled in Bryan's eyes as he looked at her for a long while. "That her papa had promised her a pony when you returned from Ireland. That her mama smelled of roses and loved to dance. And that her aunt Emmie preferred stones and books to parties and concerts."

His voice dropped so low, she had to strain to hear him despite his nearness. Captain Reilly's temperament was nothing if not mercurial. She swore she could detect the edges of his lips curling in a gentle smile through the gloom. His manner robbed his words of some of their sting.

"I am not without means, Miss Wellesley." He touched her arm in a small salute of reassurance. "I will procure our lodgings for a night or two until you can access your solicitors and set your plans in motion to return to Wiltshire. By then I will be on my way to Liverpool and cease my intrusions on your life."

Thoughts of Wiltshire and the life she would lead upon her return home sent a cold rock plummeting through her chest. Bryan was right though, their continued pretense would be best for the children's sake. She would deal with the long view of their lives once she had gotten through the next few days. "I believe the intrusion is all on my part, sir. Though if I'm to pass as your wife, even for a day, perhaps you would be so kind as to call me by my given name as well."

"As you wish, Emilynne." The sound of her name on his lips set a rebellious curl of heat spiraling through her. Their gazes locked. Their time together would be extended. Cautious relief and wary expectation pulsed through her.

Michael shook his head and tapped the remainders from his pipe bowl over the side of the ship. "Ye'll pass fer married all right, the way ye nip and tuck at one another. The both of ye—all fire one minute and polite as a parson the next. I'll go find ye a hackney."

He disappeared back down the gangplank until all that was left was a low chuckle echoing back to them from the misty billows. Lost in the tumult of her wayward feelings, Emilynne blinked

"Well, Mrs. Reilly." Bryan's smile could be quite engaging even in the gloom of night. He offered her his arm. "Shall we go below and collect the children? Then we can be off to the lodgings Michael has secured for us on Baldwin Street."

"You are quite certain you do not mind the delay of your business in Liverpool? I would hate to keep you from something urgent." She slipped her arm through his.

"My crew will head there by water once we have disembarked. I will join them by rail in a day or two." He preceded her down the hatch and reached up to help her down. "For the time being I find my business in Bristol is paramount."

Chapter Five

"Just follow me, sir. I'm sure yer missus and ye will be right comfortable during yer stay here in Bristol. My boy Peter will bring up yer bags in a thrice." Holding a lamp aloft, Mrs. Babbage led the way up a wide staircase to Babbage's Rooming House's upper floors.

Bryan shifted a sleeping Abby against his shoulder and waited as Emilynne, carrying an equally comatose Christian, followed their garrulous landlady.

"Right this way, ma'am. We'll have yer little ones tucked in, in no time. Such sweet things, sleeping through like this. They must be all done in."

Bryan turned a deaf ear to the woman's ramblings as Abby sighed against his cheek. In a gesture he found oddly comforting, she'd slipped one hand under his waistcoat to rest on his shirt just over his heart. He was amazed how their short carriage ride had coaxed both small Wellesley riptides into such peaceful slumber and doubted he would find equal serenity tonight. Or for days to come.

Now that they had landed in England, the burden of action his profession demanded lay far heavier on his shoulders than the weight of ten sleeping children.

Ah, Gran, he sighed to himself. *See what a tangle your tales of The Blessing have gifted me.*

Reilly Ship Works needed an influx of capital if it was to survive his father's failing health. The opportunity with Harland in Liverpool would remain on the table for only a fixed time now that the sharks from Belfast circled. Quin could string things out for a while on the island with grit and determination, but even that had its limitations. It wouldn't be long before they'd be forced to stop work altogether.

Bryan's honor warred with the English common sense his father had demanded he adopt. No matter how he approached this matter, tending it for his firm took precedence over his personal concerns. Chagrin chafed the irony that presented him with an opportunity to help the family business and heal old wounds, then snatched that chance away through the very responsibilities his father had hammered home to him again and again.

Mayhap the family gift was neither blessing *nor* curse, as Granny had portrayed, but blessing *and* curse, the one irremovable from the other, spiced in this instance with an added fillip of betrayal.

The flickering glow from wall sconces gleamed on polished wood surfaces as the party moved quietly down a wide hallway, their steps muffled by thick carpeting. Michael had chosen their accommodations well. Though the smell of lemon and wax added a luster of loving care to the house, they did little to lighten Bryan's mood.

"Here we are." Mrs. Babbage swung open a door on the street side of the house.

A wide four-poster thick with a feather bedcover dominated the modest room. A quick image of spun gold curls fanning the lace pillows teased Bryan's mind. He swallowed, unwilling to follow that tormenting path, and focused his gaze on the small fire glowing from the hearth at the far side of the room. The meager flames hissing there could not begin to burn away his forbidden thoughts. With a silent groan he forced himself to do a careful inventory of their lodgings.

The nimble dance of light and shadows touched a washstand and a modest wardrobe on one side of the fireplace, a changing screen on the other. A writing table and chair vied for space near a large trunk under the windows. Good solid quarters, but definitely not what Emilynne Wellesley and these children were most likely accustomed to. Still, after weeks on the run and then on board ship, it would have to do.

Mrs. Babbage set the lamp on a table by the door. "I hope ye won't mind, but I've only this one room available tonight."

The quiver of shock that ran through Emilynne was palpable as she sent a quick glance across the room and then offered Bryan a worried look from beneath the broad brim of her bonnet.

Guilt twinged over his plans for the morrow and for the doubts shining in her eyes. He'd hoped to offer her at least one night's rest before laying the facts of the situation before her. He looked back toward their landlady.

Mrs. Babbage favored them with a knowing smile and a slight wink. "I know ye wanted two rooms, but Mr. Madden, one of my regulars, returned from his sales trip a few days early. I never turn away my regulars. It is why they always come back."

The warmth in her tone forced Bryan to temper his annoyance. He'd spent many an uncomfortable night since the Wellesleys entered his life. What was one or two more? Emilynne swayed in the doorway, looking paler by the moment. He caught her elbow.

"We'll be fine," he said to the landlady as he guided Emilynne toward the bed. She cast him a look of utter dismay from eyes rimmed with dark circles of weariness.

"Let's settle the children here for now, my dear. You need to sit down." He laid Abby on the far side of the bed.

"I set a cot up fer the children over by the washstand," Mrs. Babbage offered.

"Would you be able to send up something simple for us to eat? My ... wife"—the word tasted odd on his tongue—"has not been feeling well. She, ah ... hasn't been able to keep much down lately." True enough.

Emilynne relinquished Christian to the larger bed and tugged off his shoes in silence, though her spine stiffened. Bryan slipped both children under the quilt on the bed.

"Increasing, is she?" Mrs. Babbage sent Emilynne an appraising look. "She's a lucky woman to have such a solicitous husband. A pot of tea and some nice hot rolls will help ta settle her stomach. I don't normally allow eating in my rooms, but I'll make an exception under the circumstances and given the late hour of the day."

Brilliant red crested Emilynne's cheeks as she eased Abby's shoes off. An irresistible hint of freesia wafted from her heated skin. Before she could protest Mrs. Babbage's familiarity or correct her, Bryan nodded his assent. "That would just hit the spot, I'm sure. And give our little sailor a bit to grow on. Thank you.''

He didn't need to look at Emilynne to gauge her reaction to his participation in this spontaneous addition to their deception. He was quite certain there were sparks of blue flame being shot in his direction.

Mrs. Babbage smiled. ''I'll be back directly, sir. And I'll bring a bowl of mutton stew fer yerself.''

The door clicked shut behind her, and Bryan hung his bowler on a peg beside the washstand and tugged off his bow tie. The cot looked a bit cramped, but he'd slept on worse in the past week. He lit the small lamp on the writing table to help alleviate the darkness in the room, silently awaiting a storm from his *wife*.

Emilynne tucked the edge of the quilt under Christian's chin and turned to face her *husband*.

''How could you . . . ?'' was all she managed to get out in the furious whisper she choked off rather than allow her shock to explode and rouse the children.

She took a deep breath and moved to stand all too near Bryan at the foot of the huge bed. Had he known all along they would be forced to share a room? Her fingers grazed the smooth turns of the bedpost. Heat rushed through her, followed by cold shivers even as she tried desperately to ignore the imposing piece of furniture. Had he hoped they might have to share the bed?

How would she ever get her thoughts and plans in order with his overwhelming presence provoking her at every turn? She should never have permitted this masquerade, begun in desperation in Limerick, to continue now that they had reached her destination. And she certainly didn't need him to further complicate their present circumstances, highly improper and scandalous as they were.

She'd been too ill to protest when he'd spent nights on the floor of his cabin aboard the *Caithream*, tending her with the detached care of medical professional—and too grateful for cool cloths and small sips of ginger tea to insist he leave. Now he filled the room with his wood and sage scent, and the kiss that had brought them to this place coursed temptingly afresh through her each time she looked at him.

"You were saying, my dear?" The amusement in his low tone drew her gaze up to meet the sparkle in his dark green eyes and made her realize she'd been fuming in silence rather than delivering her displeasure. Heat returned to her cheeks, mixing with a welcome prickle of annoyance.

"Why did you allow that woman to assume I . . . that we . . ." She fought back a groan. *How missish.* She couldn't even say the word. She took a breath and tried a different tack. "It is not even proper to comment on such an assumption. And you encouraged her."

He imprisoned her arms with his hands and drew her over to the table, studying her face in the lamplight. Unbidden currents of warmth streaked up her arms from his touch. She shifted her gaze from his too discerning eyes to the pulse point beating at his temple.

"Emilynne, you are not moving within the tight social circles of England's elite right now. You are trying to pass as a captain's wife. An *Irishman's* wife. Do you have any idea what others might expect of you if we are going to pull this off? Even for a day or two?"

"I am sure I can manage." She prayed her tone carried more conviction than she felt.

Truth be told, she'd little idea what life was like beyond the world of her studies. She much preferred the company of her books and scrolls, just as Robert had so often teased. Surely behavior and expectations could not be so very different between social classes. Although she was not going to admit to Captain Reilly that she never exactly fit in with the ball and tea set either. Too many viewed her bookish ways askance.

She lifted her chin. "Over the past weeks a great number of kindhearted, generous people have accepted and assisted us. Now that we are so close to home, I doubt—"

"Are you aware"—Bryan's fingers tightened on her arms—"that if you go too far from these premises, you run the risk of being sighted by those you suspect are pursuing you? Or that you chance running into an acquaintance who might inadvertently alert the aforementioned pursuers?"

The pulse at his temple increased. "Pregnancy," he emphasized the word as her cheeks burned hotter still, "provides us with the ideal excuse to shield you from exposure to too many people."

"Oh." His explanation made it all sound so simple. Why hadn't she thought of that? Yet another example of how unfit she was to guide the children on her own. She was much too tired to sort out her thoughts. She was certain he'd be glad to be rid of all three of them once the matter was in the hands of Robert's solicitors. Sweeping loneliness threatened with that notion.

At least she was close enough to Wiltshire and Richard that she had only a few more days to muddle through. For some reason, that thought provided little comfort.

She released a long sigh and met Bryan's dark gaze once more. "You are right, of course. Thank you for your quick thinking, Captain."

"Bryan, remember?" he growled as a knock sounded on their door.

"Come." He dropped his hands to his sides, leaving Emilynne alone and more than a little chilled. A shiver racked her.

His hand returned, guiding her before a second shudder could pass. "Sit here."

She sank onto the chair by the writing table as Mrs. Babbage bustled back into the room, trailed by a boy carrying two bags. Emilynne welcomed the solid support of the simple straight-backed chair more than she cared to admit. Bryan shrugged off his jacket and placed it around her shoulders. His green wood and savory spice scent enveloped her with steadying warmth.

"Here we go, sir and madam. A spot to eat afore ye turn in and ye'll feel much more the thing come mornin'." Mrs. Babbage favored them with a crooked smile as she placed the tray on the table. "I added a pitcher of milk and some tea biscuits in case the young uns awaken and are hungry too."

"Thank you." Emilynne started to rise as she untied her bonnet.

"Sit still, dearie." Mrs. Babbage picked up the cloak Emilynne had discarded on the bed and took the bonnet to dust off a few imaginary spots. "I'll hang it on the peg next to yer husband's. Ye jest enjoy the peace while yer little ones sleep."

She sailed across the small chamber past the boy, balancing their two cases. "Bring the bags over here, Peter. There's a good lad. Then off ta find yer own bed with ye."

Peter, a gangly youth with sandy hair, obediently placed the bags by the washstand and gave them both a shy grin before disappearing back into the hallway.

With a proud smile his mother watched him go, then turned back to face her newest boarders. "I hope you don't mind, sir, but I'd like ta leave yer sea chest below stairs till morning so as not ta disturb me other guests a'thumpin' it down the hall." She continued speaking as Emilynne tried to concentrate through the fog of weariness creeping over on her.

". . . Not that my walls aren't nice and thick; it is rare anything vexes my guests once they've retired. Good clean beds and a quiet resting place, that's what I'm known for." Mrs. Babbage nodded her head to emphasize the point.

The smell of the stew from the tray enticed Emilynne. Her stomach squeezed with hunger, and she could almost taste the rosemary and new potatoes the cook at Newbury Manor used in her own mutton stew—Robert's favorite supper since childhood. Tears edged her eyelids. She choked back a sob, no time yet for the luxury of sorrowing over small memories.

Bryan put his hand on her shoulder and cleared his throat.

"Yer pardon. Here I am rattlin' on, and ye with so much ta handle already." Mrs. Babbage clasped her hands in front of her apron. "Yer husband's mate told me of yer recent loss, ma'am. I'm so sorry. It is hard losin' the last of yer family like that."

The woman had a kindly way about her that Emilynne couldn't help liking. Though the landlady's face was lined with her own concern, she took the time to offer comfort to others.

Mrs. Babbage took a few steps closer and looked at Emilynne directly. "Still, ye've a new life ta think on and yer two babes ta console you." She shifted her gaze up to

Bryan. "Shall I help move them ta the cot, sir, before I say good night?"

Emilynne's heart skipped a beat as her doubts returned. Surely, Captain Reilly wouldn't carry their deception to the point of sharing the bed. Her hands went cold just the same.

"I think we can manage after we've eaten, Mrs. Babbage," he answered. "Thank you for everything else. I'm sure we'll be quite comfortable."

Relief surged, still tangled with a rebellious feeling of regret.

Mrs. Babbage nodded. "We serve breakfast at seven sharp. Downstairs and to yer right is the dining parlor. Nothing fancy, jest good, wholesome food. I'll save a bite on a tray fer ye ma'am if ye'd prefer ta get a little extra rest in the morning after all yer travels. And I could spare one of the tweenies fer a bit ta keep an eye on the children. I don't get many female guests, so I don't mind extending a little extra courtesy."

"Thank you" was all Emilynne could manage to say through the tumult of her exhaustion and warring emotions.

The older woman walked to the door. "Good night ta you both, then." She stepped into the hallway and snapped the door shut behind her, leaving them alone.

Awkward silence reigned. What next? A simple meal and then to bed? Darkness loomed outside, a dense harbinger of the long night ahead. Emilynne tried to swallow past the lump in her throat and poured them each a cup of tea. Her hand shook despite her efforts to control her apprehensions. China and silver clattered together like an alarm.

Bryan relieved her of the rattling cup and saucer she

extended to him. She couldn't bring herself to meet his gaze and have him guess the direction of her fears. She placed a napkin on her lap and reached instead for a biscuit. Perhaps some nourishment would calm the tightening of her stomach.

He took a seat on the chest and cleared his throat. "Emilynne."

His tone held gentle command, yet was spoken low enough so as not to disturb the children. She could not handle much more and fought to hold back tears by focusing her attention on the task of spreading jam on her biscuit. And should she get through this night, what of the morrow? She'd been so certain when she'd set out that she'd chosen the best, the only course, but now that she was so close, would she be able to pull it off?

"Emilynne." Louder this time, edged with the annoyance of a man used to command.

She glanced upward, unable stop herself, drinking in the easy grace with which his linen shirt stretched across his shoulders and the way his waistcoat and trousers flattered the tapers of his body. He leaned forward on the trunk, centering his attention on her as she met his gaze. The glow from the lamp and fire glinted in his dark hair and added a breath-stealing softness to his features. The little cleft in his chin was nearly hidden in the shadows. Praying he could not guess her thoughts, she had to admit her sham husband was a handsome man indeed.

"I don't know what kind of men you are used to, Miss Wellesley, but I am not in the habit of seducing the infirm, even if you were willing and there were not two young children in the room."

His not so subtle accusation was disturbingly on the mark regarding her fears. Guilt and embarrassment clutched her in equal portions. Her experiences with Thaddeus had made her suspect the worst in everybody.

"You have been nothing but kind to us, sir, going far beyond any modern code of chivalrous behavior." Although she sought to rectify any offense, she could not bring herself to openly acknowledge the veracity of his assessment. "I believe it is the strain of the last weeks that makes me appear overcautious."

His smile made her heart do a funny turn. "Overcautious is not exactly how I would describe you, Emilynne, especially given the circumstances of our meeting or the situation we find ourselves in now."

He shook his head and put his teacup back on the tray with a gentle clink. "Overcautious is definitely not how I would describe you."

"Exactly what would you say about me?" The question popped out of its own volition. His good opinion suddenly seemed terribly important to her.

He shrugged. "You seem impetuous, given your flight across Ireland. And you can be quite persuasive. Look at where I am instead of on the *Caithream* bound for Liverpool. You're well able to keep your business to yourself. Beyond the snatches of mumblings from your delirium, you've told me precious little about yourself save your love for ancient relics and your loyalty to your brother."

There, he'd practically invited her to tell him her whole history. And not with the charming but dispassionate interest of a stranger as he'd first tried when they left Limerick. Nor with the stern frown of a man certain he was headed for trouble as he'd appeared just before her seasickness struck. This time he asked with the sincere interest of an ally, a friend.

He'd brought them to England without any of the explanation she'd promised him. He'd taken care of her during her illness and seen to it that the children were safe and entertained, if the stories they'd related to her were any indication. She owed him the truth.

She opened her mouth. All the pent-up anxiety of the recent weeks on the run, and the black grief that had preceded them, rushed to her lips in a torrent. Greed, murder, and terror lurked in the tale she had been unable to convince anyone in Ireland to believe.

Did she dare tell him? Too much still lay at stake even though she was so close to home. She couldn't risk alienating him with what he would surely view as hysterics, as others had. Yet she could not refuse to tell him anything and alienate her one ally. He had been far too kind and patient as it was.

She forced herself to smile and put a casual air into her tone. "There's precious little else to tell. My parents, and then Robert, have always indulged my academic aspirations. Newbury Manor, our home in Wiltshire, houses an extensive library. Tutors, trips to Druid sites, research at special collections on the Celts—my family supported my studies and cheered my accomplishments."

He reached for a biscuit of his own and quirked an eyebrow at her but said nothing. No doubt he was horrified at the depth of her intellectual pursuits as so many others had been. At least he had the grace not to show it as he took a bite and nodded for her to continue.

"I have even had a paper of my theories published, though not under my full name. Just my initials, as no one in scholarly circles would take a woman's hypotheses seriously."

She couldn't keep the bitter tinge from her last comment. It still rankled. Too many people believed education was wasted on a woman.

"Did your brother share your passion for relics of times long past?"

She shook her head. "Not at all. He relished the intricacies of modern business. He used to tease that someone had to look after the future since I was so focused on the past. He loved to invest in small ventures and watch them blossom."

A picture of Robert reading the financial pages as the sunlight streamed through the morning room at Newbury warmed her for a moment. "He said there was no point in having money if you could not make it work for the benefit of others."

The picture of happier times faded, and the dying embers of the fire allowed a chill to creep into the room. Emilynne wrapped Bryan's jacket tighter around herself. An odd sense of comfort stole through her along with the warmth the brushed wool delivered.

"Was your family's trip to Ireland based on your interest in the Druids?" Bryan leaned forward from his seat on the chest. "Or were you visiting one of our country's best horse breeding districts in connection with your brother's business interests?"

She could not summon the nerve to lie directly. The penetrating stare Bryan favored her with as he finished his biscuit would surely see through any disemblance, even given the generous night shadows surrounding them.

"My sister-in-law grew up in County Kildare. She returned to claim her inheritance for her children's sake." Emilynne glanced over at the two small bundles under the quilt. "Now that she and Robert are gone, I am all that they have left of the family they loved."

"But not the only family member who seeks to control them, and thereby their inheritance. In both countries."

He spoke it as a statement, not a question. Almost like a prosecutor. She flinched at his implied accusation as a world of doubts opened up beneath her feet. How and what did he know? Had she babbled the entire story while she was ill? She clutched at her fears as they threatened to spin out of control.

"I did not steal the heirs and run for my own benefit, if that is what you think." Indignant heat coursed through her, chasing away the chill.

"What else would you have me think?" He practically leapt off the chest and paced the short breadth of the room before returning to the windows. She shed his jacket, which seemed confining in the face of his restless energy, and went to stand beside him as he stared off into the darkened city. Would he believe her if she dared trust him with the truth?

"You talk in circles each time you say you are going to tell me the truth." He continued in a quieter tone that dipped below her guard as he kept his gaze fixed on the rooftops silhouetted outside. "Between the children and your illness, you have never explained your fright. You may have been in a delirium from seasickness, but your desperation was very real when you begged me to protect Abby and Christian."

He turned from the window and touched her cheek. "Tell me why you fear Thaddeus Whyte."

He knew so much already, drat her weak stomach. She might as well plunge ahead with the whole truth. She took a long breath. "Thaddeus Whyte murdered my brother and his wife."

By the hiss of his indrawn breath she knew she'd surprised Bryan with that bit of information. So she had *not* told him everything.

"I have no direct proof, although I know what I overheard. Everyone else I have tried to tell put me off as if I were hysterical with grief." Bitterness twisted through her frustration over her useless efforts. "No one would believe the illustrious Mr. Whyte of Blue Hills Stud could be anything other than he seemed—a man of solid reputation who knew his horseflesh."

It was her turn to stare off at the rooftops, trying to put some distance between herself and her tale. Striving to fight the tears that welled from her soul each time she thought of the waste. All this loss over a few acres of land and some horses.

"Tell me all the facts as you know them."

She'd come this far, she might as well give him the full tale. *In for a penny, in for a pound,* as her nanny used to say. She took a deep breath and let it out slow.

"Gail's uncle Thaddeus was her guardian after her own parents' death. When she married Robert despite his objections, Thaddeus retained control over her estates through legal maneuverings and careful manipulation. He was never overt in his opposition, but he stalled them for years.

"Finally, when Christian was old enough to travel, Gail and Robert decided to confront him themselves." Emilynne balled her fists so tightly, her nails bit into her flesh. "He seemed genuinely happy to see us. Preparing to turn over the reins to Robert and enjoy his retirement, as he termed it."

She fought a shudder as she remembered how Thaddeus Whyte's wide grin and charming manners concealed his deadly intentions.

Bryan said nothing, though she could feel his gaze probing her features.

"After . . . after the accident, he was so solicitous. He offered to take care of all the arrangements, knew what I needed before I did, and let me concentrate on the children. He seemed so kind. A godsend of help in the face of tragedy."

The effort to keep all the dark memories and guilt from swallowing her whole made her knees weak. Bryan stepped behind her as she swayed on her feet and placed his hands on her shoulders, granting her a measure of silent comfort and support.

"I had no idea he'd not even posted my correspondence until I found them neatly stacked in his desk drawer," she continued, determined to get through her story and be done with it. "Along with copies of papers he'd filed with a legal firm in Limerick stating that Robert and Gail had died without drawing up a will. He sought to have himself appointed as the children's sole guardian."

She closed her eyes, remembering her shocked dismay and the horrible march out to the stables to confront him. When she overheard him speaking to one of his men, what she learned had determined the need for her to return to England at once and without his knowledge.

"He had the axle tampered with on the carriage they used for a tour of the estate. I was to go with Gail and Robert that day, as was Thaddeus. Instead, I went to visit the Piper's Stone, and at the last minute Thaddeus feigned an emergency in the stables and begged off. So they set off alone. That was the last time I saw them alive." The final sentence barely squeezed from her throat, swollen with unshed tears.

Bryan turned her to face him. "My poor lass. You've

had a very hard time of it. It is very late and you are wilting on your feet."

He cupped her cheek in the palm of his hand. Tears blurred his image as she looked at him. He hadn't called her a liar or a lunatic. He hadn't tried to comfort her with platitudes about intense grief playing tricks on the mind. All responses she'd received when she tried to expose the heinous crime to Thaddeus Whyte's neighbors in Kildare. They would not believe such wild accusations concerning their esteemed neighbor.

"You can tell me the rest in the morning."

"The rest?" She repeated his words, caught between utter exhaustion and the need to reveal all of her story. She swayed forward and he closed the gap between them by taking her into his arms for a warm embrace.

Despite all her vows of inner strength and independence, great racking sobs shook her, wrung from her core by his quiet acceptance. Without protest he muffled them with his body. She had months of anguish stored up. Enough for Robert and Gail, for their children, and for herself.

"Ah, lass. I'm so sorry." He whispered the husky words into her hair as she took comfort in the solid support of his shoulder when all her tears were spent.

A very tiny portion of her mind wondered what he was sorry for as he continued. "I've several questions I must still ask you, but they can wait for the morning. You've given me enough to think on for one night. And I don't think you've got the strength left to answer me."

For all that he held her so close, his voice seemed distant and muted. He was right, a solemn portion of herself observed, enough was enough. He lifted her in his arms, and the next thing she knew she was nestling on a cloud with Christian by her side.

"Thank you," she whispered as Bryan pulled the quilt over her. "I knew I could trust you the moment I saw you."

"Sleep now, *muirneach*." His voice came gruff as he smoothed a tendril back from her cheek.

Muirneach? He'd called her that before, a long time ago.

As she drifted away, she heard him cross the room to douse the lamps, then settle on the cot. He was not her husband in truth, but the sounds of his activities and the knowledge he was there created a deep warmth inside her, where all of her emptiness and loss resided. Comforting and intimate. Almost as good as the feel of his arms around her.

Chapter Six

Bryan tried to peer through the gray hangings of mist and smoke, looking for a hint of color to signal dawn's arrival over Bristol's gloomy rooftops. Surely this day would begin soon. Tension-choked expectation knotted his thoughts as he waited and watched from his perch by the window.

He concentrated on the discordant sounds of the awakening city echoing down Baldwin Street and tried to blot out the whispered confidence behind Emilynne's words last night. *I knew I could trust you.*

Already carts laden with country goods—eggs, milk, produce, and the like—clattered over the cobblestones on their way to market. Occasional shadowy figures, early workmen and shop clerks, shuffled by, or a carriage of late merrymakers trundled past, but for the most part he was alone with his thoughts. And a shroud of guilt.

His soul, still striving to be as one with furling sails and a trim bow cutting the waves on open water, screamed that he must find a way to satisfy his legal duties and his moral ones at the same time. The quiet logic and professional detachment he'd cultivated for years felt less a refuge and more a cage, confining and suffocating.

The sound of banging below made him wince. Breakfast preparations in Mrs. Babbage's modern kitchen, no doubt. He'd nearly forgotten how hard it was to let go of the sea and allow civilization to close in again. The flicker of the tallow candle he'd lit so long before could not begin to relieve the oppression he felt from without and within.

I knew I could trust you.

Like a lance. He hated what duty and honor would demand of him this day. Despised what it might do to two innocents. And to Emilynne. Especially if her story were true, as she seemed to believe.

And she did believe every word of what she had told him, that much Bryan could not question. Gill O'Brien will be foaming at the mouth upon hearing her allegations against his prize client.

Murder. Hardly proper behavior for an upper-class English gentleman. A barely credible accusation against someone with as sterling a reputation as Thaddeus Whyte. Yet the sincere horror of Emilynne's indictment served only to tighten the snarls of Bryan's dilemma. Legally he had an obligation to see to it that his firm's interests were protected in matters related to their client's business. As a man, he could not abandon this family to a murderer.

Add the urgency of his personal affairs, and he had the ingredients for many sleepless nights to come.

He'd tossed away the small hours of the night trying to work through the best course of action. He couldn't risk telling Emilynne of his own potential role in this blasted business, that much was certain. If her story proved false, he could not afford to tip his hand and give her a chance to slip away while he investigated. On the other hand, if her accusations proved true along with her fear of pursuit, he could not risk her being spotted with no one to protect her.

"If only I'd corrected your assumption that I was just a seaman, a captain, from the start." He swallowed back the bitterness of self-recrimination. She'd have either run from him screaming or confided the depth of her troubles while he'd still been able to hand this problem off to another lawyer at O'Brien & Mallory. He'd delayed too long on the Shannon.

Emilynne's illness as they crossed to England prevented any shared confidences, and there had been precious little time or opportunity since. He'd thought to simply turn her over to the Jefferies firm he believed Gill was working with on behalf of Mr. Whyte. But if the painful suspicions Emilynne choked out last night proved to be even half right, he was into a far different situation than he'd first appreciated—one that honor and his oath as an officer of the court bound him in separate chains.

As for his familial duty, he had the sinking feeling this matter would mean far more delay than he'd anticipated. Far more than Reilly Ship Works could afford. He could only pray that Michael delivered his proposal and he could arrive in Liverpool himself in time to persuade this investor to see the wisdom of a shipyard located on the western side of Ireland before he committed his funding elsewhere.

A sigh from the bed drew his attention. Up popped a small head.

"I'm tirsty. Mama, I'm tirsty." Little Christian shook the shoulder next to him.

Bryan strode rapidly to the bed, suddenly not ready to end his vigil and begin the long day ahead. Unwilling to face the inevitable confrontation that would come when he revealed to Emilynne his true reason for accompanying her in Bristol.

"Come here, lad." He spoke very softly. "I'll pour you some milk and you may let your aunt rest."

The boy rubbed his eyes and then held up his arms. Bryan eased Christian from between Abby and Emilynne. He tried not to notice the way Emilynne's hair spread over the pillows in long, tempting tendrils—just as he had envisioned—soft as sea foam and carrying just a hint of lemon and freesia to knot his gut.

He swore he'd not slept at all last night, but at some point she'd loosened her hair and stripped off her stockings as the hint of white toes at the edge of the quilt attested. He groaned.

Cradling the boy, Bryan moved to the tray and, one-handed, poured Christian a mug of milk. "Here we go, my lad."

Two chubby hands clasped the mug, and the boy drank greedily as Bryan settled back on the chest with Chistian on his lap. Warm from sleep, he fit against the hollow of Bryan's chest with trusting ease. Just the way his own sister, Meaghan, had done when she was a babe. It was hard to imagine her as Mother's last letter described, a young hoyden attempting to ply her fifteen-year-old wiles along the Mediterranean. Between Da's convalescence and Meaghan's determination, Mother certainly had her hands full.

And so did he, he reminded himself. His gaze sought the bed's remaining occupants. The sky was lightening enough for him to see Emilynne's outline. He fought the urge to leap up and cover those soft pink toes he knew were peeping out at him.

The irrational nature of his attraction to this slip of a woman's feet struck him anew. But then, nothing about his reactions to her or his actions in relation to her had been rational from the moment their lips touched in Limerick. Reilly Blessing, indeed. Whatever could his forebears have done to the Druids to deserve such a backhanded gift? For truly it carried all the elements of a curse meant to haunt a man to his very grave.

Granny would surely frown and lecture him for such a view if she were listening to his thoughts. But what else could he term the impulse to throw all common sense aside and do whatever was asked by the siren whose kiss bewitched him—his reputation, his family, and his soul be damned. His stomach clenched.

"Hungry." Christian stated his next demand as he waved his empty cup too close to Bryan's chin.

Bryan caught the mug and set it on the table before reaching for a biscuit. "Here you go, young sir. Pray do not make too many crumbs while you munch."

He also retrieved his jacket from the chair and settled back on the trunk, using the coat to cover them both. He'd have to add more coals to the fire to ward off the morning chill creeping through the room before he awakened Emilynne. Then again, a little bite to the air might force her to put her stockings back on and make his confession that much easier to make without the intimate distraction of her bare feet.

"That's right, Bryan. Think only of your own ease in this awkward situation," he muttered. The little head resting against his shoulder shifted. He gazed down at the solemn little eyes so like Emilynne's glittering up at him and sighed.

"Don't worry, Cap'n," the boy whispered. "Aunt Emmie makes Papa sigh too."

Bryan smoothed an errant curl away from the boy's forehead, at a loss for words.

"What's this?" Apparently finished with his biscuit, Christian must have decided to explore their covering's inner pockets.

"It is a letter from my mother." Bryan retrieved the folded linen sheets.

"Is there any pictures?" the boy asked hopefully. "I 'specially like pictures when someone reads to me."

Bryan couldn't help smiling. "If I read you my letter, will you try to close your eyes and go back to sleep?"

Christian nodded and wiggled around on Bryan's lap so that his arms tucked under Bryan's and his head nestled under his protector's chin.

Bryan drew the candle closer and unfolded the sheets of his mother's letter, though in truth he could have recited the contents from memory.

He chuckled anew as he read the loving humor laced through her recounting of his father's slow recovery from the consumption that had forced him to convalesce in Italy's warmer climate and his querulous antics with the physicians overseeing his case. Bryan knew full well his mother was not nearly as dismayed as she portrayed in telling of Meaghan's awkward transformation from girl to young woman.

His mother's concern over Quin's impatience with being forced ashore to oversee the daily operations at Reilly Ship Works sank new guilt into Bryan. Quin was used to coming and going as he pleased, sailing the world on family busi-

ness. That he'd chosen to come home and take the helm
at the shipyard while Da recuperated was a sacrifice freely
made. Still, anchoring in one place couldn't help but fray
his elder bother's quite volatile temper, Bryan was sure.
Especially with all the problems their father's failing health
had left untended.

Quin should not bear the burdens of keeping Beannacht
Island's principal employer afloat by himself.

It wasn't until Bryan reached the last page and was reading the part where Mother told him of Harland, the investor looking to Ireland as the ideal site for a modern
shipyard, than he heard Emilynne's sharp intake of breath
from only a few feet away.

"I had no idea—"

Bryan shook his head to silence her, then nodded down
at Christian, who was breathing very deeply against Bryan's
neck. She reached under the coat and gathered the child
against her, her hands a momentary softness against his
chest. Her hair brushed his shoulders. Freesia and lemon
and a wild impulse to gather her close and never let go
shook him.

"Aunt Emmie," Christian murmured as he sighed
against her shoulder, never opening his eyes.

"Yes, love. I'm putting you back to bed with your sister,"
she soothed, and headed across the room, her bare feet
making no sound over the carpeting.

"Will Mama write us a letter from heaven?"

She laid him on the pillow and kissed his forehead before
pulling the quilt over him. "I'm certain she will if she
can."

Bryan barely heard her answer, she spoke so softly. The
lad had already drifted away. Her hair rippled down her
back in shimmering white-gold waves, and she moved with

a gentle grace that stirred Bryan's not so latent desire for her.

What was it he'd said to her last night? *I am not in the habit of seducing the infirm.* Rosy predawn light combined with a few hours of sleep to banish that defense. The dark shadows of exhaustion had vanished from under her eyes as she returned to the windows and faced him.

The unrelenting black of her mourning served only to highlight her delicate coloring. He wanted nothing more than to gather her into his arms and kiss away the concern he read in her features, the fears haunting her eyes. At least the children still occupied the room with them and prevented him from giving into his baser impulses.

She tucked herself neatly onto the opposite end of the trunk and faced him with a worried look. At least her feet were covered by the folds of her skirt.

"I had no idea the scope of your business in Liverpool." The flicker of the candlelight played over her lips as she spoke, so softly he leaned forward to hear her as she continued. "So many people depend on your success, yet you are stuck with a notion that you must protect us."

Anxiety pulled the corners of her soft mouth downward. He fought the urge to smooth them back to a smile with the pad of his thumb. She looked so young and vulnerable with her sleep-tousled hair and shining eyes.

"With any luck, Michael will deliver my proposal in time. And as I told you last night, I will join him by rail as soon as you are settled," he tried to reassure her. And himself. "When the telegraph office opens this morning, I intend to send a wire explaining all."

"Has your father been ill for long?" She touched his wrist just below his shirtsleeve with her fingertips.

The warm pressure of her gesture was oddly comforting

and yet disconcerting. No one had reached out to him like this in too many years. Not since he'd refused all sympathy after nearly killing his little brother through his own foolhardiness. He hadn't deserved comforting then, he didn't now. Not from her.

He snatched his arm away and tried not to notice the light that dimmed in Emilynne's eyes as her lips tightened and she turned her attention to the windows.

"Da hid his failing health for a long time." He could at least answer her direct questions. He owed her that much after demanding she tell him the truth last night despite her own reluctance. "When he collapsed, Mother brought him to Limerick from the island. His doctors insisted he must complete a course of treatment in a warmer climate if he is ever to recover."

"He must be a remarkably strong man to have kept you all in the dark for so long." Emilynne twisted her hands together over her knees before she met his gaze again. "Your mother certainly makes your whole family come to life in her letters. You must miss them dreadfully."

Her pity drove straight into old wounds of guilt and resentment so quickly, he jumped from the chest. The fact that there was nowhere he could run from the truth halted him as it always did. He tightened his fists in frustration. There was no way to resolve the mistakes of the past. To reconcile his father's dictum and his own disastrous response.

"I have been estranged from my father for years." For an inexplicable reason he needed Emilynne to understand the basis for his odd reactions. Pale and gaunt, his da had barely been able to stand, let alone talk when he'd departed for Italy just a few months earlier. This trip to England had been Bryan's way of offering amends.

"I see Quin every so often when he's in port. And Dev passes through on his way to or from school." He fixed his gaze on the pigeons roosting on the rooftops across the street, visible in the full light of day just glowing above the roofline. "But up until they sailed for the Mediterranean, I've seen Mother and Meaghan only a dozen times since I left home."

The echo of a door slamming down the street scattered the birds. Like the dreams he once held of a different life.

He turned away from the window. Enough wallowing in his just punishment. For lack of anything else to do, he began stacking the dishes from the previous night onto the tray while he sought the right words to steer this exchange away from his personal situation and back onto the matters at hand.

Emilynne's hand on his arm halted his actions. He turned to look down into the incredible depths of her blue eyes.

"So you are alone?"

This time the sympathy she offered, so soft he barely heard her at all, held a personal poignancy. Kindred spirits. The nature and depth of her loss hit him anew. She risked so much to keep the children with her because they were all she had. In light of Emilynne's plight, his own situation seemed trivial. His family was still there for him to reconcile with.

Her expression held no reproach. He wanted to gather her close and warm himself in the sanctuary he saw there. Waves pulsed up his arm from her fingertips. He barely suppressed a groan as her silent acceptance further undermined his intentions. Conflicted responsibilities tore at him.

He glanced down and noticed the tip of one toe peeking

out from beneath the black silk of her hem. Suddenly her fingers seemed to sear his skin through the linen of his shirt, but he could not pull away.

"Aunt Emilynne, is it time to go home yet?"

They broke apart at the sound of Abby's question. He couldn't decide whether to bless or curse the child's interruption of the intimate spell surrounding the two of them.

Bryan brushed the toes of his boots on the back of his trouser legs and straightened the bow at his collar before raising the gleaming brass knocker. He sent the huge metal bar crashing against its base on the whitewashed door front of the brick office building. He doffed his hat in anticipation of gaining entry.

The deep boom echoed into the depths, but the door stayed firmly closed. Surely, the professional staff of England's legal offices included a majordomo much like the man Gill O'Brien employed to act as screener, usher, and butler.

"Come on," he muttered after another minute crawled by, and he lifted the handle for a second try. It was early yet, but he'd seen smoke from the chimney and could have sworn he detected the glimmer of lamplight in the far windows as he approached.

Before the knocker could hit its mark, the door was ripped open and a voice growled, "It is devilish early to be conducting any but the most urgent business. Who are you and what do you want?"

Bryan double-checked the brass plate by the door frame. It read Willard Jefferies, Esq., clearly enough. "My name is Bryan Reilly. I'm a solicitor with the firm of O'Brien and

Mallory in Limerick. I am indeed here on a matter of utmost urgency in regards to a client of yours."

He drew a card from his pocket and proffered it toward the darkened interior beyond the partially open door. "I must speak to Mr. Jefferies at once."

"Solicitor, eh? From Ireland, you say?" The door eased open a trifle farther. "Well, don't just stand there on the stoop. Come in and tell me the nature of your business and which client you refer to."

Bryan stepped inside. "I really need to speak to Mr. Jefferies in private."

"This way. This way."

The size of the man who snapped the door shut behind him was nearly as overwhelming in breadth as in height. Bryan's eyes adjusted to the interior gloom, and he followed the huge, lumbering figure down what looked to be a very posh hall. Several open doors on either side of the passageway revealed the firm's library with rows of neatly shelved volumes and the copy rooms where clerks would soon spend the day preparing legal documents for clients or the courts.

Bryan breathed in the odors of ink, leather, and hushed confidences, feeling very at home after the past unsettling week spent with Emilynne Wellesley on the water. At sea with too many conflicting desires. This was the world of rule and order he'd embraced long ago. A logical haven offering respite from the tumult. That last thought gave him an unsettling pause. What was he hiding from within the confines of his profession?

They took a turn near a sweeping staircase that sheltered a lavish reception area for clients, then past a double-doored office, no doubt the inner sanctum of the firm's senior partner. Bryan glimpsed a massive mahogany desk sitting on a plush red carpet, sure to impress all but the most privileged of clients.

A sense of dismay struck him when his host ushered him into the next door and he found a crowded work area with stacks of books and piles of documents scattered across the desk and floor.

"Have a seat." With a backhanded gesture toward two wing chairs in front of the battered desk, the man retrieved a large tome that dangled precariously from the corner of his desk.

Bryan swept the chaos with a quick glance. No clerk or attorney, no matter his seniority, would be allowed to keep his clients' affairs in such disorder at O'Brien & Mallory. Wondering how this firm could possibly conduct business, he settled into the nearer chair.

"Not there!" the older man barked as he sat, his weathered black leather chair squeaking in protest. "You will wrinkle his lordship's deeds."

Bryan rose with a start and sat in the far chair instead. "Perhaps I should wait in the reception area until Mr. Jefferies arrives," he offered.

"I'm Jefferies." The rotund man chuckled at the start Bryan struggled to suppress. "I like getting a jump on my morning. My clerks and associates won't arrive for another half hour, but I find this time of day ideal for ordering one's thoughts and accomplishing the most astounding rate of work without interruption."

Bryan's gaze slid toward the plush, pristine office barely visible through a connecting door. Jefferies waved his hand in the air. "I can't think in there. Too orderly. But it impresses the clients, so I keep it for show."

The man turned his steel-blue gaze fully toward Bryan, who had the uncomfortable feeling that Jefferies could look right through him and sum him up in a matter of seconds.

Jefferies himself carried an air of solid reliability and keen intellect in his open perusal. Bushy gray eyebrows and thick side whiskers edged features that exuded an aura of trustworthiness, held over, no doubt, from a time when his vest and frock coat were fashionable.

"Enough of these blasted preliminaries, Reilly." Jefferies leaned back in his chair, apparently satisfied with what he had discerned from his introductory examination. He raised one eyebrow. "Tell me why you are here, my boy."

Bryan reached into his jacket's inner pocket and drew out the note Emilynne had written earlier. They had agreed that Bryan would escort Jefferies to Babbage's Rooming House at his earliest convenience. Emilynne had really wanted to accompany him to the office, but common sense and the dilemma of what to do with the children had prevailed, to Bryan's relief. He'd barely been able to contain his shock on learning the name of her solicitor matched the one from his memory of the office discussion regarding Mr. Whyte's business. One more knot in the line.

The English barrister patted his pockets and donned a pair of spectacles before reaching over his desk.

"It is from Miss Emilynne Wellesley. Regarding the death of her brother." Bryan handed the folded paper to Jefferies.

"The devil you say!" Jefferies shot Bryan an appraising look as he sat back with a thump. "It is the first I've heard such news. I've known Robert Wellesley since he was in knee pants."

The older man's hands shook as he unfolded the note and read to himself Emilynne's message. His face flushed red and then paled as he read it through a second time. Without saying a word he laid the sheet down and bent to rummage in one of the drawers, pulling a thick set of papers out and placing them beside Emilynne's missive.

"Looks to be her handwriting all right." He nodded to himself after scrutinizing first one, then the other. Over the rim of his glasses he fixed Bryan with a piercing stare that would brook no nonsense. "Perhaps you'd best start by outlining your role in all this."

Bryan leaned forward. "Miss Wellesley approached me as I was about to depart Limerick for England on some personal business. I have escorted her here in the hope of ascertaining the validity of her claims."

How easily his words fit back into the vocabulary of his trade. "It is only recently she confided the depth of desperation that brought her home so abruptly."

How much had Emilynne conveyed in her short note? How much should he reveal at this juncture? Emilynne needed to tell her attorney her suspicions in person, then seek his advice regarding the location of the will she was certain Robert had drawn up under his guidance. Bryan had advocated this course so that he could better ascertain Jefferies's role in any of the strange tangle enmeshing Emilynne and the children.

"Are you here acting as her representative in an official capacity?"

Jefferies's pointed question sought more professional details. Like an old dog sizing up the competition for his territory. Bryan respected that. "Miss Wellesley would prefer to confer with you in person regarding the details of her situation. If you will accompany me, she awaits you at her lodgings. I will explain my role in this afterward."

Jefferies steepled his fingers and continued his appraisal

of Bryan. "Aside from Miss Wellesley's instructions, there's much else you are not telling me. What is it you wish to avoid?"

Bryan shifted his weight and admired the man's acumen. He would make a formidable opponent in a courtroom. "Miss Wellesley believes I am a sea captain. Her illness on board ship prevented me from refuting this in a timely manner. She holds a rather sharp distaste for members of the Irish legal system."

Jefferies's shoulders relaxed a fraction. "That sounds like Emilynne. Still, she trusted you enough to seek your help and to ask you to bring me to her. She'll accept your revelation right enough."

"Tell me." His tone softened. "How is she coping with this loss of her brother and his wife? They were very close."

"She grieves quietly and puts her energy into the children, from what I have observed." The picture of his temporary family as he'd left them rose. Christian splashing in the remainders of Bryan's shaving suds at the washstand while Emilynne brushed Abby's hair by the windows, the two of them bathed in sunlight. "Since this happened several months ago, the rawness has worn off to a certain extent."

"Several months ago, sir?" Mr. Jefferies exploded onto his feet. "The devil again, I say!"

He rapped his knuckles on the desk surface. "I could swear my . . . one of my . . . associates has reported being in almost weekly contact with Mr. Wellesley regarding certain business matters since his departure to settle matters in Ireland."

"Although I do not know the exact dates. Miss Wellesley is quite adamant that her brother died shortly after their arrival in County Kildare."

Florid color flooded Jefferies's face. He took a massive handkerchief out of his pocket and peeled off his spectacles. Rubbing absently, he stared down at his desk. Bryan waited with increasing agitation, unable to follow the direction of the other man's thoughts and fearing his own impressions of the older man's integrity were false.

Finally Jefferies exhaled, a sound that filled the small chamber with the hollow echo of bitter hope. "Perhaps I am mistaken."

The older man's words sounded as forlorn as his sigh, arousing Bryan's sympathy—and his suspicions that Emilynne's story was more shocking than he'd dared believe. Surely someone would have thought to contact Robert Wellesley's solicitor—to inform him of his client's passing at the very least, and to ascertain the nature and running of his affairs. He was increasingly grateful for the precautions they had taken in bringing Emilynne home.

In the distance a clock chimed.

Jefferies glanced out to the hall. "Late again. For once the fact that the associate who holds the keys to the back door this month is perpetually late works to our advantage."

He gestured for Bryan to get up and pointed toward the connecting office. "If you don't mind, I'd like you to wait for me in my inner sanctum. No one comes in here or goes there without my express permission. I'm afraid they'll mess up my order."

Bryan struggled not to look as skeptical of this last comment as he felt. He stood. "Sir, Miss Wellesley is most eager to meet with you."

Jefferies ushered him toward the other door as a slam sounded in the distance. "I have several pertinent matters to attend before I can leave. The fewer of my people who realize why you are here and where you are from, the better. For the time being at least, discretion and all that. You understand."

Bryan heard voices coming down the hall as he entered the luxurious office. The knot forming in his stomach would not be gainsaid for long. Emilynne Wellesley's kiss in Limerick had embroiled him in something far more complex than even she could imagine. Something he would not easily untangle himself from—not and live with his own conscience and Granny's strictures of The Blessing.

"Help yourself to one of the volumes in the case. Very illuminating writings some of them. I shall be back in a thrice." Jefferies pulled the door shut.

"Junior!"

Bryan heard him bellow from the other room.

"Come here at once!"

Chapter Seven

Emilynne wiped the palms of her hands on her gown and patted her chignon one last time before sliding Mrs. Babbage's front parlor door open. At least the children were occupied, happily assisting Mrs. Babbage in the kitchen while she made the afternoon scones. This was the moment Emilynne had anticipated too long, and now that it had arrived, she wished to postpone it indefinitely.

Facing Willard Jefferies, or any other of their friends or acquaintances, brought the reality of Robert's and Gail's deaths glaringly home. She'd give anything to take back these past months, to return to the days before their journey to Ireland. If only she could share one more quiet morning tête-à-tête with Robert or shop with Gail down the Christmas Steps followed by a mandatory stop to share sweets with the youngest residents of Foster's Alms House.

But those days were past and she had her responsibilities for the children to fill her future. And Bryan Reilly to free from his role as her protector. She squared her shoulders against the pang of regret that shuddered through her on the heels of that thought and pushed the pocket door open.

She kept her gaze fixed on the larger of the two men standing by the marble hearth, still fighting the sweeping loneliness she already felt knowing this would most likely be her last day with Bryan.

"Uncle Willard!" She practically flew across the room to be enveloped in one of his famous bear hugs. As always, he smelled of the peppermints he'd given her when she was a girl.

"My dear child." He patted her back and gave her the momentary illusion of her childhood, where someone older and bigger could set everything to rights.

She wanted to stay locked in his embrace, but he slipped his hands down to hers and stepped back to examine her with a practiced eye. Uncle Willard had been a schoolmate of her father's and the family's solicitor since he hung out his shingle. Robert had consulted him on all matters of business. He was even the one who facilitated the publication of her papers in academic circles, handling all the details so her gender remained a secret.

His was the first face she'd seen in months that she knew she could trust without question.

"You're a little thinner and too pale to my liking but not near as green as the time you sailed home from Paris with your parents." He favored her with an approving nod.

Looking over at Bryan, he added, "She never has been a good sailor."

Bryan had the grace to simply nod and not comment on his firsthand knowledge regarding that statement. Something about Bryan looked different this morning. He carried an air of restraint—less a captain used to command amid the wild waves and wind and more a man conforming to the constraints of a professional veneer. She found this impression unsettling, as if she didn't know him at all despite the time they had spent in such intimate company.

Uncle Willard squeezed her fingers. "Well, my girl, you've certainly had a time of it, if the hints your young man has given me prove true. You'd best start at the beginning. Tell me of Robert's first meeting with Thaddeus Whyte."

Emilynne sat down on Mrs. Babbage's black horsehair settee and swallowed. Could she tell it all without succumbing to tears? She must. Uncle Willard sat next to her, still clasping her hands in his massive fingers, patiently waiting. It wasn't until Bryan moved to stand behind them by the windows that she felt able to go on.

Grimly Emilynne recounted the events as they unfolded from the moment she set foot in Ireland with her brother and his family until she entreated Bryan's help on Limerick's docks.

"Poor Robert. Murdered. It is a hard thing to fathom. We'll do what we can to bring the blackguard to justice. But it will be hard to prove without a witness to the crime or a confession." Willard Jefferies spoke with the authoritative voice of impending justice. Music to Emilynne's ears and balm to her spirit.

"It is a terrible sorrow you've suffered, my dear." Uncle Willard patted her hands for the umpteenth time. His eyes held a distant look, as if he were already mapping strategies to avenge Robert's and Gail's deaths. Hope flooded her.

Telling Bryan her suspicions the previous night had released the pent-up doubts, worry, and grief she'd held inside for weeks, but the agonized tide washing through her had left her hollow and empty. The only thing she remembered feeling at the ebb was the security of Bryan's arms. Today her resolve had strengthened to ensure a safe life for the children first and justice for their parents second.

"I believe you did the right thing fleeing the situation." Uncle Willard reassurance drew her back to the conversation at hand. "Considerations for the children and your own safety had to come first."

He grimaced. "Still, if Whyte has begun a legal action to take charge of the children, the Irish courts may try to press a claim of precedence."

He stood and looked briefly at Bryan. When the captain grimly nodded his agreement, her attorney paced over to the hearth and leaned his arm upon the mantel, lost in thought.

Emilynne's hope crumpled to bitter fear. "There must be some way to stop him. Robert's will—"

She stopped as Uncle Willard shook his head. His face bore the burden of unpleasant news. The same tight-lipped expression Robert had worn the night he came to tell her of their parents' grave illness. An involuntary tremor shook her.

"The will appears to be missing," Bryan supplied. He placed his hand on her shoulder.

"How is that possible?" she gasped before a rapping on the door stopped any forthcoming explanation.

"Mrs. Reilly?" Mrs. Babbage's voice sounded from the foyer. "I'm sorry to disturb ye, but I think ye'd best come and see to yer boy."

"Mrs. Reilly?"

Uncle Willard's consternation barely registered as her fears over the will were replaced by more immediate concerns. A small strangled cough sounded on the other side of the door. So like the time he'd had quinsy the winter before.

"Christian!" She slid open the door without a backward glance at the two men. "What's the matter, darling?"

Mrs. Babbage held the boy in her arms, his blond head resting against her shoulder. Emilynne prayed the pallor of his cheeks was so startling only in contrast to the black bombazine of their landlady's gown.

"My throat hurts," he rasped in a small whisper.

Just as she'd feared. Christian reached for her from the shelter of Mrs. Babbage's embrace. Emilynne gathered him close. At least his skin was cool to her touch as she traced her fingers over his forehead and cheek.

"I'm sorry to disturb you and Captain Reilly, ma'am. He explained it was a most important interview." Mrs. Babbage clasped her hands together in front of her apron, a sign Emilynne had already learned meant her landlady was unsure of herself. "But I know from my boy, Peter, that a bad throat needs ta be tended to sharply. 'Specially in one so little."

"You did the right thing, Mrs. Babbage." She assured the woman and shifted Christian to a more comfortable position on her hip. "Our business with Mr. Jefferies is important. But the children are my first concern."

Mrs. Babbage smiled her approval. "It is the way of things, is it not, Mrs. Reilly. Men may concern themselves with the workings of the world, fussing over their business details—all with an eye on the future. But we mothers tend what's really important to the future, our children."

She gently tousled Christian's hair. "Would you like me ta fix the tyke a spot of tea with honey and lemon. It is what Peter favors when he feels a mite raw."

"How does that sound, dearest?" Emilynne rubbed his chin with her forefinger. *We mothers,* the acknowledgment warmed and saddened her at the same time.

"Will you come too?" Christian asked.

"I do have some rather important business to discuss with Mr. Jefferies. But I will accompany you if you insist."

Christian eyed her thoughtfully. "Papa likes Mr. Jefferies, doesn't he? He told me he was wise as that King Solomon in the Bible."

"And that is very wise indeed, is it not?" Emilynne kissed his nose but avoided answering him directly. "So, shall I go back inside or escort you to the kitchen for your tea. Afterward, I will tuck you in for a nice nap."

"Will you sing to me?"

"Yes."

"And read me a story?" A mischievous sparkle lit Christian's eyes, reassuring Emilynne that his throat was not bothering him overly much.

"We'll see." She set him on the floor. "And your decision, sir?"

"You'd best go talk to Mr. Jefferies, Aunt Emmie. You've been awful worried, so you don't know what you are doing. Perhaps he can help you."

With a laugh Emilynne patted his head. "I'm sure Mr. Jefferies will straighten me right out. Thank you, Mrs. Babbage. I shall come to fetch the children as soon as I can."

"No trouble, ma'am. I miss the days when Peter was a little un. I'm sure the tea will fix this little sailor right up. They are both charmers, that's sure. The little miss has gone to help Maisy hang sheets in the yard."

Emilynne watched them move across the foyer hand in hand for a moment before returning to the parlor.

Uncle Willard wore a deep frown as he stood by the fireplace. His face was flushed to a ruddy hue.

". . . it seemed the wisest plan at the time." Bryan spoke in the same tone she used when trying to reason with the children. She couldn't see his features, as the windows made his face a silhouette. "And in light of the missing files from your office, this ruse may prove a necessary precaution."

Neither man seemed to register her return. The peculiar florid shade of Uncle Willard's face deepened as he answered impatiently. "But posing as man and wife? Think of the scandal if this gets out! What do they teach you Irish solicitors? You can't think the senior partners at O'Brien and Mallory will approve your conduct."

Missing files? Irish solicitors? O'Brien and Mallory? The firm handling Thaddeus's ludicrous custody claim? Emilynne froze. She'd come all this way. Nearly made it home safely. And all the while the man she'd thought of as her savior worked for the enemy?

A cold rock of fear plummeted through her and was quickly replaced by anger, white hot and blinding. She'd trusted him! Told him her deepest fears when all the while he'd been so very much more than the mere sea captain he'd pretended to be and never breathed a word. He'd been a wolf in sheep's clothing.

What an idiot she was! What a bastard he was! Her soul roiled with anger and fear.

Before she could debate the matter, she was standing toe to toe with him. She slapped him hard. "You are despicable!"

Bryan flinched but stood his ground. Though he remained silent, a stubborn gleam lit his eye.

"My dear!" Uncle Willard exclaimed.

She raised her hand again. This time Bryan caught her wrist but still said nothing.

"You will not take the children away from me. I will not allow it."

Emilynne struggled to free herself, but he held firm. She would not beg him to release her. And she would most definitely not cry. For a moment they remained locked in a wordless battle of wills.

"When you are calmer, we can discuss my deception. And your dilemma." Bryan broke the virulent silence. "I have no intention of taking the children from you."

"My dilemma is none of your affair. Neither are the children. If you do not release me at once, I shall have you up on charges."

"Violence and threats will do neither of you a good turn," Uncle Willard interposed. "I suggest you return to your seat, my dear. And you, young Reilly, shall join us by sitting in that rocker there."

Bryan released her, his face a unfeeling mask marked with the hot brand of her fingers. She wanted to slap him again. Instead, she whirled away and stepped around to join Uncle Willard on the settee. Her wrist burned from the tightness of Bryan's grasp. She hoped the red stain on his cheek still stung. Bryan walked slowly over to the carved rocker, gripping the back but continuing to stand.

"I don't suppose your family crisis is any more real than your command of a ship," she flung at him, wanting desperately to crack his stoic facade as all her misplaced trust echoed back to her.

A flicker stirred in the depths of his green gaze. "The possibility of Reilly Ship Works foundering without new financing is very real. And though the title 'captain' is given to any Reilly on board one of our vessels, I don't believe you were putting too fine a point on who I was when we first met."

Embarrassment flamed through her. She had been desperate enough to throw herself into the arms of a stranger and beg his help without thought to the consequence. Idiot indeed!

"Recriminations will get us nowhere." Uncle Willard held up a hand. "The fact of the matter remains, the two of you are involved in a possibly illegal flight from Irish jurisdiction and are currently inextricably tied together until the matter is resolved."

He directed a steady look at Bryan. "You claim not to be directly involved in the matter. However, as you said earlier, having some knowledge of Mr. Whyte's hiring your firm to represent his claims in a custody matter, once your suspicions were aroused, you should have headed straight back to Limerick."

Uncle Willard patted Emilynne's hands when she gripped them together to keep them from trembling. "Claims we can easily refute once Robert's will is probated."

"However I . . . we"—he nodded toward Bryan—"are a bit concerned that several critical files, including the actual document, appear to be missing from my office."

Emilynne gasped, and her heart sank even lower, churning cold nausea in her belly.

"I changed course for Bristol since I knew Mr. Jefferies's firm is the one we were dealing with on this matter. . . ."

Bryan's voice was cold and distant, not at all the warm voice that had entertained the children with stories of his boyhood adventures with his brothers—nor comforted her last night. This was the voice of a stranger, someone she did not know at all. Emilynne pushed at the lost feeling that bloomed with those thoughts and struggled to concentrate on the information he imparted.

". . . I planned to visit his office this morning and sound him out on the matter. When you addressed your note to him—convinced he had the will—I was surprised, to say the least. I'm quite sure my firm planned to proceed to the courts on the matter of custody, since they were assured that the parents died intestate—without a will. This caused some ripples given the prominent names of the families involved."

"But, Uncle Willard, Robert showed me the will—"

"Yes, my dear." He sighed. "I retained one copy and your brother took two others. I'd like to think they are at Newbury Manor. Robert was always the orderly type, even as a young pup. But if someone can pilfer the will and all my notes out from under my nose, I'd hesitate to trust that those copies are wherever he put them for safekeeping."

"He returned the copy I saw to his desk. They must still be locked in there. No one at home would allow anyone to disturb his things."

The two men exchanged glances accompanied by mirrored grimaces that spoke louder than words. She was being naive. If Thaddeus Whyte could have a will stolen from a legal office in another country, if he could murder two innocent people just to retain control of some land and horses, surely he could arrange for someone nefarious to steal documents from their trusting retainers in Wiltshire.

There had to be some other way to refute his vile claims on Abby and Christian. There just had to be. "If the wills are gone, cannot you and the witnesses testify to Robert's desires regarding the children and his estates?"

"It is possible the Irish courts will allow such testimony."

Uncle Willard did not give that hope a strong endorsement.

Emilynne felt as if a fog were closing in, shrouding the two men. A thick, cold, merciless fog. "Could we not file for custody ourselves? Right here in Bristol. Or in Wiltshire. If I could just get the children home, surely he would not be allowed to pry them out of there. And the magistrates here all know and trust you."

"Since the matter was first brought up in Ireland, the courts here will most likely want the matter settled there," Bryan answered. "That the children's uncle is an Englishman himself will only make that decision easier for them."

Coming from Bryan, that view seemed so much more certain.

"And I am but an Englishwoman." The bitterness of the inequities her gender faced in modern society stung her with the bite of a dagger—right through her heart. How could she lose the children to a monster just because he was a man? At least in the Druid times she studied, women seemed to hold more equal footing in their society.

"Things would be a might easier if you were wed, my dear. That's a fact we cannot ignore," Uncle Willard agreed. "Not that Robert doubted your abilities. He simply did not want either Gail or you to bear the burdens of raising two children and running estates in two countries on your own. That is why he appointed a co-guardian if you were unwed."

"I don't suppose you'd be interested in making your ruse into a more permanent arrangement, young man?"

Bryan did not appear to hear Uncle Willard. His attention was centered on the windows and a loud wailing that was coming from the street.

"*Mr.* Reilly . . ."

He did glance over at her following that emphasis. Then he moved to lift the lace panel and peer out the window at the fuss. Surely whatever was going on could not be more important than the future of her children.

She took a deep breath and continued. ". . . has urgent business of his own to attend in Liverpool, Uncle Willard." She put the absurd notion of marriage between them to rest despite the rapid beating of her heart at the thought. "Now that he has turned me over to your guidance, he can be on his way. I'm sure we can straighten his involvement out later."

The wailing sounded like it was right outside Mrs. Babbage's gate. Emilynne fought her curiosity even as Bryan moved toward the parlor door. Although sympathy panged inside her, she struggled to remain focused on the serious matters confronting her.

"I'm afraid the matter is not quite so simple, child. We must consult with Richard Andrews as quickly and discreetly as possible."

Bryan slid open the parlor door just as the front door crashed open.

"Mrs. Babbage . . . Mrs. Reilly . . . come quickly . . . the little miss . . ." The hysterical wailing echoing through the foyer sent Emilynne flying after Bryan.

He caught Mrs. Babbage's maid, Maisy, by the stairs, and planted his hands on her shoulders, halting her headlong flight toward the kitchens.

"Oh, Captain Reilly, ye must come quick! Miss Abby! I'm so sorry!" Maisy burst into tears as she turned around to face him.

"Sorry for what! What has happened to Abigail." Bryan looked grim as he obviously fought to keep his voice even and thereby calm Maisy enough to say what was going on. Out of breath, the maid just panted and repeated her apologies between sobs.

Where was Abby? Please God, let her be safe!

With great effort Emilynne forced herself to halt and allow him to speak to the maid alone. The important thing was to get the information, not to goad Maisy's hysterics any further by having everyone beset her at once.

Emilynne waged her own battle with hysterics as fears about Thaddeus Whyte's evil intentions threatened to coalesce from the shadows of their flight across Ireland. What if one of his men had snatched Abby? What about Christian? Was he safe?

"Mistress sent me to nip round the corner ta the green-grocer's cart." Maisy struggled to catch her breath as she trembled in Bryan's grasp. "Ta fetch a lemon for yer boy's throat. And the little miss asked ta come."

Maisy turned pleading brown eyes to Emilynne. "It was just a little ways, and she held me hand the whole time. Good as gold she were."

"What happened?" Bryan's stern tone forced the girl's gaze back to meet his. "Is she injured? Did anyone take her?"

Maisy gulped and did not appear to notice Mrs. Babbage arriving from the kitchen with Christian in tow, though Emilynne breathed a partial sigh of relief to see his little face.

"I let go of her ta pay fer the lemons, sir. And an open carriage passed by just then. . . ."

Emilynne clutched the door frame behind her, anticipating the worst.

". . . with a beautiful lady heading down the street toward

the Christmas Steps. Miss Abby shouted 'Mama' and darted away after her.''

Mrs. Babbage's sharp intake of breath distracted Maisy from her tale. "I tried ta catch her, ma'am. Honest. But it was dreadful crowded."

"I brought back the lemons." She ended the last on a sob as she held out the fruit.

The landlady patted her maid's back as she moved by her to come and put her arm around Emilynne. Christian clutched Emilynne's skirts and looked as bewildered as Emilynne felt. She ran a hand through his hair to comfort him a little. And to comfort herself.

"Alls I could think was ta run here and fetch help. The grocer said he'd keep an eye out fer her if'n she come back on her own."

Bryan relaxed his grip on Maisy's arm. "You did the right thing. I'd like you to retrace your steps so you can show me exactly where you last saw her. Can you do that?"

"Aye, sir." Maisy nodded and swabbed her nose with the corner of her shawl. "The city's no place fer a girl alone, that's what me mum always said."

"Shall I summon the watch?" Uncle Willard said from just inside the parlor door. Emilynne hadn't even registered until then, the hand he'd placed under her elbow for support.

"Not yet, sir. We don't want to draw undue attention." Bryan was already halfway to the door, with Maisy a step behind. He paused in front of Emilynne.

"Oh, Bryan" was all she could choke out. She reached over and touched his sleeve. Abby was too little to be lost. There were too many dangerous places she could end up. Too many dangerous people. What could she have been thinking?

"Odd thing, ma'am." Maisy barely met her gaze as she handed the lemons to Mrs. Babbage. "The lady what passed didn't look nothing like ye. She had reddish hair and freckles."

Like Gail. "Oh, Abby!"

"I'll find her." Bryan touched Emilynne's cheek. "Trust me."

Then he was gone.

Trust me. Emilynne was only slightly surprised that despite everything, she did. She had to.

They arrived at the corner in short work, though not nearly fast enough to suit Bryan. Maisy panted heavily beside him as she pointed to the spot she'd last seen Abby.

Crowds of afternoon shoppers swarmed down the streets that met at this corner—scullery maids and housewives set to purchase whatever was needed for the evening or next day's meals; children and their nannies off to get an ice or lemonade after a romp in the park; tradesmen seeking supplies to continue their own work; members of the quality seeking some item of fashion. So many heads but not the small one with auburn curls he needed to locate.

He refused to even think of a little one's chances amid the thoroughfares clogged with carts, carriages, and hackneys.

A burly man with gray hair and dark chin whiskers motioned to them from beside a wagon loaded with produce while a woman in worn calico watched him weigh out some potatoes. The greengrocer.

"No sign of the girl, sir. I've kept an eye out best I could." He tied the woman's purchase up in paper and string. "I hope ye find her, sir. It weren't the young lady's fault. The child just dashed off real sudden like."

Bryan nodded his thanks and continued to scrutinize the bustling crowds. It wouldn't take much for a little girl like Abby to get turned around and not be able to find her way back. She must be frightened, especially when everything would look so tall and unfamiliar to her. Would she have any hope of finding her way back on her own? He couldn't help remembering the time Devin had been lost while they were playing Viking raiders. Quin and he'd spent hours circling the fields and woods on Beannacht Island, looking for him, while he'd been wandering in circles searching for them.

"Stay here," he said to Maisy. "If Abigail returns, take her straight back to Mrs. Babbage's. If I come back and you are not here, I will know she is safe."

"Aye, sir." Maisy nodded her understanding and set right to her task, standing on tiptoe to look up and down the intersection, her lips pressed in a grim line and fresh tears sparkling in the corners of her eyes.

Determined not to miss any detail, Bryan forced himself to walk at an even pace as he joined the flow of traffic along the street. He searched the walkways and cobblestones for blocks, pausing only long enough to peer down darkened alleyways until he was certain she'd not taken shelter in any of them.

Surely if she'd gone into one of the shops and told them she was lost, one of the clerks would have helped her find her way back to Mrs. Babbage's or, at the least, allowed her stand in the shop entrance waiting for anyone searching for her.

Doubts beset him. Would a child whose parents had been ripped away so unexpectedly, who had been threatened with losing the only other adult she loved, really trust anyone to come for her? What if she'd been confused and taken one of the side streets? He hadn't wanted to wait for help when Maisy had sobbed out her story, perhaps he should have let Jefferies summon the watch.

He fought the cold clenching of fear in his gut and continued his methodical search.

Trust me. The depth of meaning behind his promise shook him to his core. Finding Abby and returning her to Emilynne mattered more to him than anything he'd felt in a long time.

If someone associated with Thaddeus Whyte was responsible, he knew what he'd do. He'd strangle him. No one claiming to seek a child's best interest should snatch them away.

A yellow hair ribbon, trampled on the cobblestones momentarily, drew his eye, but he'd never seen Abby wear anything but mourning black. Little girls liked pretty things. When he found her, he vowed he'd buy her a dozen ribbons, all in different colors.

The crowd ahead parted slightly, and he spotted Abby sitting on the tall brick cornerpost of a posh town home's fenced-in front yard.

She smiled at him and waved, looking for all the world as if she'd been expecting him.

Chapter Eight

Bryan scooped Abby into his arms and held her close. He took a deep breath. She smelled of cinnamon and apple blossoms, better than the sweetest treat he could imagine at the moment.

"Ah, my dear. You must have had quite a fright," he whispered into her burnished auburn curls. "I know I was rather scared for a time."

"I wasn't afraid, Captain," Abigail Wellesley protested in her too serious way. But she gave his neck an extra squeeze anyway before pulling back to look at him. "I did just what you said to do. Then I knew you'd be sure to find me."

"What I told you to do?" Bryan turned and began retracing his path through the crowds, moving as quickly as he could while keeping Abby securely in his arms. Emilynne must be beside herself with worry. "And exactly what is it I told you to do?"

"Don't you remember, Captain?" The girl laid her head against his shoulder. "You told me and Christian about losing your brother when you were playing raiders."

Abby slid her hand in between his shirt and waistcoat, a gesture he found oddly comforting.

"You said," she continued, "if he'd just picked the highest rock he could find and stayed put, you'd have found him a great deal sooner."

He chuckled. "And that's just what you did, isn't it, sweeting? You're a very clever girl."

"Not so very clever," she told him sadly. "I know my mama is living in heaven now, but just for a minute I thought she'd come to Bristol to shop like we used to do. I tried to catch her before she had to go back."

She picked her head up and looked at him with a melting look in her solemn brown eyes. "You'll tell me the truth, won't you Captain?"

An adult's statement of trust more than a child's question. At that moment he felt like he would do anything she asked. "I'll try."

"People don't get to come back from heaven once they're there, do they? That wasn't my mama, was it?"

The harshness of life's realities never seemed more likely to tear his heart in two. "No, Abby. That was not your mama."

Her gaze slid downward for a moment and she nodded, then laid her head back on his shoulder. "Is Aunt Emmie very angry I ran away, Captain Reilly?"

That seemed more like a child's normal worry. "No, sweeting. She's terribly worried, but she is not angry."

The anguish shivering through Emilynne's voice haunted him. *Oh, Bryan.* He quickened his pace, weaving his way back down the crowded street. Abby gulped small breaths against his neck. No doubt fright and disappointment catching up with her.

"You know, Miss Wellesley—" He dodged a nanny with a huge wicker pram as he sought a means to divert Abby's attention. "In the spirit of honesty between the two of us, I feel I must tell you that I am not really a ship's captain. I spend almost all my time in an office or the courthouse, working as a solicitor."

"But you like being on board ship." Another observation of truth from one so young.

"Yes, I do. Very much."

"Aunt Emmie does not like solicitors much. She says they might enforce the law, but the law was not necessarily the right thing." Abby's fingers played with the buttons on his shirt. "They're not going to take her away from us, are they?"

"Not if your uncle Willard and I can stop it." The implications behind his pledge did not escape him. Surely he could accomplish his trip to Liverpool and return in time to help sort out this custody matter.

"I think I should like to still call you 'captain.' It fits you."

"If you wish." His voice came gruff as his heart twisted.

"I know you can fix this for us, just like you found me. You have a good heart." The warmth of her hand on his chest was nothing compared to the trust in her voice.

"Captain?" she asked against his neck after subsiding into silence for a moment. "What does moor-knock mean?"

"*Muirneach?* Wherever did you hear that word?"

"It is what you said to Aunt Emilynne when you tucked her in last night. I liked the sound of it."

Indeed. He'd called Emilynne his beloved. He had no

memory of ever using that endearment. He'd never imagined he would remember the few phrases from the old language his granny taught him so long ago. Let alone use them.

"It is a Gaelic word—"

"Oh, praise God! Ye found her!"

Maisy's call of relief brought their surroundings into focus. Only a block to go. The greengrocer tipped his cap as they passed by, and Bryan nearly ran the final length of Baldwin Street to get Abby home to Emilynne.

Mrs. Babbage flung open the front door to her house with a shout. "He's found her!" echoed through the foyer.

He took the steps two at a time.

The last strains of the lullaby died in Emilynne's throat, and the only sound in the room was the soft sighs of sleeping children. Just for this moment her world was complete.

Abby's small fingers were still laced tightly through her own, and she continued to rhythmically stroke the edge of Christian's brow with the gesture his mother had used to soothe him since he was borne. If Gail couldn't be here to do this for herself, Emilynne felt blessed to be able to comfort her friend's children for her.

The door to their room cracked open and then hesitated.

"Come in." She spoke softly lest she disturb Abby and Christian, but in truth once these two relaxed into their slumbers, it was usually quite difficult to rouse them. At least for the first half hour or so.

Bryan walked into the room with a silent nod and the ghost of a smile on his lips. He crossed to stand at the end of the bed, looking down at the pillows. Emilynne was struck anew with how extraordinarily handsome he was with his dark hair, smooth brow, and that little cleft in his firm chin. But it was the look in his eyes that surprised and warmed her the most as he gazed at the children. He genuinely cared for them. That belief gave her hope. He might be employed by Thaddeus, but he would carry Abby's and Christian's best interests with him. Surely he saw they needed to stay with her.

Emilynne untangled her fingers from Abby's and slid off the coverlet to join Bryan. His gaze dropped briefly to her shoes on the floor by the bedpost, which she'd taken off in order to join the children on the bed for a story and their song. She curled her toes into the carpeting.

"You should rest too." His voice skimmed through her, leaving a thrill in its wake. His gaze met hers, and behind the polite veneer she read sorrow and deep concern. "Mr. Jefferies had some matters to attend and won't return until tea."

She shook her head. "I would not be able to sleep. Too much has happened today."

She felt certain she could trust this man with their lives. But given his admitted deception in being a member of the very law firm seeking to take Abby and Christian from her, the future was an altogether different matter. And that is where she needed to untangle her thoughts. Robert and Gail were counting on her to make the right choices for their children's sake.

"There are many decisions yet to be made, which is why you should rest now." He pressed his lips together as if there were more he wished to say but couldn't.

Though she appreciated his concern, she had too many things she had to think through. Uncle Willard had been explaining that her best course in fighting to keep the children was marriage when Maisy burst into the house. The discussion had ended there as they waited in agony for Bryan's search. She needed to sort through all the reasons her original intentions to accept Richard's long-standing offer still held despite everything inside her shuddering at the thought.

She needed time alone to quell her rebellious spirit's dependence on the man standing beside her. Time away from the tender charm of twinkling green eyes and pervasive scent of new wood and sage that made her want to throw all her troubles onto his broad shoulders. The children were her responsibility. Their future, her charge.

Perhaps he was right. If she lay down, he would leave the room and she could start the process of letting him go. Bryan Reilly had done more than enough for them, sacrificed enough already.

She extended her hand to him. "I don't believe I properly thanked you for finding Abby today."

The warmth of his hand as he took hers in his firm grasp sent a rush of tingling heat pulsing through her. She took a tiny step closer, as if she were a moth drawn to the comforting glow of a bright flame.

"Abby is a dear child." He turned his head toward the pair, sleeping so soundly just feet away from them. "Aside from matters of business, it has been a long time since anyone put such innocent trust in me. I couldn't bear the thought of anything happening to her."

His answer rippled through her. She loved the sound of his voice; his soft Irish accent deepened when he spoke with such conviction. Still, there was an undercurrent of doubt and pain in his voice, and in his gaze, that troubled her.

"She is not a child who gives her trust easily. I think she chose well in trusting you." She slipped her hand from his and cupped his cheek, drawing him back to look at her. "I know I am grateful for the providence that compelled me to seek your help in Limerick."

He gazed at her for what seemed to be both forever and but the merest tick of a clock. Living doubt, wizened mistrust, and a flicker of hope warred in the depths of his penetrating gaze.

"Despite—"

She stilled his question by sliding her fingers over his lips. "We have both been guilty of dissemblance. I cannot censure your reasons without condemning my own.

"It would seem we were fated to meet over this matter." She smiled at the ironic truth as she continued. "I am grateful that at least now I trust that you seek not only the right thing, but what is right for Abby and Christian."

He closed his eyes in a long, slow blink as deep emotions flared in his depth. His hand clasped her wrist with a grip that sent shivers racing down her arm. Instead of pulling her hand away, he turned his face into it and pressed a kiss to her palm.

She flowed into him like water seeking the shore. Her arms wound around his neck as his encircled her back. For a wordless moment they gazed at each other, as if time itself held its breath. The silk of her gown sighed against his worsted suit as he pressed her closer. Being in Bryan's arms stirred feelings beyond Emilynne's imaginings. Holding him, she knew her life had changed in ways she would spend a lifetime regretting. But she would never regret this one moment.

"Kiss me," she whispered. "Kiss me as if you truly mean it."

"Gladly," he answered, his voice thick. He anchored a hand in the hair at the nape of her neck, then dragged her lips to his.

Bryan covered her waiting mouth with the intoxicating strength of his own. The taste of him sang through her blood. The music that poured from him rippled over her mind and heart in a tune her ears could not hear but made her soul dance. Lilting strains of an unseen harp. A melody she'd experienced as an echo once, yet recognized now on so deep a level, she shuddered.

He teased her lips open with the tip of his tongue, parting them on her sigh and pulling her closer still. His tongue brushed the inner rim of her mouth, sending shivers of melting desire cascading through her. His fingers cupped her chin and his thumb stroked her cheek with a dizzying caress as soft as a smile shared late at night.

She wound her fingers through the hair brushing his collar and met his demands with her own. A low moan at the back of his throat was her reward. Pressed close to him, the parts of her body that touched his pulsed with joyous life. He tasted of raw desperation and unnerving desire. He must know too that whatever passed between them only did so once in a lifetime.

Past warnings and ancient strictures about proper behavior echoed back to her in a wild blur, only to sluice away like dust on stone after a cleansing rain. To salvage her future she should thrust away from him, but to save her sanity she could do naught but meet each stroke of his tongue with her own.

"Muirneach." The name he called her that spoke to her soul pushed from his depths and shivered over her lips. Passion flared between them, so bold and hot Emilynne

could easily imagine it burning away the very floor beneath their feet.

A knock on the door broke them apart, dazed and panting.

"Beg pardon, Cap'n," young Peter Babbage called. "But me mother wished me ta tell ye that yer Mr. Jefferies has returned.

Bryan released a long breath and studied Emilynne as she tucked a stray tendril back into place with one hand while she steadied herself against the bedpost with the other. Her eyes held the stunned look of a woman who had been thoroughly kissed, but he read no shock or regret there. Rebellious relief poured through him. They'd have to talk, to make sure this didn't happen again while they were living in such intimate company. Now was not the time.

"I'll go down first. Join us as soon as you can."

She nodded and turned, hunting on the carpet with her bared toes for her shoes. He fought the urge to gather her back into his arms and turned to leave.

"Cap'n." Peter knocked again just before Bryan opened the door. He took a step backward. "Mum said I was ta sit here in the hall and bring the little ones ta her when they waked."

"There's a good lad." Bryan tousled Peter's hair. "We are in your debt."

"Oh, no, sir. Losin' and findin' yer little girl made more excitement than we had here in months. I hopes ye stays fer a long time."

Bryan hastened down the stairs to join Jefferies in the front parlor. The attorney had excused himself shortly after Abby had been restored to Emilynne's arms, saying he had a plan and he would let them know about it upon his return late in the afternoon.

Jefferies stood in front of the parlor's hearth surrounded by a sea of boxes. "Come see what I've bought for your trip, my boy." He beckoned for Bryan to join him.

"What on earth would I do with all this on a rail trip to Liverpool?"

"There's naught here for you, man," Jefferies chuckled. "It is for Miss Wellesley on your trip to Wiltshire. While you travel, I think your little family will stand out far less if they're not rigged out in black."

While the logical side of Bryan was stunned at the audacity of the older attorney's assumption that he would be escorting Emilynne anywhere, unexpected relief cascaded through his less practical side at the realization he might not need to make his farewells to her just yet.

The two views vied for dominance as Jefferies awaited his reaction, and for once since Limerick, logic won. "But—"

"I added my own missive to the telegraph you sent to Harland this morning," the older man interjected. "Wolfe and Belfast still have the upper hand in that quarter, mind, but I believe your needs can still be addressed. The carriage will pick you up here tomorrow morning, convey you and the family to Wiltshire, and then take you to the nearest railway to head to Liverpool."

"Thank you, sir." Bryan was astounded by the amount Jefferies had accomplished in so short a time and stunned that he had attempted to help with his personal dilemma.

"Nonsense. Least I could do, all things considered. You're the most discreet choice for an escort. Can't send her back alone." The older attorney waved off his thanks. "Besides, I think you'll be needed to help Andrews grasp the urgency of the situation Miss Well—er, your wife, faces."

Jefferies face reddened as he stumbled over how to refer to Emilynne. "Not exactly the sharpest quill in the inkwell, Andrews."

"Andrews?"

"Yes, Richard Andrews, her intended husband." Jefferies wrinkled his nose. "Always hoped she'd refuse the match, but her brother favored it. Boyhood chums they were."

Richard Andrews. The Richard she'd addressed in her delirium aboard the *Caithream*. The Richard whose pledge to protect the children he'd taken. The Richard she would wed and call husband for all eternity.

Bryan's heart hammered against his chest. The woman he had just kissed into glorious submission was promised to another man. He felt more than a fool.

I don't believe I properly thanked you for finding Abby today, she'd said. Cool as ice chips, like the upper-class English-woman she was borne to be. Then begged his kiss and flared into a firebrand who seared her way past his defenses.

Regret and anger warred inside him, ripping at the slender threads he held on his control. For one tiny moment he had thrown aside all that vaunted control he had worked so hard to attain. And she had been merely expressing her gratitude.

Emilynne chose that moment to join them. "What is all this?"

She surveyed the small mountain of boxes from just inside the door, looking bewildered—and dazzling. He wanted to shake her. Would he never be done with her lies and omissions? She'd had a husband-to-be lurking in the background all this time.

Kiss me, she'd said.

And he had.

"I know it is outside the bounds of propriety, dear child, for you to emerge from your mourning so soon." Jefferies advanced and took her elbow. "But I believe it will make your travel to Wiltshire less remarkable if you simply appear like another family rather than a gaggle of crows."

He escorted her to the boxes as Bryan stepped aside. "I contacted your dressmaker and requested she send me whatever she could spare to outfit you for several days until you reach home. I told her your luggage had been dampened during your crossing."

"Home?" Radiant warmth suffused Emilynne's face. "We're going home?"

Bryan's gut tightened. She was thrilled to be returning to welcoming arms of this Andrews. Mere moments before she seemed thrilled to be in his own arms. As soon as he could manage, he'd back out of Jefferies's scheme for his role as escort to this reunion. Surely he'd already done more than duty and honor should bind him to, Blessing or no.

"Not directly home. But almost as good," Jefferies chuckled. "I'm sending you to Andrews at Hampton House."

Her gaze flew to seek Bryan's briefly as this news put a damper on her obvious joy. The deep blue of her troubled gaze pierced him despite his resolution to be done with Emilynne Wellesley and the troubles plaguing her. At least on any level other than his legal obligations might demand.

"Certainly if Mr. Whyte seeks you over here, Newbury Manor will be the first place he looks," her attorney continued. "If he believes your brother's will lost, he may not know of the provisions made for you and Andrews to split the guardianship duties for young Master Christian and Miss Abigail and not look for you there."

The haunted look returned to her eyes and the color drained from her cheeks as she sat on the settee while Jefferies concluded. "At least with Andrews you will have a modicum of safety from a confrontation with the ruffians you fear while I sort out the legal tangles."

"How will we get there?" Her voice sounded as lost as she looked, a pale specter offset by both the black of her gown and the dark settee. Jefferies's idea to have her shed the elegant mourning that contrasted so well with her porcelain skin gained in stature to Bryan. Anything to return her appeal to that of an ordinary client and reduce the tug of sympathy he felt toward her.

"I've arranged for a private coach to convey you to Wiltshire beginning tomorrow. Reilly here will ride along as escort—"

"Bryan has urgent business elsewhere."

Emilynne's protest did not surprise Bryan. Damned awkward to arrive home to your betrothed with the man you'd shared a bedchamber with, no matter that she'd been ill on the voyage to England or that they were saddled with two impish chaperones.

"We've settled that already, my dear," Jefferies countered.

"Actually—" Bryan began.

"Surely there is someone else reliable enough to play escort for our journey? What about Willie?" Emilynne spoke up as if he were not even in the room. She sounded as eager to be rid of him as he was not to have to spend two or three days cooped up in a carriage with her.

"Willie is . . . well . . . Willie needs to remain here in Bristol for the time being." Jefferies looked startled by her suggestion. "I have already set my two most trusted men to tracing Robert's will. One here, and the other has already departed for Newbury Manor to see if it might be there. I'm afraid it can't be helped. Reilly is the only other man I trust at the moment."

Legally perhaps, but Jefferies was foolish to entrust Emilynne's well-being to him. Especially at a time when Bryan was torn between wanting to either strangle her or seduce her.

Emilynne's gaze slid back to meet his. Questions sparked in her blue depths. Questions and something else. Regret?

"Besides, having begun this enterprise as you have," Jefferies proceeded, "I think it the wisest course for you to continue traveling as Mr. and Mrs. Reilly and family. Far less remarkable than a single woman alone with two children."

"Bryan? Surely you cannot continue to delay your trip to Liverpool? So many people are counting on your success. I could not bear to impose upon your time any further."

Being addressed directly after all these minutes startled Bryan almost as much as her concern for his business.

"As Mr. Jefferies pointed out, chances of my shaking Harland loose from Wolfe in Belfast are slim at best. He assures me a few days will not affect the outcome." He heard himself answer with an additional pang of surprise.

She looked ready to argue so he continued. "You told me that your brother found Mr. Jefferies's business sense reliable."

Emilynne nodded. "True, but surely you do not wish to saddle yourself with us for any longer."

"On the contrary," he found himself saying, "I'd like

nothing better than to deliver you into the safety of your future husband's embrace.''

His barb struck an immediate chord in her as her cheeks pinkened in response and her gaze dropped to her lap. ''Richard is not—''

She stopped herself and raised her chin to look at him squarely. ''My marriage to my brother's lifelong friend will provide Abby and Christian with the stable home they need. It was Robert's wish as well.''

''Not to mention solidifying her guardianship as specified in the will once it is located,'' Jefferies interjected. ''It will be her best defense should matters come to a head in Ireland before they are settled here.''

Put that way, her betrothal seemed more sacrifice than deception. Or was it wishful thinking on his part that he perceived the struggle she must be enduring to make her way in the world, alone with two children. Marriage would not only appeal as another shoulder to aid her, but also as the logical course to follow in fighting Thaddeus Whyte.

''That's it, then,'' he said. ''We head for Wiltshire on the morrow, wife.''

Vowing to have as little physical contact with her as possible in order to maintain his sanity, he would only have to endure a few days of seductive torment before he could turn her over to the man who would claim her kisses for eternity.

Dublin, Ireland

''Thaddeus Whyte! Good to see you, old man. Has it really been since last year at Goff's?''

Thaddeus returned the corpulent man's handshake with

a hearty slap on the shoulder. "How are those two matched grays you outbid me for, Marshall, you dog."

They both laughed, their voices booming down the street in front of their club. It was early, but Thaddeus enjoyed getting a jump on his day, a jump on his competitors.

"They are turning out to be one of the finest pairs I ever owned. But I knew that when I saw your interest in them. You've a keen eye for horseflesh, Whyte. What brings you to town at this time of year?"

"Family business." Thaddeus sighed and plucked an imagined dust mote from the sleeve of his immaculate jacket. "Only a matter of the utmost urgency could pry me out of Blue Hills Stud at this point in the season."

"Not more bother with Gail and that rum touch of a husband of hers?" Marshall's eyes lit up as Thaddeus knew they would. The portly man loved a good tidbit of gossip, and Thaddeus was always careful to leave him with a juicy enough bone to chew over. He feigned hesitation.

"I know you don't like to discuss the havey-cavey details of her dreadful misalliance with that fellow. Wellesley is his name? But surely you can share your burdens with an old friend."

Exactly the right note, let Marshall believe he'd wheedled the information, and it would be all over the city by noon-time.

Thaddeus sighed again. "To be honest, I'm not at my best these days. I should have told you straight off that Gail is dead along with her unfortunate husband."

He paused to enjoy the gasp of surprise and condolences his news evoked. His efforts to keep the matter of the Wellesleys' deaths quiet until the time proved ripe had succeeded if Marshall had not gotten wind of the tale. "Seems the rogue fancied himself a veritable whip. Upset their carriage and killed her and himself on the estate's back hills. I had finally enticed her back to Blue Hills in the hope of getting her to see reason and secure a stable home for her two little tykes.''

"Orphaned?" Marshall's thirst for mawkish details clearly showed.

"Yes." Thaddeus favored him with a frown. "I'd hoped to do a better job by them than I did with Gail, but even that solace has been snatched from me."

"You cannot mean that the children have passed on as well!"

Marshall was eating right out of his hand. Thaddeus suppressed a smile at the ease with which he could lead this old hack to the slaughterhouse.

"Worse. Wellesley's trollop of a sister has kidnapped the children right off the farm and run away with her sea captain lover, it would seem."

He shuddered, a nice touch from the sympathy fairly dripping off Marshall. "I only hope I can locate the children before anything drastic happens to them. Gail sent me many a letter detailing that wanton chit's interest in pagan worship."

Marshall's startled gasp put paid to this business. *Let that get back to Marshall's brother-in-law, Dublin's chief magistrate.*

Chapter Nine

Hampton House
Wiltshire, England

The image of Newbury Manor scraped against Emilynne's heart as the carriage approached Hampton House. As familiar as her own home, which lay just two miles farther down the road, the crisp lines and symmetry of Richard's neoclassical house suited its owner just as the warmer brick and ivy exterior of her own home with its hodgepodge of additions fit her family. Or, rather, the family she once had.

Late afternoon shadows playing on the granite walls reminded her of so many visits through the years, for tea and picnics and other social events shared between the neighbors. If only Robert and Gail were awaiting her return with the children even now.

With a sigh she pushed those thoughts aside. Giving in

to such thinking only ripped her grief open anew and did nothing to help the children. She had to concentrate on exactly what she planned to say to Richard.

Finally faced with the reality of speaking with her brother's lifelong friend, she was caught between the safety her decision offered and the very real knot in her stomach that warned she was not doing the right thing for herself.

She stole a quick glance at Bryan's resolute chin, suffering an odd swirl in her stomach that seemed to happen only when she looked at him. He carried an air of self-possession she envied, refraining from even mentioning his knowledge of her future plans the whole of this trip together. He had been far from self-possessed when they kissed in Mrs. Babbage's upper guest room. The swirl in her stomach tightened anew, somewhere between pleasure and pain.

She smoothed the sleeve on her pointed basque traveling dress and tried to picture her arrival without Bryan. This journey by carriage had passed far more quickly and pleasantly than she expected as they exchanged childhood stories and examined the differences and similarities between the Celtic legends of both their countries.

Bryan was the first man who managed to look interested when she waxed on about Stonehenge, the Heel Stone, and whether the monolithic circle had been some sort of calendar or a place of ritual sacrifice. He'd even tested her knowledge with his questions and keen observations, none of which helped assuage the sense of loss their arrival and his imminent departure evoked.

Now that they had arrived, he would be leaving to complete his business in Liverpool. As he should—he'd been delayed by her long enough. She would, however, miss him far more than she should. Far more than any woman about to marry another man should. Would she ever see him again? Her stomach spun again, but the feeling was far different this time, like disappearing into the dark fathoms of a bottomless pit.

The carriage rumbled to stop and her heartbeat stumbled to the same abrupt halt as her blood chilled. A gust of wind whooshed by the carriage whispering an insistent rhythm, like a distant drone of warning.

"We're here." Bryan's words barely registered before he'd opened the carriage door and alighted. He turned back to help Abby and Christian down before offering his hand to her.

Emilynne slipped hers into his warm grasp. Despite the gloves she wore, his fingers seemed to burn a searing blaze of regret straight through her. She must stop thinking like this. She stood and he slid his hands to her waist for support. The children scrabbled up the steps toward the front door.

"Thank you." As he helped her down, she slid against him. Her breath caught in her throat. Every contact between them seemed to simmer in her blood. Heat washed into her cheeks.

He held her a tiny moment longer than was necessary, and his gaze, dark and unfathomable, caressed her lips. Her heartbeat quickened, erratic and expectant. Her lips trembled with the remembered demands of his mouth on hers, his tongue meeting hers.

"Aunt Emilynne, should we knock?" Abby's voice shattered the intimate haze between them. Emilynne was all too aware of the touch of his fingers against her waist. Perhaps it was a good thing that he would soon be gone from her life. A rebellious tugging on her heart belied that thought.

"Aye." Bryan released her and answered Abby with a wink. "Knock, Abby. It is why we've come all this way, after all."

Before Abby could raise the heavy brass knocker, the wide door sprang open. Richard prided himself on his staff's efficiency, and their arrival had no doubt been noted from the moment they first came into view from Hampton House's stately windows. Abby did not hesitate to speak up. "I am Abigail Wellesley. Is my uncle Richard in?"

Emilynne had to smile as Abby's girlish voice raised the eyebrow of Richard's servant.

"Indeed?" Stephens drew himself up, standing even straighter in his starched collar and pressed day coat. The butler's disapproval made Emilynne all the more aware of their dusty appearance and their arrival outside the normal hours for social calls.

Emilynne stepped forward. "Quite so, Stephens. Please show us into the sitting room and tell Mr. Andrews we have arrived."

Stephens paused for a moment longer, clearly caught between the desire to close the door and have nothing to do with the rumpled children trying to peer behind him into the hallway and his duty to see to his employer's guests.

Bryan met the cold curiosity of the butler's stare with a raised eyebrow of his own.

Stephens nodded to Emilynne. "Of course, Miss Welles-ley, this way please."

The man turned without further word, his heels clicking smartly across the parquet floor of the foyer as he led them toward the front room. He had never been anywhere near approaching warm or solicitous, so his manner did not surprise her. She supposed she should be flattered he remembered her name. It had been a long time since she had called on Richard, regardless of the fact that he was Newbury Manor's closest neighbor and her brother's boyhood friend. Richard's proposal, carefully couched to Robert almost two years earlier, had put a damper on her own desire to spend time with him until the question was settled.

Stephens opened the door. "In here if you will, Miss. I shall send word of your arrival to Mr. Andrews."

"Thank you, Stephens. And if you could bring us some tea and some lemonade for the children, we'd appreciate it. We've had a long journey."

Stephens sniffed but nodded his ascent to this demand. He took her bonnet and Bryan's bowler without comment. Why Richard kept this butler on staff in the country was beyond her. The man was definitely trained for duties among society's elite. The ice in the bottom of her stomach grew as she thought about living here and facing the man on a daily basis.

Emilynne shepherded the children into a room of warm cream and soft peach tones. The influence of Richard's mother still held here. Emilynne had always liked this room. For the first time in too many months she felt like she had come home. She sighed over the lump rising in her throat and slid into one of the wing chairs by the fireplace. She stripped off her gloves and ran her fingers over the smooth silk of the chair's arms, a habit left from childhood visits to this room when her parents and Richard's had been friends.

Christian and Abby peered out the bow windows that looked over the grounds, giggling with delight as they watched the sheep gamboling on the lawn as they headed in from their daytime pasture. As Robert and Richard no doubt had done during their early years as playmates.

Bryan paced the room's confines, stopping to handle

a porcelain fawn. Next he perused the signature on the painting of Richard's father with his favorite hunter. Even Stephens's arrival with the refreshments she had requested did not seem to interest Bryan. He clasped his hands behind his back and seemed intent on looking anywhere in the room but at her. A small frown crinkled between his brows. Did he realize this was possibly the last opportunity they might have to speak in private?

Whether he did or not, she had some things she wanted to say before he disappeared from her life. She pushed from the chair and joined him in the far corner, where the window heralded a view of Hampton House's front lawn.

"Bryan." She touched his sleeve.

He transferred his gaze from Richard's grounds to her face. Why did she feel so awkward beside him after all they had been through together?

"Aye?"

That one low syllable did strange things to her stomach. She'd the insane notion she would never again hear the gentle lilt of an Irish tongue without thinking of this man's green eyes and the desire sparkling deep within them like a deep green flame. She looked away and dropped her hand from his sleeve.

"I want to thank you for all you've done for us. I'm quite sure we would not have made the journey safely without you."

"No thanks are necessary, Emilynne." He traced her cheek with his fingertips, drawing her gaze back to his. "It is not every day a beautiful woman entices me off to adventure and intrigue."

Heat blazed in her cheeks. She would never forget him.

It would be impossible with the taste of his kiss so indelibly imprinted in her memory.

"I am sorry we delayed your own business." She covered his hand against her cheek with her own. "If there is any way I can repay . . ."

The door opened behind her. "Em, what a pleasant surprise."

"Richard." She stepped away from Bryan, feeling caught and guilty as she faced the man she intended to marry. Not an auspicious beginning. She tried to greet Richard's smile with one of her own.

Richard's eyebrows hitched up a bit as his gaze measured her flushed face and then traveled to Bryan, but his smile didn't waver as he continued toward her. "I repeat, a pleasant surprise."

He took her hands and brushed a cool, dry kiss against her hot cheek. Something inside her shuddered in dismay, but she squeezed his hands, reminding herself that the children were more important than her own wayward responses.

"Sir." Richard nodded toward Bryan.

"Forgive me." Renewed heat steamed into her cheeks. "This is Bryan Reilly, a solicitor with O'Brien and Mallory in Limerick. Bryan, this is my brother's dear friend, Richard Andrews."

Richard's eyebrows shot up again as she made the introductions, but he offered Bryan his hand just the same.

"Uncle Richard!" Abby and Christian hurried toward him.

"Hello, ducks." Richard patted them. "Go into the kitchen. Cook's made raspberry tarts for after dinner. I'm sure there are plenty to share with special guests such as yourselves."

"Yummy," Christian pronounced.

Abby looked to Emilynne for permission.

"Go ahead, darling." It would be better to give her explanations to Richard without the children having to listen. "But make sure Christian doesn't make a mess."

"I will, Aunt Emilynne." Abby took her brother's hand. "Come along, Christian."

The adults watched the children leave hand in hand. Richard turned back to face Emilynne. Keen interest added a spark to his gray eyes. The thin mustache over his lips twitched. There was an uncomfortable distance here, but whether it truly existed or was just her imagination, Emilynne couldn't tell.

"Are Robert and Gail already so immersed in manor business that they couldn't spare an hour for an old friend?" Robert spoke a shade too jovially to ring well in the ears. "Tell me of your adventures in Ireland and why you have called on me accompanied by one of the legal profession."

Her heart sank. "Then you did not receive my letter?"

"No, my dear." Richard shook his head. "What is it, Em? What's wrong?"

"Oh, Richard." Tears welled in her throat and she choked them back. Thaddeus's perfidy had seen to it that she would have to tell everyone herself.

"My dear." Richard slid a arm around her shoulders and drew her toward the settee.

"Please do sit down." He managed to include Bryan in the invitation.

She sank onto the cream silk cushions and faced Richard. "There is so much to tell you. Quite frankly I'm not sure where to begin."

"Em, you make this sound so serious."

"Very serious." She gripped her hands together in her lap and took a shaky breath. "Robert and Gail are dead. I have taken custody of the children, and we are here because Robert set the two of us up in his will as shared guardians."

Richard paled. The smile died from his lips. "What? Robert is dead? When did this happen? How? And what about Gail?"

"There is so much to tell you. I can scarcely bear to begin."

"But, my dear, you are not even dressed in proper mourning. Surely this cannot be true." An incredulous frown formed between his brows.

"It is true all right." Bryan's agreement held deadly intent; he nodded encouragement when Emilynne glanced his way.

In for a penny, in for a pound. She took a steadying breath.

"I believe they were murdered by Thaddeus Whyte, Gail's uncle. Afterward, he virtually held us prisoner on Gail's estate in Ireland and confiscated all my correspondence, telling no one what had occurred. I was afraid he intended to kill the children as well."

Richard shook his head. "But—"

"We have been running for over a month," Emilynne continued, unwilling to let him stop her now that she had begun. "You and I are Abby's and Christian's guardians, Richard. It is up to us to protect them. And to do whatever we can to bring Thaddeus to justice."

"But"—Richard shook his head again, agitation further knitting his brows—"how can this be? I received a letter from Robert's man of business only last week."

Emilynne glanced toward Bryan again.

"I observed firsthand some rather seedy-looking characters searching for Miss Wellesley," Bryan offered in what she had learned was his solicitor's manner.

Richard focused on Bryan, his frown increasing. "Who the bloody hell are you, sir? And what has a solicitor from Ireland got to do with any of this?"

"Richard."

"I've asked myself that question on more than one occasion." Bryan's lips twisted over the words.

"Please, Richard." Emilynne's cheeks heated again as her anger flamed at his manner. "Bryan not only provided us transportation out of Ireland at his own risk and expense, he has escorted the children and me to you. He has delayed his own urgent business to assist us. He has been a godsend. I am very grateful to him."

Her rebuke sent Richard to his feet.

"Indeed." He stalked over to the windows. "Then it seems I must be grateful as well."

Richard stared out into the evening mist for a moment before turning back toward Emilynne. "Em, you will allow this tale seems a bit fantastic, won't you?"

His words jabbed cold fingers of dismay into her stomach. She swallowed hard, struggling to put herself in his place. "Perhaps. But the story remains all too true."

"I cannot believe it." Richard raked a hand through his thin, sandy hair. "I just cannot. You are sitting there pretty as can be in your blue dress. Not at all suitable for one so recently bereaved. How could anyone as impractical as you possibly elude a pursuer for such a length of time? It is unfathomable to me."

Emilynne's temples throbbed, and she could feel her strength ebbing out through her toes.

"Belief is not what matters. What counts is the truth."

Bryan's tone held a decided edge. "I can substantiate most of what Miss Wellesley has told you. You are aware of Robert Wellesley's will, are you not?"

Richard eyed Bryan. "Yes, I know everything about Robert's will. He is . . . *was* my best friend."

"Then you understand why Miss Wellesley felt it necessary to come to you."

"Indeed." Richard turned to Emilynne. "Em, I can believe there has been some kind of accident and that Robert and Gail have died. God rest them both. Please don't misunderstand me. It is the other parts of this tale I find hard to believe. Such a story, out of the blue. Surely you can understand my shock."

"Yes. I understand. Would that it were not true, any of it." Her voice cracked on that last prayer.

"Come now, Em." Richard returned to the sofa and took her hands in his own cool clasp. "I know you think you've had a hard time of it. You look worn out. No doubt it has been a very long journey for you and the children. Would you like a glass of sherry?"

"No, thank you, Richard." She concentrated on the touch of their hands, wishing she could feel one iota of the wonderful things she felt when Bryan touched her. "I think it best if I just get the children settled."

"Certainly." He patted her hands and released them. "I'll have my horse saddled and escort you myself. I cannot let you go home alone to Newbury Manor, not at this time of night."

"She cannot go to the manor." Bryan's tone precluded argument.

"I beg your pardon." Richard's voice was flat.

Bryan pushed away from his stance by the fireplace. "Regardless of your belief, or lack thereof, Emilynne and the children are in danger. The one place Thaddeus Whyte will expect her to go is home."

Richard bristled beside her, but Bryan ignored the reaction as he continued. "Even coming here was taking a risk, but with you as co-guardian, it was imperative that they seek your assistance."

"We've come to entreat sanctuary from you, Richard." Emilynne tried to diffuse the tension rising between the two men. "May we stay?"

Richard turned away from Bryan. "Em, you know you are always welcome here. It has been my fondest wish that you would learn to call Hampton House your home. Of course you may stay."

Emilynne swallowed, grateful for the respite. Yet here was the last hurdle to be approached. "That brings me to the other reason we have come."

Two pairs of eyes turned toward her.

"According to the terms of Robert's will, we must work together to care for the children. I fear we are far from having things settled with Thaddeus, and there is the possibility we will never be able to prove him responsible for Robert's and Gail's deaths."

Richard started to look away. She placed her hand on his sleeve. "No, let me finish this, Richard, please. This doesn't sit well with me either. In that event, we will be facing a custody battle for the children. Thaddeus will claim he should be their guardian just as he was Gail's."

"That will not matter. Any dispute will be settled here."

"It may matter." Bryan interrupted Richard this time. "Thaddeus started custody proceedings before the children left his care."

Again Richard favored him with a displeased glare. "And you would know this because?"

"My firm is handling the case."

Emilynne could have groaned aloud. This telling was only getting muddier and muddier as they went along.

Richard's brows furrowed again, and he shook his head. "What *are* you doing here?" The cold glare he sent Bryan would have cracked a lesser man. Bryan returned the frigid regard measure for measure but said nothing.

"I told you that already." She caught back an impatient sigh. "Richard, the important thing is that we must work together, provide a united front. The other provision in Robert's will is that I be sole guardian to the children should I be married."

She succeeded in gaining his gaze back to her.

He frowned again and glanced quickly down at her ringless fingers. "And?"

She took a deep breath. Best to get this over with before she lost her nerve. "I believe we should marry at once."

Richard's face paled yet again. She could almost see his very correct and proper moral sense recoil in horror from her bald proposal. What young woman of good quality would do such a thing?

With the perfect sense of timing inherent in children everywhere, Abby and Christian returned from the kitchens. Despite the smear of raspberry jam across his cheek, Christian looked pale and tired. He snuggled into Emilynne's lap and rested his clean cheek against her shoulder.

Richard's blank gaze went from Emilynne to Abby to Christian and back again. Emilynne felt at a loss. This had been his idea, hadn't it? It certainly had seemed so when Robert had put it to her again a few months before. She had agreed then to announce her decision upon their return from Ireland.

"Perhaps it would be best to settle the children." Emilynne strove for calm in the face of Richard's silence. This was hardly the reception she had expected or envisioned, but at the moment she was far too weary to worry about it.

As though her words released him from a stupor, Richard stood. "Of course. I shall have Mrs. Bennett ready rooms immediately."

He strode from the room, the strained look on his face emphasizing what his haste had already said. He was horrified by the whole idea. Horrified. His reaction more profound to the idea of marrying her and acquiring a ready-made family than to the news that his best friend was gone.

Emilynne tried to push the thought away. How could she be so uncharitable? She had thrown enough at the man within the last few minutes to warrant a state of shock. She longed for Robert's comforting presence as tears burned at the backs of her eyes.

Bryan's hand touched her shoulder and she nearly jumped. "Are you all right?"

"Yes, yes, I'm fine." She blinked back the telltale moisture in her eyes, trying to ignore the way his hand warmed her clear through to her skin. She had tangled him in her problems long enough. She would straighten things out with Richard because she had to. There was no other choice.

She offered Bryan a smile. "You should be going, shouldn't you?"

"Aye, I should." Bryan held her in his dark gaze for a moment. She couldn't help wondering what he was thinking. "It is too far into the day though. I'll go but not until tomorrow."

Hope soared unbidden and her heart skipped a beat. "Tomorrow?"

"Aye, it is too late to reach the railway this night. I'll leave early in the morning."

Richard appeared in the doorway. "Of course." He had a smile pinned to his features that did not reach his eyes. "Emilynne, Mrs. Bennett and Kate will escort the children upstairs for you."

"Oh, no, I'll take them."

"I think we need to talk privately for a few moments." Richard's determined manner underlined his polite request.

"I'll take the children, Emilynne." Bryan scooped Christian from her arms. The boy slung his chubby arms across Bryan's shoulders with complete trust. "Come along, boy-o. We'll continue that tale of Cuchulain at the Avon Dia your aunt began for you last night. I'll tell you of his exploits in my country."

He offered his arm to Abby. "If you please, my lady."

"Aye-aye, Captain." Abby smiled as she took his arm. Emilynne heaped silent blessings on his dark head and Gaelic charm as he left the room.

Richard watched Bryan's departure with a cool gaze and said nothing until the door closed behind them.

"Who *is* that man?"

"I told you . . ."

"I know what you told me, but that doesn't really answer the question."

"Bryan . . . Mr. Reilly, has been of enormous assistance in helping me to return home. To reach you. Isn't that enough for now?" She was too tired to try to tell Richard all she owed Bryan.

Richard sighed and raked a hand through his pale hair. "I'm sorry, Em, this has all come as quite a shock."

He joined her on the sofa once again. "I am so sorry about Robert."

She drew in a soft breath and knotted her hands in her lap. "So am I. Thank you for letting us stay."

He nudged her chin with his fingers, bringing her gaze up to meet his. "Em, you know how I feel. How I have always felt. I just never expected the proposal to come from you instead of me." He smiled, and the old Richard, her friend, peeked out from behind the staid gray of his eyes.

The tight knot of tension in her chest eased just a bit.

"I know how you feel about such spontaneous events, Richard, but in this instance it cannot be helped."

He was quiet for a long while. "Em, I shall do whatever I can to help. And if you truly feel there is some merit to your charges about Gail's uncle, then I will have them looked into for you."

Emilynne suppressed a shudder. His words too closely mirrored the empty assurances she had received from Thaddeus while the man furthered his own plans. *But this is Richard,* she reminded herself, *not Thaddeus.*

"Em?"

She looked up at him as he placed his hands on her shoulders.

"I am glad you're here. I look forward to discussing our future." He pulled her toward him and pressed his lips to hers. Cool, dry, impersonal, his kiss stirred none of the wild desire and heated longing Bryan could rouse with just the touch of his hand. And his mustache tickled her lip.

The thought of the further intimacies she would share with Richard once they were wed served only to make her cringe inside. With an effort of will she relaxed against him and tried to return his kiss, hoping that somehow her willingness would engender the feelings she sought. Feelings she would need to warm the future she faced. He pulled her closer and increased the awkward pressure of his mouth against hers. Her heartbeat throbbed a slow death knell in her ears.

"I've missed you." He sighed as he released her.

"I missed you too," she told him truthfully.

He smiled again and kissed her forehead. "You look tired, darling. I'll see what's keeping Mrs. Bennett."

Emilynne leaned back against the sofa and stared up at the ceiling molded in soft tones of vanilla. At least this was a beginning. Now that Richard knew the truth, she had someone else to fight alongside her permanently. Someone to help her bring Thaddeus to justice and protect Robert's children.

Weariness ached in every inch of her body. She closed her eyes, trying to picture her life, her future, with Richard as her husband.

But the image that formed in her mind had dark wavy hair and intent green eyes.

"I'll send Stephens to fetch you, Mr. Reilly, when the other rooms are ready. Kate will sit with the children until they're asleep." Andrews's housekeeper had frosty blue eyes and a straightfoward manner befitting her station. All the members of this household seemed a bit too high in the instep to suit him. He could not imagine Emilynne and the children living in such a sterile place. The halls and rooms looked more like a museum than a home.

"Thank you, Mrs. Bennett." Bryan closed the door behind him. Christian and Abby snuggled together in a big four-poster, managing to look both lost and safe at the same time. He could not picture Emilynne married to the dispassionate individual who had greeted the news of his best friend's death with barely a flicker of emotion. A man who viewed the prospect of being her life mate as though it were a responsibility. An obligation.

His own obligation had surely come to an end. He'd brought her to safety. Delivered her into the very lap of her intended. He started down the steps as he tamped down uneasy doubts.

His duty to reach Harland and persuade him to finance Reilly Ship Works tolled inside him like an alarm left ringing too long. Each delay loomed like shoals behind him. He should have smooth sailing from here. So why did he feel compelled to linger?

He opened the door to the Andrews's front room. Firelight flickered over the Persian rugs and drifted over Emilynne's sleeping features as she reclined against the settee's silk cream perfection. Perfection that did not hold a candle to her own.

There's why, a sarcastic part of him argued.

Deep inside him everything tightened in response to the sight of her. He crossed the room, drawn irresistibly toward her. Tendrils of shining blond had come loose from her coiffure. Even in repose a slight frown marred her smooth brow. His fingers itched to ease away that tightness and assure his erstwhile wife all would be well.

After so much time, an eternity, it was hard to surrender to the inevitable. It was no longer his responsibility to make it so.

Knowing he would soon walk out of her life, he gave in to the impulse and soothed his fingers across her skin.

She released a sigh that ended on a tiny moan of protest. He smiled. She would not easily release her concerns even in sleep, not to him, and he suspected not to Richard Andrews. If only he could ignore the cord inside him that tightened at the sight of her, or the invisible bond forged between them.

"What am I to do with you, Emilynne?"

"Is Miss Wellesley ill?" Concern laced Andrews's voice from behind Bryan.

Bryan tightened his lips and straightened. "She is exhausted."

He turned to find relief etched on Richard's pale face.

"Thank heaven." He raised a brow at Bryan and stopped, turning his gaze to Emilynne instead. Bryan recognized that Andrews did not care for him in the least. Which was just fine, because he returned the feeling.

"Em." Richard sat on the sofa next to her and patted her hand. "Wake up, Em, darling."

The endearment grated on Bryan almost as much as the man's insufferable proprietary manner.

Emilynne blinked at both of them before straightening with a touch of pink in her cheeks. "I'm sorry."

"Your room is ready, Em." Richard smiled at her. "And yours as well, Reilly. Follow us."

"Thank you."

Looking dazed, Emilynne stood and Andrews escorted her toward the door. Bryan followed, aware of each time the other man touched her and struggling to ignore the burst of angry jealousy that burned hotter with each intimate contact.

As they reached the top of the stairs, Andrews turned toward him. "Your room is to the right, Reilly. Third door on the left."

"You're over here, Em." He guided her in the opposite

direction. "Across from the children. Mrs. Bennett will send up a tray for you."

"Thank you, Richard." Emilynne stopped and turned back as Andrews led her toward the opposite wing.

"Good night, Bryan." Light flickered over her features from the gas lantern on the wall. Her eyes sparkled, luminous and dark.

A sudden rush of loss tightened Bryan's throat as he looked at her. He'd grown used to having her in the same room with him at night. He would miss the soft sounds of her breathing and the scent of her perfume. She turned away and was swallowed into a patch of darkness as she moved down the hallway with Richard Andrews. The lucky man who would truly claim her as wife.

He entered the room assigned him and closed the door, putting the solid oak panel between them like a shield against the yearnings she evoked in him.

"Good night, Emilynne, sleep well."

Chapter Ten

A knock on the door a few moments later forced Bryan to open the barrier once again.

"I'm afraid the evening has been too much of an adjustment for me." Richard Andrews's tone, hollow and grating despite his attempts at civility, crawled along Bryan's spine. "Stephens is even now drawing me a bath so I may relax and recover from all the agitation. Then I shall retire."

Bryan nodded with a demeanor he hoped would pass as understanding. At least they would not be forced to make idle small talk during a chilly meal.

"Mrs. Bennett will supply you with a late supper tray if you wish, or you may ask Stephens for whatever you require. Feel free to make use of anything in my home this evening. Avail yourself of whatever you like, Reilly."

Andrews barely disguised loathing practically oozed from him even in the dimness of the empty hall. "I'm afraid I shan't be up to see you off in the morning. And

I sincerely doubt Miss Wellesley will be up to an early start either."

"I believe I'll be able to manage on my own," Bryan returned with equally empty courtesy. "You are a most gracious host."

"Good night, old man." Richard nodded and left Bryan outside his door, his host's haste toward the other wing displaying a complete lack of the exhaustion he espoused.

Bryan's lips twisted as he descended the steps toward the lower floor, relieved to be away from Emilynne's intended husband. He felt in need of some reading material to distract him from the solitary emptiness of his chamber while the family he had begun to think of as his own slept in the other wing.

Chagrin chafed him that such an insipid fellow as Andrews would soon claim Emilynne for his own. He could not picture them together, at least happily. And yet his mind did nothing but picture them together in lurid detail, making him wish he already possessed time and distance away from this place.

Why had he lingered?

Because he simply had been unable to leave. Not when the woman who struck such chords deep within his own soul seemed nothing but a problem to be resolved by the man she planned to spend the rest of her life with. Not when Thaddeus and his thugs might lurk somewhere in the darkness, ready to wreak havoc upon her and the two children he'd come to care about.

He was bound to be in error no matter what he did. Perhaps Mother was wrong to have shared her tip about Harland's investment with him. The information should probably have been passed on to Quin for action.

Even now he should be in Liverpool before Harland's

deal with Wolfe in Belfast was sealed. He'd put his family mission in drydocks for far too long, turning a deaf ear to his responsibilities in order to protect Emilynne and the children. Emilynne was now safe. The children's father had apparently seen something in Richard Andrews that he did not. But he could not seem to release himself from the bonds he'd knotted together on their behalf.

He paused at the windows framed in dark brocade and turned his gaze out into the darkness surrounding the house Emilynne would soon call home. Moonlight spilled onto the carefully manicured lawns. Black shadows from trim hedges etched across the smooth expanse just as doubts clawed his soul.

"Enough." He retraced his steps and headed for the billards room and the promise of more potent distraction. He'd spied a whiskey decanter with a newspaper folded on the table beside it earlier. He suspected the newspaper was there only for show. Andrews did not appear to be the sort who cared overmuch for the world outside his pristine walls.

Whiskey would deaden the uncertainties plaguing him, at least enough to get him through the night. Tomorrow he would be gone and Emilynne Wellesley and her problems would be naught but a tantalizing memory.

Moonlight flowed across the polished floor from tall windows leading to the garden. He found the whiskey decanter and poured himself a healthy draft.

"My felicitations, Mrs. Reilly." He raised the tumbler and downed the contents in a single fiery swallow. He poured another and prowled the room, blessing the liquor's welcome heat as the tension inside him began to uncoil.

He opened one of the windowed doors, letting the cool

night air waft over him as he sipped his second whiskey with a little more respect for fine liquor.

A breeze ruffled the edges of the newspaper on the table. He plucked it up and leaned his hip against the hearth, letting the whiskey do its slow, comfortable work on him as he perused the pages by the light of the lamp glowing on the mantel. Several articles drew his gaze, and he read in silence for a few moments, content to have something on his mind beyond Emilynne.

Just as he started to relax a bit, a small article on page three leapt up at him like hot brands, searing his breath. Burning into him with a vengeance! *Financier Harland to Invest in Belfast Shipyard*

He read the article as numbness seeped through his mind and froze his heart. Harland's decision was already made. "Hell."

He crumpled the damning paper in his fist and downed the rest of the whiskey in his glass, the liquor's burn a pale thing beside the recriminations searing his mind.

He failed.

Failed again.

And for what? A beautiful woman who'd snagged his heart and made him imagine he'd heard the Reilly Blessing. Blessing indeed. He'd found the curse and would now pull the rest of the Reillys down with him as well.

The weight of his family's expectations and needs fell against his shoulders like one of Emilynne's ancient stones, reducing him to the boy he'd been. At fault yet again for following his impulsive nature rather than aligning himself with logic and rational decision-making.

"Damnation."

His mother had been very wrong to trust him with this errand. Very, very wrong.

He headed back toward the whiskey decanter with the paper roiling in his palm. Good thing the decanter was full when he entered the room. He was quite certain it would be quite the opposite when he climbed back up the stairs.

He grabbed up the whiskey and headed out into the mockingly precise peace of Andrews's gardens, a far cry from the wild, windswept hills of Beannacht Island and the home he had exiled himself from due to rash behavior.

After another long swallow he looked back at the newspaper, reading the headline again and imprinting the condemnatory phrase on his soul. A small sidebar offered further culpable testimony that Harland had made his decision based on an apparent lack of interest on the part of any shipyard located on Ireland's western coast.

"Lack of interest."

He tossed back more whiskey in an empty salute. "Hardly that, Mr. Harland. I allowed the call of a blue-eyed siren to throw my better judgment out the nearest window."

He sighed and crumpled the paper before tossing it from him in loathing. He subsided onto a carved marble bench and pressed the crystal whiskey tumbler to his forehead as he sprawled against the cool back.

Regret stung like acid. How familiar this feeling was! How many times had he promised himself he would never feel this way again? How many years had he struggled to tame the beast of his impulsive actions?

Only to be faced with terrible consequences.

Again.

"Elegant proof of the Reilly curse." He spat out the words with a groan and drained the remainder of the whiskey in his glass.

So much for Andrews and his untrammeled cleanliness.

The playful sound of water from the fountain at the heart of the garden scoffed at his dark mood. Cool night breezes mocked him with the soft scents of freesia and lemon.

Emilynne.

"Bryan, I saw you from the windows when I went to check the children. Are you all right?"

He froze with his hands pressed against his eyes. Her voice, soft and soothing, so filled with concern, ripped him open inside. He didn't want her pity. Would not accept her solace.

He clenched his fists at his side.

"Go away, Emilynne." His words came harsh and low. "Go back to bed."

The rustle of her gown against the flagstone told him she ignored his directive. And made him think how soft her skin would be beneath that gown.

"What is it?"

"My concerns are my own," he told her, not bothering to hide his irritation. He needed her to leave. Now while he could still control the wild impulses raging inside him.

She was silent for a moment while he wished her elsewhere.

"You've been drinking." Her observation came without judgment, but anger roiled through him anyway.

"Aye."

"That's not like you."

He laughed without humor. "How little you know me."

"I know enough to discern there is something terribly wrong with the man who came to my aid and saved the lives of my niece and nephew." Her hand touched his shoulder. "Let me help."

Fire burned beneath her touch. Desire and raging passion. He jumped to his feet and turned to face her, then wished he had not.

She stood clad in some voluminous creation of finely laced silk as dark and blue as her eyes. It covered her white linen nightgown to her hips. Her hair was loose, pale and soft against her shoulders. Seductive. Her feet were bare against the thick grass. Intimacy personified.

He swallowed as a hot stab of desire pierced him in spite of the knowledge that she now belonged to another man. And that his very attraction to her was responsible for the debacle he now found himself in.

"Bryan, what can I do to help?" she prodded.

He groaned. "Go away, Emilynne."

"Why?"

Why did she look so damned beautiful? Smell so damned good? Why did everything inside him scream to possess her? To make her his and to hell with the outcome?

"I'm not fit company." And that was putting it mildly.

She smiled and moved closer. "You've seen me at my worst."

The need to retreat welled within him. Anger that even then he couldn't dismiss her from his thoughts augmented the acidic regrets burning inside him. He stood his ground. If she wanted to press her luck, let her.

She searched his features in the moonlight. "What has happened?"

I've failed my family. "Nothing to concern you."

Another step and the crackle of crumpled newspaper sounded beneath her bare feet. He turned away as she bent to retrieve the paper he'd discarded.

He could almost feel her scanning the paper as easily as she read him. Was he always this transparent? Or was it just in her company? Only this woman, who saw through all his defenses and undermined the barriers he'd so carefully erected.

"Oh, Bryan." Her voice broke over his name.

He steeled himself against the sympathy in her tone. "It doesn't matter. I'm certain my family expected me to fail."

"Of course it matters. You missed this chance because of us, because of me. All those things you wanted for your family, the people on your wonderful island." She moved closer, a bare whisper of sound that twisted his insides in a vise.

"Aye." He didn't try to deny it. "I knew there would be a price. There always is."

She was quiet for a moment. "A price?"

"Aye." He could feel her close behind him. His mind provided hot images of ravishing her soft curves, finding surcease for the pain and regret in the silken warmth of the embrace he knew her capable of giving. Seeking to submerge his failure, just as he'd sought to drown his worries in whiskey.

He tamped the urge back and cursed his empty glass.

"What do you mean?"

He said nothing even as she touched his arm. His lips tightened as anger and desire warred within him, a beast straining a whiskey-thinned leash. "Go away," he urged through clenched teeth.

"What price?" Determination laced her soft tones. "Bryan, look at me."

He turned. Teardrops sparkled against her cheeks. She was too close, too soft, and he was in no shape to resist her. The empty whiskey glass fell to the grass forgotten as he grabbed her shoulders and hauled her up against him.

She gasped, her eyes wide and fathomless. Full of questions he didn't want to answer.

"The price of folly." He growled the words at her, not bothering to soften the raw need in his tone. "Consequences for actions not thought out in advance. The price for following your heart instead of your head."

Anger struggled for dominance against a deeper urgency. His failure rang in his mind and heart, plunging him into darkness. The feel of her in his arms offered the only ray of light even as it mocked him for feeling the way he did. He wanted to make love to her. Right there. Right then. The thought was like lighting a match to dry kindling. Everything in him flamed.

He searched her face as the primitive beast raged within him. Their gazes locked for a moment, moonstruck blue with storm-tossed green.

"Muirneach." The endearment tore from him like a curse as he tightened his arm about her waist. "Why did you not leave when I told you to? Why did you stay to twist my honor as easily as rigging within a gale?"

"I don't understand."

"It does not matter."

With a groan he captured her lips with his own, slipping the leash. A soft sigh parted her lips beneath his, and he tasted her, thrusting his tongue inside her mouth to test the depths of her sweetness. Wild desire tightened within him, heavy, sweet, unbearable.

She twined her arms around his rigid neck and pressed herself closer, welcoming him. Her tears dampened his skin and seeped into his blood—rain on parched earth. His heart began a determined thud that echoed in his ears.

She felt so good against him. So damned right. Heaven and hell within the confines of his embrace. Impulse and consequence. Blessing and curse.

She released a little moan in the back of her throat. But it was not protest. That certainty burned through him, making short work of any restraint he still held claim to.

He swept the length of her back with his hands, pressing her fully against him, not bothering to hide the fierce weight of the desire she stoked in him. He molded her hips through the silken mantelet, urging her closer still. Her softness cradled him. Desire pounded sweet and heavy in his blood.

Let her feel what she did to him with her soft words and kind heart.

He anchored her hips with one arm, allowing the other hand freedom to roam her softness, testing, teasing, stroking in time with the hot blood pounding through him. He needed her, needed her soft compliance. Each little moan she released echoed through him.

He edged the lace covering aside to test her tempting curves through her night shift. Her breast swelled against his palm. She shuddered. He released her lips and pressed his mouth to her throat, nibbling and licking, tasting the softness of her skin.

Her mantelet was too much between them, too much between what he wanted and what he would never have. He pulled at the silken cord tying it below her neck and the garment fell open, giving him free rein to the soft warmth within.

Her sheer linen gown revealed the ripe curves of her hips and waist, the tips of her breasts tightened to fine points. Logic told him he should cover her and send her back to the house. What use was logic on a night such as this? At a moment such as this?

"My God, you are so beautiful, *muirneach.*" He pulled her hard against him, the gown but a whisper-thin veil across her body as his hands slipped the blue mantelet from her shoulders. She shimmered in the moonlight, an angel in gossamer linen and sparkling white-gold hair.

He cupped the fullness of first one breast and then the other, swallowing her gasp of surprised pleasure in a long, hot kiss as he caressed her, thumbing her nipples into even tighter nubs.

She was an educated woman, but her body was untried and innocent. She shivered beneath his hands and clutched his shoulders but did not pull away.

When mere touch was no longer enough, he anchored one arm about her waist and released her kiss-ravaged lips to taste a hot pathway over her cheek, her throat, and into the tempting lace-edged V of her gown. Her skin, soft and fresh beneath his lips, tasted far too good. Her breath skimmed over his ear, teasing and tantalizing him as did the locks of her hair that caressed his face. He blew hot air against the tight peak of one breast, and she shuddered.

With a husky laugh he pressed his open mouth against her breast through the thin garment and wet the fabric with his tongue. She shuddered again and clung to his shoulders as though her limbs could no longer support her. He teased and licked and nipped her, enjoying each smothered gasp, each tiny moan his attentions drew from her.

Dimly, honor and propriety screeched at the liberties he was taking, but they seemed pale echoes beside the passion clamoring inside him. He couldn't stop himself. She was in his blood like the whiskey.

He lifted her against him and pulled her down with him onto the bench he'd vacated just a short time before, inhaling a harsh breath as she fit over his lap. Her thighs parted and slid alongside his as her hands kept their grip on his shoulders. She exhaled, her eyes luminous and dark as she gazed at him, her lips parted.

"Oh, Bryan." Her words, a whispered plea. For release? For further surrender? The desire written on her features caught his breath. Everything in him tensed.

"Tonight you're mine, *muirneach.*" He meant every word.

"Yes."

Her answer sighed through him, more felt than heard, though her eyes told him everything he could ever need to know. More than a man could ask for in one lifetime.

He covered her mouth with his and made love to her with his lips and tongue, slowly, thoroughly. Mating on a level somewhere beyond mere passion as he slipped his hands between the two of them and touched her intimately, stroking her until she shivered in his arms.

She whimpered in the back of her throat and clung to him as he continued, swallowing each soft sound as she trembled near the brink. Teasing her further and driving himself mad with the exquisite hot silken feel of her. She writhed atop him and a long series of shudders racked her slender body.

"Bryan."

"Aye, darlin'." He rasped against her neck as she trembled against his shoulder. "But that is not the half of it."

He would have her now and damn the consequences. He lifted her in his arms and bore her into the darkened confines of the house, finding his way more by instinct than by sight.

He carried her easily. She fit against him as though she had been made just for his arms, just for his caress. He took the stairs two at a time and paused at the top.

His room? Hers?

Did it matter?

Feel free to use anything in my home, old man. Sanity knifed passion's blaze with a jagged blade of ice as Andrews's words echoed in his mind.

Her future husband.

Somehow he doubted Richard Andrews's offer extended to the less than tender use of his betrothed's body. Bryan gritted his teeth in the darkened hallway. Wasn't foundering his family's future enough for one night? Should he sink hers as well? Fail her?

Passion would not help Emilynne come the morrow when he had gone and her maidenhead had become a thing cheaply bartered. For what? To salve his pride? To make him feel better about himself and the choices he had made? The price she would pay on her wedding night would not be worth one night's surcease for one such as he.

He could not be the one responsible for further endangering the life she had chosen for herself.

He held her closer still and turned toward her room, ignoring the painful tightness that demanded he take all that she offered and more. That he make love to her until neither one of them could move.

Contemplating her bedroom door in silence, he let her feet slide to the floor. She tilted her face to his, dazed by the passion he'd evoked in her

"I want you, Emilynne, very badly." He offered her the truth in the darkness as he tipped her face up to his.

He kissed her one last time, slowly, hot, and thorough, unable to resist the tempting mixture she presented of untouched innocence and newly awakened sensuality.

He regretted the absence of her mantelet. "You are too

much for any sane man to resist." He took a shaky breath.
"For what I've done tonight I should be horsewhipped."

Her cheeks glowed red in the splash of moonlight, a
perfect match for her kiss-bruised lips and tousled hair.
"Bryan—"

He pressed his fingers over her mouth, uncertain if she
meant to argue or agree but knowing his tenuous hold on
his control could not stand the strain.

"You were not the only participant," she offered against
his thumb.

Her tart tone startled a chuckle from him and tightened
an invisible cord around his heart.

He brushed his lips against her brow, not trusting himself
to taste her mouth again. "Sleep well, *muirneach.*"

Everything within Emilynne screamed in protest as he
turned and disappeared into the darkened depths of
Hampton House. With grim determination the urge to
call him back stayed locked behind her lips, though she
wanted to do just that very much.

She swallowed over the tight lump in her throat. She
had known the nights they'd spent together as a family
had bonded them in some unspoken connection. The
untapped strength of that union shook her to the depths
of her soul.

Every part of her body ached for him, as if his touch
had awakened portions of her she hadn't known existed.
So this is passion. The thought seared her already flushed
cheeks as she closed her bedroom door behind her. The
intimacies of the garden and the liberties she allowed
him—no, encouraged him—to take, echoed within her.

The thought of doing with Richard any of the things
that had passed between them, allowing any other man

such intimate contact with her body, made her quake and provided a sudden chill to her heated blood.

She could imagine no lover save Bryan.

She groaned, paced to the windows overlooking the moonlit gardens below, and froze as she realized the view from her window offered full sight of the area she and Bryan had just occupied. Each touch, each forbidden caress, echoed through her thoughts. Had anyone seen them together? Had Richard?

Her cheeks burned all the hotter.

No, surely if he had seen them he would have presented himself immediately. Richard was nothing if not correct. A trait Robert had always admired about his friend—his innate sense for the proper response to any given situation.

Imagining his angry response to witnessing her betrayal by encouraging Bryan's passionate lovemaking made her stomach churn in slow, icy circles.

She pressed cold fingers to her cheeks as recriminations tore through her mind—Robert's voice, Richard's—raised in furious accusation. She clutched the quilted bedcovers about her body as she sank onto the bed, feeling every bit the wanton her thoughts proclaimed her to be, yet unwilling to block out the demands of Bryan's hands against her flesh.

She shuddered beneath the weight of her own condemnation. Her actions and ungoverned responses added further support for Robert's decision to select someone to help her guardian his children. Someone he could depend on more than he could his sister.

"I am marrying Richard." The words rasped out of her on a shaky breath as pain locked in her throat. "I owe him my loyalty, my honor, and respect."

But it feels so wrong.

"Thank heaven Bryan leaves tomorrow." Her words echoed through the depths of the bedchamber, lifeless and hollow, as empty as the marriage she now contemplated. But that aspect of her future didn't matter. The only things that did were Christian's and Abby's safety and bringing Thaddeus Whyte to justice.

She slid farther down between the crisp sheets of the big four-poster, cool and stiff as Richard's kiss, and tried to focus on positive thoughts of their future together. She bit her lip to still a telltale trembling as hot tears began to drip onto her pillow.

Her love for Bryan Reilly was something she would overcome in time. The wonderfully passionate sensations he'd wrought from her that night had come from within her. They echoed still within her and held their genesis in the time and tribulations she had shared with this man. Surely when she transferred her affections to her husband, her physical desires would shift as well.

She tried to quell the certainty that Richard would never be able to touch her heart, her mind, and her soul with the intensity Bryan had just ignited.

Long into the night she prayed she was wrong.

Chapter Eleven

"Miss Wellesley." Mrs. Bennett bustled into the bedroom with the barest of knocks as Emilynne twitched the neckline of her lavender sprigged pique day dress into place. "You'd best come right away."

Alarm tingled down Emilynne's spine, displacing the drowning pool of sadness as she turned her back toward the mirror. It was long past time for her to make her way downstairs. Putting off the inevitable would not negate Bryan's impending departure.

"What is it?"

"The little one, ma'am." Richard's housekeeper disappeared back the way she had come with Emilynne hustling behind her. "I don't like it. And Mr. Andrews will be most upset."

Mention of Richard calmed some of Emilynne's fears. If it was only her employer's upset worrying the woman, then Christian was probably fine. She slowed her pace a bit.

"What has he done to upset Richard?" Broken some treasure no doubt or disarranged the bric-a-brac as he explored a tantalizing display.

"Oh, no, miss." the housekeeper contradicted as she waved her hand to encourage more urgency. "The lad's done nothing. But you must know Mr. Andrews abhors any kind of illness. Will not tolerate it the household. I just packed off the downstairs maid after she started her morning duties with a fit of sneezing."

Emilynne swayed against the wall but caught herself. *Mr. Andrews abhors illness.* She hurried on toward the children's bedroom door. *Christian was ill?*

The thoughts collided to knock the breath from her lungs. She felt light-headed as a sudden wave of dismay knifed her.

The room was slightly darkened, the curtains drawn against the bright morning light. Huddled in the big four-poster lay one little form. He'd been fine the previous day. Completely fine.

"Christian." She rushed to the bedside and sank onto the mattress. No, fine was not exactly how she would describe him on their carriage ride to Wiltshire. He'd been content to listen to Bryan spin outrageous tales of Fian warriors or to have her softly sing to him. But for all the confinement of riding for two days in a small space, he'd not been his usual bundle of irrepressible energy.

He lay against the pillows here, pale and drawn. His little cheeks flushed a high pink at odds with his general pallor. She'd put his lassitude off as exhaustion from the weeks of travel, and instead he'd been coming down with an illness. She should have recognized the difference. She should have known the difference. Gail would have.

"Aunt Emmie." Her name came in a thick whisper as his eyes rolled in an effort to focus on her.

She took his little hand in hers. Fear wedged deeper into her heart. He was hot to the touch, far too hot. She swallowed around the lump threatening to choke her.

"I am right here, darling. Don't worry." She stroked her free hand over his forehead. He closed his eyes with a small, whimpery sigh.

"I've already summoned the doctor, ma'am." The housekeeper stood at her elbow. "And sent Kate to fetch some cool tea for the lad to sip."

"Yes, thank you." Emilynne struggled to get a controlling grip on the fear inside her. She must think clearly. *Thank heaven Richard's housekeeper is thinking ahead for me.*

"I can't like the looks of this."

Emilynne tore her gaze from Christian. "What do you mean?"

"The fever, ma'am." Mrs. Bennett favored her with a worried glance as she whispered her answer.

Chills coursed over Emilynne's shoulders and settled in her belly like jagged cuts of ice.

"I've seen it before. My mum and a couple of me cousins had fevers that came on sudden like after sniffles or a sore throat." She shook her head and dabbed at the corners of her eyes with a handkerchief. "The younger two—"

"Please." Emilynne held up a hand, willing the woman to stop before she gave voice to what already shouted through Emilynne's heart. She couldn't bear the thought of losing Christian. "How long will it take the doctor to arrive?"

"I sent a boy over just before coming to fetch you,

ma'am. Provided he's not on a call elsewhere, he should be here within the hour."

She paced over to the window and took a quick peek outside. Sunlight struck Emilynne's hand, a momentary warmth, and then as quickly vanished as the curtains fell back into place.

"We'd best stop that Mr. Reilly from leavin', at least until the doctor's been here," the woman continued, "for if it is what I fear, we could all be stuck here together for up to a fortnight."

Quarantined.

"I forgot about Bryan's departure." How quickly her attention had turned from the thoughts that had kept her awake all night. Emilynne bent down and pressed a swift kiss to Christian's hot cheek, wishing the ice inside her could soothe him. "Have you spoken to Richard yet?"

"No, ma'am." The woman shook her head. "I came to you straightaway."

"I will inform them both. It is best they know as soon as possible." Richard might abhor illness but surely not in a child under his care. And the news over the expansion of Belfast's shipping at least cooled the urgency behind Bryan's departure. The awkwardness of them all keeping company for a while longer was a minor inconvenience compared to her worries over Christian. He was so little. He'd been through so much.

She straightened Christian's bedclothes around him and ventured another soft kiss as the protective instincts inside her screamed in protest.

"Perhaps the doctor will pronounce this no more than a minor thing." She spoke as much to comfort herself as to Mrs. Bennett. "Where is Abby?"

"I sent her down to breakfast, ma'am. I thought it best

she not be present or think anything amiss until I spoke with you."

"Yes, thank you." *Bless this woman and her commonsense approach to the whole situation.*

"As soon as the doctor arrives—"

"Aye, ma'am, I'll send word to you."

"I will be back very soon, dearest. Drink the tea Kate brings you like a good boy."

Relinquishing Christian back into Mrs. Bennett's care, Emilynne left the room.

She reached the foyer and nodded a hasty good morning to Stephens. The butler inclined his head slightly and continued on into the billiards room.

Bryan's bag by the door stood mute testament to his plans for imminent departure. Despite the intimacies they had shared, had he hoped to leave before she came down? She realized it had taken a supreme act of will for him to turn away from the freedoms she had given him, from the passion they had built together. Had he thought to spare her, to spare himself, an awkward good-bye?

"I am sorry," she whispered, and walked toward the sound of male voices.

"Good luck, old man," Richard was saying as she entered the front room.

"Thank you." Bryan's dry reply.

Richard could have no idea that Bryan had essentially turned his back on his family mission in order to protect her. And being the man he was, Bryan most likely had no intention of enlightening his host.

They stood by the hearth, Richard a pale, elegant porcelain figure next to Bryan's vibrant coloring and vitality. It was obvious both men couldn't wait to see the last of each other, judging by the tension emanating from them. She wished she had better news for them.

"Em, darling. What a lovely frock. Is it new?" Richard's tone grated as he came forward to greet her. He took her hands and kissed her cheek. She received the distinct impression his actions were more a show for Bryan than a true desire to touch her.

Bryan's gaze met hers over Richard's shoulder. Hot memories seared through her in that instant. The feel of his hands against her flesh, the taste of his mouth, the incredible intimacies they had shared in the moonlit garden, flared inside her in vivid detail as Richard's dry lips and mustache brushed her skin.

Bryan's brooding gaze seemed to share her thoughts. Green fire blazed in their depths. Her breath caught and she looked away.

"Good morning, Richard." She backed away as he released her hands. "I am afraid I have some bad news for you both."

"Bryan." She flashed him a quick glance. "I fear you cannot leave Hampton House just yet."

"Why on earth not?" Richard didn't bother to hide his irritation.

"What is it, Emilynne?" Bryan dropped his casual pose and came toward her. A frown knotted his dark brows. "What's wrong? The children?"

How easily he read her. How had he known?

"Yes." She swallowed hard around a truth that stung. "I am afraid so."

She had both men's attention now. She took a deep breath. There was no skirting the issue. "Christian is ill. Seriously so, if Mrs. Bennett is right."

"Ill?" The slightest tremor seemed to go through Richard.

"Ill with what?" Bryan moved closer still.

"I am not sure yet. We have sent for the doctor." She couldn't keep her hands still as they worked together in a knot of worry. "He is running a fever."

Richard took a step back. "A fever? Good God."

Bryan gripped her hands. His own were warm and solid against hers, gone suddenly cold. She fought the urge to throw herself against his shoulder and find solace as tears burned the backs of her eyes.

"But you're not sure yet, Emilynne. It may be nothing serious." Bryan squeezed her hands. "Children often seem deadly ill one day and are up and running about the next. Or so the fathers at my office tell me."

Bless him for trying to lighten her load.

"Let us hope that is the case here." Richard paced over to the windows. "Still, perhaps we'd best keep everyone away from the boy until we know for certain one way or the other. You can never be too cautious. Children can be so . . . contagious. You haven't been near him, have you, Emilynne?"

"Well, of course I have been near him." She struggled for patience. Richard was not used to children, that much was obvious. "Richard, he is ill. He needs me."

"Oh, dear." Richard's face paled beneath his sandy brows. "You . . . touched him?"

She could almost see Richard going over his recent contact with her and evaluating it for possible dangers. Something cold twisted her stomach, followed by a shiver of nausea.

"Yes, Richard. And I will go on touching him. He is my child now." *Soon to be yours,* she screamed silently. "I cannot ignore him any more than I could cease to breathe by will alone."

"No, of course not." Richard took a step toward her and then stopped himself. "I didn't mean that you should, Em."

"Sit down." Bryan drew her toward the sofa. "You're a bit pale yourself. Are you feeling all right?"

"Yes, I am fine." He sat beside her, close enough for his warmth to roll toward her in comforting waves. Selfishly she was very, very glad he was here. "Just worried. I am so sorry we have delayed you yet again."

Their gazes met. His lips quirked up at the corner. "It no longer matters."

Everything that had passed between them in the night echoed here in the sunlit parlor. Heat curled into her cheeks. She would always equate the scents of newly cut wood and sage with the passion they had shared so briefly.

"Excuse me." Mrs. Bennett appeared at the door. "Mr. Andrews, the doctor is here." She nodded toward Emilynne. "Miss Wellesley."

"Thank you." Emilynne was on her feet immediately. She hurried toward the door. Without being asked, Bryan was beside her. She silently blessed him for being as worried as she and tried not to judge Richard for his apparent lack of concern.

"Let me know what you find out." Richard's voice followed them into the hallway.

Emilynne didn't answer as she and Bryan took the stairs behind Mrs. Bennett. The doctor was ahead of them in the room, bent over Christian.

"Dr. Harris." His presence gave her a sense of home and eased her fears just the tiniest bit.

"My dear Miss Wellesley. So good to see you home. Or

nearly so." Harris nodded in her direction, his face grave. "How long has the boy been ill?"

"Since this morning as far as I know. Mrs. Bennett found him like this when she came to rouse them."

"Has he had a recent soreness in his throat?" The doctor threw the question over his shoulder as he peered at Christian.

Guilt struck hard in Emilynne. "Yes, a few days ago, but it was quickly gone."

"And his appetite?"

"We have been traveling, sir," Bryan answered. "None of us ate much, due to exhaustion."

"The maid tells me he barely touched his supper last night, Doctor," Mrs. Bennett supplied. "We put it off to the raspberry tarts he ate when he first arrived."

"Hmmm." He gave no other response to her answer except a slow shake of his head.

Dr. Harris turned away from the bedside and motioned Emilynne toward the hallway. Her heart sank at his solemn demeanor. Bryan steadied her with his hand at the small of her back as they followed the doctor out of the room.

"Miss Wellesley, young Christian appears to have scarlet fever. The disease can follow after a putrid throat."

Guilt speared her heart again. Would Christian have avoided this if she had stayed put at Mrs. Babbage's? "We have just come from Bristol. That's when he complained of the soreness in his throat."

The doctor nodded. "Are the lad's parents still in Bristol, or have they gone on to Newbury Manor."

"Mr. and Mrs. Wellesley died recently while in Ireland." Bryan supplied the news Emilynne dreaded repeating to all her acquaintants, especially the doctor who had attended both her and Robert's births.

"I must say—" Dr. Harris looked shocked. He paled beneath the white of his beard. "Was fever involved?" he asked sharply.

Emilynne shook her head. "There was a carriage accident."

"My sincere condolences, my dear. Your brother was a fine man. I know he would be proud of the care you show toward his child."

"Will Christian be all right?" She had no time for hovering grief. She needed to concentrate on the living.

The doctor nodded again. "Well, that will depend on the lad's determination to fight. The whole house will be placed under quarantine. Scarlet fever is extremely contagious. It usually begins with a sore throat and progresses from there."

Emilynne swayed again. Bryan's hands closed over her shoulders. Warm, solid, dependable. "Could we have prevented—"

"No, my dear." The doctor smiled briefly behind his beard. "You could not, but we can prevent further contamination by keeping the household contained."

"What will happen to Christian?" The question came through numb lips.

"It's always hard to say, my dear." Dr. Harris ran a hand over his beard. "He looks to have been a healthy child in other respects."

"Yes, very."

"Then there is every reason to hope he will survive the outbreak."

"Hope?" That's all he could offer?

"What can we do to help ensure his recovery?" Bryan took control as Emilynne's fears raged out of control.

"I don't believe we've been introduced, sir." The doctor looked him up and down quickly.

"I'm Bryan Reilly, a solicitor from Limerick." Bryan shook Dr. Harris's hand.

"Escorted her home in the aftermath?" Dr. Harris queried. "Very good."

"Have the boy bathed with cool water to lower his fever." The doctor instructed Bryan to Emilynne's relief. She was terrified she'd miss some significant detail on her own.

"Some of my colleagues still advocate bleeding, but I've found the baths and plenty of fruit juices work best. I'll send around a mixture of yarrow concentrate and catnip, which should also help."

Dr. Harris leaned closer to Bryan. "If . . . when the lad's fever drops, I'll also provide a remarkable powder my cousin in Boston sent me, claims it works wonders on just this illness. It's made from the roots of a flower found there, purple coneflower or the like."

Bryan nodded his understanding and Dr. Harris turned his attention back to Emilynne. "Are there other children in the house?"

"Abby." A new fear.

"How old is she?"

"Just seven."

"Then she will be the one to be watched, aside from the young man in there." He thumbed toward the bedroom door. "She will be the most susceptible."

"Will you come back to check on Christian?"

"No, my dear. Too much danger of cross-contamination. I'll send a lad with fever medicine and the powder for afterward. He'll come around for daily updates on the boy or to deliver any advice I can share. Aside from that, I dare not return and risk further spread of the illness."

"I understand." She heard the words leave her mouth as everything inside her shrieked violent protestations. There should be no understanding, not where her family was involved. All their losses were too recent, too raw for her to understand anything beyond a need for an immediate cure for Christian and certain safety for Abby. She had not brought them all this way from Kildare to lose them within two miles of home. Or before they had both led long, happy lives.

After quickly repeating his instructions and precautions to Mrs. Bennett, the doctor retrieved his hat and bag and left Emilynne with a reassuring pat on her shoulder. She gripped the railing and watched him exit the house without further word to anyone. She realized she was holding the rail in a death grip only when Bryan gently pried her fingers away and turned her in his arms.

"It will be all right, Emilynne. We'll make him all right." His words coursed over her raw heart, threatening to release the tears she'd been holding back all morning. She bit her lip, fighting the temptation to throw herself against his shoulder and sob out all the fear that whirled through her.

"I truly hope so." She blinked hard and withdrew herself from his embrace. She'd risked enough last night. She could fight only so many battles this morning, and Christian's was paramount. "I must tell Richard."

"I'll tell Andrews." His husky tone shivered over her arms. "He'll have to make arrangements for supplies and such."

"No." She shook her head. "The children are as much his responsibility as mine now. We will have to make the arrangements together."

Bryan watched her move away from him. She looked so lost, so alone—deliberately holding herself that way.

Damn him and his inability to keep control. When she might have turned to him for comfort, for help, she must pull away. No longer able to trust herself with him.

Well, he'd be damned if he'd let her face Andrews alone simply because she wished it so. She needed help with that cold fish. Since he couldn't leave, he might as well give her whatever support he could. He followed her silently down the steps, keeping a pace behind and vowing to retain his control.

"Emilynne." Andrews's voice welcomed her, and Bryan cringed inside. How was it Richard Andrews managed to make her name sound so intimate and so impersonal in the same breath?

The man cast Bryan a quick cold glance, not bothering to hide his ire that he accompanied Emilynne. "What did the doctor say?"

"Christian has scarlet fever." she offered in a dull tone. She did not acknowledge Bryan's presence, but he grimly determined to stay within earshot if she needed him.

"Oh." Andrews's gaze went back and forth between them. "And?"

"And?" she echoed.

"What is to happen now? Do we send the boy away to a cottage on the estate? Are we all in peril of our lives? What?" Richard raked a hand through his hair.

"Richard. He is too ill to be sent anywhere even if I would allow it." Her voice gained a bit of strength. "Christian is the one in danger at the moment. No one else."

"What do you mean, no one else? Is my household not quarantined?"

"Yes—"

"Then I repeat, how much danger are we in?"

"The children—"

"Are the biggest contagion. Is that it? We'll have the servants care for them. Mrs. Bennett must have dealt with this before. She's an excellent choice. Then neither you nor I have to be in close contact with them until this is resolved."

Bryan's hands tightened into fists at the other man's tone. He held them rigidly at his sides, determined not to allow the anger rushing through him to gain dominance. He was speaking about children with no pity or thought for them at all.

"No, Richard," Emilynne disagreed. "I will care for Christian myself. If Mrs. Bennett offers her help, I will gladly accept."

"I cannot allow that, Emilynne." Andrews's tone was cold, harsh, and commanding.

Emilynne's spine straightened to the point Bryan feared it would crack. His urge to pound the haughty demeanor right off the other man's thin face burned like a white-hot flame.

"I did not ask your permission." Emilynne's tones were cool but determined.

Good girl. Bryan applauded her spirit, knowing Andrews was swimming way out over his depths if he thought he could dissuade her where the children she regarded as her own were concerned.

"You are to be my wife." Andrews threw the verbal gauntlet at her, daring her to argue his future mastery. "Robert made the children my responsibility. I will not have you endanger our future, theirs as well, by putting yourself in harm's way."

Emilynne's struggle with her temper was written in the

set of her shoulders. The sharp sense that if she lost control now, she would lose more than her emotional equilibrium pierced Bryan like a blade. That her fight for control equaled his own threatened to shake whatever tenuous hold he retained.

She swallowed carefully and gripped her hands together in front of her in an effort he recognized as one she used to force an outward show of calm. "Our future may very well be in danger, Richard. But understand this, I am the closest blood family those children have left. I stole them out of Ireland from beneath Thaddeus's nose and I brought them safely to England. I am not about to relinquish my care of either one of them simply to assuage your fears of infection.

"Without them we do not have a future," she concluded.

"I cannot—"

"Neither can I." Emilynne's tone grew soft again but was just as determined as before. "This is a pointless argument, Richard. We are not married yet, and you cannot stop me from caring for my nephew."

Andrews had the grace to show a tiny bit of shame. "Em—" He came toward her and took her hands in his for a moment. "I'm sorry. I sound like a bastard when you put it that way. It's you I'm thinking of. You've been through so much already. Why torment yourself when there is the possibility the boy may die?"

How heartless to think let alone express that fear when the boy had only begun to fight this illness. Bryan was outraged.

"Christian will not die, Richard."

"Emilynne, darling." Andrews smiled at her though no warmth touched the cool gray of his eyes. "I understand how you feel, but we must be prepared for the worst."

"No. I will not give Christian short shrift by readying myself for anything but his recovery." She took a long, slow breath and then continued in a gentler tone. "Richard, I would ask that if you feel this way, you stay as far from the sickroom as possible. Christian is very sensitive. I do not want him picking up anything negative that could affect his struggle."

Andrews's blank expression fairly screamed the news that he had never had any intention of going near the sick child. In fact, the farther away he stayed, the better. But for once he seemed to realize that information would be unwelcome.

"As you wish, my dear." He nodded. "When will the doctor return?"

"He is not coming back."

Andrews's eyebrows shot up beneath his hair like tiny rats scurrying for cover. "Not—"

"No." She sighed and relinquished the tiniest bit of her rigid posture, a concession more felt than seen. "He does not plan to return because he does not wish to risk danger of further infection to the community."

As her lips closed behind her brave words, the slightest tremor quaked over her body. Bryan realized she was braced, as though facing a high storm at sea, for any recriminations Andrews might offer her. Everything in him coiled tight, waiting for her betrothed's reply.

A moment of silence passed while tensions pulsed in the room like the ticking of an overwound clock.

"I see." Andrews's eyebrows returned to his forehead, now etched in a deep frown. "Well, I cannot say I am at all happy with this turn of events, especially with your refusal to heed my requests. You endanger not only yourself with this foolish display of misplaced loyalty, but me and my household. As well as Abby, and even Reilly here."

Bryan doubted his host would spare even a second grieving for his unwanted guest should illness stalk him.

"Richard—"

"But"—Andrews held up a hand to forestall any protests she might wish to voice—"I can see you are unwilling, or unable, to listen to reason at this juncture. Taking into account your recent losses and state of mind, I can only concede in the hopes you will soon tire of the exercise and manage not to exhaust yourself in the process."

"See if you can talk some sense into her, Reilly. You will both have to excuse me." He bowed ever so slightly and left the room.

Silence reigned as the door closed behind him.

"The man is plainly an idiot." Bryan couldn't keep the guttural anger from his voice.

Emilynne laughed softly but with little humor. She turned toward him. Tears sparkled in the deep blue of her eyes.

A sudden yearning to gather her to him and hold her close, protecting her from anything that might hurt her, seized him, locking his breath inside his chest. The Blessing played a distant, haunting melody through his mind. Knowing his desires would do nothing to help her, he leashed the impulse tight and kept his hands rigid at his sides.

"He is not as bad as his words make him out to be," she offered.

Bryan wondered if she really believed her words, but he held his tongue. She didn't need a dissertation on what he considered to be Richard Andrews's considerable lack of fortitude. Family was everything. No matter what. Somehow that small bit of moral foundation was lacking in the man she now sought as her husband.

"Thank you, Bryan."

"For what?"

"For understanding my need to care for Christian. And for supporting me just now."

"I said nothing."

"I know." She smiled as a single tear tracked over her cheek. His gut tightened again. "But I could feel you there behind me and I knew what you were thinking. It helped more than you know."

Her words shook him. He'd stood there feeling everything she felt, supporting her yet holding himself in reserve. It had not occurred to him that she would feel a similar connection.

"Emilynne." He took a step toward her.

"I must go back to Christian." She backed away. "Bless you, Bryan." She whisked herself out of the room in a flurry of lavender skirts, leaving the tantalizing scent of freesia and lemon in her wake.

He'd need her blessing all right, need all the blessings he could muster, cursed as he was to spend the rest of his life wanting another man's wife.

Chapter Twelve

Emilynne hurried up the staircase, unwilling to examine her uncertainty over whether she ran more toward Christian or away from Bryan and everything about the all too handsome Irishman that undermined her determination to marry Richard and provide safety and security for the children.

Just the look in Bryan's eyes was enough to burn her good intentions to cinders by inflaming her memories of the previous night in the gardens, searing her with forbidden yearnings. She needed all her concentration to focus on Christian and the battle he waged.

"There you are, Miss Wellesley." Mrs. Bennett's quiet greeting held a tiny hint of censure for Emilynne as she reached the top of the stairs. Had she been gone too long? Or did the housekeeper reflect the head of the household's distaste for this disturbance in his ordered existence? They would all have some adjustments to make if they were going to provide a happy home for the children.

"How is Christian? He'll be so frightened if someone is not with him should he awaken."

Mrs. Bennett clicked her tongue, a condemning note harking back to Emilynne's refusal to fetch the children's nanny from Newbury Manor, no doubt. Richard's former nanny's disapproval had bordered on obstinance when she reminded Emilynne in a firm tone that women of her station did not spend their time caring for their own children.

She'd fairly bristled when Emilynne had asked her to be certain word of their arrival at Hampton House did not get out among the neighborhood.

Mr. Andrews's staff prides itself on our discretion. We never stoop to idle gossip still rang in Emilynne's ears. She could almost picture the older woman mentally adding up the tally against her.

A child's illness couldn't help but strain this staid household and Mrs. Bennett's less than patient attitude. But Emilynne still couldn't afford to explain why Mr. Jefferies and Bryan insisted that as few people as possible know of their arrival home in Wiltshire. Especially members of her own staff at Newbury.

"He's been awake, then asleep and a wee bit restless, but he's a fighter, that one," the housekeeper answered her immediate concern.

Emilynne nodded. "So was his father."

The thought of Robert panged a hollow chord inside her. Robert had usually shrugged off illness. But she recalled the time his horse threw him and he'd spent many weeks recovering from a shattered ankle. He'd amazed Dr. Harris and their parents with the speed and completeness of his recovery.

"Thank you, Mrs. Bennett."

She continued into Christian's bedroom with the housekeeper in her wake. Christian lay much as she had left him. A small sick boy in an oversized bed. Her heart twisted within her.

"How did Mr. Andrews take the news?" Mrs. Bennett helped her straighten Christian's covers with deft movements.

Anger washed through Emilynne with surprising strength. Richard's reaction, so insensitive as to be stunning in its sheer lack of concern for Christian's and Abby's welfare, stung her deeply. The security she'd so hoped to find when she started her journey to Hampton House now seemed a hazy dream at best. Reluctant to unleash her anger in the sickroom, Emilynne tamped it back with an effort. Letting Mrs. Bennett hear how Richard's cool demeanor and cavalier attitude had hurt her would accomplish nothing beyond further sinking herself and the children in the housekeeper's graces.

"Richard has never spent much time with children." The words came out plain and clipped as Emilynne sat at Christian's beside. "He will learn how precious and fragile they are when he has more time with them."

Unbidden, comparisons rose in her mind. Bryan had cared for the children from their first meeting. Memories of him carrying Abby on board his ship, telling them tales of his home and life aboard ship, his white-faced response and quick actions that had brought Abby back to her safely in Bristol.

She smoothed her hand along Christian's forehead, trying to control the worry that rose in wake of the heat she felt there. He was far too hot. And there was far too little for her to do but wait and watch.

"I'll keep an eye out for the little miss." The housekeeper turned away.

"Thank you, Mrs. Bennett."

The older woman turned back as she reached the door and her detached manner relaxed just a little bit. "I've some recipes for a cool bath with comfrey and lady's mantle that could help the little one. If you like."

Emilynne would gladly accept help from any quarter. Though unbending in her support of Richard, the woman obviously had a caring heart.

"That would be good." Emilynne bit her lip as the woman turned back toward the door.

"Mrs. Bennett?"

"Yes, Miss Wellesley?"

"Thank you."

The housekeeper nodded and shut the door behind her, leaving Emilynne alone with her fears and hopes for Christian's recovery. She stroked his forehead again.

"Mama?" Christian's eyes rolled as he searched for the familiar face he would never find.

Emilynne's throat tightened. "No, darling."

"Aunt Emmie." He focused on her with an effort.

"Yes, my love." She stroked his cheek and waited for his struggling gaze to settle on her again. "Christian, you are going to have a couple of very tough days ahead and you need to be a strong little boy. Think about all the things you would like to do when you get well and all the places you would like to go. Can you do that for me?"

"Yes." His eyes rolled again and her heart tightened as he gulped several deep breaths. He was already trying so hard. "I want to go sailin' with Jimmy and the cap'n."

"Yes, I know you do." Emilynne swallowed hard, determined to preserve a loving and positive attitude around him. "We will discuss that with Captain Reilly as soon as you are well. In the meantime, I will be right here with you, sweetheart. I promise."

"Aunt Emilynne." Abby's voice, healthy and strong but a little hesitant, sounded behind her.

Emilynne's heart sank as her fears for both children collided inside her, shredding her calm anew. She could not allow Abby anywhere near Christian and risk more exposure than the girl had already suffered.

"What's wrong with Uncle Richard? He's acting very strange. Has Captain Reilly left? He didn't say good-bye. And why is Christian still in bed?"

"Sick," Christian offered in a rusty squeak from amid the bedclothes, though he did not open his eyes.

"Come with me, Abby, and I will explain." Emilynne kept her voice low as she drew her niece with her back into the hallway.

"I will be right here, Christian." No answer as he drifted to sleep again. She offered a quick prayer as she closed the bedroom door behind her.

She led Abby to the cushioned window seat at the top of the stairs. Did she look a trifle pale? Or was that the first flush of fever on her cheeks? Were her eyes too bright? Fears plagued Emilynne.

"What's wrong, Aunt Emilynne, you have your worried face on again." Abby frowned at her.

"Do I?" She supposed she'd worn that look more often than not of late. She'd have to watch that.

"Come here, dearest." She drew Abby into her lap and cuddled the girl's soft warmth against her, enjoying the clean-scrubbed child scent with just a hint of apple blossoms that lingered in her hair. Though prevarication tempted her for just a moment, Emilynne had long ago learned that with Abby there was nothing for it but the truth.

"I am worried, Abby," she offered after a moment. "Your brother is very ill with something called scarlet fever."

"He's going to die, isn't he?" Abby's stalwart tone held more acceptance than question, ripping fresh wounds in Emilynne's heart. This child was far too young to be braced for death and loss at a moment's notice.

Emilynne pulled Abby against her shoulder and rocked her back and forth. Sunlight spilled in the windows, warming them both.

"No, Abby. He is not going to die," she said firmly, praying she told the truth, determined to hold tight to any hope she could.

"Are you sure?"

"Yes, Abby, I am quite sure."

Abby digested that in silence for a few moments and then pushed back to hold Emilynne's gaze with her own serious brown ones. "Very well, then, what can I do to help Christian get well?"

"Abby." Emilynne stroked the girl's cheek and smiled. Her skin was cool and soft. No sign of fever. "Thank you for offering, but what I need from you is going to be the hardest part. You must stay away from Christian until he recovers."

"But—"

Emilynne stilled Abby's protest with her fingers. "I told you it would be very difficult. You are so used to helping with your brother. You have since the day he was borne. No boy could ask for a finer sister. But in this instance you will do more harm than good by staying near him."

"Why?" Abby's auburn curls gleamed with vitality in the sunlight. Surely she would not get sick as well.

"Because what Christian has is very contagious. He could give it to anyone, but most especially to other children. I couldn't bear it if you were sick too."

"But Christian will get well?" A doubtful tone laced Abby's hesitant question.

"Yes, Abby, he will." Emilynne forced every bit of assurance she had into those words, both for herself and for her niece. Neither one of them was ready to face another loss.

"What about Uncle Richard and Captain Reilly? Must they stay away as well?"

"I can't answer for your uncle, Abby," Bryan answered as he ascended the stairs, looking far too handsome in his white shirt and black trousers. His jacket was slung over this shoulder. "But I'll be around to help your aunt."

"You didn't leave without saying good-bye." Abby jumped off Emilynne's lap and ran to him with her arms wide open. "I knew you wouldn't, Captain, even if Mr. Stephens said grown-ups had no time for such childish nonsense."

Sunlight glinted in his hair as he scooped her into his arms and spun her around. "Of course I wouldn't leave without saying good-bye to you. And as it turns out, I don't have to say good-bye at all right now. We're quarantined, you know.''

"Quarantined?" Abby's brows knit together over the word as he set her back on her feet.

"It means nobody else can come in and, for the time being, we are all to stay together in your uncle's house." Bryan managed to make it sound like some kind of wonderful game.

Abby's brow cleared and she smiled up at him. "Oh, then, you won't be leaving today?"

"No, sweeting, I will not." He smiled back at her, a devilish twinkle in his green Gaelic eyes. "And since I'm to stay for a while, I am in desperate need of a guide who can show me around the estate. Do you know where I can find one?"

"Oh, yes, I would be happy to do that. I'll take you myself."

More than happy by the glow in her eyes. Emilynne caught back a sigh. Abby seemed to have lost her heart to the charm and dark good looks of her sea captain. She knew just how her niece felt. Even when not directed at her, his charm held much too much sway over her own emotions.

Abby smoothed her sprigged muslin skirt in a very feminine gesture. "Where would you like to start? In the gardens or at the stables?"

The gardens. Emilynne's heartbeat quickened as a traitorous thrill spiraled into her stomach.

"He has already seen the gardens." The words left her lips of their own volition as heat stung her cheeks and burned there like a beacon.

"Aye." Bryan's gaze locked with hers. A world of passion

dwelt in the banked fires behind his dark green gaze. "I have at that."

He held her regard for far too long before turning back to Abby. "The stables should do, my lady. Shall we?"

He bent his knee, offering her his arm with a great flourish, and Abby giggled before accepting him with the unusual mingling of maturity and youth that was hers alone.

"Please be careful," Emilynne admonished as they started down the stairs.

"We will, Aunt Emilynne," Abby's voice trailed back, unconcerned.

Don't worry. Bryan mouthed the words as his gaze met hers again.

"Easier directed than accomplished." Emilynne sighed as they disappeared out the front door.

Blessing him for thinking of an occupation for Abby and allowing her to keep her thoughts and energy on Christian, Emilynne crossed the hall.

A light breeze carried the mingled scents of new roses and white gardenias as Bryan and Abby began their impromptu tour. Walking the estate was the first thing that sprang to mind as he'd watched Emilynne struggle to keep her own fears in check while not engaging her niece's in the process. But, he had to admit, the idea held merit beyond occupation for his charming young companion. He needed a mental map of Hampton House's grounds, in particular where it adjoined Newbury Manor.

He wouldn't put it past a man as perfidious as Thaddeus Whyte to have his minions skulking about the perimeter of Newbury Manor in the hope of coming upon Emilynne and the children unawares. Whyte's hand would be much easier for him to play if he actually had possession of the children. And Andrews did not seem to feel the least compunction to take the very real alarm of his betrothed to heart in regard to the custody matter sure to be looming on their horizon.

"The gardens are over that way," Abby informed him, following his gaze as she gestured with a delicate finger. "They are quite beautiful, in an orderly fashion. Or so my mama used to say. She preferred bouquets of meadow flowers."

"Indeed. I believe I prefer wildflowers myself." He didn't need any reminders of Andrews's trim garden. The way Emilynne colored just then had been enough to fire his blood—uncomfortably so. She'd been so warm and giving, so womanly in his arms on the garden bench, driving the last ounce of respectability he'd ever laid claim to right out of his head.

Everything in him tightened anew, and he groaned inwardly, shouldering those unfulfilled desires away. She had allied herself with another man. Worse yet, though he sensed her hesitation, he had taken advantage of her vulnerability and her grief to gratify his baser needs and blot out his failures. Well, he wouldn't fail to protect her again, especially from himself.

"The stables are down this way." Abby slipped her fingers into his and tugged. "Come along, Captain."

He turned away from the gardens and his haunting thoughts of Emilynne and fell into step beside Abby.

"So, you are very familiar with Hampton House, Miss Wellesley?"

She giggled, as she always did when he addressed her so formally, the sound ruffled merrily over the grass. "Oh, yes, my father spent lots of time here with Uncle Richard. Uncle Richard says that I shan't be Miss Wellesley until Aunt Emilynne and he are wed. I'm just Miss Abigail to him until then.''

Abby talked on, and Bryan let her voice trail away as his thoughts turned to his own inner struggles, shoals yet to be navigated. The possibility of Harland's backing might have dried up, but the problems facing Reilly Ship Works still existed. Quin was a master at commanding men on board ship, steering them through the roughest water, but after a while even his formidable talents would be unable to hold things together at home. Without money for fresh lumber and supplies, let alone to pay the workers on the island for whom the Reillys were the only support, the shipyard faced closure.

A clear picture of his father's face should that deed come to pass tightened his gut and almost stopped him in his tracks. He could not let that happen. He would have to find other financing. He could seek some direction from Jefferies once he was free of the quarantine. Emilynne had mentioned that her brother had relied on the old attorney for advice in his own business dealings.

Purely selfishly, he wished Robert Wellesley had not died in Ireland. Hadn't she said her brother preferred investing in struggling businesses, enabling them to grow to benefit others? Just the kind of investor his father would approve. But if Robert had not gone to Ireland, Emilynne would never have sought his help and he might have made it to Liverpool in time to persuade Harland. What a tangle what-ifs created.

He sighed as he thought of how his mother had closed her last letter to him, urging him to set aside the past by concentrating on the future for the sake of his family and sail for England as quickly as possible. *Once you make the choice, son, only you can direct your course to joy or sorrow.*

Once free of Hampton House, he would have to redouble his efforts for Reilly Ship Works. Which led him right back to his need to be certain Emilynne and the children would be safe and happy when he was gone from their lives. A tangle indeed. A knot like the Celtic symbol entwined under the family signet ring he wore.

He shook his head and tried to concentrate on the chores he had set while giving his attention to Abby as she continued. "—pond over beyond those trees. Christian likes it there, although why he likes to play about in the mud is beyond me. Mrs. Bennett told our nanny she shouldn't let him make such a mess of himself."

She made a most unladylike face and Bryan smothered a laugh. "Ours is much nicer and we have fish in it. Or, at least, we did. Do you suppose Nanny Stewart will have to listen to Mrs. Bennett when we live here all the time? She won't like that much."

"What's through there, Abby?" He gestured to a break in the row of hedges lining one side of the estate and then could have kicked himself as her face paled.

"Home." Her answer came quiet and sad, as though she were realizing afresh that although the building might be the same, the home she had known would never be there again.

"Papa and Christian and I always came through the bushes. It was our own special way, one no one else could take. Not even Mother."

"I'm sorry, Abby." Bryan's throat tightened over the inadequacy of words in the face of her losses. What did one do to console a child? His own memories of his little sister Meaghan at this age consisted mostly of her climbing trees and tearing her dresses as she chased after boys. Little help there.

Abby turned away from the break in the hedges and resumed her journey toward the stables. They walked in silence for several minutes.

"Captain?"

"Aye, lass."

"Do you think Christian will get well?"

Her question froze his thoughts for a moment. He glanced down at her, hoping to gain some insight from her face, but her head was bent and her hair shadowed her features.

"What did your aunt tell you?"

"She said he would."

Abby stopped and looked up at him with a curious mixture of childish innocence and world-weary experience. "But Aunt Emilynne thinks she has to protect me. So she would tell me that even if she feared it wasn't true."

Wise girl. She would run circles around some poor, hapless lad someday. He wondered if Emilynne knew just how perceptive her niece really was.

He dropped to one knee to bring himself level with Abby's somber brown gaze. At this vantage point he could see the desperate hope and fear colliding behind the brave facade she presented. His heart wrenched in his chest.

"Aye, Abby." He told her what she needed to hear. What he most needed to believe. "Your brother is a strong boy, he will get well."

She searched his eyes for a minute with the sobriety of a magistrate passing sentence. Only the slight tremor of her lips betrayed the child she was.

"Oh, thank you," she told him in a rush. She flung her

arms around his neck and sobbed against his chest as if her heart would break.

He wrapped his arms around her and stroked her hair, letting her cry out all the fears and frustrations that had built up inside her over the months since her parents' deaths. So much suffering in one so young.

"Hush, *mavornin*," he whispered as her sobs at last began to lessen. "It will be all right, sweeting, you'll see. You've been such a help to your aunt. And to Christian. And to me. In a few days Christian will be well and driving you to distraction while trying to convince me he's ready to captian his own ship."

She hiccuped against his neck and then giggled softly. "A Reilly ship?"

"Aye, lass." He kissed her cheek. These Wellesley women had a way of getting straight to the heart of a man. "A fine Reilly ship."

" 'Cept for Christian being sick, I'm glad we're quarn'ted today. I like your kisses, Captain." She smiled.

"They don't tickle like Uncle Richard's. He has a mustache and it scratches." She traced a line along his upper lip. "My papa had a mustache, but his kisses were soft and made me warm, like yours."

With the mercurial recovery of the child she was, she pushed away from him further and smiled again, an impish grin that lit her eyes. "Do you still want to see the stables? Uncle Richard has horseflesh even Uncle Teddy would approve."

"Aye, I'd love to see the stables." He brushed her cheeks with his fingers and tapped her nose.

Bristol, England

"What news do you have of the lightskirt's whereabouts?" Thaddeus Whyte paced over to the hearth of his hotel room and poured his guest a portion of the whiskey the establishment provided its better-paying clients.

"Nothing direct." Willard Jefferies, Jr., doffed his hat and accepted the tumbler proffered him with an triumphant gleam in his eye. "My pater's keeping a tight grip on any information he might have, despite nosing about looking for Wellesley's papers and trying to pin the loss on all and sundry."

He chuckled. "Of course, I've been ahead of him for months, so everyone just thinks he's getting forgetful in his dotage. He's no threat to our business."

"If you have no news beyond the fact that the vessel she left Limerick aboard docked in this harbor briefly, why did you summon me to Bristol?" Thaddeus made no attempt to cloak his annoyance in a more palatable veneer, the gold he paid old Jefferies's son to betray his father more than covered any need for pseudo-civilities.

"The old bird must have seen her, and he undoubtedly knows her whereabouts." A smug smile edged the young solicitor's lips as he took a hefty swallow from his glass. "Cagey just ain't in his nature. I intercepted a letter from a Mr. Richard Andrews of Hampton House regarding a matter of utmost delicacy in the business of his being named co-guardian to the Wellesley brats."

So, the little weasel did have news. "Just where is Hampton House located and what do you know of this Andrews?"

Jefferies, Jr., drained his glass. "He's a sap-skulled country bumpkin. His estate marches side by side with Wellesley land in Wiltshire. Seems he and the late Mr. Wellesley were boyhood chums. And a match was once proposed between him and the Wellesley tart."

The fine edge of triumph warmed Thaddeus. "She's most likely gone to ground there."

"I've already sent a messenger to Wiltshire, supposedly from you, looking to make certain she had arrived safely." Jefferies, Jr., held out his tumbler for a refill. "And a secondary missive to the men keeping an eye on Newbury Manor, just in case she headed there."

Thaddeus poured himself a healthy draft as well. Handing the whiskey to the younger man, he clinked glasses. "To a rewarding partnership for both of us once my great-niece and -nephew are returned to my tender care."

"Aye," the younger man rejoined. "You keep the brats and the land in Ireland and I'll manage the estates here. You did secure the necessary documents in Dublin, did you not?"

Thaddeus touched his breast pocket. "I keep them close to my heart. My petition for guardianship and the order forcing Miss Wellesley to explain her flight from justice to the Irish courts."

"Excellent." Jefferies grinned. "We should receive confirmation from Wiltshire within the next day. Then we can conclude the matter."

"You're quite certain none of Wellesley's personal bequests or documents survive."

"I burned both my father's copy of his will and the one recovered from Newbury Manor myself. All I retained are the means for us to continue draining his estates until the boy comes of age. Or meets with his own tragic fate."

"Excellent." Thaddeus drank to the coming fruition of all his efforts.

"Wilkins!" He bellowed for his assistant, asleep in the other room. "Begin preparations for a journey to Wiltshire. I wish to make ready to leave at a moment's notice."

Chapter Thirteen

Emilynne frowned and relinquished Dr. Harris's half-empty apothecary jar to the cool surface of the nightstand. She'd been holding the bottle so long, staring down into its murky depths and praying the remedy it held would prove to be what Christian needed, she had warmed the thick glass with the heat of her hand.

Her faith in the good doctor, a holdover from her own childhood illnesses, had been shaken by her anxieties for Christian. The past few days, caught on tenterhooks of uncertainty and fear, only heightened her distress, skewering her anew each time Christian's fever rose or he turned his head away from the sips of broth and fruit juice she knew he needed.

"Robert, Gail—help me. If there is any way at all, help Christian. I know you miss him as much as he misses you. Please help him stay with me a little longer. I will make things right for him. I promise."

She doubted they could hear her, but despair's grip was strong and painful and she was willing to try anything, beg grace from any quarter imaginable.

She'd yet to see any positive changes in Christian's condition. The raised rash covering a good portion of his cheeks, neck, and chest, rough to the touch as though coated with a fine sand, could hardly be viewed in a favorable light to her thinking, although Dr. Harris's note had told her these were signs of the disease's progression. And she was certain Christian felt warmer than he had before. What if Dr. Harris were wrong and this wasn't scarlet fever?"

"Christian, darling." She brushed her fingertips along Christian's cheek, praying he'd feel cooler. "Look what Abby has sent you to cheer you up. She thought you would like to play with the unicorn that Jimmy carved for her on Captain Reilly's ship. She said to tell you that she is keeping the birds and other animals he carved safe until you are better, but that the unicorn was magic and special and it should keep you company."

No response.

Emilynne looked over at the small figurine on the nightstand by the medicine jar. If only he would rouse a little to see how desperately they both loved him and needed him.

"Too soon." She sighed and pushed loose strands of hair from her forehead. He needed her to keep her worries from escalating out of control. "It is just too soon."

But how much longer would it take? How long could she expect Richard's patience to hold out before he fretted at her again to leave Christian be, to let strangers tend him.

Her stomach swirled at the thought. She had to stop seeing Richard as the enemy. She gripped her hands together, desperate to control her own rising panic, her emotions far too raw with worry to come easily to heel.

"This will not do." Her harsh whisper broke the silence. "Think rationally, Emilynne."

True to his nature, Richard had yet to come near the sickroom. She doubted he would anytime in the near future. He avoided anything that marred the accepted perfection of his existence.

In fact, the only people anywhere near Christian so far were Kate, the shy little maidservant, too afraid to speak, and Mrs. Bennett, whose crisp decisions and serious nature Emilynne blessed with every appearance despite the sting of censure that still lingered in her unspoken opinion that Emilynne should be more amenable to Mr. Andrews's wishes.

And, of course, Bryan Reilly.

A stalwart companion through the hours of vigil, when he was not at her side, he entertained Abby, relieving that anxiety at least.

Abby openly adored him, but then, Abby could afford to lose her heart to a pair of dark green eyes and a kind smile. Truth be told, her own heart was far too attached to the Irishman. Another thing that could not be, yet was.

Catching herself twisting her hands together, Emilynne wrung out one of the damp cloths she'd been using to bathe Christian and replaced the one on his brow, already toasted with the heat radiating from him.

The door creaked open behind her, probably Mrs. Bennett on her nightly rounds. Guilt seized Emilynne; the housekeeper surely had enough duties without waiting on her in the dead of night, regardless of how welcome her late visits were. "Mrs. Bennett, you need not—"

"It is me, Emilynne." Bryan's low whisper stopped her.

He stood in the doorway, silhouetted by the gas lamp burning low in the hallway. A figure, dark and shadowed, but comforting as summer shade. Somehow his presence never failed to raise her flagging hopes.

"How is Christian?" Expectation and concern underscored his question.

"Sleeping. At least for the moment." Emilynne tried to still the rush of gratitude welling inside her for his return to the sickroom. "He still alternates between restless discomfort and a sleep so sound, I think he'll never rouse. I cannot decide which one worries me more."

She tugged the coverings smooth over Christian and forced herself to turn to her other concern. "How is Abby?"

"She fell asleep in her supper." Bryan laughed, the sound low and intimate as he stepped into the room.

The door swung almost closed behind him, leaving only the barest sliver of light, his unvoiced concession to propriety. "Mrs. Bennett gave her a proper tucking up before going off to bed herself. Although perhaps she stopped by to tuck up her nursling, Andrews, on her way."

His gibe startled a quick laugh from Emilynne on which she could only blame her own tightly strung tensions. "Oh, what a horrid thing to say."

"Indeed, yes, you are quite correct." Bryan came closer, his tone not the least bit repentant about his lack of respect for their host. "It was a horrid thing to say, and I would take the words back except they made you laugh and so it was worth it."

Would she ever have a conversation with this man that did not set her cheeks to burning and churn wild, unwanted longings inside her?

"Mrs. Bennett has known Richard since he was a babe,"

she explained, trying not to dwell on the twist of his lips and what the sight of that slight curve in his chin did to her, especially in the intimate dimness of the chamber. "She was Richard's nanny before she became his housekeeper. You will find none more loyal to him or better able to anticipate his likes and dislikes."

"I knew there had to be a reason," he told her with a devilish wink.

Emilynne bit her lip as he looked down toward the bed.

"Poor lad." He stroked Christian's cheek with gentle fingers before his gaze came back to Emilynne.

As she met his look, she realized he was standing far too close for comfort. She closed her eyes with an effort to blot out the images from the gardens, to stem the raging passion that had surged between them and threatened to swamp her even in these dire circumstances.

"And poor lass." He stroked her cheek now, so lightly she might be imagining his touch and the lingering scent of wood and sage it carried. "You're as pale as parchment. You could use some rest. Would you like me to sit with him for a while?"

"I dare not leave." She shook her head, the idea was unthinkable, the illness far too serious.

"You cannot sleep in a chair for the third night in a row. You'll be sick yourself. Do you really wish to give Andrews the satisfaction of proving his dire predictions true?"

He gestured toward the door to the adjoining room. "Mrs. Bennett moved Abby across the hall to your bedroom to allow you to get some rest in that room. You cannot continue to sleep in a chair in here."

He waved away her protests as if he understood and didn't need to hear her reasoning aloud. "Abby will sleep better surrounded by your things, and you will do Christian far more good when you have rested than by collapsing by his bedside.''

What little energy she had drained away, leaving her light-headed as she thought of the bed waiting in the other room. She should have eaten more of the supper Mrs. Bennett sent up. ''I must be here when he wakes and calls for me. He is not used to being alone and he should not be cared for by strangers.''

''I am not a stranger.'' Bryan loomed over her in the semidarkness and she stifled a swift longing to find comfort in his arms. He was no stranger to any of them anymore. When had he become more friend, more necessary, than the man she had come running to Wiltshire intending to marry?

''And I'll leave the door open,'' he coaxed further. ''If you are anything like my mother, you will hear each cough or sniffle no matter how soundly you sleep.'' He pulled her gently to her feet.

The urge to snatch a few quick moments lured her, warring against her responsibility and her very real need to retain some small shred of control over the grim situation. On the one hand, Bryan was right, she couldn't continue her vigil if she did not at least try to rest.

Bryan's hand cupped her elbow as she swayed on her feet, and the contact warmed her straight to her toes. She wished in vain for a way to make herself stop responding to him like kindling just waiting a flame.

''Let's get you there before you fall down.''

''But—''

He turned her to face him. ''Emilynne, do you trust me?''

From the depths of my soul. She bit back the answer her

heart gave too hastily and with surprising intensity. A tremor quaked through her. "Yes."

"I promise not to leave. I care for Christian too. I will pay attention as if he were my own." The words he spoke were so simple and yet they wrapped around her heart, tempting her to release her worries just for a little while. He offered such a broad, capable shoulder for that release.

"You will wake me if—"

"You are one stubborn lass." He raised an eyebrow at her. "I will wake you if he so much as peeps. Now, lie down before I have to do something drastic."

The look in his eyes was just serious enough to make her believe he meant it.

"Very well, Captain." The title came out before she could catch it back. "I mean—"

"I know very well what you meant." Humor laced his husky tone, though his expression hid his thoughts. "And if it is what it takes to make you listen, then so be it. I shall bark orders each time I need you to attend me."

She realized he'd escorted her to the doorway of the adjoining bedroom as they spoke. He was subtle but determined, she'd give him that. She eyed the welcoming bedstead with its fluffed lace quilt and pristine pillows, grasping just how utterly weary she really was.

He nodded, going to take up a position at the foot of Christian's bed. Something about his stance, feet braced apart, arms akimbo, marked him every bit the born-and-bred captain he denied himself to be. Someone who could steer a ship through the murkiest fog and find safe harbor despite the sea devil's fiercest storm. Such knowledge and command had been transferred to him by blood—a bond strong enough to tear him from his comfortable life as a prominent solicitor and set him on a course in search of salvation for the Reilly shipyard.

Who better to watch over Christian? Yet somehow she couldn't discount the feeling that her very presence, her watchfulness, helped Christian fight his lonely battle. She could not relax, even though her eyes burned and her limbs ached with weariness. The tension wound so tight inside her would not be gainsaid for the sake of a few moments of peace.

She took a deep breath and stepped back into the bedroom.

"Nay." Bryan's tone brooked no arguments, catching her intentions before she progressed any further.

"I cannot—" she began.

"You will," he told her, coming to stand above her with all his captain's authority. "Even if I have to put you there and hold you down myself."

She straightened her spine and stood toe to toe with him, frustration and anger ripping asunder her tenuous hold on her emotions. "I cannot just lie there and do nothing. You do not understand. I have given Dr. Harris's medicine and tried the baths Mrs. Bennett made. There must be something else I can do.

"Christian and Abby are the only family I have got left. I have a responsibility to them both." Hearing the desperation in her own tone didn't help as her voice broke over the words.

"I understand, Emilynne. Believe me, I do. Family is what sent me on this God-cursed errand in the first place. Responsibility. Ties that should not be broken." He raked a hand through his hair.

Then, as though a decision had been made, he cupped her chin and held her gaze to his. "When I was younger

I took my brother Devin sailing even though I'd been forbidden to touch the ship Quin had built. I knew better. Common sense held no sway. I didn't need to listen. I could handle anything by will alone, or so I thought.''

She caught a glimpse of desperate boy glinting in his gaze. "A storm came up while we were navigating this ship I was unfamiliar with handling. And I learned just how foolhardy my bravado was. In the end I destroyed Quin's ship, almost cost Devin his life through near drowning and then pneumonia, and lost something very precious to me—my father's respect. All because I wanted to prove something to him. And I ended up proving just the opposite.''

He sighed, and the hurt lurking behind his eyes carved into her like a hot knife. "Since then it has been my goal to heal the breach I created, to make amends for what I'd done, and to remain cool and even-keeled in the process.''

He shook his head and stared down at her with a rueful expression. "I don't always manage, but the goal remains steadfast in my heart.''

His soft words tore at her. She had pulled his chance from him without any understanding of the enormity of what she had done. More than guilt raged inside her, pain gnawed afresh, and she wished she could undo the complications she had thrown into his life.

"Bryan—''

He placed a finger over her lips. "I didn't mean to tell you the story for any reason but to show you that sometimes you need to ignore the dictates of your pride and your heart and listen to a little common sense. And you, my dear Miss Wellesley, need to lie down before you fall down.''

How neatly he had trapped her. Yet she could not deny him after he revealed the source of his own pain.

"You sound like Richard," she offered as meager defense, her voice husky with the emotions he'd churned loose inside her.

He gave her a lopsided smile that squeezed her heart. "Mayhap, in this one instance, the man is right."

"Mama?" The little call from the bed washed through Emilynne like cool water, pulling her from the intimate warmth that throbbed between her and her reluctant rescuer.

"Christian, Aunt Emilynne is right here." She knelt by the bed and straightened his covers again.

"I'm thirsty," he offered in a scratchy, irritable little voice, and then he yawned so big and so wide, she had to catch herself from echoing the gesture.

"Here, boy-o." Bryan offered a glass of water and Christian eyed it with interest.

"Little sips," she coaxed as he held the glass with two hands. She smoothed his hair out of his eyes and touched his cheek more out of reflex than any expectation of relief.

"Bryan."

"Aye?"

She was almost afraid to answer. "Feel his cheek."

His gaze locked with hers for a moment, but he didn't question her. His hand went to Christian's cheek.

"He's cool."

"Yes." She leaned down and kissed Christian's cheeks, his brow, his fingers.

"You'll make me spill," Christian threatened from within the confines of the water glass.

She couldn't hold back the laugh burgeoning up from the deepest depths of her soul. Relief was blessedly sweet, overwhelming, after the worry she'd nursed. "Oh, Christian, how do you feel?"

"Still thirsty." He held the empty cup out to her. "More?"

Bryan scooped the cup from Christian's fingers and refilled it as Emilynne fought giggles of pure delight.

"And your throat?"

"Okay." Christian frowned up at her. "Why are you crying?"

"Just happy, darling, just happy." Emilynne stroked his hair and straightened his nightshirt as her vision blurred. She just couldn't stop touching him. Obediently, he allowed her to fuss until he'd finished the second glass of water and satisfied his immediate needs.

"May I go back to sleep now, Aunt Emmie?" He yawned again, wide and unabashed, as only children do. "I'm still tired."

She laughed again. "Of course, Christian." He lay back amid the pillows, and she tucked the covers close against his chin the way he liked them. She kissed his brow, lingering to inhale the warm little-boy scent of him. And the mercifully absent waves of heat that had rolled from him until then.

"Your aunt will be right in the next room, sleeping herself, okay, boy-o?"

"Aye, Captain." He yawned again. "G'night."

When his breathing had returned to a deep, even pattern and they both had listened in awe for several minutes, Bryan pulled her, still giddy with relief, into Abby's bedroom. He all but closed the door behind them as Christian drifted in restful sleep once more.

"And now, Miss Wellesley—"

"He's all right. Oh, Bryan, he's all right." Without thought, she looped her arms around his neck and kissed him full on the mouth with her own still parted with laughter, his soft and warm in surprise.

A tremor of shock rippled down his arms and echoed the length of her spine as he closed them around her. The kiss, begun so innocently, deepened into something raw and open and hungry. Totally out of control. A need unleashed, a passion burning bright beneath the concerns that once held it at bay.

He groaned as his tongue slid against hers in a slow, primitive rhythm older than time itself. Pleasure rippled through Emilynne in a hot wave. He tasted so good, felt too good as his broad chest pressed tight against her breasts. All the pain and need—the fears, betrayal, and doubts—rushed from her soul, burned into oblivion by the passion flaming between them.

Nothing mattered but this time, this man and the yearning inside her to somehow heal them both.

He turned with her in his arms and braced them against the wall behind her, sheltering her against his body, pulling her closer and then closer still as his mouth moved over hers in a lazy sensual haze that left her dizzy.

"Emilynne." Her name came rough with need to rasp across her heart. And still he kissed her, deeper, harder—as though he could draw her inside himself and still it would not be enough. His fingers tangled in the buttons of her gown.

She could feel the burgeoning pressure of the desire she roused in him heavy against her belly. The knowledge that she had but to kiss him to produce this wondrous passion was a heady drug as he molded her lips beneath his. Tender, gentle, ardent. And she did not want him to stop.

He released her mouth though his body stayed pressed

to hers and traced her brow, her eyelids with his lips. "Sweet Emilynne, how I want you."

His words shot a spiraling spark of pure fire into her middle, and she shuddered in his arms. He locked his gaze to hers and slid his fingers into her hair, loosening it to fall around her shoulders. "I knew you would be like this, *muirneach*. All fire and passion. All silken softness. More than any man could ask for. But—"

"No, please don't stop." She couldn't bear to have him walk out of her arms a second time.

"Darlin', you don't know what you're asking." Torment fringed his tone.

"Yes, I do." She kissed the edge of his mouth.

"Nay." He groaned as she pressed her mouth to his throat, daring to trace a path over his skin and echo what he had done to her.

"I cannot hold you like this, kiss you, and not want to make love to you." His breath shivered over her cheeks.

She trembled at his honesty. "I know."

"Nay, you do not."

"The garden—" she began, her cheeks flaming at the memory and the unspoken promise of what she had yet to experience.

He chuckled harshly. "The garden was nothing compared to the way I feel right now.

"Tonight." His gaze met hers again, hiding nothing of the intentions burning there. "You would be mine."

"Yes." Emilynne breathed the word, and fire lit Bryan's mind.

"Nay." He swallowed and grit his teeth, holding tight rein on the ungoverned desires riding him like a beast from hell.

Desperately, he held back, gripping the ragged scrap of

sanity that screamed he should not do this. Should not take from her what could be given only once. Certain that for the rest of his life the heated scent of freesia and lemon would drive him out of his mind.

"Make love to me, Bryan." Her words locked the breath in his chest. "Life is too short and too easily lost not to cling to something wondrous when you find it."

"Emilynne." Her name was the only word that made sense as he claimed her mouth again and again. To her, he was something wondrous. The knowledge destroyed both his barriers and control in a instant. He was lost. Tasting her, delving into the depths of her sweetness and knowing she wanted more, wanted all of him.

And he wanted her more than he had ever wanted another woman.

Fractured light and fragmented colors coalesced around them. The lilting strains of a distant harp poured over and through him. The Blessing. Like on the docks but deeper and more vibrant. *The choice once made cannot be undone.* How could he do less than love her when she was already his? *The decision once forged cannot be altered.*

Their fingers met, tangling and stroking and somehow making short work of her bodice, stripping the garment from her and dropping her bulky skirt and petticoats to the floor as well, until she clung to him in naught but sheer, indulgent linen. Slender and soft and womanly. Perfect.

He laced his fingers through hers and drew her arms up over her head, holding them against the wall as he kissed her. Long, slow, thorough, feeling the slight tremor that raced through her as he stoked the fire between them. Tasting her acquiescence as he sipped from her mouth, making leisurely, passionate love to her with his lips and tongue. Their bodies pressed together in a promise of what was yet to come.

She moaned as he braced himself fully against her. He could only echo the sentiment. She felt so soft and yielding, so hot and sensual. With deliberate slowness he kissed and licked and nibbled a pathway over her cheek and throat, dwelling on the pulse point below her ear as she whimpered.

"Aye, love, aye." He continued his slow torment, aching to have her as he tasted the soft skin of her shoulder and nudged aside the fabric of her chemise, coaxing ragged breaths from her as he dipped lower and lower in his quest.

"You are beautiful, *muirneach.*" He breathed the words against her skin. Her breasts, clearly outlined, strained the sheer fabric covering them, her nipples tightened to fine points of desire.

With an exquisite leisure that tortured them both, he pressed featherlike kisses to first one taut crest and then the other.

"Bryan." His name was a plea on her lips.

"Aye?"

"Please." She squirmed in his grasp, her body eager and questing for what she knew he could give her.

A feral growl escaped him. "As you wish."

He released her arms long enough to tug down the straps holding the damned shift in place. The fabric pooled around her waist. She was perfection, rosy-tipped, golden perfection. He pressed the open heat of his mouth over one breast, exulting in the feel and taste of her as well as the shuddering moan of pleasure that racked her slender frame.

He laved her nipple in long, lazy circles and grazed her with his teeth, teasing her, teasing them both with exquisite care—savoring her every tiny gasp and moan and the unfathomable way she made him feel as he held her.

When he transferred his attentions to her other breast, her knees went weak. A husky laugh of pure male triumph escaped him as he scooped her into his arms and carried her toward the bed, his own knees a trifle shaky.

He would never get enough of her, not in a thousand lifetimes. The knowledge blazed through him in a fireball of truth. Whatever his intentions had been when first her lips touched his, now he yearned to make love to her until they were both too weak to protest, too spent in pleasure.

Consequences be damned, she was his, his so completely, he could not imagine that it had not always been so.

Her legs encircled him as his own knees weakened and he sat on the edge of the bed. Sitting in his lap, she slid her fingers into his hair and kissed him with a wild passion hot enough to melt steel and strong enough to make him shudder.

She tugged at his shirt, her hands quickly loosening the buttons until she could part the fabric and run her hands over his chest as he fondled her breasts and teased the delicate softness between her thighs.

Their breaths mingled in the sliver of moonlight that kissed them both as their gazes locked one to the other for a moment, time out of time. An unspoken question, a wordless answer.

When he took her lips again, he knew there was no going back, no stopping this time. She was his and she knew it, nay, welcomed his possession. A muffled knocking somewhere in the distance served only to echo the pounding of his heart.

Cold light splashed onto them from the hallway as the

bedroom door opened. A shocked gasp held them immobile.

"Miss . . . miss." The housekeeper struggled and stuttered. "Miss Wellesley." Shocked dismay accented each syllable of Emilynne's name with clipped precision.

Chapter Fourteen

Emilynne shivered, unable to deny any recriminations Mrs. Bennett wished to heap on her as the gaslight flickered over her, clearly highlighting her intimate position in Bryan's lap. Guilt washed over her in violent waves.

In a quick swirl Bryan covered her nakedness with his shirt, still warm from his body. Somehow that only heightened their predicament.

"Did you need something, Mrs. Bennett?" Bryan's question came in a normal tone of voice, completely out of place with the whole situation. Emilynne stifled a hysterical desire to laugh.

"Miss." The housekeeper drew herself to her full height, managing to look dignified despite the late hour and the sight that had greeted her. She turned on her heel, taking her candle with her without another word and disappeared back down the hallway, tempting Emilynne to believe it was all a hallucination.

But it wasn't. And neither was her state of undress. Or Bryan's. Or the very real heat of him still throbbing intimately against her. There couldn't have been any doubt in Mrs. Bennett's mind what they were about. None. And that only made matters worse.

With an effort Emilynne met Bryan's gaze, her own blurred with tears she couldn't shrug away. Certainly she would find at least some measure of disrespect gleaming there as well. What had seemed so right, so undeniable just a few moments before, was now blackened by the knowledge and condemnation in the housekeeper's eyes.

Worse still would come. Emilynne was quite certain the woman would tell Richard everything. She squirmed in Bryan's lap.

"Oh, Bryan—"

"Hush, *muirneach*." He cupped her face in the warmth of his hands, stilling her frantic movements with his touch. "I would not take back the last few moments between us for anything."

His gentleness served only to coax the tears she'd been holding back to spill over his fingers. He kissed her then, a soft, yielding kiss of such exquisite tenderness, her heart broke anew.

"It will be all right." He pressed her cheek to his shoulder and rocked her against him as the sobs she just couldn't hold back shook over her.

She had surely run the gauntlet of emotion this night. Between Christian's bedside and Bryan's arms, her mind and heart spun in a million directions. Gradually, her own weariness took its toll and offered a small measure of quiet. It felt good to be held and to convince herself, even if only for a few moments, that all would be well.

"Things will be difficult in the morning," she offered

in a watery tone against his neck. She hadn't the strength to move from the shelter of his arms.

"Aye, they will be that, lass." A short rumble of laughter shook his chest and he pressed a kiss into her hair. "But it will still be all right. I'll make certain of it."

She drifted away with his words a hazy comfort in her mind.

Bryan held Emilynne for a long time after she had fallen asleep.

It was not the first time he'd offered his body to serve a woman's comfort, but it was certainly the first time he'd rocked one to sleep like a babe. His own body ached with the pain of unfulfilled lust. Not the first time for that either. And with Emilynne Wellesley, he was beginning to suspect, this was just the beginning.

She shifted in her sleep, and his shirt dipped low across the upper swells of her breasts. She was too soft and warm and womanly. He groaned, silently enduring the ultimate torment of holding the woman he desired in his arms and being unable to do anything about it.

He shifted position to ease her onto the bed, best to let her have a peaceful sleep while she was still able. The morrow would be more than difficult. She whimpered a protest as her warm, bared flesh came in contact with the cool bed linens, curling her fingers around his neck. Holding on to him even in her sleep.

He sighed and settled her, half on the bed and half atop him as he reclined against the pillows. It would be a long night, and yet for all the trials they would face in the morning, one thing stood clear in his mind. What was done was done, even though it was not well and truly completed. A riddle that held the answer. He already knew what course to steer to bring them through the muddle he had created in their lives.

And though it promised to tangle them more tightly together than before, he couldn't help but smile as it brought him a modicum of peace. Once Andrews was dealt with, there would still be Thaddeus Whyte to face.

Only now they would face him together.

Emilynne woke with a start. Bright daylight stretched across the floor. It was late and her head felt foggy. Why had she slept so long? And what room was she in?

In a rush it came back to her. Christian was well and she and Bryan . . . She caught back a gasp as she realized the warm, hard pillow she was intimately snuggled against was not a pillow at all, but a far too real Bryan Reilly. In the bed with her.

She pressed her knuckles across her lips and shuddered as he reflexively cupped her bared breast in his sleep, branding her with the heat of his fingers. Should she wake him?

Lazily, his hand molded and caressed her breast. Low fire warmed her belly despite the difficulties they had yet to face.

"Bryan." His name whispered out of her mouth in a husky tone she didn't recognize. She cleared her throat as her nipple pebbled against his palm and tried again. "Bryan, you must wake up."

He rolled toward her, not quite asleep but not yet awake. His hand became more purposeful at her breast, teasing her taut nipple as his lips nuzzled her throat. The fire in her belly burned hotter, threatening to consume whatever rational thoughts she still laid claim to. She struggled against the passion welling so easily at his touch as his other hand swept the bared length of her back to stroke her buttocks.

"Emilynne." Longing enveloped her name as it came from his lips.

Her cheeks flamed as he pulled her beneath him.

"Captain." She forced a little of the heat bursting inside her into her tone. "Please wake up."

A low chuckle was her answer. She looked up to find herself locked within the sleepy dark green confines of his gaze. "Ah, better than a dream, for it is reality I hold in my arms. Good morning, *muirneach.*"

She squirmed as the husky timbre of his voice cascaded through her. He groaned softly and she went still.

"You'd best be careful, my love, or we will be fully occupied should someone come to the door once again."

She gaped at him, uncertain if his words were mere teasing or a threat, and unable to find humor in the current situation. She could not wholly blame him for the position she now found herself in. She had begun the episode last night by flinging herself into his arms and igniting the banked fire sleeping in them both.

"Things are bad enough already. Please do not make them worse."

"From my position, darlin', they'd not be worse." He pressed an irreverent kiss to the tip of her nose, then snatched another from her lips.

She tried in vain to ignore the way his touch made her feel. Even the taste of his breath on her tongue caused lazy spirals in her middle. And this could not be. Not in the bright light of day. Not with the impending doom hanging over her head. Not with the children at stake. And next door.

"Don't worry, Emilynne." The teasing note vanished from his tone as if he'd read of her thoughts.

"I have to—"

"We'll handle this together." He levered himself off the bed, leaving her grateful for the meager covering of a sheet and unconscionably bereft without the pressure of his big, warm body against hers.

What did he mean by that statement?

"Bryan?"

"I suggest you get dressed." With that, he quit the room barechested before she could question him further.

Handle what together? Her need to check on Christian? Her complete lack of morals? Her confession to Richard?

She was not looking forward to the discussion she was bound to have with her intended husband. She could only hope that Richard would be able to somehow look beyond the emotionality of the moment, remember he was Robert's friend, and still help her with the children.

And now that Christian was on the road to recovery, where did that leave Bryan? On the road back to Limerick and his legal practice? Or would he go in search of other financial backing for Reilly Ship Works? And what would become of the hole he would indelibly leave in her life?

She pushed from the bed and began a search for her discarded bits of clothing, scattered in mute testimony to the passion she'd shared with her handsome solicitor only a few hours before.

Her cheeks burned hotter with each garment she retrieved from the floor, the foot of the bed, and amid the tangled bedding. How on earth could she possibly explain any of this to Richard? Or to Mrs. Bennett? Or to herself, for that matter? Thank heaven she didn't have to

explain it to her brother as well. She shuddered to think
what either he or Gail would have said.

She splashed cold water from the basin over her hot
cheeks and forced herself to dress, reaching deep inside for
the bravado that had always been there when she needed
it. She had demanded to study alongside her brother,
published her research and findings for all the world to
see, and smuggled her niece and nephew out of Ireland
beneath the very nose of one of the most influential men
on the island.

She'd made it this far, and she could endure this confrontation as well. After all, whatever Richard had to say
couldn't possibly be worse than the time she had spent
with Thaddeus Whyte or her very real fear that he would
somehow gain control of the children once again.

That must remain her main focus. Not a life together
with Richard, nor unconsummated passion with Bryan, not
reclaiming her own pursuits, but safety for the children.
Surely even Richard would be able to see that far, wouldn't
he?

After she'd fussed with her hair, she couldn't linger in
the bedroom anymore. "Come on, Emilynne, face him
and be done with it."

She gripped her hands together and left the room, closing the door silently behind her. The hallway was deserted.
Her first priority remained the children. It was not coward-
ice that prompted her to check on them. At this hour it
was long past time for them to have eaten and started their
day. Christian was obviously feeling much better, because
his room was empty when she peeked into it. A relief and
a concern at the same time.

She made her way down the stairs and met Stephens at

the bottom. "Have you seen the children, Stephens?" she asked him when he finally deigned to look at her.

"I suggest you ask Mrs. Bennett, Miss Wellesley," he sniffed, and continued on his way.

She spied Mrs. Bennett just leaving the front room.

"Miss Wellesley." The woman's tone, once almost supportive, was cool and distant with displeasure, laying to rest any remote hopes Emilynne might have harbored that she had not told Richard.

Emilynne lifted her chin. "Good morning, Mrs. Bennett."

"Mr. Andrews is waiting to see you in the front salon."

That felt like an order.

"Indeed. Where are the children?"

Mrs. Bennett gave her a frosty stare that fairly screamed the children were none of her concern.

Emilynne swallowed back a tremor of fear and held her ground, determined to wring an answer to her question if only by her silence.

"They're in the back garden with Kate. The fresh air will do Master Christian some good. Mr. Andrews thought it best they not be in the house when he interviewed you."

Emilynne nodded, unsettled further by this information but determined not to let the housekeeper see how rattled she was. She took a deep breath, resisted patting her hair one more time, and opened the door to the salon.

"Good morning, Richard."

"Good morning, Emilynne. I trust you slept well." There was nothing in his tone to indicate his mood, but she couldn't stop the hot color from creeping into her face. He came toward her, took her hands, and just barely brushed her cheek with his lips.

No sense waiting. "Yes, Richard. I—"

"I've missed you, did you know that?" Richard interrupted her, his tone musing and distant. "Always expected that someday our two families would join. You and I, commingling two very proper bloodlines and prospering from there."

"Richard—"

"Of course there were always things about you that would have to change." He gave her a cold little smile. "That disreputable habit of studying things a woman has no business being interested in, for one. How your father ever agreed to your education is a complete mystery to me."

His statement made her catch her breath.

"And Robert?" He shook his head and took a tiny step backward. "I cannot count how many times I tried to convince him to put his foot down and force you to behave properly, according to your sex. Any female children the two of us might have produced would lead far more decorous and ladylike lives. I can assure you of that."

A touch of anger began to burn behind Emilynne's determination to be humble. Such a life as he was suggesting would be abhorrent to her. Didn't he know that?

"I'm sorry you feel that way."

"Are you?" As he came closer again, she could see his cool disbelief gleaming in his eyes. "Are you really? Is that why you chose to make a mockery of our engagement? The very engagement that you proposed when you reached my doorstep. What a mockery you made of the honor I was willing to bestow on you. Arriving with your paramour in tow."

"He is not my paramour." She didn't think her cheeks could possibly get any hotter than they were just then. "We have never been lovers."

"Do you mean to tell me that Mrs. Bennett is prevaricating in following her duty to me? That you did not take this man, Reilly, to your bed?"

"I . . . I . . ." What could she say to that question? She had, hadn't she? And she felt guilty of the very actions he was accusing her of despite the fact they had not come to fruition. Her cheeks heated.

"You betray yourself, as well as me, too easily. Things will definitely be changing around here, Emilynne," he continued without giving her time to formulate a response.

"What do you mean?"

"I'll not allow Robert's children to suffer the same spurious fate you now face. And, although it pains me greatly, I am willing to marry you in spite of what you did last night in an effort to fulfill the spirit of the role Robert wished me to undertake."

"You are?" It was too much to take in.

"Yes, your brother Robert was the best friend I had in the world. One of the reasons I intended to marry you was out of respect and friendship for Robert. He seemed to feel that you would eventually find your way, but I fear he was wrong in this instance. I always knew that studying like a man could only do you damage. And now you have proven me right."

Suddenly it made sense. Richard was ready to marry her because he believed her actions had proven the perfection of his own intellect. How could she have ever thought she would be able to adjust to life with him?

"I do not know what to say."

"Em, I'm willing to forgive you. To help you through this." Richard touched her cheek, his fingers cool against her hot skin. "It's time to face the truth."

"And what truth might that be?"

Emilynne jumped as Bryan entered the room.

Richard's frown seemed enough to freeze fire.

Bryan ignored both reactions as he came toward her. "Good morning to you both."

He smiled at Richard, and Emilynne smothered a groan, certain she could cheerfully strangle him for appearing at just that moment.

"Bryan, I—" Emilynne began.

"We were discussing her indiscretions of the previous evening." Richard's cool tone grew frostier still.

"Richard," she tried again.

"Actually that would be *our* indiscretions, wouldn't you say?" Bryan sounded amused.

Emilynne wanted to crawl into the nearest hole and stay there.

"Emilynne." Crisp command now from Richard in a tone that made her blink in surprise. "Perhaps it would be best if you went back to your room. You do not need to be present for any discussion between Mr. Reilly and myself."

"Richard, I am so sorry."

"I'm glad to hear that, my dear." His features softened just a trifle as he sent her a glance. "We'll continue this later."

"No, you don't understand—"

"She's not going anywhere, Andrews, and you'd best get used to the idea."

She groaned aloud, and both men looked at her. "Neither one of you seems willing to let me get a word into this conversation."

A moment of silence passed.

"You have the floor, Emilynne." Bryan crossed his arms over his chest and raised an eyebrow at her.

"Richard, I am very sorry things are turning out far from what you had hoped for. And I am grateful for your kindness, but—"

A knock at the door interrupted her, followed by Stephens's voice as he opened the door a trifle. "Excuse me, sir. There are some men outside from Bristol. They said you were expecting them."

Bristol? The word sent a peal of fear through Emilynne. Her glance collided with Bryan's as she prayed the men had no connection to Thaddeus.

"Show them in, Stephens."

"What men?" Emilynne barely held the question back until the door had shut behind the butler.

"Who are these men, Andrews?" Bryan's query came close behind hers.

"I did some of my own checking to ascertain the truth of your story."

"You what?" She could only gape at him.

He gave her an unruffled glance. "Em, look at it from my point of view. You landed on my doorstep with a hysterical story of violence and mayhem. Did you expect me to swallow that whole without even trying to find out all I could?"

"No." Anger underscored Bryan's answer. "She expected you to be someone she could trust. A friend who would care for her and the children, first."

"Indeed." Richard raised his eyebrows. "And I expect the woman I plan to marry to remain true and virtuous to me and not flaunt her lover in my face. The fact that you coupled with her under my very roof shows how little breeding you have and how gullible she is. Of course I would need to ascertain the truth of her story."

"This way, gentlemen." Stephens appeared in the doorway.

"Ah, Mr. Andrews, how kind of you to invite us in."

That voice. A cold shock of panic knifed Emilynne, and the room seemed to tilt out of control. She swayed and clutched at the back of the sofa as Thaddeus Whyte advanced into the room, dispelling all the safety and distance she thought she had achieved. After all the running. It was like a bad dream.

Behind Thaddeus came a man she recognized from Blue Hills and a man who looked to be Willard Jefferies's son, Willard, Jr. How could that be?.

"Bryan." His name barely escaped her.

"And Emilynne. You are looking a tad pinched." Thaddeus came toward her with a false smile twisting his handsome features. "I have been so worried about you and those dear little ones."

As he reached for her hand, her skin crawled with revulsion. For a moment she couldn't breathe. She pulled back, but he managed to trap her hand in his anyway. The smile he gave her as he touched her iced her blood. "How are you, my dear? I was quite put out with you, leaving as you did without so much as a word."

He managed to sound concerned and just a bit chiding, as though she ought to know better than to upset him that way. "I had Wilkins scouring the countryside for you."

Wilkins, the man she'd seen at Blue Hills discussing her brother's carriage accident with Thaddeus, tipped his hat. Willard, Jr., held a small sneer at the corner of his mouth as he looked her over.

Thaddeus released her only when Bryan moved to her side. The warmth of Bryan's hand at the small of her back was like a lifeline. She clung to the slender hope he seemed to offer, determined not to show weakness in the face of the enemy.

"I don't know you, sir." Thaddeus bowed cordially, his eyes as sharp as a ferret's.

"Bryan Reilly."

"From O'Brien and Mallory." Thaddeus nodded, looking pleased. "A pleasure to meet you as well, Mr. Reilly. Your senior partner, Gill O'Brien, assured me you would help in any way possible in this matter. I'd no idea you would be here waiting for me when I arrived. I am most pleased."

"Indeed?" Bryan's cool tone managed to sound polite and skeptical at the same time.

"Of course one would hope that would not be necessary. After all, it is fairly clear by now that the children must be my responsibility."

"Never." Emilynne couldn't stop herself. The word came out laced with venom. "You will never have my children."

"Emilynne." Displeasure dripped in Richard's tone. She was upsetting his little gathering.

Thaddeus offered a small moue of distaste. "My dear, they are hardly *your* children. I had hoped that this flighty dash across the water would have exhausted your ridiculous fears, but it appears that is not the case. If anything, you are more confused than before. Such a pity."

As though signaled, Willard, Jr., spoke for the first time. "A difficult situation, I'll warrant, when Miss Wellesley is obviously unwilling or unable to face the truth. This can happen in times of severe stress, particularly to females who are high strung in nature."

"High strung?" Emilynne barely held her anger in check as pain throbbed in her temples. The whole situation was unreal. "He murdered my brother and my sister-in-law. If that is severe stress, then yes, I am definitely under it."

"There, you see." Willard, Jr., transferred his raised eyebrows to Richard. "I was told this was her attitude. I understand she's led a very sheltered existence and really has not had much experience outside the world of story-books."

Storybooks. He made her sound like an inept child. And Richard was actually nodding his head in agreement.

"As the children's uncle," Williard, Jr., continued. "Mr. Whyte's claim to them holds true. Mr. Whyte is even willing to overlook Miss Wellesley's recent transgressions and welcome her back into his home along with the children. He understands the need for a close family and applauds Miss Wellesley's loving, if misguided, heart."

"That is, unless the two of you have reached the understanding I know both Robert and Gail so fervently wished for her sake." Thaddeus flattered Richard with an ingratiating smile. "In which case you may visit the children as often as you like."

"No." Dizziness hovered at the edge of Emilynne's range of vision, and she clung harder to the back of the sofa as Bryan's hand squeezed her waist. He was waiting for something, though heaven knew what, and she could only pray he had some idea, some legal trick to pull out of his bag. At this point she'd agree to anything to stop this farce from going any further.

"Why, Em"—Richard sounded relieved—"perhaps this would be the right thing for all of us, given our current circumstances."

"No." The word trembled out of her as she clung to her anger as a means of support. "We cannot accept this, Richard. Regardless of what you may think of me, we cannot send the children back to Thaddeus. He will murder them. He would have killed me along with Robert and Gail if I had not had other plans that day."

"Miss Wellesley," Willard, Jr., protested. "You really have no other choice. Your brother's will, if it ever existed, has not been properly executed. Mr. Whyte has legal documentation granting him both the right to take the children and to have you arrested.

She refused to wilt.

"Emilynne." Thaddeus managed to look more hurt than offended. She had to struggle to keep from screaming.

"You forget that Gail was my beloved niece and ward," he prosed on. "I raised her after the death of her parents. No one could have been more destroyed by her death. I seek now to gift her children with the same love and devotion I always showed Gail. They are all I have left of her."

"That seems most reasonable." Richard nodded, sending Emilynne a glance that plainly revealed his conviction that she had been hysterical and out of her senses since she arrived.

The very earth beneath her feet seemed to have turned to quicksand, miring her ever deeper in Thaddeus Whyte's well-laid plans.

"Excellent, Mr. Andrews. I cannot tell you what a help this is. We shall retrieve the children and be on our way."

"Somehow I doubt that." Bryan's words cut through the rising anticipation in the salon and drew the gaze of the other men.

"Mr. Reilly?"

"The children will not be going anywhere unless they go with their aunt and me."

"Please remember that your firm supports Mr. Whyte's endeavors."

"Indeed. Reilly, you go too far. Again." Richard narrowed his gaze. "Under the circumstances, I doubt you have any say whatsoever regarding the outcome."

"I'm afraid I do, and it supersedes any jurisdiction or dictates from O'Brien and Mallory."

"And just what might that be?" Richard didn't bother to hide his sarcasm or his irritation.

Emilynne said a quick and fervent prayer that whatever he had to say would be enough.

"In accordance with her brother's wishes, Emilynne has the right to take the children anywhere she wishes at any time. There is nothing anyone can say to stop her. She is their sole guardian as set forth by the duly witnessed will and testament of Robert Wellesley."

"But—," Willard, Jr., tried again.

"And I share that responsibility," Bryan continued, allowing no one to stop him. "Because she is my wife."

Chapter Fifteen

Emilynne swayed as Bryan's bold declaration achieved the effect he hoped for. His words seemed to echo through the suddenly quiet salon from the cream-colored walls to the long, stately windows. He slid his hand to Emilynne's arm and tightened his fingers at her elbow, willing her to stay on her feet and praying she would follow his lead.

"Preposterous," Andrews scoffed after finding his voice.

"That is not possible." This from Whyte's man.

"She is my wife," Bryan stated again, using the successful courtroom tone Gill O'Brien had trained him for. As always, he enjoyed every moment of the unsettled looks on his opponents' faces. "We were married weeks ago, according to ancient Brehon Law."

"What are you talking about?" This from Andrews, who was eyeing Bryan as if he were a rare and disgusting species of insect.

"What trickery are you trying to pull here, Reilly? The interests of your firm—"

"Do not supersede the interests of my family." Bryan cut off Whyte's blustering and pulled Emilynne closer. The intensity of his own words lodged securely in his chest like a pledge, undeniable and more powerful than he ever expected.

"I apologize for any inconvenience this causes you, gentlemen," he continued. "Had you communicated with me first, I could have saved you the trouble of coming all this way for nothing."

"Not for nothing. For Mr. Whyte's wards." The little weasel he recognized from Jefferies's Bristol law office glared at Bryan with a gleam of triumph.

"The Wellesley children are not his wards. Robert Wellesley's will clearly states that the children should be in the sole guardianship of his sister, Emilynne, and her husband."

"There was no will," the weasel snarled, but there was a touch less bite to his tone. "We have in our possession letters of writ giving Mr. Whyte sole charge of the children. You cannot discount them with your fictitious will."

Worried, are you? Bryan bit back a laugh. Gill always said the best defense was good research, obviously a stratagem this scrawny little fellow was unfamiliar with.

"Robert Wellesley's will is far from fictitious. You have only to check with the head of your own firm to verify its existence and validity. I'm sure Willard Jefferies will be very interested to know you are acting in direct opposition to the lawful will and testament drawn for one of his best clients."

"Mr. Jefferies—"

"You cannot be her husband." Whyte's eyes narrowed a bit as he cut off his own minion.

"I am."

"Emilynne, deny this ridiculous sham." Andrews's tone held equal parts cajolery and disgust, his face a perfect pasty match for his fashionable dove-gray trousers and cream-colored waistcoat.

Bryan held his breath. Under the ancient cadre of laws passed down by the Brehon, she had only to deny him publicly and their tenuous marriage would dissolve along with any hope of saving the children from Thaddeus Whyte's determined clutches. Not to mention, saving her from whatever penalty the Irish courts might impose for her flight from their jurisdiction. There was no way to communicate this to her except through the urgent pressure of his fingers.

"I am sorry, Richard, I cannot," she answered after a moment.

"Under what circumstances do you claim this Brehon marriage?" The little weasel stepped forward.

"It was publicly declared and acknowledged on Limerick's docks. My crew will stand as witnesses." Bryan smiled. "Since then we have lived publicly as man and wife before numerous witnesses."

"And the consummation of this marriage?" The little weasel was beginning to annoy him.

"Is none of you affair," Bryan stated before Emilynne could answer.

"I beg to differ, Mr. Reilly." The weasel had gumption, Bryan had to give him that as he chewed this bone. "But as a solicitor yourself you will understand that this point must be verified. To claim the matter publicly is one thing, but let us not forget that Brehon Laws are merely tolerated by modern British statutes. You cannot divorce the one from the other, nor can you expect any reasonable British citizen to do any less."

Whyte's weasel demonstrated the reason he had been recruited to engage in Thaddeus Whyte's business in the first place.

Bryan shrugged, forcing himself to remain nonchalant. "What exists between myself and my wife is no one's business but our own."

"Perhaps you would like to answer these questions before a magistrate?"

"That is not necessary." Emilynne spoke with more fire than her trembling led him to expect. "My husband came to my bed last night. Right here in this house."

Her cheeks flamed a brilliant rosy hue as she lifted her chin and faced them. "You have only to question Richard's housekeeper to discover the truth. She walked in on us while we were together."

Andrews paled still further and narrowed his eyes at her pronouncement. "Then why did you appear on my doorstep and all but beg me to marry you?"

Bryan held himself in check with an effort, hoping Emilynne's quick intake of breath had been audible to him alone. He could cheerfully have driven his fist through Andrews's indignant face.

Repeatedly.

"A ruse, old man." Bryan forced a relaxed chuckle he did not feel. "Sorry we couldn't let you in on the deception, but it was necessary for us to spend a few days close to Newbury Manor without anyone suspecting we were nearby. Any copy of Robert's will that he had retained there needed to be located."

Andrews stiffened at his explanation, and Bryan continued his attack. "As you can see, Whyte's trained dogs managed to sniff us out anyway."

Andrews offered him a glare clearly designed to slice him in two.

"Then, you maintain this?" The weasel again.

"Aye."

"And are you willing to come back to Ireland and declare this in court?" Thaddeus's other trained mutt spoke.

"Bryan." Emilynne's voice broke over his name, her fears threatening to call a halt to the whole procedure. Her hand slipped into his and he laced their fingers together as tightly as their fates, feeling her mounting trepidation in the cool dampness of her palm.

Going anywhere near Thaddeus's sphere of influence after her struggle to get away must feel like losing the battle before it had truly begun.

He could only hope she would continue to trust him because there was no escaping the certainty this would be the best—the only successful—way to handle the situation in the long run. To put an end to Thaddeus's legal control over the children and Blue Hills. And in the process they just might be able to do something about the crimes the man had committed against the Wellesley family.

"Aye, we are prepared to do just that."

"Emilynne?"

"You can put an end to this, Miss Wellesley." The weasel tightened his thin brows and gave her a stern look. "I worked closely with your brother. I'm certain he wouldn't have wanted your entry into this ill-advised misalliance."

Emilynne's hand tensed against Bryan's at the reference to her brother. She turned her gaze to his and searched his soul in silence for a few brief moments. In her eyes he read fearful hope and a tenuous trust he dared not break.

He gave her the slightest nod he could and tried to let her read the honesty of his own intentions.

"You should address me as Mrs. Reilly now, Junior. A name I am proud to bear. I believe I know best what my brother's intentions were. Pray do not speak for him again. Does your father have any idea the depths to which your own intentions have sunk?"

The weasel was Willard Jefferies's son, Willard, Jr? No wonder files and papers had been so easily misplaced. No wonder Willard, Sr., had been so disturbed by the perfidy from within. Bryan groaned inwardly but remained certain the senior Jefferies had not been complicitious in this matter.

Emilynne nodded to the semicircle of men awaiting her answer, her head held high and defiant. "As my husband said, gentlemen. We will return to Ireland and allow the courts to settle this once and for all."

Whyte did not so much as bat an eyelash at the thwarting of his plans. He had surely come to England and to Hampton House with the intention of spiriting the children away with a minimum of fuss. The true current of his objectives must run deep indeed, hidden to all but himself.

The weasely Willard, on the other hand, looked ready to throw an apoplectic fit. "You will release the children at once. Mr. Whyte cannot be expected to travel without his wards in his custody until this matter is legally settled."

"I think not." Bryan relaxed and pulled Emilynne into the crook of his arm, never taking his eyes from Thaddeus Whyte's face.

"You must concede this point."

"I suggest we all travel together." Whyte's quiet tone stopped Willard, Jr.'s, wordy posturing in mid-breath.

"Safety in numbers, as they say. And, after all, we are family."

Emilynne shuddered within the confines of Bryan's arm. He brushed her fingers with his own.

"Very well. We shall travel to Dublin together. I should have a ship waiting in Bristol harbor." Bryan smiled. "The *Caithream* is one of my family's finest vessels. You could not be in safer hands."

"Ah, yes, you're connected to the famed Reilly Ship Works." After a moment of silence Thaddeus returned Bryan's smile with a small upward arch of one brow. "Pity the recent financial downturn to your family business. Any truth to the rumor the owner has fled his creditors and is hiding out on the Continent?"

A surge of anger nearly shook Bryan's nonchalant mask. Emilynne's fingers tightened on his, but he was sure no one else heard her hushed breath at the backhanded insult Whyte had just delivered.

He forced his stance to remain casual. Too much lay at stake to allow this wily bastard to draw him out. "No truth whatsoever. My brother has the shipyard well in hand while my parents enjoy a well-deserved rest. A man such as your-self should know better than to pass such rumors without verifying them."

"Indeed." Whyte nodded. "This should prove an inter-esting voyage. Wilkins, make our carriage team ready. We've a long way to go."

"Aye, Mr. Whyte." The younger man disappeared into the foyer.

"Mr. Andrews." Whyte's cool demeanor was back in place. "I still offer you my sincerest thanks. Without you my men would yet be desperately searching for the chil-dren and Emilynne."

Bryan might have guessed Andrews had revealed their whereabouts. Mayhap if he had worked harder to overcome the animosity he'd felt when they arrived, he could have emphasized the need for their host's discretion. The man might be an ass, but even Bryan believed he would not deliberately place Emilynne in harm's way. If not for her sake alone, for her brother's friendship.

"I'm sorry things have proved so complicated." Andrews had the grace to look uncomfortable over this revelation. "Your missive certainly conveyed your urgent concern over the welfare of all parties involved."

"Indeed." Whyte smiled again. "Perhaps we could avail ourselves of your hospitality for a few moments before we depart? It has been a long ride already."

"Of course." Andrews's pale skin colored as the fact that he had allowed a guest in his home to go without came home to him under Whyte's prodding. "Please come right this way, gentlemen. I'll have something light prepared for you."

He rang for Mrs. Bennett as he shepherded Thaddeus and his weasel out of the salon.

"You'll wait your departure for us, of course." Whyte didn't bother to turn as he exited the salon.

"Of course." Bryan watched him until the door closed behind the three men.

"Bryan—"

"Shhh." He placed a finger over Emilynne's soft lips, unwilling to let even a hint of her true fears free anywhere a man of Thaddeus Whyte's formidable talents might latch on to them.

"You did well, Emilynne." He smiled at her, trying to lighten the tense atmosphere still lingering in the salon.

"Married?" she managed to whisper around his finger.

He couldn't contain a chuckle at the consternation on her features. "Aye, my sweet lass, it is the only option I could think of to protect the children and save your reputation in the process."

"What is this Brehon Law? And when were we wed by it? How can we protect Abby and Christian now that we have agreed to return them to Ireland? Must we go through with this?" She peppered him with her whispered concerns.

"By calling me husband when you first entered my arms on the docks in Limerick, both our lives turned upside down with that single kiss. If a copy of your brother's will can't be located, Mr. Jefferies can at least testify to his intentions." He answered her questions in the order they'd been presented.

"Returning willingly, as a couple who have nothing to hide and who hold the law as on our side, is far preferable to being dragged there in chains," he concluded, and tried to give an encouraging smile.

Her cheeks grew paler as she closed her eyes and swayed forward. He pulled his new wife against his shoulder for support. *Wife.* He could barely absorb the idea himself as he tried to soothe her palpable anxiety.

"I've more than enough experience with the magistrates in and around Limerick and Dublin to be able to hold my own through any courtroom maneuverings. The Brehon Laws, though ancient, are still respected and upheld in my country. We'll not be the first such marriage to pass through the system, and we'll not be the last. It is the best hope the children have."

"It seems an awful chance to take with their lives. I don't want them anywhere near Thaddeus, let alone traveling the countryside with him. And when Willard, Jr., suggested

Thaddeus take immediate custody . . ." She shuddered, and he tightened his arms around her.

"But he didn't take them, Emilynne. We've already won that battle." Lemon and freesia wafted from her hair to mingle with his resolve to protect her, to protect the children she loved at all costs.

"Isn't there some way we could settle this here in England? Must we go back to Ireland?" The hopeful tremble in her voice betrayed the strain of her struggle to keep her fears in check.

He cupped her face in his hand and pressed a gentle kiss to her lips, resisting the urge to deepen the caress. "Emilynne, if we fight here and now, our chances of winning will be much worse. Whyte is English. He may have lived in Ireland for the past thirty years, but he is an Englishman to the core. If we fight on English soil, he will win."

"But I am English too."

"Aye, but you are a woman who dragged her niece and nephew away from a secure environment and thrust them into uncertainty. Declaring our marriage is risky enough back home, but it will at least even our odds. Here, it could be used as further evidence of instability."

"No." She pulled out of his arms to face him.

"That's how it will look to the courts here." He needed her to be completely behind this defense, to realize it remained her only option.

"It is how it will look to an English magistrate. To any English-minded soul we come across, even Robert's friends. You have only to sample your friend Richard's reaction to see how quickly they will flock to Whyte's line of thinking. We'd be very unlikely to hold up any kind of marriage under that strain, and the ancient Brehon Laws will not be an arguable option, they will be a mockery."

"So we must?"

"Aye, Mrs. Reilly. Trust me. You are my family now. I will not let you down."

Doubt edged the glance she gave him; then she lowered her gaze and studied her fingers clasped together in front of her.

"Would you have brought up this matter of the Brehon marriage if Thaddeus had not arrived today?" The look of stark anxiety she shot him after forcing this whispered question told Bryan how desperately she needed him to answer correctly.

"If your affections were truly engaged to Andrews, I might not have thought about it at all," he told her truthfully.

He lifted her chin and caressed her cheek with the pad of his thumb. "But your heart does not belong here, and Whyte's arrival before Jefferies could come through forced my hand. This is the best chance you have of retaining your niece and nephew."

"But what of you?"

"I gain a lovely and desirable wife and a ready-made family. We'll sort the rest out later."

She searched his face for a moment, looking intently at each feature as if the set of his brow or the firmness of his chin could tell her what she needed in order to believe him. Finally, she nodded, a brisk gesture.

"I guess I had better ready the children." She sighed and pressed his hand. "Thank you, Bryan. You did not have to put yourself out for me. And yet you have done so since the moment I met you."

"I could do nothing less."

The Reilly Blessing demanded it so. Someday, he would have to tell her about Granny's legends. *The course once set cannot be altered.* Someday, when the matter at hand was resolved and he could speak freely to her about their future.

She pressed a small kiss to his cheek in answer to words that rang from his heart. With a grim smile she left him standing where he was and departed the salon.

He watched the determined swish of her skirts as she went in search of her two young chicks. Somewhere along the way Miss Emilynne Wellesley had welded herself deep within his heart. He wondered how long it would take her to realize that, once proven, their Brehon marriage would be as legal and binding as any accomplished in a church.

"Good-bye, Richard." Emilynne held out her hand, determined to remain cordial for the sake of all his years as Robert's friend, if nothing else.

And truly, after the way she had landed on his doorstep and behaved throughout her stay, she could not blame him for any lingering feelings of ill use he might harbor.

"Em." Richard took her hand. "I hope this all turns out to the good."

She supposed that was the closest he could bring himself to any show of support. But for Richard it was a grand admission. He must be feeling some twinges over his promises to his old friend.

He pressed a thick envelope into her hands. "I wish you

would have confided more to me upon your arrival. And I suppose it is a little late to offer my felicitations."

Thaddeus and his helpers appeared on the stoop behind Richard and she couldn't stand there any longer. His packet of money was the last thing she needed, but in his own way it was probably the only help he could think of to offer. She'd see it returned once everything was resolved.

"Thank you, Richard." She brushed his cheek with her lips and hurried toward the carriage. Before she could step into it, Thaddeus appeared at her elbow. Cold pierced her stomach, straight from the icy depths of his gaze.

"My dear, let me offer you a friendly hand."

His words doubly chilled her. She froze, unable to continue into the carriage or back away from him as he grabbed her arm. "You've shown far more spunk than I ever expected from such a bookish miss. Your pet solicitor just might prove amusing, Emilynne. His claims regarding your marriage are a nice touch. I congratulate you."

He leaned close enough that the fumes of Richard's brandy on his breath wafted over her. "Nonetheless, you only delay matters. I've been patient, and more than understanding regarding the confusion your grief caused you. But I'll not wait much longer. It would be wise of you, and expedient for all, if you reconsidered your position."

Darkness edged her vision as fear closed in on her.

"Let go." She struggled to free her arm from his grasp.

"This could be a minor problem between the two of us, Emilynne. Easily resolved for the sake of those dear little ones. I'd hate for you or your new husband to experience just how precipitous accidents can be in the godforsaken hell that is the Irish countryside."

"I believe yours is the other carriage." Bryan tipped his

hat politely, though his tone caused Thaddeus to release his tight grip of her arm immediately.

"Indeed?" The silky manner was back in Thaddeus's voice. "I was only being solicitous of Emilynne's welfare. Do have a care stepping into the carriage, my dear. I wouldn't want any accidents to delay our trip."

"I can assure you, Mr. Whyte, I won't allow any harm to befall my wife."

Emilynne couldn't suppress her shudder and bit her lip as Thaddeus's gaze flicked over them both before he strode away. This all felt so wrong, so impossible. Going back could not be a good idea. She was trusting the children's futures, all their futures, to some ancient laws she was not even familiar with.

Yet, Bryan was the only part of this that did feel right and good or solid. If anyone could bring them through this, it would be Bryan Reilly. He was the only one left in her world she dared trust.

Her husband handed her into the carriage. She lifted her skirts as Abby and Christian settled themselves in the carriage with Bryan's help. To look at Christian, you'd never know he'd just recovered from his fever. Still, Emilynne hesitated about dragging him on another voyage so soon.

"The sea air will do him good."

She glanced up to see Bryan had followed the direction of her gaze and her concern.

"Mrs. Bennett said Nanny Stewart's comin' too," Christian piped up. "Is she nice? I don't 'member her."

"Of course you do, you silly goose." Abby favored her brother with a look of utter scorn. "She took care of us at home ever since we were babies.

The child turned her serious gaze up to the adults. "Aunt Emilynne, are we truly going back to Ireland?"

"Yes, Abby."

Abby mulled that over in silence for a moment. "Must we go back to Uncle Teddy's?" The tremor of fear lurking in Abby's voice tore at Emilynne's heart.

"No, my love, we must not." Emilynne struggled to keep anger out of her tone as she answered. The children did not deserve another uprooting to satisfy a murderer's greed.

Pray God this would be the last of the matter and she could concentrate on raising the children as their parents wished and seeing to it that Thaddeus Whyte was brought to justice for his crimes.

"Then, why do you have your worried face on again?"

Bryan settled next to Emilynne. He cupped her chin and turned her face to his, offering her a wink that made her smile in spite of the fear lodged in the pit of her stomach. "She's got you there, Emilynne. You were definitely wearing your worried face."

"Abby, your uncle is a very determined man," Bryan told the child. "We are accompanying him because it is in your best interest for us to settle a matter once and for all."

"Are you sure he cannot take us to live with him?"

Emilynne's heart wrenched anew.

"Aye, darlin'." Huskiness edged Bryan's answer. "I'm quite sure."

Abby thought in silence again as Christian perched on the seat and looked out the window. "Are you a good solicitor, Captain?"

"Aye, I am."

"Even though you love the sea more than the law?"

"What makes you think I love the sea more than the law?"

"Because it is there in your eyes and your voice whenever you talk about Reilly ships. And it is not there when you discuss the law. You might respect the law, but you do not love it."

She spoke in a straightfoward tone. "Am I not right?"

"Aye, lass. I've a great pride in Reilly ships. There was a time when I would have done anything to put to sea and stay there. But when I had to make a choice, put to sea or serve my family, I discovered I loved my family more. I've learned to turn my talents toward the law."

"Oh."

"And, lass?"

"Yes?"

"You and Christian and your aunt are part of my family now."

Again a long silence while Abby digested this information. A frown tightened her brows. When Emilynne had told her of their journey and the marriage, Abby had accepted both without comment. Now, when the words came from Bryan, somehow things sounded more real. There was something about the inflection in his voice that made Emilynne feel dangerously unsettled, yet safer than ever, at one and the same time. Perhaps Abby felt the same.

"I think I like that," Abby said at last. She smiled at Bryan. A wide, happy grin that had been missing for too many months.

"Thank you." Bryan's formality seemed only to heighten the unreality of the past twenty-four hours.

"Reilly ships," Christian quipped to no one in particular as he continued to look out the carriage window, and

Emilynne could only wonder just how much of what was happening he really understood.

"Aye, lad. Reilly ships." Bryan ruffled Christian's hair and turned toward Emilynne.

The glow in his gaze went straight to her heart and lodged there, a painful, unreasoning hope. For whatever reason, this strong and purposeful man had fallen in love with the children and made them his own. That truth burned like an ambient and unfailing flame in the depths of his green eyes. He would guard them with his life if need be.

No wonder he was willing to risk his future by claiming marriage to her. The knowledge eased some of her fears, though it could not temper the slight twinge of disappointment that followed. What had she expected? A pledge of undying devotion?

She could not forget a different glow lighting those same green eyes. A passionate fire that had fueled her own and continued on inside her, banked but viable, ready to ignite at the slightest provocation.

"Feeling better?"

"Yes." She glanced out the carriage window, unwilling to share the telltale heat in her cheeks with him. Reluctant to be even more vulnerable than she already felt.

He took her hand and laced her fingers with his, squeezing gently. "We've a fight ahead of us, but we'll win, Emilynne. I promise you that."

Warmth flooded her along with his statement, solidifying her growing hopes for the outcome of this whole debacle. Her heart might never be the same when Bryan Reilly finally left her life, but at least the children would gain safety and a chance to have their lives return to some semblance of normality. Since that was her goal at the start of this whole mess, she would be content with that.

She swallowed around the tight lump in her throat. "I believe you, Bryan Reilly. I believe that we will win."

He touched her chin and turned her to face him. "That's all I need."

She could drown in the deep green depths of his gaze. He tipped her chin and brushed her lips ever so lightly with his. She caught back a sob at the taste of his breath on her tongue and the need that welled inside her to stay, held tight, in his arms.

"We must go forward and present a united front. And to that purpose, my lass, remember that you are no longer Emilynne Wellesley. You are Emilynne Reilly."

Sudden fear and forbidden pleasure shot through her at his statement, so easily said amid their turmoil as the carriage pulled away from Hampton House, leaving Richard behind forever.

"My wife." He growled the last in a low tone that shivered over her skin, unleashing a wild tumult of longing in her stomach, a tight mixture of checked passion, and fears she couldn't name.

No, didn't want to name.

Not now, when everything else in her life was out of kilter and in danger of staying that way. And for how long would she be his wife? A week? A month? She couldn't bring herself to ask the question. How long were Brehon marriages? Were they like ancient handfastings, good for a year and a day? Like the ones described in Druid texts, from harvest to harvest? The answer mattered far more than she wanted it to, far more than she could ever possibly admit.

"Emilynne Reilly," she returned, her own voice husky

with the effort to remain calm as he watched her. "I shall try to remember that, Captain."

He smiled then, a soft and wicked smile that quickened her heartbeat. "See that you do, Mrs. Reilly. See that you do."

Chapter Sixteen

"Thank you for coming, Uncle Willard." Emilynne returned his hug as Willard Jefferies engulfed her in his massive embrace.

"Good to see you again so soon, my dear." Sunlight filtered through wispy lace curtains, dotting Mrs. Babbage's fashionable front parlor with dancing lilies as Willard Jefferies settled himself in one of her best chairs. Bryan winced as the chair creaked under the older man's girth.

"You as well, Reilly," the portly solicitor continued. "I've heard nothing but good things about you. Your senior partner thinks very highly of you. Very highly indeed, as his correspondence attests."

"Thank you, sir." Bryan stood behind Emilynne's chair, somehow not at all surprised Willard Jefferies had taken the precaution of checking his references. The man owned the kind of investigative thoroughness Gill O'Brien always prized. So how was it his own son had been able to blindside him? Most likely he'd answered his own question.

"Now, what is it I can help you with, Emilynne? Especially since you have chosen to ignore my advice and remain sequestered in the countryside until I could send for you." His tone belied the censure of his words.

"Both of us this time." Bryan had only begun the words when Jeffries's keen blue eyes pinned him with curiosity. Those eyes would be a definite asset in any courtroom. "We've a slight problem."

"And what might that be, young Reilly?" Jeffries leaned forward slightly. The chair creaked again as though underscoring the question.

"Uncle Willard." Emilynne put a hand on his arm. "You know it was my intention to marry in order to satisfy the requirements of my brother's will."

"Indeed." The man didn't take his gaze from Bryan as he acknowledged Emilynne's words.

"Well, it did not work out with Richard." She blushed crimson as she gained the older man's attention.

"I mean, it turned out not to be necessary for me to marry Richard." She stopped and blew out a long breath.

"It turns out that I already am married." She gulped. "Oh, bother."

She started again. "Dear Uncle Willard, I cannot marry Richard Andrews because I have already married Bryan Reilly."

"Indeed?" That keen blue gaze snapped back to Bryan. "And just when did this happen? I do believe I suggested that when the two of you were here originally. And you both turned me down."

He peered at Emilynne again. "Had a change of heart, did you?"

"I—" Emilynne floundered beneath that probing stare.

"Circumstances dictated the need." Bryan offered by way of rescue. "Thaddeus Whyte made an unscheduled and very unexpected appearance at Hampton House, complete with one of his hired thugs and letters of writ from the magistrate in Dublin endowing him with guardianship of the Wellesley children."

"Did he?" Jeffries rubbed his thick sideburns and frowned at them both. "Yes, I can see where that would pose a most untenable issue."

He paused for a moment, and the chair creaked again as he shifted positions. "Was there anyone else with him?"

"Aye." Bryan locked his gaze with Jeffries's. Reluctant as he was to cause hurt, the respect he held for the other man warranted nothing but the truth. "Young Willard was there as well."

Jeffries accepted that in grim yet unsurprised silence. Bryan could almost read the dreams gone awry as Jeffries shook his head and released a heavy sigh. "I suspected as much. That boy disappoints me more every day."

"I have the depositions prepared from the witnesses to your brother's will. I can only hope they may be of some use with the courts. I have seen to it that Junior no longer has access to my firm's offices or resources, at least."

After another short silence, he made an effort to shake off his own personal regrets. "But how did Whyte know where to find you? I thought I instructed both of you to make no unnecessary contacts."

"You did, sir," Emilynne told him in a soft tone. "But we neglected to figure Richard into that equation."

"Andrews?" Those bushy eyebrows snapped together.

"Mr. Andrews found our story of Whyte's deeds less than plausible," Bryan supplied. "He decided to investigate on his own. Someone put Whyte and Andrews in contact with each other."

"Botheration." The old solicitor slammed his fist on the table and Emilynne jumped.

"I'm sorry, my dear." He offered her a contrite look and patted her hand. "I thought Richard Andrews was Robert's friend. I've a few things I would like to say to that boy."

He sighed again and lapsed into silence for a moment as though contemplating exactly what he would say the next time he cornered Richard Andrews.

"Well, it is water under the pass at this point," he said, shaking off his muse. "Is that when you decided to get married? Excellent idea. I could see the two of you would make a good match. Can't wait to tell Mrs. Jeffries; she is a romantic soul at heart." Jefferies chuckled over thoughts of his wife, a soft twinkle lighting his eyes.

"That is not exactly how things transpired." Emilynne glanced toward Bryan and bit her lip.

"Are you familiar with Irish Brehon Law?" Bryan decided to take the offensive.

"What? Brehon Law?" The winsome twinkle left the older man's eyes. He frowned and stroked his sideburns again as he studied them both. "Do you mean to tell me you're using ancient law to support your marriage? A common law marriage?"

"Aye." Bryan offered the one-word response, knowing protestations would be useless by the squint of Jeffries's eyes.

"Emilynne Wellesley!" Jeffries cleared his throat and managed to continue in less than a shout. "My dear, this will not suffice. What idiocy convinced you this would enable you to hold on to your children?"

"Mine." Bryan leaned forward himself and raised a brow at the older man.

"Indeed, sir, it is well you confessed it." He pointed a thick finger in Bryan's face. "You cannot possibly expect such a marriage to hold true in a modern British court."

He pounded a fist on his knee. "What possessed you to try such a tack? Surely you know better than that. How junior allowed you to get this far is beyond me. You can thank your lucky stars the Brehon Laws are no longer required study on this side of the empire."

"We do not intend to support the marriage here. The letters of writ are from a magistrate in Dublin. We intend to fight on Irish soil."

"I see." Jeffries held his peace for a moment, almost closing his eyes as he pondered the information they had given him.

Emilynne's worried look was back in place as she caught Bryan's glance with her own. He squeezed her shoulder in silence, unwilling to break the older solicitor's train of thought.

"Well, there is nothing else for it that I can see. It is a very good thing you sent for me directly." He favored Bryan with a small nod of approval.

"Yes?" Emilynne prodded when he seemed indisposed to enlighten them further.

A smile creased Jeffries's broad cheeks. "You must also wed according to English law. A proper wedding, a proper marriage." He spread his hands in a gesture to indicate perfect balance. "Then there will be no disputing who the children's lawful guardians are."

"Oh, my." Emilynne's stomach swirled and her fingers grew icy cold as she gripped them together in her lap.

Marry? In truth?

She doubted this could be anywhere near Bryan's precise intentions. And heaven knew she had already turned his life upside down and spun it backward. She cleared her suddenly tight throat. "I do not think Mr. Reilly—"

"When?" Bryan broke into her protest, his gaze fixed on Willard's face, his mouth a tight line of purpose.

"As soon as possible." Jeffries nodded, pleased with Bryan's apparent grasp of their situation. "In view of Emilynne's prior decision to marry Richard Andrews, I already have the required licensing in my possession."

"I really do not think—" Emilynne tried again as the cold numbness in her fingers seemed to spread up her arms.

"Mr. Jeffries, you are indeed a thorough man." Bryan offered a grin as he nodded at the older man.

"Indeed." Willard smiled, pleased. "Preparation is more than half the battle, my boy."

"But—" Her teeth began to chatter.

"When can you be ready, Emilynne?"

Willard Jeffries's piercing blue gaze pinned her, demanding an answer she wasn't ready to give. Was she?

She took a deep breath and then blew it out over a slow, shaky count to ten. "Bryan offered his help, Uncle Willard, which I am more than willing to accept if it will guarantee the safety of my family."

This would be so much easier if he were not standing so close to her. She could inhale the wood and sage scent that was his alone. If he were not in the room at all. "I am quite certain he did not come to England with intentions of marrying anyone. Least of all me. The time he has given so freely has already squashed his personal goals and jeopardized his family's situation. What you are proposing is a much more permanent solution than the condition the two of us had agreed upon."

"My dear." Willard frowned at her as he took her hand, shelving his jovial personality like an outdated law book. "If you wish to hold on to your children, you will do as I suggest without delay. When I encouraged you to marry Richard Andrews, I did so for very solid reasons. Though your choice of mate has changed, the reasons still stand. If you return to Ireland, you may very well win your challenge there on the strength of the Brehon Laws.

"Though I would beg leave to dispute that." He raised his brows at Bryan, who nodded agreeably.

"However, if you do secure your rights there, Thaddeus Whyte will still have the opportunity to pursue and win his case here, in England, with little to no opposition."

"But—" She was shivering now.

"He is English," Willard continued as though she hadn't spoken. "The children are English. No Brehon marriage, no matter how well consummated, will stand up against a man with Mr. Whyte's formidable reputation."

A frisson of fear dashed through her as he underscored the same justifications Bryan had given her. She glanced at Bryan, half afraid to read what she might find in his face.

"Emilynne, marry me." He spoke in a low tone that moved such incredible warmth through her, she forgot for a moment they were not alone.

"Your family—" she began with the only protest that came to mind.

". . . will be thrilled I have found a woman worthy to bear my name."

Her breath caught in her throat. He couldn't mean the things he was saying. Could he? She couldn't bring herself to ask. If Willard was to be believed, she really had no other choice at this juncture. If the pounding of her heart was to be believed, she could give no other answer to this man.

"Can we do this now, Uncle Willard?" She seemed unable to extract herself from the dark green confines of Bryan's gaze. "Before I begin to doubt your wisdom?"

"Consider it done, my dear."

Done indeed.

The golden Reilly crest that had first identified him to her in Limerick now rode her finger, an outward sign of the validity of their marriage. She traced the Celtic knot etched beneath the raised *R* on his ring. Their lives intrinsically tied together. For all time?

Emilynne's head spun from the small sips of champagne Mrs. Babbage had unearthed from the depths of her larder.

"Always be prepared, my dears," the landlady chirped happily as she poured sparkling wine into hastily dusted flutes. She'd been more than pleased to stand as witness to the *repledging* of their vows as Willard had dubbed it in order to avoid any unexplainable questions.

Romantic soul that she was, Mrs. Babbage actually had produced a voluminous handkerchief from her pocket to wipe away tears and sniffle into quietly while the minister Uncle Willard procured led them through their vows in the voice of a born orator.

The fact that their fellow guests at Mrs. Babbage's had wandered in only highlighted the unreality of the whole situation for Emilynne. But Willard and Bryan both seemed pleased by the turnout of witnesses. A solicitor's matter, obviously.

Having Abby and Christian beside her had proved her rock of security. Anchored by Bryan's steady intent.

Emilynne buried her nose in the graceful curve of her champagne flute again and swallowed the dry liquor, wishing it would somehow defrost the frozen lump of apprehension that had settled in her stomach as she changed gowns. The lavender sprigged percale gown, though lovely, was hardly the wedding gown fantasized by little girls.

Her gaze traveled the length of the parlor to light on her new husband, clad in black trousers that followed the line of his body, a crisp white shirt, and green velvet vest, beneath his dark jacket.

She sighed. Now, he, on the other hand, was enough to satisfy the dreams of any girl, no matter what her size.

She caught herself giggling foolishly at the thought and deposited her empty crystal flute on a side table, deciding she'd had more than enough already.

"How wonderful it was, Mrs. Reilly." Mrs. Babbage was at her elbow with the champagne again. "And you looked every bit the bride in spite of your . . . delicate condition." She whispered the last with a knowing smile, and Emilynne caught back a groan as her cheeks heated.

"Why, thank you, Mrs. Babbage." Bryan saved her from replying. "You've no idea how pleased we were that you were able to stand our witness."

Mrs. Babbage turned a becoming shade of pink. "Mr. Reilly, you are a flatterer. My dear, he is worth every moment you've given him."

She fluttered away to attend her other guests.

"There now, wife." Bryan's gaze, a deep, glowing green, touched Emilynne's. "We have well and truly married. Whyte cannot have the children now and Jefferies will take care of any other paperwork involved in our marriage this day."

"Thank you, Bryan," she managed to say over the tight lump in her throat, wishing she could voice the conflicted questions churning inside her. "I do not know what else to say. Your generosity and selflessness in reworking your life at a moment's notice is quite overwhelming. I wish there were a way for me to repay some small measure of what you have done for me. And for the children."

Bryan touched her hand. "My dear Emilynne, I assure you, my motivations are not completely selfless."

His dark, smoldering look threatened to burn her to a cinder right there in Mrs. Babbage's parlor, regardless of how many people might be looking.

She shivered, beset with the liquid heat his gaze had kindled inside her.

"Oh, Mr. Reilly." Mrs. Babbage waved frantically from the other side of the room as the other guests began to filter out.

"You have a devoted admirer there." Emilynne tried to laugh, but it came out husky with the need and longing Bryan never failed to churn within her.

He nodded to the landlady.

"I'll be right back." He squeezed Emilynne's waist and left her standing there, wishing idly for things that could never be.

Uncle Willard appeared at her elbow. "Are you happy, my dear?"

She smiled at him, watching as Bryan escorted the landlady from the parlor. "I am satisfied with the notion that we have secured safety for Christian and Abby, but I cannot help but feel I have done nothing but take unfair advantage of Bryan Reilly since the moment I met him."

"I've been meaning to speak with you about that, Emilynne." Uncle Willard stroked his bushy sideburns. "There were some papers—"

"You will not circumvent the law with this no matter how prettily you've managed." The cold ice of Thaddeus Whyte's voice sliced through Willard Jefferies's words.

Emilynne's stomach swirled and her vision darkened as though a thick fog had rolled into the room. Thaddeus and his thug, Wilkins, strolled in Mrs. Babbage's parlor, uninvited guests to their impromptu wedding. Emilynne struggled to bring her sudden trembling under control.

"Thaddeus," she managed to say in a whispered warning to Willard, grateful she was not alone to face her nemesis.

"Indeed?" Uncle Willard seemed unruffled. "Mr. Whyte, I presume."

"You presume too much." Wilkins offered Emilynne a sly smile, then eyed Uncle Willard as though trying to decide how much of the old man's bulk was muscle.

Thaddeus waved his hand, and his pet thug subsided. "You are quite correct."

He summed Uncle Willard up in a glance and dismissed him as unimportant, fixing his cold stare on her instead. "Emilynne, it is a bit late in the day to solidify your position with an actual ceremony."

His gaze trailed over her from head to toe.

"I—" The icy swirls of nausea in her stomach seemed to cut off all thought from her brain.

"It is no business of yours what has transpired here today, Mr. Whyte." Uncle Willard's imperious tones drew Thaddeus's gaze once more. "Indeed, the children are of little interest to you. I would suggest that you would better occupy your time by lining up your defense for the numerous charges yet to come. Or at the very least by finding yourself some other place to set up residence once you lose Blue Hills Stud. The battle you think to fight here has already been won.''

Thaddeus eyed him in silence. For once Emilynne felt he had actually been surprised. She wondered if it had come home to him that he had chosen the wrong solicitor to deal with at Jefferies's firm.

Thaddeus smiled. "Your *son* has been an immeasurable help to me.''

That silky tone she so loathed crawled over her skin as he directed his evil darts at Uncle Willard.

Willard Jefferies took a slow breath and she winced inwardly, knowing the pain that one statement must have caused him.

"Junior has always been an apt pupil in all that he has experienced.'' The frost in Uncle Willard's eyes could have frozen a lesser man. "It is my hope that learning shall continue whatever his circumstances.''

"Let us hope so.'' Thaddeus offered a congenial nod, as though discussing something of mutual interest. "He has proven to be a great asset to me.''

"This is a private party, Whyte.'' Bryan's voice cut through the tense atmosphere brewing between the other men and forced Thaddeus's gaze to him. "I suggest you and your assistant leave my wife and me to our celebration.''

"Reilly.'' Thaddeus's narrowed gaze marked him. "Your family enjoys an excellent name. I should hate to see that come to an end. I'm sure you are aware how tenuous and delicate a thing reputations are.''

He raised an eyebrow as Bryan fixed him with a stony stare. "I merely wished to inspect the premises housing the children. Their nanny assures me you have provided adequately for them. Far be it from me to spoil the last night of freedom you will enjoy on this soil for quite some time. Good day, Emilynne."

Thaddeus left on that note with his minion following carefully in his wake.

"Bryan." Emilynne choked on her fears.

"That man is quite something," Uncle Willard pronounced.

"Aye." Bryan glared at the now-shut parlor doors as though his very gaze could skewer Thaddeus and make him pay for his crimes. "It should make for a very interesting day in court."

"If you make it to court." Uncle Willard stroked his sideburns again.

The speculation in his eyes sent a chill over Emilynne. "What do you mean?"

"I've a feeling he doesn't mean to see you in any court, whether English or Irish. He intends mischief."

Willard frowned and patted Emilynne's hand protectively. "That blackguard had a history of solving his problems in his salad days with violence when backed into a corner. If I were you, young Reilly, I would watch myself and my family very, very carefully."

"I intend to, sir," Bryan assured him in a quiet tone that elicited pointed gooseflesh along Emilynne's arms. "I intend to."

Willard's words were still echoing through Emilynne an hour later as she entered the bedroom she would now share with her legal husband. The wedding supper Mrs. Babbage had managed for them was long since consumed, along with a bottle of soft white wine.

Abby and Christian were tucked safely to bed, Mrs. Stewart, their nanny, watching over them. Mrs. Stewart was a plucky woman, who had received strict orders to open the door for no one save Emilynne and Bryan.

Mrs. Babbage had taken the liberty of turning down the crisp white bed linens and sprinkling dried rose petals across the lace pillows. Such bridal ado only made Emilynne's stomach spiral with a hot mix of anticipation and fear she couldn't hold back. Would they truly consummate their marriage? Did Bryan intend to remain her husband? In fact as well as in name? And what was his motivation in all this?

No words of love or commitment had ever been exchanged between them beyond their vows that afternoon. So what did he seek? What did he gain?

All questions she should have asked him before their vows but just hadn't been able to vocalize.

"Too late now, my girl." Her voice came out shaky and high. There was no escaping the knowledge that tonight was her wedding night, and regardless of what private arrangements they might make, in the eyes of God and man Bryan had all the rights to her body he needed.

She pressed a hand over her stomach to still the wild butterflies such thoughts let loose. All the rights she needed him to have.

The sheer nightdress laid out across the bed offered mute testimony to what was to come. Bryan had seen this before the night she'd gone to him in the gardens of Hampton House.

She shuddered with remembered sensations at the memories as she lifted the nightdress from the bed and traced the delicate fabric with her fingers. His hands, his lips, he was more than familiar with the feel of her body, even the taste of her skin.

Flames seared her cheeks and she dropped the gown,

wishing she had swallowed gallons more of the various wines Mrs. Babbage had seemed so determined to fete them with.

A cowardly urge to run welled up inside her, to run from the strange, complicated mess she had made of her life over the past months. The change from spoiled, book-laden spinster to new bride and mother was dizzying in retrospect and all too frightening. Her hands were cold, and she rubbed them together.

This is necessary, she reminded herself, inescapably necessary. To be well and truly binding, a marriage must be consummated.

She rubbed her hands over her arms, trying to chase her fears away and find somewhere deep within herself the woman strong enough to carry forward with her new responsibilities. To find the woman who had published her paper on Druid symbols despite the fact that she was female. The one who had dared Thaddeus Whyte's study and when confronted with the horror of his misdeeds had stolen the children away and spirited them to safety.

With a determined lift of her chin she began unbuttoning the small row of buttons fastening her gown. She would be ready for Bryan when he came to her. She would not stand there like a cowering miss and beg him to refrain from truly making her his wife. If that was his intention, so be it.

And if it were not? She swallowed a hot pang of unreasoning disappointment as her fingers stilled.

She would deal with that as well.

Chapter Seventeen

Bryan tore himself away from Mrs. Babbage's insistent company with a extended sigh of relief. As much as he appreciated the woman's adept handling of their wedding, her enthusiasm had gone far beyond what necessity dictated.

He started up the staircase, his footsteps slower than one might expect from a new bridegroom. To be honest with himself, he had to admit he'd accepted the landlady's verbose companionship only as an excuse to delay going up to the bedroom he would share with Emilynne.

His wife.

In truth this time, instead of the ruse they shared when last they stayed beneath Mrs. Babbage's well-appointed roof. Though their circumstances had changed, the feelings Emilynne Wellesley, nay Emilynne *Reilly*, churned loose in his gut remained the same. He wanted her more than he had ever wanted another woman, but the sheer haste of their wedding had precluded the gentle wooing and careful persuasion he imagined usually accompanied marriage.

How would she receive him?

Did she even now eagerly await him in their bridle bower, as Mrs. Babbage had insisted on dubbing their room? Or was she fully garbed and pacing the confines, ready to assault him with all the questions he'd noticed swimming in the depths of her deep blue gaze.

Questions she had every right to ask and ones he wasn't sure he held any answers to.

He sighed and rubbed a hand over the back of his neck, loosening his collar as he continued up the stairs. Did she truly understand that he had entered this marriage with every intention of making it a real one? That he'd chosen to make her his wife in every sense of the word? That he wanted to make her his wife in deed as well as in the eyes of the law? Or did she harbor, somewhere deep in her woman's heart, a hope that he would solve her problems and then disappear like mist on the Shannon in the bright light of day?

His questions throbbed painfully at his temples as his thoughts chased one another around in circles, achieving no answers and offering no respite to the doubts plaguing him. He loosened the top buttons on his shirt and shrugged out of his jacket as he reached the landing.

Standing before the tall window overlooking the street below, he tried to bring some order to his tangled thoughts. Baldwin Street lay dark and quietly empty, devoid of the answers he sought.

He couldn't help churning over his failure with Harland. While he'd arranged their disaffected party's travel to Dublin on the *Caithream*, Michael's news of the financier's welcoming manner and sincere regrets about not backing Reilly Ship Works did nothing but add salt to an open wound, honing Bryan's guilt all the keener for the loss.

When Emilynne's issues were finally settled, he could at last turn his attention to his own family's difficulties. In spite of all his good intentions when he left Limerick, he had nothing to show for his leave of absence from O'Brien & Mallory except a major upset to the petition of one of Gill's prize clients.

And a wife who'd never intended to marry him. The thought twisted in his chest, a painful tightening he refused to name.

I never intended to marry anyone. Her words repeated in his mind like a tune he couldn't forget.

But she *was* his wife now. Despite what hopes she might secretly shelter, no law on earth or in heaven would deny him his rights as a husband. Small comfort that if the woman he hoped to exercise those rights with chose to believe otherwise.

Her obvious reluctance to follow through with Jefferies's suggestion still chafed. The fact that she had fully intended to marry that milk-and-water oaf Richard Andrews and attempt wedded bliss with him for the rest of her life rubbed raw against his pride.

Her final consent had only followed through with her motivation since the moment he met her, safety for the children. Abby and Christian came first in her life. An admirable trait, and one he understood completely, yet it did little to offer him hope for their future as man and wife. It seemed to matter not at all whom she married so long as she wed quickly and thwarted Thaddeus Whyte's schemes.

That thought galled most of all.

He groaned and turned away from the tranquil street, unwilling to follow the dark pathway in his mind that led to just why it bothered him so. Damnation, she was his wife. She belonged to him. It was time simply to face that fact. Tell her straight out and be done with it. They would be leaving for Dublin in the morning. If they were asked in court about the state of their marriage and its consummation, they would need to be able to answer in the affirmative.

Emilynne might not like the idea, but there it was, pared down to the lowest factor.

With a grim twist of his lips he advanced toward the bedroom and his reluctant bride.

He knocked once and then entered, unwilling to wait any longer and torture himself further with delays. It was best she face the unpleasant truth as soon as possible.

"Emilynne—" he began, and then stopped short at the sight of her. His mouth went dry and dusty.

"Oh, Bryan." She stood by the foot of the bed, clad in the sheer nightdress and midnight-blue mantelet she'd worn during their unforgettable encounter in the gardens at Hampton House. The gown swirled about her in a whisper of gauzy material, hinting at all her charms beneath and freeing a torrent of memories while freezing his breath in his chest.

At the hemline her bare feet peeped out as though taunting him for the angry thoughts that had goaded him down the hallway.

He swallowed and swept the length of her with his gaze from her small, appealing toes to the tip of her pert nose. And back again. She clutched the mantelet together at her throat with delicate fingers. Her lips were parted in greeting, begging his kiss. The blue of her gaze was soft and warm and focused on him.

Hot blood surged through his veins. He swallowed as desire's tight fist punched him hard in the gut, showing no mercy.

"Hello, Emilynne." He closed the door behind him and leaned against it.

"Hello." One husky word as she clutched the blue lace mantelet tight across her shoulders. A delicate pink stained her cheeks and she cleared her throat.

"There are questions we need to answer." The cool, precise tones of a scholar soared across the room toward him.

He held back a smile. She had chosen a mixture of the possibilities he had imagined. Sweet siren awaiting him and inquiring miss, ready to barrage him with questions.

"Indeed?" He met her gaze. "And what might those be?"

"I—I need to know just what your intentions are." She twisted her hands together in front of her, caught herself, and stopped.

"My intentions?"

To make hot, sweet love to you. The certainty burned through his mind as desire leapt inside him, scorching him with the needs she invoked so easily.

"Yes." She fiddled with her hair, still snug in its cool chignon. His fingers itched to undo the pins along with the calm reserve she was trying so hard to portray.

"I . . . we . . . never discussed any of this." She gestured to the bedroom with its invitingly turned-down bedcovers sprinkled with rose petals gleaming in the romantic glow of beeswax candles. Mrs. Babbage again, no doubt.

He crossed his arms over his chest. "And what would you like to discuss about the matter?"

Her cheeks pinkened again. "I just want to clear up any confusion there might be."

"I see." He tossed his jacket on the nearest chair and she jumped. He hid a smile and relaxed back against the door.

"What part of the act confuses you?" he asked in a helpful tone.

Her color deepened adorably. He looked forward to a lifetime of provoking just such blushes.

"Oh, it is not that." She stopped herself and took a deep breath before continuing. "I do not wish to discuss, I mean I do, but not the . . . the mechanics."

"The mechanics?" He bit back a groan at the slow torment she was putting him through. "If there are mechanics involved, perhaps it is you who will have to enlighten me."

She licked her lips and his gaze centered on the slow motion of her tongue.

"I need to know if you intend . . . well, if you intend to consummate our vows." She nodded primly after this outrageous statement.

"Aye." Unable to stand the distance between them anymore, he pushed away from the door. "Fully."

"Oh." She paled. Apprehension glittered in her dark eyes as he drew closer, but she did not retreat. "I see."

"Do you?" He stopped as he reached her, allowing his gaze to play over her flushed features.

"I . . . I think so." A shuddering whisper.

"You are beautiful, Emilynne Reilly." He stroked one finger over the heated curve of her cheek as the scent of skin-warmed freesia and lemon drifted into him with each breath. "More than beautiful, you are intoxicating."

"Thank you." Polite to a fault, his beautiful wife.

"I intend to make you mine. Completely."

"Oh." The pink glow in her cheeks burned brighter still.

"This is no stopgap measure to assure Christian's and Abigail's safety. Or to satisfy the whims of any court, Irish, English, or West Mongolian," he told her, refusing to hold back now that he had started. He reached out and pulled the pins from her hair, watching as it sluiced over her shoulders, a rippling waterfall of white-golden silk. "There will be no going back."

"None." She offered a stiff little nod of agreement. "I understand."

"Nay, my sweet lass, I don't think you do." He slid his hands beneath the lacy edges of her mantelet and placed them firmly on her trim waist, drawing her to him.

He brushed her lips with his, feather light and gentle. "There will be no stopping this time, Emilynne. No interruptions." He punctuated his words with more teasing touches of his mouth against hers.

"Yes." She breathed the word against his lips, firing the urgency building inside him. "No stopping."

He squeezed her waist and slid his hands over her back, drawing her more fully into his embrace. Her hands slid up his shirt.

"You are mine, sweet Emilynne. From this day forward."

"Until death us do part." She echoed the words coaxed from her earlier. This time the husky timbre in her voice sent desire spiraling straight through him.

"Aye."

He captured her lips then, tasting her willingness as her mouth opened beneath his. Their tongues slid together in slow, intoxicating circles as the need burning in his blood grew hotter still. He would go slow, he must, for her, but the effort would surely drive him mad.

He rubbed his thumbs back and forth across her hips and down across the gentle curve of her stomach as she twined her arms around his neck. The slight pressure of her body against him was not enough.

Her fingers slid through his hair as their lips parted and met, parted and met. She felt so good in his arms, as if this was where she was meant to be. He would never need anyone ever again the way he needed this one woman.

His fingers tangled in the lacy ties of her mantelet as he released it, dropping the garment to the floor.

His gaze held hers as he traced one finger over the simple lace-trimmed neckline of her gown. Each individual lace filigree gave beneath his touch, so that he stroked not so much the gown but the warm, tender flesh beneath.

Her eyes darkened and her nipples tightened to fine points as she shivered. "Bryan." Almost a plea.

"Aye?"

"Are you sure this is what you want?" Her soft words tore at the control he was struggling so hard to maintain, whipping to a frenzy the rough, wild lust throbbing deep inside him. "That I am who you want?"

It is what I require to make me whole. The answer welled from deep within him.

"Aye, *muirneach.*" He pulled her against him as white-hot fire lit his mind and burned low in his belly. "It is more than what I want. It is what I need."

He threaded his fingers into the thick silk of her hair, tilting her head to better accommodate his hungry kisses and the passion threatening to destroy him if he didn't assuage it completely—and soon.

She moaned into his mouth as he laved his tongue

against hers and moved his hands over her soft, supple body, tracing the lush curves of her buttocks, the indent of her waist, the slim length of her back, the rounded fullness of her breasts.

He pressed her hips against the painful need of his arousal, torturing a groan of pleasure from her with the brush of his thumb across each taut nipple. He sipped soft sounds from her lips as he fondled her, delivering slow, sweet torment for both of them.

"My God, Emilynne, I want you," his voice rasped out, harsh and unrecognizable against her cheek.

"And I you," she whispered in return as her fingers made short work of the remaining buttons on his shirt and spread it open, moving her hands over his heated flesh. They blended a mutual groan of pleasure into a kiss of white-hot passion.

He scooped her into his arms and carried her toward the cool bed linens awaiting them. Releasing her onto the bed, he shrugged out of his shirt and shucked off his boots and trousers. She straightened, perching on the edge of the mattress and watching his progress with an intent curiosity that nearly unmanned him as her bold gaze traveled downward over his body.

"Oh, my." Her gaze flicked back to his, doubt centered in soft lapis blue.

He gritted his teeth and once more warned himself to go slowly with his virginal bride, but it would be a difficult matter with his passions riding him hard.

"Emilynne." He held out his hand. She slipped hers into it without a moment's hesitation, flowing to her feet to stand before him.

Naught remained between them, but the soft, gauzy fabric of her gown as he pulled her against him and kissed her. What was meant as a soft caress quickly became a primal mating, driven by the hunger goading him to near madness with wanting her.

She did not flinch from the fires raging inside him. Nay, she stoked the flames, sliding her hands over his shoulders and down his back in teasing caresses and then lower still to test the firm flesh of his buttocks.

He sucked in a breath as her questing fingers sought his manhood and traced his hard length thoroughly.

"You play with fire, *muirneah*," he warned her, his tone hoarse with his effort to keep himself under control beneath her touch.

"Indeed?" Her smile, a bewitching blend of moonstruck innocence and fire-bright sensuality, made short work of what little control he still retained.

With a groan he molded her tender curves against him in a fierce agony of longing. Savoring the wild sweetness of her lips, he grasped handfuls of the gauzy stuff of her gown and tugged the flimsy garment slowly down over her shoulders. It pooled for a moment at her waist and then whispered to the floor in a long sigh, leaving her in nothing but the fire's warm glow.

Her skin felt more exquisite than silk to the touch as his fingers roamed her softness with no impediment. He held her still, his hands at her waist as he kissed her in slow circles from her shoulders to the fine, tight points of her breasts. Her fingers slid into his hair as he laved first one taut nipple and then the other, sucking her thoroughly, teasing her with his teeth.

"Bryan." A more urgent plea now as he rasped his teeth over her again and again, tugging and nipping, tormenting them both.

He slid his hands to the soft V of curls at the juncture

of her thighs, coaxing her legs to part for him so he could gain access to the moist flesh within.

She was slippery and wet for him, almost ready for the lovemaking he planned to give her. She shuddered as he stroked her slick folds, parting her softness and easing his fingers inside her tight, velvety sheath.

"Oh, oh, oh." Her wordless cries built in sweet rhythm with the slow invasion and retreat of his fingers. In. Out. In. He watched her eyes widen, so deep and pure a blue, he could shatter to pieces from looking into them.

"I just can't." Breathless and desperate. "Oh, Bryan."

"It is all right, my love, I will hold you." He teased the engorged little nub of flesh beneath his thumb in a tight circle.

She stiffened against him and cried out, a look of wonder in those beautiful eyes as he took her over the edge. Her knees buckled and he scooped her into his arms, tasting her pleasure on her lips as he kissed with all the hunger straining for release inside him.

"You are mine, beloved," he told her as he bore her to the bed. "Mine as you have been from the moment we kissed on the docks in Limerick harbor."

"Yes, Bryan, oh, yes." Tears sparkled in her eyes as he eased her down, following her in a fluid motion.

The feel of her beneath him, soft and warm and willing, tore a ragged groan from him. Her legs parted without any coaxing, and he settled against her.

His breath came jagged in his chest as he struggled for sanity. Somehow she had twined herself around his heart and woven her essence into the very fabric of his soul.

"I cannot wait any longer, beloved."

"Then, take me," she urged him softly. "Take me now, husband."

It was all the invitation he needed. He pressed himself against the slick wet heat of her body and pushed. Slowly, lowly, the warning sounded distantly in his brain, but she would have none of his patience. In a movement that stunned them both, she arched upward, impaling herself fully on his hard length.

Her groan and his echoed in the room, a hot mix of pain and pleasure, blending inside him with the distant ripple of ancient music and the surge of wild, unearthly colors he'd seen when first he kissed her.

A blessing come home and fully accepted.

He held himself still, fighting the raging drives inside him that demanded the aged rhythms from his all too willing body. Despite his own desires, he couldn't bear the thought of hurting her.

"Emilynne, beloved, are you all right?"

"Aye, my husband," she whispered, her sparkling gaze catching his. "You have not hurt me. Is there more?"

A short chuckle escaped him at her question. "More? Indeed, yes, my fine lass, much more." He moved inside her, slow and gentle, watching her expression change from teasing smile to a tight mask of passion.

A moan escaped her, deep and husky, but it was not pain he read in her face, it was a wild desire to match his own.

He surrendered then to the unbearable yearning inside him, moving inside the hot sweet velvet of her body. Accepting what was between them in all its enticing fiery and silken wonder as their mouths melded together in kiss after hungry kiss. Forging their hearts, their souls together in the heat of the passion that dwelt between them.

"You are mine, beloved." He punctuated his words with each thrust of his body. Filling her with his heat. Accepting and receiving an age-old blessing in the sweet friction of his body against hers.

"Yes, yes," she whispered against his lips as she clung to him. Her fingers threaded his hair as her silken limbs twined his. With a soft moan she squirmed beneath him, so innocent of the very act and yet so innately sensual, he couldn't hold back his groan as she arched against him, driving him deeper and deeper into her body as she caught his rhythm and echoed it.

Then, in a flash of pleasure, he gave her his soul, shuddering over and over as she welcomed everything he had to give.

In the aftermath she gifted him with the finest kiss he'd ever tasted. The finest kiss he could ever want. A kiss from the woman he loved beyond measure. His life's blessing indeed.

Emilynne struggled with the buttons on her gown for the tenth time in as many minutes. She was all thumbs and sore in places she'd never known existed before. Catching herself daydreaming over her night in Bryan's arms again sent hot color over her cheeks.

He'd been blessedly gone when she awoke, leaving only a hazy memory of soft kisses and Celtic endearments as he coaxed her to awaken and make ready for their journey to Dublin.

Now that she was dressed, well, almost, forcing the last few buttons to fasten, she couldn't dismiss the awkwardness she was feeling about seeing him in the bright light of day.

The intimacies they had shared left her breathless. She sat on the edge of the bed as her knees weakened. He'd been part of her last night, one heart, one body striving together. She pressed her cold fingers over her cheeks. It wouldn't do for him to see her blushing like a shy child when she went downstairs.

She took a deep breath and counted slowly to ten, no, she extended that to twenty. There was still the sea voyage to Dublin to face and whatever might happen to them once they arrived.

She shuddered. If only she didn't have to take Abby and Christian back to Ireland, she would actually have been happy despite the unresolved questions between herself and her husband.

Did he love her or desire her? Did he know that she loved him? Did any of that matter considering what else they shared?

She forced herself to her feet, checked that she'd left nothing behind, and hurried down the hall to the children's room.

"Och, there ye are, Miss—I mean Missus." Nanny Stewart greeted her at the door as Christian and Abby cheered her appearance.

"We're ready, Aunt Emmie," Christian piped in, bounding off the bed to join Nanny at the door. "Captain says we're to sail on a Reilly ship. Just like you promised when I was sick."

Nanny took his hand firmly. "Not yet, young master. We've your sister to wait for. We'll be down in a thrice, Miss—I mean Missus. It will take a bit of getting used to."

"Bring them down when you're ready, Nanny." Emilynne patted the older woman's hand, waved to Christian, and forced herself down Mrs. Babbage's long staircase.

Bryan met her at the bottom.

Fire leapt in her stomach as she met his glowing gaze. "Good morning, Mrs. Reilly." His low tone shivered ver her.

"And to you, Captain," she offered in return, deliber- tely bestowing his title on him along with a wide smile to ide her nervousness.

"You'd best watch yourself, *muirneach*. Or we'll not make 1e ship when she sails."

Heat spiraled through her, leaving her breathless as he ʋok her hand. How odd, the analytical scholar in her bserved, that giving in to one's desires only served to ʋeighten the problem. When a knock sounded at the front ʋor, she couldn't decide which was stronger, relief or isappointment.

Maisy opened the door to admit a cool gust of air and smiling Michael McManus.

"Captain." He grinned at Bryan as he removed his pipe ʋom his mouth. "And *Mrs.* Reilly."

He bowed formally to her, though the merry twinkle in is eye belied such polite society.

"Captain McManus." She bobbed a short curtsy, won- ʋering just how long it would take for her to accustom erself to the reality of her new title and stop blushing very time someone used it.

"The ship is ready when you are, sir," Michael offered, ʋrning his mischievous gaze back toward Bryan, thankfully noring her reaction. "We're rigged fer yer guests and mily."

He winked at her. "And well stocked with ginger tea."

"Thank you, Michael." Bryan swung his gaze to her. Are you ready, *muirneach*?"

"I hope so." She couldn't hold back her grimace both

at thoughts of their destination and manner of transport. She heard Nanny Stewart and the children on the stairs behind them.

Bryan cupped her cheek, warming her soul with his touch. "Don't worry, it will be a much briefer voyage than the last."

Mrs. Babbage and Maisy waved to them from the porch as they left after extracting assurances that they would be sure to return there when they arrived back in Bristol. *If* they arrived back in Bristol. Emilynne couldn't help the silent doubt.

Willard Jeffries stopped them as they reached the carriage out front. The children, Nanny Stewart, and Michael preceded them inside.

"Here are the depositions I promised you." He handed a packet to Bryan. "Lock them up tight on the voyage. I've included a letter to your senior partner expressing my gratitude for your handling of this matter given the delicacy of your position."

The two men shook hands.

"Thank you, sir," Bryan said.

"My dear." Uncle Willard puffed over to her side, looking harried and rushed. "I wanted to offer you my best wishes and hopes this turns out well for you all."

"Thank you, Uncle Willard." She pressed a kiss to his rounded cheek and fished in her reticule for the packet Richard had given them. "I'm glad you're here actually. Richard gave this to me when we left Hampton House."

"What is it?"

"Money, I believe. I cannot accept it but couldn't tell him so at the time." She pressed it into his hands. "Will you return it for me?"

"Indeed, I will." Willard nodded. "I've a few things to talk over with that lad."

He ran his fingers over the envelope. "But this does not feel like currency. May I?" He looked to her for approval.

"Of course."

He tugged open the envelope and withdrew several sheets of parchment. "Ho, ho. I don't think you'll want to be returning this anytime soon, eh, young Reilly?"

He handed the papers to Bryan, whose mouth spread in a grin of acknowledgment. "No, I think not."

His gaze focused on Emilynne. "You've been carrying around one of the items Mr. Jefferies has been searching for." He turned the papers toward her and she could plainly read the scrolled letterhead from Uncle Willard's firm.

"It is Robert's will, Emilynne."

"Thank heaven." She grasped the papers with a sigh of relief, and tears sparked as she read Robert's bold signature at the bottom. "Of course he would have given Richard a copy to hold. And Richard probably thought nothing about it until Thaddeus arrived."

"Aye. It will help shore up our defenses in the coming legal battle. Excellent work, my wife."

"Keep that close, my friends," Uncle Willard warned them in a low tone. "It is the only copy at this point. Don't let Whyte or Junior even suspect you have it."

Bryan nodded, tucking the packet back into the envelope with deft fingers and dropping it back into Emilynne's reticule.

"Thank you, Uncle Willard." Emilynne hugged him hard.

His cheeks colored. "I did nothing, my dear. You had the will."

"You've been an immeasurable help," she told him.

"To both of us," Bryan added, shaking the older man's hand.

"Be gone, both of you," he scolded in a thick voice. "Trying to upset an old warrior with your sentimentality." He waved them toward the carriage. "And remember to let me know the outcome right away."

"I promise," Emilynne called out the window as the carriage pulled away.

The ride from Mrs. Babbage's was all too short as Emilynne struggled not to betray her growing apprehensions to her husband or to the children. Despite having Robert's will solidly in her possession, she dreaded the coming ordeal.

She didn't realize just how strongly she was hoping Thaddeus would not appear until they reached Bristol's busy dockside. Nanny Stewart helped Christian and Abby alight as Emilynne looked toward Bryan's ship. The *Caithream* looked far too small to carry all of them without spending any time in Thaddeus's company. She groaned aloud.

"You have your worried look again." Bryan's low whisper, forced her gaze to his, dark green and full of understanding.

"I can't seem to help it," she told him as she gripped her cold hands together. "All of his cunning and evil trickery keeps running over and over through my mind."

"Think about this instead." Before she could guess his intent, Bryan covered her lips with his and kissed her so thoroughly, she forgot everything. Time, place, circumstances, faded away beneath the sensual taste and feel of his mouth against hers.

"Better?"

"Much." Her answer came huskily with the turbulent desires he loosed inside her and earned her a warm chuckle.

"Come, *muirneach.*"

She trailed up the gangplank behind him and came face-to-face with Thaddeus as she set foot aboard the ship. The urge to run surged so quickly, she grew light-headed and was more than grateful for the feel of Bryan's strong arm about her waist.

"Lovely." Thaddeus drawled out the word as his cool gaze trailed over her flushed face. "Every inch the blushing bride. I'm glad to see you made it, my dear, none the worse for wear. It wouldn't do for you to miss this voyage or escape your destiny in court."

Anger washed through her in a white-lightning flash. "It is your destiny that should concern you, Thaddeus, not mine."

His eyes narrowed. "I see married life does not agree with you after all. But then, perhaps it is just your choice of mate that makes you shrewish. You would not be the first sweet young miss to decide too late she's made a mistake."

Bryan's grip on her waist tightened as tension ran the length of his arm. "I suggest you go below and make yourself ready, Whyte. The *Caithream*'s crew needs no distractions while we cast off."

"As you wish." Thaddeus nodded, his eyes cold. He turned to go with his lackey Wilkins and young Williard Jefferies in his wake. "Perhaps your crew's lack of expertise is one of the many reasons your family business faces ruin, Reilly."

Emilynne smothered a gasp.

"That'll be Captain Reilly," Bryan informed him, pride ringing strong in his voice. "And we're not ruined yet. Now, get below before I toss you off my ship."

Chapter Eighteen

The shuffle of their feet on the wide marble steps was lost in the hum of the crowd and whirl of faces they passed on their way into Dublin's Hall of Justice. Emilynne tried to concentrate, but her thoughts kept veering off toward the awful possibilities that could come to fruition today.

What would she do if Thaddeus prevailed? What would become of Abby and Christian? Her heart twisted within her, and she forced herself to remember the assurances Bryan had given her. Thaddeus could not win against the defense Bryan would present. He could not win against the truth.

Trust in Bryan was the only thing holding her together as they approached the courtroom.

"Here comes Uncle Teddy," Abby whispered, her hand tightening within Emilynne's grasp. Emilynne suppressed grimace as the bailiff held open the courtroom door. There was no going back now.

An impression of dark aged wood and tall leaded windows assailed Emilynne as Bryan squeezed her other hand and drew them into the courtroom. The Hall of Justice smelled of ink and the dust of ages. The enormity of the procedure they were embroiled in made her knees weak. She caught Abby's astute gaze on her and forced a smile as they advanced down the center aisle.

They stopped at the last row and Bryan turned toward her. Definitely not a sea captain today, her husband was dressed in fine gray worsted wool suit, a crisp white shirt, and freshly polished boots. The very air around him seemed to crackle with precision and authority. He was eager for the proceedings to begin. That thought surprised her.

"Trust me, Emilynne." He stroked his thumb over her palm and she had to resist the urge to fling herself into his arms.

With my soul.

"I do," she told him softly but with far more strength than she felt, unwilling to provide any distraction or doubt from the purpose he had set for himself. For all of them.

A dark gleam lit his eye, but he said nothing as he turned away to take his place. Quickly, he donned a long black robe and gray woolen wig.

He nodded toward the solicitors at the opposing table. Gill O'Brien, she guessed from Bryan's description, senior partner in his firm, was already dressed for this appearance before the magistrate. Behind Gill came Thaddeus and Wilkins along with Williard Jefferies, Jr., and a few men she did not know.

"Why does the cap'n have that thing on his head?" Christian whispered. "He looks like one of Uncle Richard' sheep, not a proper sailor at all."

Abby suppressed a giggle while Emilynne soothed them both to quiet. "Today Captain Reilly has other duties to attend, and this is how he is required to look."

Across the aisle from them, a man nodded in greeting. He looked so much like Bryan, she had to examine him more closely. He winked and smiled broadly under her perusal. Yes, he looked enough like Bryan to be his twin, from the black of his hair to the breadth of his shoulders, alike save for the scar across his left eyebrow that would have given him a rakish look. And for the fine lines of fatigue etched in his tanned face.

He winked at her with unmistakable Reilly green eyes.

She leaned forward. "Bryan—"

"It is my elder brother, Quintin," Bryan explained, catching the direction of her gaze before she could finish her question and nodding to him.

"Why is he—"

"The high court of the city of Dublin will now come to order." Words echoed in a censorious tone through the high-ceilinged room as the bailiff pounded his metal pole against the floor.

There was a general scuffle as everyone rose to their feet. "The honorable magistrate, James Wingate O'Connell, presiding."

A man in flowing black robes entered from a side door with great ceremony. He wore a long powdered wig atop his head and held himself erect as he advanced toward the high platform in the front of the room.

The magistrate seated himself and the bailiff thumped his pole again, signaling the rest of them to return to their seats.

"Can I have a pole like that?" Christian leaned across his sister as he asked his question.

"Don't be silly," Abby offered as she frowned at him.

"Hush, now, my loves. We'll discuss this later." Emilynne soothed a hand over Christian's forehead and rubbed Abby's back, wishing the whole nightmare were already over.

The judge placed a small pair of spectacles on his nose and shuffled through the papers in front of him before clearing his throat. "This is a matter of family custody?"

Bryan and Gill stood.

"Aye, your lordship, in part." Gill spoke first. "It is part a matter already addressed by this court over a fortnight ago and also a matter of potential kidnapping charges."

"I see." The magistrate pursed his lips and thumbed through his papers again. "Mr. O'Brien, you may refresh me on the matter."

"Aye, your lordship." Gill slid a sideways glance toward Bryan, a look bordered with a mix of reluctance and determination.

Emilynne bit her lip, realizing what Bryan must have already known. Despite their friendship and the mutual respect of their business relationship, Gill O'Brien intended to do his very best to win this case.

He stood in his barrister's box and cleared his throat. "My client is Mr. Thaddeus Whyte of Blue Hills Stud in County Kildare. He came to me some time ago on a matter of the utmost importance to him. It seems his beloved niece, Gail Whyte Ryan Wellesley, for whom he had been sole guardian and support for many years, died in an unfortunate carriage accident along with her husband, Mr. Robert Wellesley of Newbury Manor in Wiltshire."

The magistrate nodded but made no comment.

"The young couple left behind two small children, Abigail and Christian, who are now Mr. Whyte's only living relatives. Keenly feeling his niece's loss, and determined to carry through the familial trust long ago bestowed upon him by both English and Irish jurisdiction, Mr. Whyte requested formal custody of his orphaned niece and nephew."

Thaddeus nodded from behind Gill O'Brien, managing to look both self-important and concerned at the same time. Emilynne gritted her teeth and struggled not to show the anger and fears roiling inside her as Gill's description made him sound like the perfect patriarchal figure for the children.

"Indeed?" The magistrate nodded again. "Very good, Mr. O'Brien. Your information supports the decision already effected in this matter."

"There is more, your lordship." Gill shifted his posture. "While Mr. Whyte was in the course of petitioning for said custody, Miss Emilynne Wellesley, also of Wiltshire, the spinster sister of Robert Wellesley, absconded with the two children, having neither rights nor legal writs to support her precipitous and ill-considered actions."

The magistrate leveled a frowning stare in Bryan's direction. "Is this the same woman you now represent, Mr. Reilly?"

"Aye, my lord." Bryan nodded. "But your lordship needs to know that at the time the decision was rendered, there were other factors of which the court was not aware."

"Evidence withheld?" The magistrate beetled his eyebrows.

"Nay, your lordship." Bryan spread his hands, his actions controlled and smooth. "Merely evidence my learned opposing counsel was summarily unable to present due to it being withheld from him."

Gill leaned over and said something to his client at

this revelation. Thaddeus slid a glance at Emilynne but continued to look unconcerned.

The magistrate frowned and peered into the audience. "Is Miss Wellesley present?"

"Aye, my lord." Bryan's answer, still smooth and unruffled. He turned to face her, caught her gaze and nodded.

Emilynne gained her feet despite her trembling knees. She lifted her chin, refusing to look either meek, guilty, or unfit.

The magistrate eyed her in silence for a moment, his intent gaze roaming both her face and her person. She held herself motionless beneath this wordless interrogation, seeing Robert's face in her mind and reliving her desperate vow to protect his children.

The magistrate nodded again. "You may be seated."

She sank back onto the bench, feeling as though she had just been give a very important examination and having no clue as to whether she had passed or failed.

Two little hands sought hers, Abby and Christian, neither truly understanding, yet both needing the contact. She linked their fingers in both of her hands and smiled down at them, unable to offer any verbal reassurance.

"Mr. Reilly, you may proceed."

"Thank you, my lord. Emilynne Wellesley had knowledge of her brother's wishes and those of his wife, Mrs. Abigail Wellesley. Neither of the parents wished Mr. Whyte to have any control over their children. Robert Wellesley had set Emilynne and his best friend and neighbor, Richard Andrews, as co-guardians in the event of his and his wife's deaths, with the proviso allowing for any eventual marriage. If Miss Wellesley wed, then she and her husband become legal guardians of the children."

"What reason had they for disbelieving Mr. Whyte to

be a good and proper guardian? Be brief and to the point, since they cannot testify nor be cross-examined."

"Initially their concern dealt with the long-delayed transfer of Mrs. Wellesley's estate into their authority. It was the reason for their finally making the journey here. Mr. Whyte had offered to complete the transaction provided they appeared in person."

"How long a delay do you refer to?"

"More than ten years, my lord," Bryan stated firmly. "But with no proof of negligence or willful misconduct, they felt they had no recourse but to accede to his demands."

"They suspected him of negligence?"

"Indeed, my lord, and other misconduct as well."

"What other misconduct?"

"My lord"—Bryan lowered his tone—"I hesitate to bring the matter fully before this court with the Wellesley children present in the courtroom."

Thaddeus whispered furiously to Gill O'Brien.

"For what reason?"

"It will be unnecessarily distressing for them both, my lord, given their tender years."

The magistrate considered this for a moment. "Very well, Bailiff, escort the Wellesley children to the waiting area."

"May I suggest your inner chambers, my lord, with a guard to protect them."

The magistrate's thick gray brows shot up toward his wig and he frowned heavily at Bryan, who returned the man's stare without flinching.

"That arrangement suits Mr. Whyte, your lordship," Gill concurred.

"Bailiff, escort the Wellesley children into my chambers."

"Must I go, Aunt Emilynne?" Abby whispered as the bailiff started toward them. "Captain?"

"Yes, Abby, but don't worry, I'll come to get you soon." Emilynne prayed she spoke the truth.

Abby's face looked pinched as she held Christian's hand and trailed out through the silent courtroom behind the bailiff.

"May we continue now, Mr. Reilly?" The magistrate's tart question came as soon as the door shut behind the children.

"Aye, my lord. I place before the court the fact of my marriage to Emilynne Wellesley. I seek custody of the Wellesley children for myself and my wife according to the lawfully executed dictates of Robert Wellesley's last will and testament."

Thaddeus tapped Gill on the shoulder and held another short whispered conference. He looked relaxed but annoyed. The thought reassured Emilynne despite the empty feeling of the seat next to her.

Gill stood. "My lord, I object. Mr. Reilly makes vague injurious references against my client and now seeks custody with a nonexistent will and a marriage that was not in effect at the time Miss Wellesley fled Ireland."

"Mr. Reilly, I will caution you to present sufficient evidence to support your claims."

"I fully intend to do so, my lord." Bryan bowed slightly.

"Your lordship." Gill stood again. "My client does not wish to take up the court's valuable time with a protracted legal battle. It was his original intent to bring Miss Wellesley up on charges of kidnapping due to the possibility the children had come to harm. Since that has not occurred, and due to her fragile emotional state, he is willing to drop those charges. He wishes only to have the children returned to his care."

"I object, my lord." Bryan didn't wait for a reply from the magistrate. "Mr. Whyte's claims are superseded by the express desires of Robert Wellesley."

"Hearsay alone," Gill stated. "Robert Wellesley died intestate."

"Nay, sir, he did not."

Willard, Jr., gasped. "Impossible."

Thaddeus turned a reddish hue of displeasure.

The bailiff's pole thumped through the exchanged stares Gill and Bryan locked.

"I will have order in my courtroom, gentlemen." The magistrate frowned at both of them.

"Mr. Reilly, can you present Robert Wellesley's duly executed will?"

"Aye, my lord." Bryan pulled the packet of papers Richard had given Emilynne from his pocket. "I have the will here in my possession."

He handed the papers to the bailiff, who stepped forward to convey them to the magistrate.

Emilynne stole a glance at Thaddeus as Robert's will at last made it into the hands of the authorities. His face tightened and he began another animated discussion with Willard's son. Junior's face was flushed and he looked far from happy.

Hope rose with a surge of warmth in Emilynne's heart. *Oh, please, please let this truly work.*

"I am familiar with the seal of the Jefferies firm in Bristol," the magistrate intoned. He handed the will to the bailiff and gestured the man to show the papers to Gill.

Gill read them in silence for a moment before handing

them back to the bailiff. "In view of the disappearance and then sudden reappearance of Robert Wellesley's supposed will, we ask that you uphold the previous decree from this court until the signatures can be verified."

"You doubt your eyes, Mr. O'Brien?"

"Nay, my lord, but Mr. Willard Jefferies, Jr., here, is late of the Jeffries firm in Bristol." He gestured toward young Willard, Jr., who stood pale and aloof.

"He has sworn, as an officer of the courts in his county, there was no will for Robert Wellesley. Indeed we were in contact with the firm almost immediately after the Wellesleys died, directly with Willard Jefferies, and have signed documents informing us of this fact."

"My lord." Bryan spoke, his cool tones echoing to the ceiling. "I too have a document from Jefferies, signed and sealed by Willard Jefferies, senior partner of the firm but three days ago. Williard Jefferies, Jr., is no longer employed by the firm due to some malicious negligence he practiced while in his father's employ. He faces disbarment when he returns to Bristol."

Willard, Jr., paled still further and sat abruptly as Bryan produced more papers for the bailiff from the box he had carried into the court.

Hope fluttered in Emilynne's heart to join with her faith in her husband, a hope she prayed was not premature.

"These papers appear to be in order. Mr. O'Brien. It would seem you have been duped."

Gill turned back to the magistrate. "My lord, in light of this evidence, we no longer dispute the will of the late Robert Wellesley."

Thaddeus made a sound of protest, but his solicitor

ignored it. "However, it is Mr. Whyte's belief, delivered to him in letters from his niece, that Miss Wellesley . . . is not a fit guardian for the children. And the charges of kidnapping, not yet withdrawn, must be addressed."

She knew it was too early to hope this was over.

"It is Mr. Whyte's considered opinion," Gill O'Brien continued his attack, "that Miss Wellesley is not capable of dwelling fully in the realms of society to which the children must gain access. She has spent most of her life researching old ruins and fantasizing pagan history. Further, the will seems to indicate even Mr. Wellesley's concern."

Emilynne could feel the color drain from her cheeks, replaced by icy cold as her own actions weighed against her.

"Robert Wellesley did not doubt his sister's abilities to raise his beloved children. He did not wish for her to shoulder the burdens involved alone." Bryan's commanding tone offered a lifeline and she clung to it. "The charges of kidnapping are spurious at best. They were filed subsequent to her marriage. Miss Wellesley and I wed before we left Limerick, invoking the clause in Robert Wellesley's will making Emilynne and me the children's sole legal guardians and nullifying the filing from Mr. Whyte's representatives."

"It was not a legal marriage—" Gill began.

"My lord," Bryan interrupted, clearly chafing at Gill's continued arguments. "It is legal in every sense of the word. By the ancient laws of this land, we joined our lives in Limerick, dwelt as man and wife both aboard my ship and at a well-respected boardinghouse in Bristol. I can offer you signed statements to that effect."

Silence reigned as the magistrate digested the information in Bryan's documents, broken only by the variegating rumble of discussion between Thaddeus and his team of lawyers.

"My lord—" Gill's words were cut off as the tall doors leading into the courtroom opened with a bang, drawing the gazes of everyone in the court.

"Good God," Thaddeus whispered as two men appeared in the doorway.

"Beggin' yer pardon." It took a moment before Emilynne recognized the larger man. Michael O'Toole from Blue Hills Stud stepped into the courtroom. "We be lookin' fer Mr. Thaddeus Whyte."

"You've found him," the magistrate intoned with belabored patience. "What is your purpose here?"

"We've been riding fer the past two days." Mr. O'Toole dusted his clothes and motioned to the boy by his side. "But it was important we reach ye. Young Timmy, here, has news ye'll need to hear."

"These are laborers from my estates," Thaddeus rumbled in an angry tone. "They do not belong here. O'Toole, take your son and be gone immediately, lest I send your whole family packing."

"Mr. Whyte, do be silent in my courtroom," the magistrate cut through Thaddeus's rising bluster. He turned his gaze back to O'Toole and motioned him forward.

"What you have to say had better be of the utmost importance to justify the interruption you have caused to this proceeding."

"It is that, sir." O'Toole grabbed young Timmy by the scruff of the neck and the two of them approached the magistrate. "Go on, Timmy, tell the magistrate what ye know."

"Mr. Wilkins killed them people." Timmy O'Toole's voice was barely audible, but it was enough to raise the fine hair at the back of Emilynne's neck.

"Nay, it ain't true." Wilkins stood, losing his thin veneer of propriety as he glanced at Thaddeus.

The magistrate did not so much as bat an eye. "Be silent, Mr. Wilkins. What people?"

"Them Wellesleys. I was in the stable when Mr. Wilkins come in. I weren't supposed ta be there, so I hid. Mr. Wilkins don't like it when I take care of the horses. I give them extra oats and brush their coats real fine." Timmy O'Toole drifted away for a moment and his father gave him a shake.

"So I hid. And that's when Mr. Wilkins did something ta the axle on their carriage. I didn't think anythin' of it till after they didn't come back. Then, when I said somethin' to Mr. Wilkins, he just smiled kinda funny and suddenly I was workin' for the ferrier down in Fermoy."

Everything inside Emilynne screamed to hear these details relayed in the open courtroom. Tears dripped onto her hands. She struggled for calm and blessed Bryan for sending the children to safety. Christian wouldn't understand, but Abby would have comprehended all too well.

"You cannot take the word of this . . . crofter!" Wilkins's voice ended on a high squeak.

"Either be seated, Mr. Wilkins, or suffer the consequences." The magistrate motioned to a couple of officers stationed near the now-open doors.

They came forward, stopping when they reached Mr. Wilkins as the magistrate continued. "I shall not caution you again. You may continue, O'Toole."

"Sent my boy away." The elder O'Toole nodded. "Without even a by-your-leave, savin' Mr. Whyte tellin' me it was fer his own good. I reckon he'd have had an accident real soon too if'n Mr. Whyte hadn't been so busy lookin 'fer them little uns."

"I'll not swing for this alone, Whyte." Wilkins leapt to his feet.

"Be silent, fool," Thaddeus hissed.

"Nay, I'll not." He pointed a finger at Thaddeus. "He wanted 'em dead, not me. I did only what he asked me to do. Said he'd pay me well for getting them two out of his way. He intended to do the same to the children after a bit."

Emilynne's stomach churned at the thought.

The magistrate made a slight motion with his hand.

"It weren't just me," Wilkins squeaked as the bailiff advanced toward him and took his arms. "Mr. Whyte made me do it."

"I believe you, Mr. Wilkins," the magistrate intoned. With another motion of his hand, more men in uniform filed in and stopped beside Thaddeus.

"You cannot arrest me no matter what you believe." Thaddeus stood and offered the magistrate his iciest stare. "I am English and a man of sterling reputation. It would take more than the word of one down-on-his-luck crofter and a surly ex-employee to support such a move."

Emilynne shot to her feet without conscious thought. "You have forgotten me, Thaddeus."

Thaddeus leveled his malevolent stare in her direction, but she refused to be cowed, returning his stare with every ounce of strength she had.

"Sit down, girl," he bit out, a rat finally cornered.

"Miss Wellesley, have you something to add to this . . . carnival?" The magistrate's gaze pierced her again, reminding her of Willard Jefferies.

"Yes, my lord, although I am rightfully Mrs. Reilly now."

Finally released, all the righteous indignation and pain inside her roiled to the surface. "Thaddeus Whyte is fully responsible for the deaths ... no, the *murders* of my brother, Robert, and his wife, Gail. He lured them to Ireland with no intention of handing Blue Hills over to them just as he has no intention of caring for the children."

She favored him with a hard stare before continuing. "I'll admit I was drawn in by his charm and his solicitous manner, but eventually even my suspicions became aroused. When I discovered my unsent letters in his desk, I went to confront him in his precious stables.

"There I overhead him and Wilkins discussing the success of their plans! *The success!*" Her voice broke over the words as Bryan reached her side.

"As if Robert's and Gail's deaths meant nothing." She shuddered and took a deep breath before continuing. "It was at that point that I escaped with the children as fast as I could manage. It is my very strong opinion, my soul-deep knowledge, that we would be dead even now if I had not done so."

"Indeed." The magistrate raised an eyebrow and focused his gaze once again on Thaddeus. "And is it still your opinion that I have no recourse here, Mr. Whyte?"

"She is not a credible witness," Thaddeus snapped back.

"I believe she is." The magistrate made a third motion with his hand and the bailiffs flanking Thaddeus took his arms.

"You cannot do this." Through clenched teeth Thaddeus hissed at them. "I will not be done in by a simple girl with ridiculous notions in her head. Not after all this time. Not after all I've accomplished."

He focused his hate-filled gaze on her. "You should have died with the others."

"That's enough, take him away."

"No! This cannot be!" Thaddeus struggled, but their grip on him could not be shaken.

"Do something, you idiot!" he shouted at Gill. "What do I pay you for?"

Gill spread his hands with a slight nod to Bryan. "Nothing anymore."

Thaddeus turned a fiery red and continued his vociferous protests out the door, which the bailiff mercifully closed behind him, cutting Gail's uncle off in mid-complaint.

Emilynne's knees went weak with relief as Bryan's arm slid around her waist. "Well done, *muirneach*," he whispered against her hair. "Well done."

The magistrate cleared his throat and looked at them over the rims of his spectacles. "On the matter of your marriage, Mr. Reilly, have you anything else to add?"

"Aye, my lord, one more thing." Bryan caught her gaze with his, a deep, glowing green. "I have given my heart and my soul into Emilynne Wellesley's keeping by a law deeper and more ancient than the precepts that will recognize our bond here today."

Warmth sluiced through Emilynne as his words echoed inside her.

"Well put, Mr. Reilly. Your papers appear to be in order. The marriage of yourself and Mrs. Reilly is recognized in this court. It woud seem the children belong in your care, indeed."

Pure white relief burst inside Emilynne.

"Thank you, my lord." Bryan nodded formally, though the grin on his face displayed his pleasure as his arm tightened at her waist.

"This is over?" Emilynne couldn't hold back the question as the bailiff's pole thumped once again. Words had never tasted so fine.

"Aye, *muirneach,* we've won."

He shed his solicitor's garb and kissed her then, soft and full of promise.

"Excuse me, boy-o, but I think it only right and proper that you introduce me to my new sister."

Bryan released her mouth but retained his arm at her waist.

"Indeed, Quin?" They clapped each other on the shoulder. Bryan glanced back down at her. "This rather rude interruption is my elder brother, Quintin Reilly. Quin, this is my bride, Emilynne Reilly."

Quin Reilly bowed over her hand, a roguish twinkle in his eye, so like Bryan's. "Lass, you're a welcome addition to our family. There's many of us thought Bryan might never marry, he'd become such a staid, withdrawn fellow. Shall I ask if you heard The Blessing, boy-o?"

"You may ask," Bryan answered with a slight smile.

Quin narrowed his eyes and then reached into his pocket, withdrawing a small leather bag. "I think I'll pass for the moment. I hope this is what you were looking for."

He handed the bag to Bryan.

"Thank you." Bryan squeezed Emilynne's waist as he tucked the bag away.

"I also found this among the things on Da's desk." Quin handed a packet of papers to Bryan, who opened them.

"I recognized the name from your correspondence and thought I should bring it along."

"What is it?" Emilynne asked.

"It is an offer from your brother." Bryan handed her the papers.

Robert's neat script covered the pages, blurring her eyes with tears. It was like touching him again. She blinked and struggled to focus as tears dripped onto her hands.

"It is an offer to invest in Reilly Ship Works," Bryan explained. His fingers brushed at her tears as he cupped her chin and turned her face to his.

"It would have been a real help." Quin shook his head.

"It still will be," Emilynne told them softly, gaining two pairs of inquisitive green Reilly eyes in her direction. "This is something Uncle Willard told me about. Robert had already set things in motion with Willard before his death. He was planning to visit Beannacht Island after completing their business with Thaddeus. I wanted it to be a surprise for you."

In Bryan's eyes she read the same thing that had occurred to her when Willard told her. They may very well have met anyway, for Bryan said he planned to return to the island as soon as he completed his business with Harland.

As the heat leaping in her husband's gaze warmed her cheeks, Emilynne forced her gaze to his brother. "So you see, Quin, I may have sunk your brother's efforts with Mr Harland, but this investment will come through."

"It will help, indeed." Quin squeezed her hand. "You got lucky, Bryan, better hold on to her."

"I fully intend to."

Quin chuckled. "I must go now, boy-o. There's enough waiting for me back at the island to make me quite certain I've been gone too long already."

Quintin focused his gaze on Emilynne. "You'll bring him around for a visit, won't you? He's been gone far too long already. I just might have a surprise of my own for you, brother mine."

"I will do my very best," she offered, ignoring the raised brows of her husband.

"You'd best catch the tide, Quin, if you're going. And remember, stay alert for The Blessing. It can sneak up on you when you least expect it," Bryan added helpfully.

Quin offered a quick snort of laughter.

"Good-bye, Mrs. Reilly." He pressed a quick kiss to her cheek.

"Take care, boy-o." Quin disappeared through the courtroom doors as Bryan's gaze caught hers.

"What did you mean, stay alert for The Blessing?"

"Later, *muirneach,* first let's go rescue our children." He held out his hand.

Our children. She linked her hand with his, quite certain no sweeter words had ever been spoken in any courtroom.

Hours later, when they finally closed the door on the two sleeping whirlwinds so close to her heart, Bryan offered her the bag Quin had given him.

"Are these yours, Emilynne?"

Her breath caught as she emptied the bag's contents into her palm. "Mother's cameo and Gail's ring! I was certain I'd lost them forever when I pawned them. But escaping with the children was so vital."

"I thought you might want to give them to Abby and Christian one day," Bryan offered. "When we first landed in Bristol, I sent word to have Quin scour every pawnshop in Limerick until he found them."

He arched a brow at her. "You are quite an astute salesperson, *muirneach*, at least according to the shopkeeper and my brother."

"Oh, Bryan." Tears sparkled in her eyes, and she wound her arms around his neck. She kissed him, reveling in the sweet passion that rose so easily between them. "I cannot thank you enough for all you have done for the children and for me. I'm only sorry that you had to restructure your life so to do it."

"Indeed." His dark, glowing gaze enraptured her as he pulled her closer. *"Muirneach*, have you still not realized why I have done all that I have done?"

His tone made her shiver with anticipation. "No."

"With everything that is in me, I love you, Emilynne." His husky words unlocked a flowing sweetness in her heart as he continued. "I married you because I wanted you for my wife. It was mere coincidence that it solved your problems as well."

He teased her lips with his own. "It is my hope, someday, you will love me in return."

"Oh, Bryan." Tears burned her eyes and tightened a painful lump in her throat. "I do love you. I think I have from the moment you kissed me on the docks in Limerick harbor."

He smiled and kissed her then, melding their mouths together with fire and passion as he swept her into his arms and started toward their bedroom, kicking the door closed behind him before he let her slide the length of his body.

"You still haven't told me what you meant when you told him to stay alert for The Blessing." Her own words came raggedly now as he kissed a path from her brow to her collarbone.

"It is a long story, my love." He unfastened the lacings of her gown and petticoats, which pooled at her feet, leaving her in nothing but her linen shift.

"Have we not a lifetime before us?" she teased as she nibbled his lip.

"Aye, *muirneach.*" He shuddered as she undid the buttons of his shirt and pressed kisses over his chest.

"Then tell me," she coaxed, enjoying a heady haze of power as she teased her lips over his chest and down his belly while he groaned.

"It is a tale of an ancient blessing given by the Druids to my family. We know when we have met our life's match, be it blessing or curse. Emilynne." He groaned her name as she undid the buttons on his trousers and tugged them down.

"And have you heard this blessing?"

"Aye." He gripped her shoulders before she could continue her torment and pulled her up for a long, drugging kiss. "I heard it, and saw it, and felt it, tasting it on the docks in Limerick when I kissed a sweet lass in widow's weeds. It is you, beloved. You are my blessing."

She held his gaze. "Did you never think I was a curse?"

He chuckled at her question as the glow in his eyes flared brighter. "Aye, at first, but I have learned since then."

"What have you learned?"

"That a seeming curse can be a gift if you aren't afraid of it. That following the laws of your heart can lead you to your deepest desire." He kissed her long and slow and thoroughly as his hands began their hypnotic spirals over her body. "I bless the day you ran into my embrace."

She flung her arms around his neck, all words forgotten as the desire between them blazed anew.

Bryan took her onto the bed with him, reveling in the unrestrained passion of his sweet wife as the distant strains of an unseen harp played through them both.

If you enjoyed REILLY'S LAW, be sure to look for Elizabeth Keys' next release in the Irish Blessing series, REILLY'S GOLD, available wherever books are sold December 2000.

When youngest brother Devin Reilly sets off to sample America's possibilities, he never expects to lose everything he owns—or to experience the Reilly family "blessing" when he stops a runaway carriage and saves Margaret Brownley, daughter of the city's anti-Irish party leader. Working as a stable hand for her father is far from the fortune-seeking adventure Devin imagined—until Margaret convinces him to take her to her grandmother's home in Maine, and he discovers that some things are much more valuable than gold. . . .

<u>BOOK YOUR PLACE ON OUR WEBSITE</u>
<u>AND MAKE THE</u>
<u>READING CONNECTION!</u>

We've created a customized website just for our very special readers, where you can get the inside scoop on everything that's going on with Zebra, Pinnacle and Kensington books.

When you come online, you'll have the exciting opportunity to:

- View covers of upcoming books

- Read sample chapters

- Learn about our future publishing schedule
(listed by publication month *and author*)

- Find out when your favorite authors will be visiting a city near you

- Search for and order backlist books from our online catalog

- Check out author bios and background information

- Send e-mail to your favorite authors

- Meet the Kensington staff online

- Join us in weekly chats with authors, readers and other guests

- Get writing guidelines

- AND MUCH MORE!

**Visit our website at
http://www.zebrabooks.com**

We're sure that you have enjoyed this BALLAD romance novel and we hope that you are looking forward to reading the other wonderful stories in this series, as well as sampling many of the other exciting BALLAD series.

As a matter of fact, we're so sure that you will love BALLAD romances, that we are willing to guarantee your reading pleasure. If you have not been satisfied, we will refund the purchase price of this book to you. Send in your proof-of-purchase (cash register receipt with the item circled) along with the coupon below. We will promptly send you a check.*

Put a Little Romance in Your Life With
Hannah Howell

__**Highland Destiny** 0-8217-5921-3	**$5.99**US/**$7.50**CAN
_ _**Highland Honor** 0-8217-6095-5	**$5.99**US/**$7.50**CAN
__**Highland Promise** 0-8217-6254-0	**$5.99**US/**$7.50**CAN
__**My Valiant Knight** 0-8217-5186-7	**$5.50**US/**$7.00**CAN
—**A Taste of Fire** 0-8217-5804-7	**$5.99**US/**$7.50**CAN
__**Wild Roses** 0-8217-5677-X	**$5.99**US/**$7.50**CAN

Put a Little Romance in Your Life With
Betina Krahn

Merlin's Legacy

A Series From
Quinn Taylor Evans

__**Daughter of Fire** $5.50US/$7.00CAN
    0-8217-6052-1

__**Daughter of the Mist** $5.50US/$7.00CAN
    0-8217-6050-5

__**Daughter of Light** $5.50US/$7.00CAN
    0-8217-6051-3

__**Dawn of Camelot** $5.50US/$7.00CAN
    0-8217-6028-9

__**Shadows of Camelot** $5.50US/$7.00CAN
    0-8217-5760-1

Call toll free **1-888-345-BOOK** to order by phone or use this coupon to order by mail.

Name _____
Address _____
City _____ State _____ Zip _____
Please send me the books I have checked above.
I am enclosing $_____
Plus postage and handling* $_____
Sales tax (in New York and Tennessee) $_____
Total amount enclosed $_____
*Add $2.50 for the first book and $.50 for each additional book.
Send check or money order (no cash or CODs) to:
Kensington Publishing Corp., 850 Third Avenue, New York, NY 10022
Prices and Numbers subject to change without notice.
All orders subject to availability.
Check out our website at **www.kensingtonbooks.com**